WARRIOR'S BETRAYAL

M.M. CHROMY

SIDELINE
THUNDER
PRESS

To all the women who are told they're too much. Too impulsive, too loud, too dramatic, too intense, too sensitive, too fill-in-the blank …
fluff that noise.
You are glorious.

Also to my Aunt Stephanie.
While you were not the only one asking (oh, so patiently) for this book, you were by far the most persistent. It truly got me through the hard times.

SAM

Magically induced comas sucked. Especially when said coma was induced by a Dark Warrior on a revenge tour. Waking up from having my brain on lockdown by the Mage was life changing. As I struggled back to consciousness, I found myself in a familiar bed, inside a familiar farmhouse, with a familiar pit bull snuggled up to my side.

But I was far from comforted.

An IV and all sorts of tubes and lines tethered me to machines. With my Warrior of Light anointing, none of this should have been needed. My Powers came from Heaven. I healed at a rapid rate. I was stronger, faster, and more powerful than a normal human. But poisoned demonic stab wounds could bring even the toughest Warrior to her knees.

The injury in my side gave a nasty throb, making me wince. Bear, my brindle pit bull, snuggled closer to me on my good side. Half of my mouth tugged up and I rubbed one of his soft ears.

"Thanks for keeping me company, bud," I murmured.

He grunted and continued snoring.

With a careful sigh, I leaned my head back against my pillow and studied the swirls of plaster on the ceiling. My mind was fuzzy, filled with cotton, as I thought back to the events leading up to my current predicament.

The last thing I recalled was running out of a restaurant like my ass was on fire, leaving my boyfriend Camden with more questions than answers. *Why had I left?* Snippets of my memory surfaced, but again, they were hazy. I remembered my phone buzzing with several texts. That I'd been annoyed over the stream of messages. That something in that conversation had left me in a blind panic.

The longer I focused on recalling what happened, the more difficult it became. And after several minutes, a sharp pain lanced through my temples.

"Ouch! Shit!" I rubbed the sides of my head. "It's gonna be like that, huh?"

Doubling down, I tried wrangling my fractured memory. Someone important had texted me. *Who? Why?* Another ice prick of pain pierced in my brain.

"Nooooo," I wailed. Bear's head popped up, so I patted his thick-barreled side. "I'm okay. Maybe. Just, ya know, an entire chunk of my life is missing."

My dog did one of those faux sneezes, lowered his face back to the mattress, and shifted to make himself more comfortable. Again, I started digging at the recent memories that wanted to stay hidden. I *would* out-stubborn them.

Pain.

Sweat beaded on my brow.

Throbbing.

My face flashed hot, then cold.

Stabbing.

Nausea swirled in my gut.

Agony.

"STOP!" Leticia yelled in my mind, her shout reverberating to all parts of my being.

I froze with only my chest heaving. *"Letty! Angel mine."*

"Brave One, Warrior mine," my inner angel gently chided, her tone suggested she was unenthused. *"Are you done ignoring me? Let's handle this together, shall we?"*

"Ummm... okay? Sorry," I said. *"Any thoughts on where my memory's run off to? I'm taking suggestions."*

She let out an audible sigh. *"If you hadn't been Heaven-bent on trying to fight the Mage's magic just now, maybe you would have heard what I said."* I swear I could feel her cross her arms.

"Sorry. Again." Really. Truly. I didn't like to disappoint Letty. She was the one constant no one could take away. The conduit of my Power. The literal angel on my shoulder. My built-in conscience. *"You were saying?"*

"I've been scanning your body since you woke. There was some residual effect from the Mage's abominable blood magic." Letty let out a hiss. *"That vile creature constructed a wall warding off your memories.*

I pursed my lips and narrowed my eyes. *"Awesome. Do me a solid and bulldoze that sucker."* No more than a breath later, a violent shiver ran down my neck, along my spine, and into my legs. *"What the fire fart are you doing in there? Did you push a button? Am I being reset to the factory setting?"*

"Let me focus, Brave One," Letty chided, using her more normal patient tone rather than the shouty one from a moment ago. I settled back into the pillows and waited. After a moment she gasped. *"This wall—Good Heaven—this wall is sentient!"*

That couldn't be good.

More tingles ran throughout my body as she did more examinations. I knew when to keep my mouth, er, thoughts quiet. Being a Warrior of Light was a rollercoaster of fun, folks. Demon fighting, getting stabbed, being recruited by the most powerful Dark Warrior of all time—oh my.

"*It's an alarm system,*" Letty finally stated. "*Both Dark Warrior and demon's blood were used to construct it. Dominic's demonic taint is woven all through this dark magic. If I pull it down, the Mage will know you've woken.*"

Oh, geez. No biggie.

I quirked a brow. "*When did that evil overlord have time to do that? I booted their asses from my head.*"

"*Who knows when the barrier was erected? Could have been before they gained entry.*" Letty chuckled without humor. "*But I guarantee the Mage was counting on you wanting to tear this down immediately upon your waking.*"

"*Gross.*" I lifted a lip in disgust. The Mage got its powers from a Greater Demon instead of an angel. That demon was Dominic. He was an enigma of his own kind with proper manners, stellar hygiene, and an obsession with me. It made sense that the Mage used his blood. But the thought still gave me the heebie-jeebies. "*I don't want a literal bloody wall in my head. The Mage wasn't wrong to assume. I want my memory back.*"

Letty said nothing, but her conflict over my choice was palatable. I chewed the inside of my cheek. During my seven-day coma, while the Mage and Dominic had my consciousness on lockdown, Letty had been trapped inside with me. Only she hadn't been able to sense me. I could see her, but she couldn't see me. This current situation with the wall served as a stark reminder that, for all Letty's power and might, she'd failed to protect me.

At least that was what she believed. Though she didn't say those words, I knew. She was as close to me as my own thoughts. I didn't blame her. The Mage's blood magic was powerful as hell. Dominic wasn't some bottom rung demon; he packed a wallop in the Power department.

"Letty," I said out loud—gently, quietly. "I need to know."

"It won't be painless, Brave One."

"I don't care. Do it." I wasn't above begging. *"Please."*

"All I ask is that you take a moment to think over the consequences, but ultimately, I'll do as you ask. Besides, there is someone who wants to speak with you—"

"Samantha!" my Warrior Guardian roared from the place where he lived in my soul. A real horse, but inhabited by some Heavenly being, his consciousness became linked to mine when I became a Warrior of Light. His sacred duty was to safeguard and serve me.

"Maximus Prime." I loosed a breath. My loyal old copper Thoroughbred. My protector. My Best Friend. My Max.

And, boy howdy, was he in a rank mood.

"I thought you to be dead!" His indignation ricocheted inside me, as if my coma was a personal affront to him. *"You were gone, ripped away. I had no awareness of whether you lived and breathed. They tried to show me your body, but you were not here, in our place. I am unaccustomed to such emotion."*

All my immediate concerns evaporated. I'd scared the shit out of my poor grumpy Guardian. *"Oh, Max, I'm so sorry."*

He dragon-snorted again. *"As if that is sufficient. I have never—"* Another offended snort. *"Do not spook me in such a manner ever again."*

I chuckled, winced, and shifted uncomfortably in bed. *"I'll work on that."*

"Come see me," he demanded. *"These humans have returned us to our modest dwellings. Though, I rather prefer the one with finer accommodations."*

"Grew accustom to Xavier's place pretty quickly there, huh? I didn't even get to see the barn in person. Only through your eyes." Our living quarters at Adviser Gerena's property were lush and ostentatious. Andrew's farmhouse was far humbler in comparison. *"I don't know if I'm allowed out of bed right now. We'll see if Leigh or Harper will help me out."*

"See that you do. Now, if you don't mind, I have not eaten in a week. There is breakfast I must attend to."

"Haven't eaten in—Max!"

He didn't acknowledge me, having already gone dark, and a wave of horror washed through me. He was bound to be a sack of bones with a chestnut hide slung over his skeleton. *Good God.* I shuddered. It hurt my heart that my coma had taken a toll on my poor horse.

"Letty?"

"Brave One?"

"Take down the wall."

There was a pause followed by, *"As you wish."*

Those damn tingles went down my body when Letty pressed on the barrier. Her Power grew warm pushing against it. The prickles turned into hot pokers. I gritted my teeth. As Letty worked, her Power burned hotter. Brighter.

I cried out, my back arching off the bed, and the hole in my ribs felt like it split me in two. Bear leaned into me and whined. Then the dam broke. The weight of her Power vanished. The heat vaporized to a cool mist. One breath. Two. Angel and Warrior waited. Then an eruption of images and color burst forth, spewing like a geyser in my brain. I thrashed at the onslaught of the sudden return of my memory.

Breakfast with Camden. Text messages from Judy. She'd been captured. Harper speeding to Milton's Feed & Tack. His command to not be a hero. A trap. Ambrose biting into Judy's neck. Judy bleeding out. Enyo's attack.

Our battle. Her poisoned sword. She wore me down. The phone call to Harper. My plea for him to save me.

Crushing grief coupled with hideous pain twisted me up, tore at my heart. *Judy's dead!* I let out an unearthly wail. *She's dead, dead, dead.* Unbidden tears streamed down my cheeks. Enyo's blade flashed in my vision. Pain seared my side. *I'm dying.* I felt *his* hands on my wound. Warm blood leaving my body. I gasped, desperate for air.

"Harper!" I wrenched myself out of bed. Bear leapt to his feet with a startled yelp.

"No!" Letty yelled.

Stumbling sideways, I caught the edge of my side table for balance, slipped, and wiped out everything that sat on top with a flailing arm. Bottles, washcloths, medical items littered the floor. Bear jumped from the bed and with a soft huff ran from the room.

Fear gripped my throat. My chest heaved. My heart pounded. The tubes connected to me itched and burned. I ripped out the IV in my arm and pulled off the wires attached to me. The pain didn't register. The heart monitor's steady beeps turned into a flatliner's wail.

"I beg you to stop," Letty pleaded.

Judy was gone. Ambrose murdered her. I'd watched her die. Wracking sobs overtook me. Wheezing gasps brought me to the floor. I curled into a ball, crying and shivering. I couldn't save her. A trickle of blood ran down my left side. Down my arm. I choked on hot tears and snot. Even Letty's soothing warmth did nothing to calm me.

"I'm so sorry, Judy," I moaned.

"Sam!" The semi-familiar voice of a girl cut through my panic. "Oh, my God!"

I focused on the sound of feet rushing over the carpet. Sensed her kneeling beside me. Jolted when her small hands gripped my shoulders. I looked up, meeting Delaney Hayes's concerned green eyes. Xavier's adopted daughter. Child prodigy. Genius. Pixie with a wide smile. Though there was no hint of good humor now.

"Judy—it was a trap—couldn't save her."

Confusion and concern filled her face. "Why are you out of bed?" She scanned me with her eyes. "You busted your stitches. And your arm? What did you even *do*?"

"I failed," I wailed, and agony stabbing me in the ribs.

"Crap! Daddo!" DH yelled over her shoulder. She gripped my arms and tried to haul me to my feet, but her small strength was no match for my muscled Warrior frame. "I can't pick you up, Sam. This is bad." She turned her head again and shouted at the open door. "Nigel! Jax? Adviser Holland? Anyone! Help!"

I grabbed DH by the front of her shirt, gaping at her before I crumbled in a mess at her feet.

"No, no, no. Sam, get up. I'm not strong enough to help you." DH leaned away, and a moment later she pressed something soft to my side. One slim arm around my shoulders. "Shhh, shhh, it's okay. I'm here. You're safe."

I sobbed, soaking her shirt while she stroked my hair. Bear reappeared and huddled close to me, licking my flesh wherever he could.

"DH, I heard you shoutin'," said a baritone voice steeped in the deep South. "Oh, shit."

Jackson Bozeman, my fellow Warrior of Light, stopped short. His blue eyes widened for a fraction of a second before he spurred into action. In one long, smooth stride he scooped me up, cradled me against his chest, and said, "DH, go get your daddy. He's in Adviser Shaw's study down the hall. Harper's gon' be pissed when he sees her this way. See if Adviser Gerena can buy me a couple more minutes to at least get her back in bed."

"On it!" DH hopped up and sped from my room.

Jax scooped me up and carried me to bed as if I weighed nothing. I was limp in his arms, spent from my burst of emotions, waning adrenaline, and horrifying memories. Judy was gone and it was my fault.

"Jax," I whispered. More tears leaked out.

"Yes, Miss Sam?" Jax sat next to me, pressing the towel to my ribs.

"I asked Letty to bring down the wall. She warned me. Even she didn't know what would happen."

"I haven't the foggiest idea of what you're tryna tell me," Jax's slow, southern drawl soothed me warm honey, "but it's alright, sug', I got you." He picked up my own hand and put it on the towel. "Can you hold this? I gotta pick up this mess before Harper gets here."

Numb all over, I nodded, did as he asked, and watched the big, blond Viking of a Warrior collect everything I tossed. Bear jumped back in the bed, settling at my feet, and kept his brown eyes pinned on me.

"I'm sorry," I said, not entirely sure if I was talking to Jax or Bear.

"You've been in a coma," Jax said, righting the lamp. "Everyone's been real worried about you. Gave us all a scare, but Harper more than most. I don't reckon I've seen a man so determined to save someone's life." Jax's hands stilled and he raised his eyes to the door. "Good. DH was able to get to Adviser Gerena. They are all at the back door."

A freaking seven-day coma. Time lost that I'd never get back. I tried tapping into my Warrior hearing, expecting to hear as Jax did, but the response was a spasm of pain from my open wound. I gasped. Jax whirled towards me with grace no one his size should have. Conversations that should have been crystal clear were muffled like under-water words.

"I can't hear them," I murmured.

"What?" His brows furrowed and he moved. He felt my forehead with the back of his hand. "You're clammy. Breathe. In through your nose, out your mouth."

I did as he said. Once. Twice. Three times.

"That's it," Jax coaxed. "Gonna be okay."

But fear had a death grip on my heart. In two years, I'd *never* had my Power fail. It always worked without so much as a glitch. *"Letty, am I broken? Is this—is this from taking down the wall? Shit! Is it permanent?"*

"Let me look," she said and I shivered as she scanned me from head-to-toe, a fresh round of tingles radiated from within my chest. *"Ah, I see it now. Your wound is interfering with your ability to connect to your Power. When it heals, you'll be fine. But for now—"*

"I'm useless and healing like a normal human."

"I wouldn't go that far. You can still call on your Power, but until your wound heals it won't be as strong normal."

"And triggers a million daggers to stab my insides." I rubbed my forehead, weary and more than annoyed.

"Your head hurt, too?" Jax asked, his eyes filled with compassion, kindness etched on his face. "Do you need some water?"

What did the world do to deserve this man? I lifted my hand. "No, I'm processing. My brain is scrambled."

"Now that you're awake," Letty interjected, *"I can speed up your recovery. Enyo's poison did a number on your body."* She pushed her soothing warmth out into my limbs, which worked more now than when I was having a complete meltdown.

"The average Warrior wouldn't have survived what you've been through. You're made of pure tungsten, Brave One."

Enyo—the demon bitch who stabbed me—got bumped up to *numero uno* on my "to kill" list. I didn't know how to end a demon permanently, but I would find a way or die trying. She'd *never* harm another Warrior with her poison if I had any say in the matter. Ambrose, the midnight black demon that who'd kicked my ass before and had murdered Judy, was number two. My heart seized at the mental image of Judy's bravery in the face of certain death. Letty's warmth staved off any mounting panic. I failed once, I wouldn't fail again.

And even though Light Warrior law forbade me from killing humans, I would find a way to execute the Mage. Dominic—the red-skinned, conniving bastard—earned himself a reprieve until I dealt with his friends. I had my memory back. My angel was working on repairing me from the inside. I would heal. I would rise. And Hell would pay.

The group of voices, which had been far away at the back door, grew clearer as they entered the hallway outside of my room. I took a careful breath and looked at Jax.

"What's goin' on, Miss Sam?" Jax asked, his tone wary.

He's too perceptive. I shook my head. He didn't need to know the depth of my rage.

I gestured to my bedroom door. "On a scale of one-to-ten, how much trouble will I be in?"

"Everyone's gon' be happy you're awake, but Harper?" Jax flinched. "He's gon' lose his shit."

I patted the duvet covering me flat and smoothed the wrinkles. "Show time, then."

No sooner were the words out of my mouth than Harper darkened my door. He was a solid wall of muscle; his stout, rugby-player build filled the entrance. His hands were fisted at his sides. My gaze slid up to his face. A shadow beard covered his clenched jaw. His mouth was pressed tight and his brow was furrowed. His sapphire-blue eyes burned dark. For not being a Warrior of Light, he sure oozed absolute authority.

Oh! I attempted a smile. *Letty's white wings* "Hey, Harper. How ya doing?"

2

HARPER

"Goddamn it, Sam," I growled.

She's awake. She's awake. She's awake. The one thought pounded in time with my heart. Her stormy eyes met my mine and never wavered. How many times had I imagined that she'd regain consciousness? How many scenarios?

I drank her in. Her fine blonde hair was a mess. Her pale-skin had a thin sheen of sweat, but her cheeks were flushed pink. I swept my gaze down, soaking in the details, until I got to the blood. Fucking blood. My stomach lurched and my thoughts tried to lead me down recent memory to when I'd first saved her from Enyo. She had been bleeding out.

"Fuck!" I took three long strides to get to her side.

"I can explain," she said, holding a crimson-stained towel to her ribcage. Tacky blood streaked her arm. "Just don't be mad."

"For Heaven's sake alive!" Leigh Kestler, Sam's best friend and Warrior partner, exclaimed from behind me. "I left you alone for fifteen minutes."

Stubborn, impulsive little shit. My temper flared to life in my gut. I ran a hand over my face, down my chin, and along the back of my neck. "Don't know why you're so surprised, Kestler. This is Samantha Fife after all."

"Miss Fife, it's good to see you amongst the living," Xavier said, sweeping into the room. He laid a hand on Sam's shoulder and gave a gentle squeeze. For being just over three-hundred years old, he didn't look a day over fifty, with broad shoulders, salt-and-pepper hair, and a thick goatee. "Even if you fell out of bed, pulled out your IV, and ripped your stitches, I much prefer you wreaking havoc than in a coma."

The Spaniard wasn't wrong. I might be infuriated by whatever stunt she'd just pulled, but at least she was conscious and raising hell. My fury ebbed as a wave of relief washed over me. This past week had been the longest of my twenty-four years. But seeing her conscious and speaking unshackled all worry and dread from my shoulders.

"I gotta reputation to uphold," Sam said.

Rolling my eyes, I pulled the towel away and lifted her shirt. Her dressing was completely red. "Jesus, Sam."

"That bad?"

I glared at her. "You're a menace."

"I'm sorry," she whispered, then bit her lip. A tear slipped down her cheek.

Ah, fuck. I wiped the tear away with the pad of my thumb. *How can someone be so damn infuriating and endearing at the same time?* Sam turned her head away from me, but her shoulders shook as she wept.

I sighed through my nose. Sam was no stranger to physical pain. But inner angst? She tried to hide that behind a mountain of bravado. Even when we were kids, she always tried to keep people from seeing her cry.

Sam and I had grown up together. After my parents were killed, Andrew and Judy Shaw took me in and raised me. Sam's family spent so much time with the Shaws that they were as close as two families could be without a blood relation. They treated Sam like a grandchild.

She'd spent her free time at the farmhouse. Even though she was four years younger than me, she had worshiped the ground I'd walked on. And I'd adored her as one would a sister. Until that fateful day when I discovered the truth behind my parent's deaths.

Thomas and Elaine Tate had been the most powerful Warriors of Light in recent history. They'd avoided the initial Warrior slaughter lead by the Mage, and were the only ones to remain alive under Pop's ranks. Then that traitorous Dark Warrior came for my parents and ended their lives in a bloody, gruesome display of violence. I'd been four years old and they'd hidden me in a closet, but I heard everything.

Pops kept all that information from me in hopes of— well, I still didn't understand his reasoning for all the goddamn lies. At eighteen, I'd learned what had happened. I stormed away from my adoptive home, leaving a sobbing, heartbroken Sam behind. To keep my guilt at bay, I'd steeled my heart and left with no intention of returning.

I'd been gone for six years and never contacted Sam during that time. I never let her know that I'd kept tabs on her through Ma's weekly phone calls. That little blonde spitfire had a grip on me that I could not escape. Then I got the call from Pops that he needed me. And like some well-trained dog, I came home.

Only to return and find Sam a grown-ass Warrior of Light filled with bitterness, distain, and unresolved anger towards me. While I had moved on with my life, her wounds had festered. She'd fought me at every opportunity. I'd thought her impulsive, willful, and disobedient. A liability.

But I'd come to see her in a different light as of recently. Before her coma, we'd taken strides to repair what was damaged between us. Almost losing her put shit into perspective for me.

"I got you, Sammy," I murmured to her.

I turned around. DH, Sam's fellow Warrior Leilani Kalakaua, Bozeman, Xavier, Kestler, and even Nigel crowded into Sam's room—all eyes on her. I'd be willing to bet all of them witnessing her breakdown filled her with embarrassed shame.

"Everyone get the hell out," I barked. "I can't work with you people breathing down my fucking neck."

Xavier gave me a considering look. The man was as sharp as the Heavenly steel he forged and his gaze flicked to Sam before returning to me. He nodded.

"I'm sure we're all thrilled Miss Fife is awake," he said to the room, "but let's give Mr. Tate room to tend her wound." Xavier started herding everyone towards the door. He beckoned for Bozeman, who stood at the end of Sam's bed. "Visitation hours will be later."

Everyone filed out, but when Bozeman passed by me, I stopped him with a gentle forearm across his chest. His brows shot up.

"Thank you for helping her," I murmured. "Don't know what happened, but the blood on the carpet didn't escape my notice."

Bozeman glanced at Sam. "We may have only known y'all for short amount of time, but I reckon we're family. A long-lost, complicated family. She's my sister-in-arms."

"Good man." I patted him hard on the chest.

Bozeman was as dependable as they came—former military man and genuinely good guy. He'd been on clean up duty with Nigel when Sam had been attacked and Judy, my adopted mother, had been murdered. Bozeman had mopped up their blood at the scene, fabricated the lie that Ma had died from an animal attack, and had spent sleepless nights patrolling the farmhouse's weakening borders ever since.

"Kestler, you stay," I muttered as Bozeman lumbered out of the room.

"Wasn't going anywhere, despite your bossy demands." A hint of a smile tugged her mouth and she clasped her hands behind her back. "What do you need?"

"Go to the medical supply room. Get me Lidocaine, Ketamine, and Life Elixir." I glanced at Sam. Her skin had taken on a grey pallor. Each of her breaths seemed to make her wince. "Hopefully we can get her shitfaced enough with meds to help with the pain before her metabolism burns it off."

"Got it." Kestler gripped my shoulder. "Don't stay mad at her. She's alive and awake and, for once, I don't care about whatever asinine thing she's done. I'm relieved that the fight between us wasn't the last thing—"

"Think about that later," I said without heat. "Stay on task."

"Right." Her eyes turned glassy. "Be right back."

Everyone was gone now.

I turned to Sam. My gut clenched at the fresh blood on her side. *Help her, you idiot.* "We're alone. Start talking."

"Thanks," Sam said, meek and quiet. "Letty took down a wall in my mind. It kept me from remembering what happened before—before you saved me." She reached out, her hand finding mine. "Thank you for that."

Well, fuck. I tightened my fingers around hers and squeezed. *I'd save you every time.* "That why you ripped our your IV and—what?—fell out of bed?" I let go of her and pulled a medical tray next to said bed.

"When my memory came back it was too much. Everything hit me at once. I got overwhelmed." Her voice dropped. "I remembered what happened to Judy—"

My jaw tightened and eyes burned. I focused on laying out needles, syringes, a suture kit, and fresh gauze pads. Ma had only been dead a week. But how could Sam have known that? She was a week behind everyone in terms of grieving.

"That's not the worst of it," Sam whispered. "The wall was an alarm system. The Mage knows I'm awake now."

Jesus. Fuck. I froze. The Mage was bound to find out one way or another, but *fuck.* That bitch now had advanced notice. I blew out a tight breath, comforted that as long as Pops lived, the divine borders around the farmhouse would hold—however feeble. I shook my head, pulled up a seat, snapped on a pair of latex gloves, and started removing her soaked bandages. The neat row of sutures had popped in several places and blood pooled in the gaps.

"I should use wire thread this time," I said. "Maybe it could withstand your impulsiveness."

She blinked once. Twice. "I didn't mean to, but it was an avalanche in my brain. I forgot where I was."

"Next time you remove walls in your head, make sure you aren't alone."

Sam flashed a cynical smile. "How about I not get myself into any more magical comas in the first place? No coma, no walls, no flailing about. Simple math."

"Jesus." I dropped my eyes to the running sneakers on my feet and shook my head.

This damn woman. Her actions were so impetuous, so raw, but so goddamn typical. Part of me couldn't believe she'd done it, and the other half wanted to grab her by the shoulders and shake the shit out of her.

I lifted my head to peer at her. "You're a piece of work, know that?"

"Yeah, but never boring." She lifted a shaky finger into the air emphasizing her point.

I growled low in my throat. Sometime during her coma, I must have blocked out just how fucking snarky Sam was. *God help us all.*

"You mad?"

"I'm fucking furious, Sammy." I resumed examining her wound. "But I've spent days hoping, and praying, and being an unbearable asshole to everyone while we waited for you to wake the hell up. But I'm so—" I wet my lips. "—so fucking relieved you're back with us. Plus you're a grown-ass woman. You don't need a lecture from me. Though you deserve one."

"Oh." She chewed the inside of her cheek.

Kestler cleared her throat from the doorway. I glanced over my shoulder. Her arms were loaded. "I hope I'm not interrupting." She crossed over and set the items on the bedside table.

"Leigh." Sam lifted her head. I pushed her back down with a finger.

"Hey there." Kestler peeked over top of me and smiled down at her.

"W-where is Camden? Is he okay?" Worry haunted her eyes.

"He hasn't left your side," Kestler said. "He set up camp in Andrew's office. Been working here instead of at his restaurant. Unfortunately, he caught a call about an hour before you woke up and had to leave."

"By himself?" Sam's brows pinched in concern. "Is that safe?"

Pure, unadulterated resentment rattled in my chest. *Fucking Bennett.* I didn't trust Sam's boyfriend. How someone could just start seeing the supernatural realm at twenty-two did not sit right with me. Either people were born Seers from birth or they were Warriors of Light. Sometimes Seers became Warriors. But one didn't suddenly develop the ability unless weird forces were at play.

I tolerated Bennett's presence this past week, but it wasn't out of the kindness of my heart. Xavier allowed him to stay. Kestler, for some reason, backed his innocence every time he came up in conversation. I respected their opinions, and to his credit, Bennett had toed the line. He'd kept watch over Sam when no one else could.

Kestler must have felt my tension rise, or heard me growl, because she laid a steadying hand on my shoulder. To Sam she said, "Jax offered to go with him. Cam said no. He insisted it would be a quick trip."

"Does he know I'm awake?" Sam asked, her voice cracking. "I wanna—I need—we need to talk."

The emotion in her voice over that asshat called up a rage in me that I didn't expect. *But* of course *she'd want to see him. I'm fucking unhinged.* Forcing myself to be rational did nothing to abate the unexpected, irrational anger at Sam's inquiry. Kestler's hand tightened to an uncomfortable pressure on my shoulder. I schooled my face, and tried maintaining an indifferent expression. But the white-knuckle grip I had on the forceps in my hand probably gave me away.

"I left him a message before you went and ..." Leigh gestured to Sam's wound and my medical tray with her chin, "did whatever you did. I'm sure he would have turned around mid-drive if I'd actually spoken to him."

"Can you try again?" Sam said. "Humor me, please?"

"Sure hon. I'll be right back." Kestler leaned in, forcing me to move aside, and kissed Sam's temple. When Kestler drew back, she hissed low in my ear. "Calm down, caveman." I barked a laugh at the unexpected name call.

"Get going," I murmured. "Call the asshat."

Sam and I were alone once more, and if she'd heard my slur against Bennett, she didn't react. I cleared my throat—trying to let go of residual anger—and turned to the supplies Kestler brought. I drew up a syringe of medication. "This should numb you enough to get patched up. Won't work the same as it does on a normal human, but it'll help you sleep. And since your IV catheter offended you so much, and you're now awake, it'll be easier to have you take regular oral doses of Life Elixir."

Sam gave me a small smile. "The IV was an unintended victim."

Shaking my head to hide my answering smile, I poured amber liquid into a dosing cup and set it beside her. She tried to sit up, hissed, and let out a string of swearing that would have made Kestler turn scarlet.

"Easy, little spitfire." I caught her before she collapsed back to the mattress. "Let me help. You'll get blood everywhere. Again." I supported her shoulders so she could take the Life Elixir.

After laying her back down, silent moments ticked by as I meticulously cleaned the crook of her arm of all blood and gave her a shot of Ketamine. I moved to her side and administered Lidocaine around her wound. Sam watched my movements without speaking.

Atypical.

"What's on your mind?" I settled into my seat and

opened a suture package. "We have fiveish minutes before you're shitfaced."

"Where to begin?" she asked.

"Start talking. You'll find your way."

Sam licked her lips. She was lost in thought for a moment, then anger flashed like lightning in her eyes. "The Mage trapped me inside my own consciousness. Dominic and the Mage kept me locked in my own damn head. They tried to get me to join their band. I don't know how many ways I have to tell them to *fuck off* before they get the message. I don't think they know the definition of the word no."

A muscle twitched in my cheek as the overwhelming urge to flip shit burned my chest. *How fucking dare they?* A breath puffed out of me while I kept my hands busy with removing busted stitches, held my tongue, and checked my temper.

"Do you remember when we were kids and we'd go up to the mountains in North Carolina?" she asked.

I nodded, keeping focused on my task, unsure where she was going with this.

"The Mage accessed those memories and tinkered with them. Dominic took Judy's form and acted like my spirit guide. We made a trip down memory lane. And then! Then the Mage implanted some memories of a woman named Cheryl. Like those are mine now. I can't get rid of them."

All the air left my lungs. *Sam knows about Cheryl Talbot.* I shrank back from the bed. *Has she put two-and-two together that Cheryl is the Mage? Jesus H. Christ.* I went to rub a palm over my mouth but stopped when I saw the blood-fleck latex covering my hand. The Mage implanted her memories in Sam. Fuck. Questions bombarded me. *How much does she know? What do I tell her? Do I tell Xavier?*

"Harper?" Sam's voice pulled me from my spiral.

"Hmm?" *Get your shit together for Christ's sake.*

"Are you okay?"

No. "Yeah. Fine."

I recognized Kestler's footfalls as she reentered the room. Sam looked over my shoulder, her countenance brightening, almost hopeful.

Fucking Bennett.

"No answer," Kestler said. "I even called Cam's restaurant and left a message with his executive chef, Renard."

Sam deflated and laid her head back on the pillow. I felt her disappointment in the deepest recesses of my heart. I wanted to hunt Bennett down and drag his ass back here to ease Sam's anxiety or shoot him on sight for existing—the later was more tempting.

"Hooboy," Sam said, interrupting my murderous thoughts. "Harper gave me the good stuff. I'm not sure if I'm supposed to be a Pegasus flying around the room, but here we are."

Ketamine's kicking in.

"You're a Warrior, all drugs work differently in you." I pressed near her wound. She didn't react so I picked up the suture thread and leaned in. What I didn't bargain on was Sam continuing to talk. Working as fast as I could, I listened with half an ear.

It wasn't long until Sam grabbed my wrist and looked at me wide-eyed. "Dominic told me how they became demons, that being outside of Heaven mutated them. He also told me about a governing body in Hell. What did he call it?"

She squinted, not letting go of me. Not realizing I was mid-stitch. "Shit," I whispered.

"The Infernal Order!" Sam shouted. "Do you know about them?"

"A little help?" I asked, my voice tight.

Kestler carefully inserted her long, lean frame into the bed with Sam. Bear popped up from where he'd been lying and joined Kestler. Sam's best friend took her hands and held them in her lap.

I met Leigh's eyes. "Keep her distracted."

Kestler nodded. "Sam, tell me more about this Order. Did Dominic say anything else? When did the Mage show up?"

"Wooooow, the room is spinning," Sam said.

"Focus on me. Tell me what happened," Leigh said.

I sutured faster than I preferred but as neatly as possible while Kestler kept talking. Dominic told Sam how he'd thrived in Hell by modeling his behavior after the five members of the Infernal Order. I made a mental note to research the Order in Pops's files and in Xavier's library archives. And though Sam's words slurred, and most of what she said made no sense, Kestler and I caught the important parts. Eventually, Sam's wild thoughts became unintelligible mutters. When I reached the end of my stitching, I made a quick suture knot and set everything aside.

"I should go tell Xavier all of what she just yammered on about," Kestler climbed from of the bed. "He may already know much of what she told us."

"Mmhmm," I mused. The demons had been *too* quiet while Sam was out of commission. Local crime had been down, Bozeman and Kalakaua reported no Greater Demon sightings, and everything was fucking Mayberry around town. I took off my gloves, tossed them onto the medical tray, and rubbed a hand over my face. Sam had mentioned a sentient wall which she had asked Letty to remove. A wall which alerted the Mage to Sam's return to consciousness—

"Fuck." I shot to my feet and ran my fingers through my too-long hair. It was touching my ears at this point, which further agitated me.

Kestler's attention snapped to me. "What? What's wrong?"

"The Mage now knows Sam's awake. The demons have been quiet, but it's not going to stay that way. Some serious shit is gonna hit the fan."

"You think they'll attack?" Kestler asked, her brows raised high.

"The borders are weak. Pops is just going to continue to decline without Ma. Go, talk to Xavier. I'll finish up here and join you." Kestler wasted no time and was gone before I turned back to Sam.

Her soft snores filled the silence while I applied a dressing to her wound, and just as I pressed the last strip of tape down, Sam caught my hand. I froze, looking up at her. Her eyes were surprisingly clear despite the fuckton of Ketamine pumping in her veins. She smiled at me. My stomach clenched.

"I heard you in my coma." Her words were soft. The pad of her thumb rubbed the back of my hand. "You asked me to come back to you, so I did."

Emotions I shouldn't have ever felt towards Sam bloomed in my chest. She was alive, awake, and functioning, but it had been *me* that woke her? I sucked in a breath and ran the back of my knuckles down her cheek.

Don't look at me that way, Sammy. I'm no hero. "Go to sleep."

"I trust you. With everything. All of me." Then her eyes turned glassy again, stoned off her ass. "I keep hearing birds. Where are the birds, Harper? How did they get inside?"

"It's the meds. The birds are outside. Now get some rest." I laid her hand on her belly, but she wouldn't release me.

"Don't leave," she begged, her words nearly inaudible.

My heart tripped at her desperate request. I gave her fingers a quick squeeze.

"Need you, Harper."

I closed my eyes for a breath then glanced up at the ceiling, desperate to look anywhere but at her. I grabbed my chair and sat. And stayed sitting even when she nodded back off to sleep.

She's back. Relief swept through me, sweet and cool against my burning soul. I brushed hair from her face and traced the line of her jaw. *So strong and so fucking beautiful.*

She'd fought the Mage in her head, obtained memories that didn't belong to her, and experienced true loss for the first time in her life. She'd bounce back—if Sam was anything, it was resilient—but a tangle with the Mage like that was bound to leave its permanent mark. Only time would tell how this affected her in the long run.

Her breaths deepened and grew longer, so I stood and gave Bear an ear scratch before leaning over and pressing a kiss to Sam's forehead. I was certain of one thing; she wouldn't go through the next phase of her life alone. I'd be there at every step, whether she wanted me there or not.

3

DOMINIC

Dominic strolled the long hallway of his Master's invisible bastion, heading towards the throne room. The passage was dimly illuminated by gas-lit sconces bolted to the limestone walls; some of their wicks had fizzled down, and ominous shadows danced in the meager light of the cavern. The working lamps snapped and hissed with flame, and in the distance, water dripped with slow *plunks* into a larger pool. The only other sound was Dominic's steps echoing through the barren hall. His mouth puckered in disgust. He hated this fortress and its lack of luxury.

As he neared a massive set of heavy oak doors, a scream from the other side pierced the quiet, followed by a thud. Angry shouting arose and Dominic sighed. *Here she goes again.* He paused before entering, laying his hands on the door handles. He hadn't seen his Dark Warrior in such a temper in many years, and it always promised drama would ensue.

But this was to be expected after being ejected from Samantha Fife's mind with such force. How the young

Light Warrior was able to break a powerful blood spell confounded and fascinated Dominic. The Mage had taken quite a bit of damage from being ejected, and her magic was now erratic and dangerous within their compound. Outside of their pocket of Hell, the Mage's magic had become mere embers of what she could do. Her battle with Samantha Fife had caused unforeseen damage to her Powers.

And thus, they were holed up in this miserable place until the Mage healed. Dominic had sent out numerous demons to collect Samantha Fife's body, but all of them came back with the same news: the protected borders of Andrew Shaw's land still held, though weakened, and there were no holes in the veil to allow an invasion.

Yet.

At current, a tingle from his connection to his Warrior alerted him that she was about to use a powerful burst of magic. With supernatural agility, he moved backward, and at the same time the heavy doors banged open, slamming back against the walls of the hall with a mighty crack, which echoed along the corridor. The wood splintered up the middle. Glacial air poured into the stuffy, humid hall. A dusting of frost coated the hair on his arms.

"Wonderful," Dominic muttered. His brethren had failed his Dark Warrior one too many times. She was livid and he, himself, was the only one who could mollify her rage.

"You useless cretin!" she shrieked. "How dare you show your face after your impressive display of incompetence." The Mage's cold, unnatural voice ripped through Dominic. He winced at the offending screech.

"Master, I have no excuse," the deep voice of Ambrose responded.

"I asked you to complete one simple task: bring the

girl to me." The clack of the Mage's shoes stopped. "And where is she? Not here!"

Harper Tate's infuriatingly human interference had been something neither Dominic nor his Warrior had counted on. Shooting Enyo with a man-made bullet had been a small stroke of genius on the boy's part. A head shot from a mundane firearm would warrant a brief respite to Hell in order to recover.

Another magical inkling trickled down Dominic's spine, and he stood flush against the limestone wall. He watched as several demons were expelled with unseen force from the room. They landed in a heap at his shiny black shoes. Mild irritation rankled him as they scrambled in a panic to get as far from the main hall as quickly as possible.

"You had one job!" the Mage screamed so indignantly that her words were nearly indiscernible.

Dominic sighed again. While he generally appreciated his Warrior's ruthless aggression, he didn't love when she took it out on his Greater Demons. His kinsmen. Those who fell from Heaven with him. It was better to keep his Warrior calm, lest she actually start killing them, in which case they would cease to exist, not returning to Hell to mend.

He swept into the throne room. It was a massive space of rock walls, barren floors, and large gaslit chandeliers. A red runner carpet led from the entrance, along the floor, over a low-lying platform step, and ended at an obsidian throne. And it was before this throne that the Mage stood, bent at the waist, seething in blind fury. With a deep breath, she heaved herself upright and picked up an agitated pace, passing back and forth before her profane seat of power.

The Dark Warrior's robe hood had been lowered,

revealing a head of long white hair and white eyebrows. Every inch of her body was tattooed with an intricate pattern of red swirls and whorls. The visible marks on her face, neck, and arms glowed in her fury, burning bright against her porcelain skin.

Ambrose, the overgrown brute, kneeled before the Mage. Head bowed with his fists clenched and planted on the floor. Dominic strolled past him, sparing only the briefest of glances, and rolled his eyes. For all Ambrose's brawn and strength, he really was an idiot. *Perhaps he deserves his punishment.*

Dominic sauntered the length of the carpet, suppressing his annoyance that in his Warrior's rage, she kept several of his lesser kin cowering along the walls. It irked him that they were petrified of his Warrior, but he understood their fear.

She could be terrifying when enraged.

"My sweet," Dominic crooned, stopping just before the low stage.

The Mage ceased her agitated pace and whirled, nearly tripping over a cowering hellhound. She hissed and kicked the beast, sending it flying. The animal crashed against a wall and yelped. He wasn't down long and leapt to his feet. Flames erupted from his paws in his agitation. He snarled and snapped at the Mage before limping out of the throne room.

"Dominic," she sighed out his name, placed tattooed fingers against her forehead, and drew in a steadying breath.

"It's been—what?" Dominic smoothed his tie. "Twenty years since I've seen you in such a delightful mood?"

He scanned the great hall. There were three slain Lesser Demons, their bodies lying a few yards from the stage. Their rib cages had burst open and black blood pooled on the sandstone floor. She'd been performing magic with his demons—which never worked as well as human blood. Dominic refocused on his Warrior out of concern that she would resume her murderous rampage on his fellow fiends.

"I'd be better off," she lowered her trembling hand and glared at Ambrose, "if I could get competent help around here."

Dominic went to his Warrior's side, grabbed her elbow, and steered her sit on her throne.

The Mage tossed a rigid hand at Ambrose, who was still kneeling. "This buffoon failed to bring me Samantha Fife's body! Pathetic waste of breath!" Her tattoos flared bright, and the temperature dropped even further.

"Patience, my sweet. You know she's heavily protect-ed." Dominic kept his tone soothing. Violent rage simmering through their connection. He moved to her side. "Easy now."

The Mage huffed, lifted her chin, and ran her fingers through her pin-straight hair. She turned her red eyes on Dominic and said, "That *girl* thwarted my blood magic. I used her own blood. No one breaks my curses!"

Snow flurries floated around the throne.

Instead of speaking, Dominic reached over and traced the line of one of his Warrior's tattoos along the back of her neck. He whispered a word in his demonic tongue, invoking an enchanted tranquility, and the spot where he touched her glowed faintly. In the time they'd been together, his touch was typically enough to assuage her without the magical enhancement. His spell made it work faster.

The Dark Warrior shuddered under his fingers, and her eyes flashing before she lowered her lids, and rocked her head back against her throne. The snow stopped and the great hall warmed a few degrees.

She looked sidelong at Dominic. "What do I do with this useless sack of hellhound dung?"

Ambrose flinched and grunted but remained rooted to his spot. Dominic cocked his head.

Has she frozen him in place? Dominic continued to trace the glowing red lines of his Warrior's tattoos, along her neck and shoulders. Through his fingertips, he focused on pulling out the more violent parts of her anger, drawing out her desire to slaughter and maim anything within a hundred yards. He absorbed it into himself, while simultaneously invoking soothing vibes. His Warrior's chaotic emotions fed his demonic hunger, much like savoring a decadent dessert —luscious and delectable—an extravagance he didn't need, but enjoyed nonetheless. He rarely fed from her.

It was, however, a mark of Dominic's demonic superiority that he could take his Warrior's savagery and, in return, infuse her with positive warmth. He could lull anyone into a state of ecstatic bliss. Lull them into trusting him. He alone had this ability and had masterful control over his drives, impulses, and hungers.

A wistful sigh came out of his Warrior as she melted deeper into her throne. She slipped up a hand and gently grasped Dominic's fingers. "I forget myself when you leave me. Where did you go?"

"My apologies," Dominic murmured. He smiled. As unstable as she could be, he was rather fond of his Warrior. His sweet. His *pet*. He lifted her hand to his lips and pressed a chaste kiss to her skin before letting go. He continued his soothing touch along her tattoos. "I was collecting a gift for you."

The sound of running feet brought their attention up

as a brown Lesser Demon skidded to a halt before them. He was humanoid and scrawny, with his bones jutting out from under his skin like a crack addict.

"Bodhi," Dominic addressed him cooly.

Bodhi timidly skirted around the still-kneeling Ambrose to stand in front of the throne. He cast nervous glances at the demons cowering along the walls, behind him at Ambrose, and then at Dominic.

The Mage bolted upright in her seat, spine rigid, and shooed away Dominic's hands. He tucked his arms behind his back.

"Enyo has arrived, my liege," the peon-level demon relayed.

Ambrose's eyes grew wide, but he remained mute, head bowed, frozen before the throne of the Mage. Dominic lifted an amused brow. *She* did *freeze him. Quite ingenious of her.*

"Why?" the Mage snapped. "I did not summon her." Heavy snow started to fall.

"Easy, my sweet," Dominic muttered for his Warrior's ears only. "I had her run an errand for me. She comes on my behest." The indoor blizzard eased.

"Master of mine," Enyo's melodious voice called from the entrance of the throne room. She sashayed in. Her glossy black hair hung in loose waves down around her navy-blue shoulders. She'd replaced her armor with a black silk dress and was barefoot.

The Mage pulled in a deep breath; her red eyes narrowed in suspicion. Fat snowflakes drifted down, melting in the pools of black demon blood. Ice crept over the arms of her throne.

"What is happening?" she asked.

Enyo walked past Ambrose, pausing long enough to

throw him a small smirk. Snow collected on his back. His body shivered but he couldn't move.

"My Queen," Enyo curtsied before the Mage and met Dominic's eyes. He nodded and Enyo continued, "As the girl's body is behind enemy lines, I come bearing a different gift."

"The only reason you're still standing here is because Dominic invited you," the Mage snapped and stabbed a finger at Enyo. "The point," she hissed. "Get to it." Ice crept out from the throne and along the carpet runner.

"As you wish." Enyo clapped her hands and said, "Bring him!"

Purple and orange Lesser Demons came through the throne room doors, dragging a lean human male between them. His blond curls were plastered to his head and his green-gold eyes were unfocused. His tailored shorts and linen button down had rips in them, and he was missing one of his boat shoes.

The Mage barged to her feet. "Dominic, you—you orchestrated this? You brought him back to me."

Dominic joined the Mage's side and ran his knuckles down her arm to taste her emotion, but focused on the human before them. His Warrior had been dosing the boy with a cocktail of wine, her blood, and Dominic's blood for the past two years. It thinned the veil between the natural and the supernatural. He was ripe for the picking, and all Enyo had needed to do was allow herself to be seen by the boy just as she'd stabbed Samantha Fife. It was the chess move Dominic had been hoping for.

Enyo stepped to the side and held her arm out. The Mage swooped in and grabbed the boy by the chin, tilting his head up. Her eyes glowed and the air felt a little frostier. "Did you harm him?"

"Tut, tut, my sweet," Dominic soothed. "I would

never allow that to happen. But I rather think it's time I take matters into my own hands. *I* will not fail you."

The Mage met his eyes. She licked her lips. "I would trust no one else with him but you."

"It's my honor." He bowed before his Warrior.

The Mage glared at Ambrose with a malevolent smirk. "It seems Dominic and Enyo earned you a reprieve, you blundering dolt." She waved a hand and the big, midnight black brute collapsed on the floor, panting.

She turned back to Dominic and with her fingernail, she cut a line on her forearm. She smeared the blood on Dominic's forehead, uttered a few demonic words, and Dominic's form diffused into red smoke. With a flick of her wrist, Dominic poured into the boy's body, possessing him.

4

SAM

I saw a movie once about a man forced to relive February 2nd on a time loop until he learned whatever lesson the cosmos was trying to teach him. I only saw it once, during movie night with my parents in my pre-Warrior years, but it made an impression. Waking up the next morning, in my bed with Bear snuggled next to me, made me feel like I'd been dumped into yesterday's waking moments. But there was a sense of calm where chaos had reigned.

The room was cool and quiet. The brindle burrito must have sensed I was awake since he shifted and his tail thumped quietly against me. My side ached but I reached down and gave him a subtle scratch on the head anyway. A gentle sigh brought up my attention. Leigh sat on a roll-away cot at the foot of my bed. I propped myself up on my right elbow to get a better look at her and bit back a pained hiss.

Her long dancer legs were folded under her, her brunette hair was swept up in a messy ponytail, and in her hand was a book. Engrossed by whatever novel she'd chosen, she didn't hear my gasp. I suspected that this had been her nesting spot while I'd been out of commission.

"This is deja vu," I said quietly.

Leigh started and her head snapped up. It took her a second, like she had to come back to the real world. A smiled brightened her face. "Maybe you should stop putting yourself in situations that warrant moments like these?"

I chuckled, winced, and said, "Help me sit up?"

"Sure." Leigh set down her novel and hopped off her cot to join me. "How are you feeling?"

"Foggy." I ran my fingers through my greasy hair. I needed a freaking shower. "Like my brain is filled with smoke."

Leigh hooked an arm under mine. Together we got me propped up against the headboard. She filled a glass of water from the pitcher on the bedside table and handed it to me.

"Slowly," she cautioned. "Don't chug it."

One sip. Two. A longer third. The cool liquid felt like Heaven on my Sahara-dry throat. "At the risk of sounding like a broken record, how long was I out this time?"

"Eighteen hours. Long enough to get us into Tuesday."

I massaged my eye sockets with a thumb and index finger and lamented, "More time gone."

She took the glass from me. "If you hadn't gone berserker, we wouldn't be in this situation."

I huffed and pursed my lips. Leigh crossed her arms, returning my fierce glare, and quirked a brow as if to say, "You really wanna go there?"

"Maybe I do?" I snipped.

Leigh smiled before her expression fell into pensive melancholy. She carefully settled next to me and gripped her own hands in her lap. She opened her mouth and shut it.

"You look like someone's kicked your dog. Why so serious?"

"Do—do you remember much from before?" At my evident confusion, she hurried to clarify. "What I mean to say, is do you remember that we—you and I had—we, ah ..."

I tilted my head, flipping through what I could recall. The further back I went, the clearer the memories got. And I landed on The Fight. My jaw dropped in a silent, "Oh."

The day before I'd walked into the trap at Milton's Feed & Tack had been hellacious. After finding out Andrew had lied by omission and kept pertinent information from the two of us, I'd reacted differently than Leigh had. We had gotten into the worst fight we'd ever had. We disagreed about how to deal with the aftermath of Andrew's epic screw-ups. She'd said I was disrespectful, undisciplined, and selfish—all true—but she'd also called me an asshole.

I'd apologized. She hadn't.

But if there was anything I'd learned recently, it was that I needed my people. They grounded me. Made me a better person. Helped me think beyond myself. When the Mage had pressed me to turn on those I loved, Leigh had been the first person I couldn't betray.

I traced one of the grey feather swirls on my duvet and said, "We didn't have a chance to sort that mess out, did we?"

Leigh gasped before stilling my hand with hers. "I'm so sorry. Shouldn't have said all those things. Should've remembered you handle hurt differently—"

"We're sisters." I squeezed her fingers, but not able to meet her eyes. "We fight. We move past it."

"Still," she huffed. "I almost lost you."

"Leigh." My tone caught her attention and her eyes finally met mine. I smiled. "You were *right*."

Her shoulders slumped and a small, relieved sigh slipped from her. "That's what Harper said, too."

I chuckled. If I'd only listened to Leigh that day at Xavier's house, in the hallway outside his war room, maybe I wouldn't have gone off to save Judy half-cocked and with no Warrior backup. Harper was good at many things, but he didn't have the juice to fight demons, let alone Enyo.

Maybe I would have sat down with Andrew and he'd have explained everything. But no—I couldn't do anything the easy way. Shame bloomed wild in my chest and I looked everywhere in my humble room except at my best friend's face.

"Judy may have died because of me," I mumbled.

"Don't," Leigh commanded. Her hand sliced through the air. "Only one guilt-ridden, self-flagellating, ill-tempered human is allowed in this house and Harper takes the crown. I won't let you go down the 'I got Judy killed' road. From what we've pieced together, they would have killed her whether or not you showed up. You, of all people, know the Mage's capacity for malice."

I flinched. *How can she be so blunt about Judy's death? Just how much did I miss in my week-long siesta?* Not ready to unpack either of those thoughts, nor wanting to dwell on our fight, I changed the subject to something—*someone*—rather conspicuous in his absence.

"Has Camden come back?" My heart stuttered. *Does he not care about me?* Unaccustomed to feeling insecure, I bristled at the emotion.

If my abrupt change in subject surprised her, Leigh

made no outwards signs, and said, "He called me while you were asleep. Said the emergency at Sorcerie would keep him longer than he wanted. Didn't give me much detail as to what happened. He did tell me to tell you that he's so relieved you're awake and can't wait to see you."

I chewed on the inside corner of my lip. Something was off with Camden. I knew it in my gut. He would have fought hellhounds to get back to my side. There was also that tiny detail that Dominic had been stalking Camden. If he was not here, then my boyfriend wasn't on shielded ground and had no Warrior protection.

Wait.

My gut clenched in panic. I pawed at Leigh's shirt and gave her a wild look. "Cam saw me get stabbed by a demon, right? He knows what I am?"

"Ah, yes. That was interesting." Leigh *smiled*. Actually, freaking smiled. My brain short-circuited.

"When you fled from your breakfast date with him in a panic, he followed Harper. Camden saw Enyo stab you at the same time Harper shot her. And maybe it was a good thing he'd been there, even though it put him in danger. Having that second set of hands helped Harper administer aid. While he worked to keep you from bleeding out, it was Cam who drove like a wild man to get you to the farm house."

I gaped at her. "And he—what? Just took it like a champ?" I snapped my fingers. "Just like that?"

"No." Leigh chuckled without humor. "He demanded to take you to the hospital."

"Bet that went over well."

"He tried to fight Harper over it. Like, physically fight him. I'm talking, chest-bumping male throw down. Adviser Gerena slid in and diffused situation before it became a *thing*. He took Cam aside, told him what we are and what we do, then had me go full Warrior in front of him."

My eyeballs damn near bugged out of my head. When a Warrior of Light tapped into their Power, their bodies glowed golden from the real, undiluted light of Heaven refracting out through them. Cam witnessed Leigh go full Warrior and stuck around? Stunned. I was one-thousand-percent stunned.

"He handled it pretty dang well," Leigh said, interrupting my thoughts. "And thus, Cam's been camped out next to you ever since."

Not exactly how I would have introduced him to our world, but here we were. I scratched my fingers along my skull. "Remind me why y'all let him leave without protection?"

Leigh stood and busied herself straightening the mahogany side table. "We didn't *let* him, Sammy. He just left without saying anything. I told him I'd have Jax go with him, but when we came back he was gone."

My heart turned to ash in my chest. My mouth went dry.

Cam, for the love of Heaven, why did you do that? I leaned my head against the headboard. *Why haven't you come back? Where are you? This isn't like you.*

Cam was kind and considerate. He truly cared about people. Cared about me. He could have freaked out when he saw Enyo stab me, but he didn't. He could have dropped me like a bad habit when he got a crash course on the Warriors of Light, but he didn't run. No, he'd been ready to pick a fight with Harper over me. Stayed by my side. He didn't leave me.

So why the fire fart was his ass not on his way back to me? Yes, fine, not everything was about me. I got that, but something about his absence didn't feel right.

"Leigh, I know you're not worried, and you've spoken to him, but I'm concerned." My gut twisted. "Something's wrong. I know it."

Leigh crossed her arms. Her face said, "I'm listening, but you'll have to convince me," but otherwise, she stayed silent.

"Maybe I'm being ridiculous. Perhaps being held hostage in my own head has made me paranoid, but I need to see Camden with my own two eyes. Touch him to know he's solid and real and safe."

The lines on Leigh's forehead softened.

"Best case scenario," I continued, "I'm wrong and he's fine. He'll laugh it off. Worst case—" I swallowed, unable to complete that thought.

"Worst case is he's dead," Harper said from where he leaned against the door. "But the asshat's hard to get rid of, like a cockroach."

My heart did such a stupid flip-flop at the sound of his voice that I almost missed *what* he'd said. I glared at him. "Cam is *not* a bug."

Harper shrugged, walked into the inside, and Leigh stepped out of his way. While his words were gruff, his touch—his fingers—were gentle as he checked me over.

In a much softer tone he asked, "How you feeling, spitfire?"

"It hurts but I'll live," I said.

"Let me look?" He continued with that private voice and his hands paused at the hem of my shirt. He was so close, his hand so warm on my side. His familiar scent of sandalwood and clove hit me hard. I nodded, giving him permission to proceed. His fingers brushed over my bandage with a whisper-light touch.

After a moment, he said, "Looks good. I'll change your

dressing later." He looked at me, his dark eyes gentle. "Glad you're awake. Damn near killed me."

A confession. A rare confession.

My heart took a skitter step. "Good to see you, too."

I'd spewed all my guts to him the day before—albeit in drug-induced ramblings I don't completely remember. My cheeks flushed and heat raced up the back of my neck. I did remember telling him I freaking needed him. Some alien must have confiscated my brain because, oh my God, I was not ready to unpack my Harper luggage. And that sucker was jammed full. Like, I'd be paying extra for weight overage.

I wrenched my eyes from Harper and spoke to both him and Leigh. "I'm worried about Cam, sooooo I want y'all to drive over to Sorcerie and see what's going on. It's been eighteen hours. He should be here. He would want to be here. I'm not some self-absorbed brat. He's seen some serious crap this week, right? Come on, guys. You gotta agree." My worry kindled my temper. "Did no one check on him? Why am I the only one having a shit-fit about this?"

Leigh and Harper glanced at each other. It would seem that my best friend and my—whatever Harper was—were co-conspirators? *What the hell happened while I was out?* It didn't matter. Cam's whereabouts did.

"Sam, he's been texting me regularly," Leigh said. "Cam *wants* to be here, but he's been tied up at his restaurant. I didn't think it was my place to pry into his business. We don't have the man-power to send out a search party for him, especially if he's been communicating with me."

These people. They don't understand. Anxiety threatened to choke me. The Mage was bound to be furious with me. I expected them to retaliate knowing that I was awake. Fear jackhammered my sternum.

"Brave one," Letty warned, trying to break through my ramping-up anxiety.

"I'm going nuts!" I snapped at her. *"Everyone is calm and I'm freaking the hell out. Why is no one on high alert?"*

"Perhaps they are and don't want to disrupt your recovery? You have *exhibited outwards signs of dangerous panic."*

"I got your panic right here, angel woman."

If I could see her, I'd put money on it that she just rolled her eyes at my sass. But since this was a new-and-improved Sam, her words gave me pause. My lips pursed. I *did* have her rip down a magical wall in my head. I *did* leap out of bed, tear out my IV, and obliterate my stitches. I *did* rant and rave like a lunatic. I sighed. Loud and heavy.

"What if something happens to him?" I said ask, calmer and not like a malfunctioning mongoose. "Dominic is out there." I threw a hand in the air. "Cam could be in danger."

"Sam—" Leigh started.

"Look, if you two don't go," I flipped the covers off my legs, gritted my teeth, and made motions to get up, "I'll do it myself."

"No fucking way," Harper growled and pushed me back down.

"You wouldn't dare," Leigh hissed, stepping up to my bed.

I raised my hands. "Fine. I'll stay put like a good little girl. But do this for me? The invalid." I sought both of their eyes. "Please?"

"What I was about to say," Leigh said, "before you cut me off, was that Harper and I discussed this with Xavier while you were asleep."

"Oh." Relief and embarrassment whooshed through me. *Aren't I a horse's ass?* "Thank you."

"Kestler and Bozeman volunteered to check things out," Harper said.

"Are you going with them?" I asked.

"Wasn't planning on it." His shoulders went stiff and his expression told me he'd rather be served Rocky Mountain Oysters than make sure Camden was okay. *The hell happened between these two?*

I fiddled with my duvet. If Camden were hurt in a ditch and hanging on for dear life, Harper, with his kickass paramedic background, would be my boyfriend's best chance at survival. He wasn't a Warrior, but he was someone I trusted without question. Harper needed to go, too. I slipped my fingers through Harper's, and to my surprise, he firmed up his grip. He finally looked down at me, studying me, when a fleeting smile ghosted his face.

"You want me to go with them," he said softly, reading my mind. I nodded. He grunted.

Leigh tilted her head towards Harper. "You think a demon will attack?"

"Always a possibility. Demon activity has been suspiciously low lately. But if the idiot got himself in a bad situation, I should be there to help." His squeezed my hand once. "We'll go check on your boyfriend. Rest and recover, and for Christ's sake, no more crazy shit."

With his help, I scooted back down into my bed and watched them leave. I laid my head back against my pillow, worry bubbling in my guts. Bear snuggled right back next to me and sighed. *At least someone's content.* I might have been out of my coma and on the road to recovery, but I couldn't shake the feeling that shit was about to hit the proverbial fan."

Brace. Brace. Brace.

5

CAMDEN

C amden woke sitting in a plush chair facing floor-to-ceiling windows overlooking Tampa Bay. According to a pamphlet on the low coffee table in front of him, he was in a five-star high rise hotel suite with no recollection of how he'd gotten into the room. In one hand he had a glass tumbler of whiskey. With the other he mindlessly rubbed a button on his shirt between his fingers. The whole time, he racked his brain trying to come up with a reason for this lapse in memory.

Don't panic, he thought. His knee bounced as his thoughts raced, and he leaned back to stare at the ceiling. The last thing he remembered was walking towards his restaurant.

"How did I get here?" He looked down at himself. "Why am I dressed like this?"

He wore a fitted black blazer that had the outline of red roses stitched into the fabric. His black slacks were slim-cut, black derby shoes shiny, and the ridiculous red button-down he wore was made with silk. Everything fit like he'd been stitched into the suit. Cam rubbed his cheek, expecting the rough feel of blond scruff, but his fingers met smooth skin. He froze, eyes widening. The last time he remembered shaving was before Sam's coma.

When did I do that? His stomach cramped with anxiety. *This is too much.* He stood and set his whiskey on the coffee table. An involuntary groan escaped him. He felt like one big bruise.

"Son of a bitch," he gasped. "What the hell? Was I in a goddamn brawl?"

Camden was no stranger to the bodily after-affects of fighting. He pressed a fist to his right kidney. The muscles in his shoulder tightened against the movement. He doubled over, bracing himself against the arm of his chair until the shock wore off. After taking a deep breath, he straightened once more, carefully this time, and went to the bathroom. It was a gold and grey marbled affair that had a sunken jacuzzi tub.

His reflection in the mirror looked like him. Well, a polished and posher version of himself, but Camden none-theless. He touched his blond curls, which were cut shorter than yesterday. He didn't recall getting a haircut. His green-gold eyes looked keen and clear, starkly different to how he felt inside. Camden smoothed his hands down the lapels of the flamboyant blazer he had on and drew in a deep breath, all the while his heart thundered against ribs.

He turned the tap on high, cupped his hands under the strong stream of cold water, and splashed his face few times. Grabbing a white hand towel, he dried himself off while walking back into the suite. He tossed the towel onto the bed.

"Alright, Bennett, there has to be a clue in here some-where," Camden muttered, trying to rationalize his circumstances to himself.

He opened every drawer, door, and cabinet in the

room. In the night stand next to the bed, he found his wallet, keys, Rolex watch, and a filigreed silver lighter. His brow furrowed, eyes narrowing. He didn't own a lighter.

Camden flipped open his leather billfold. All his credit cards, identification, and three hundred dollars cash were right at home where they were supposed to be. He closed the wallet and stowed it in his back pocket, along with his keys. He put on his watch with deliberate slowness.

He picked up the lighter, turned it upside down and saw the initials C.R.B. *Camden Remington Bennett.* Shock numbed his fingers and he nearly dropped the stupid thing. Tossing it on the bedside table, not wanting to even hold it, he searched further back in the drawer.

"Where's my cell?" He pinched the bridge of his nose. *Why can't I remember anything?* Camden's frustration rose. He glanced at his wrist. It was a quarter past nine in the morning on Tuesday. *Where did Monday go?*

Cam snatched the landline phone receiver and dialed his restaurant. The line rang and rang. "Pick up, damnit."

"Sorcerie kitchen, Jackie speaking," said a female voice in a crisp tone. While Camden's sous chef was a good friend, she was not who he needed at the moment.

"It's Cam. Is Renard there?"

"Boss!" Her voice warmed but morphed into an offended demand. "Where have you been? Are you alright? We've been worried sick. Renard ended up having to call your mother about the leak in the wall. She's furious, by the way."

Cam grimaced, glanced around his hotel room, and muttered, "You wouldn't believe me if I told you."

"What was that?"

"Nothing. I'll deal my mother. Do I need to do anything about the leak? Is everything okay now?" He rubbed the back of his neck, guilt and confusion gnawing at him. *What happened to me?*

"No, Renard took that bullet. You owe him a raise, or something, because your mother is a maniacal bitch."

Camden would have laughed if it weren't so true. Aerona Bennett was a piece of work. Ruthless and cold-hearted, she terrorized his staff regularly. He wasn't looking forward to speaking with her, but she had never treated Renard with any respect. Camden's executive chef deserved more than a raise. *I should make him a partner.*

"You there, boss?"

"Yes. And noted."

"Good. Now, back to why you haven't returned any of our calls or texts. Are you okay, boss?" Jackie asked, lowering her voice.

"It seems I've misplaced my cell." Cam patted his pockets as if it would magically appear. "As soon as I get a new one today, I'll shoot you a text."

"Sounds good. Are you still at the farmhouse?"

Camden's heart tripped a beat. *Sam!* "No, I'm ..." He ripped a hand though his hair and scrubbed his face. "I had to runs some errands."

"Gotcha." There was a pause and then, "Are you okay, boss? You sound a little stressed."

"Dammit, I—" *Woke up in a hotel with no idea how I got here and the last twenty-four hours are missing from my memory.* "I'm heading over to see Sam now."

"Alright. I hate to ask, but will you be coming back to the restaurant sometime soon?"

Camden's eyes narrowed. Jackie wasn't prone to invasiveness. "What's wrong?"

"It's just—" A long pause filled the airwaves. "Yesterday's run-in with your mother wasn't the first incident we've had while you've been gone. She's popped in much

more often than normal. Each time she does, she micro-
manages everyone. That sweet hostess girl we hired a
month ago quit. Aerona reduced her to tears because her
shirt wasn't tucked in tightly enough and her earrings were
too dangly."

"Shit. Was it that red-head college freshman girl?"

"That's the one," Jackie confirmed.

"I'm sorry." Camden shook his head, guilt punching
him in the gut. "I promise I'll handle her."

"It's okay, Cam. You look out for all your staff like
family. No one wanted to tell you because you had enough
to deal with."

"You give me more grace than I deserve." Camden
glanced at his watch. "Listen, I still need to speak to
Renard. Is he there?"

"Sir, it's Tuesday. His day off. Remember?"

Shit. Shit. Camden rubbed his brow with his fingertips,
a headache exploding behind his eyes. "It can wait. I'll be
in touch. Call the farmhouse for me? Let them know I'm
on the way."

"You got it."

After Jackie hung up, he set the receiver back in its
cradle. *Sam.* Camden closed his eyes for a moment. He
wanted to kiss her, to hold her, to tell her that he didn't
care if she was a Warrior that battled demons. And more
than anything else, he wanted to know what the hell
happened to him.

He grabbed up his meager belongings and headed out.
Down in the hotel lobby, Cam walked up to the front desk.
He had no bags. "I'm—I guess I'm checking out."

"Mr. Bennett! Was everything to your liking? Is there a
problem with the room? Was your second steak perfect? I
hope they found the wine you wanted." The concierge's
brown eyes held wonder and fear. His name tag said Raj

Reddy. He gulped. "I'm sorry we couldn't put you in the penthouse."

"Ah, well," Cam ran a hand through his hair and coughed. "The room was perfect," he lied with a dazzling smile. "Unfortunately, something has come up and I'll have to be on my way. I don't need a refund. Just a receipt."

"Of course, sir." Raj returned Cam's smile as he tapped away at his computer. A printer hummed to life behind him. "I understand. Shall I have valet bring up your car?"

"That would be great."

As Raj made a call, Camden turned around and leaned backward against the counter. He chewed his lip. *Steak? Wine?* This whole experience confounded him. He watched the people of the lobby come and go. A child chattered to his parents and they were clearly enamored. A fountain bubbled. Chandelier crystals sparked. *But how did I end up here?*

"Mr. Bennett?"

Camden turned at the sound of his name and forced a pleasant expression into place—his hospitality face. "Yes? What did you say?"

"We can charge it to the credit card you provided when you checked in."

"That's fine." *Just hurry up.*

Raj Reddy handed Camden a receipt and pointed at the bottom line. "Please sign here."

Cam glanced at the date but signed the paper with a flourish, not even bothering to look at the amount owed. When he saw his signature, he jerked back, pen suspended in hand. *The hell? This isn't my handwriting.*

He needed to get to Sam and needed to do that now, before he lost all sense. He took several steps backward. Remembering that he had to keep his shit together in public, he thanked Raj and jogged out of the circling glass door.

A young man with an unfortunate case of acne was at Cam's side a moment later. "Got your stub, Mr. Bennett?"

"Stub?"

The pimply kid held up half of a yellow slip, one edge perforated where it had been ripped in two. "For security. That's all."

"Oh!" Camden patted his chest, pants pockets, and then pulled out his wallet. *Please be in here.* The ticket's twin was tucked in with the cash.

"Here ya go, kid." Camden handed it over. "Sorry 'bout that."

"Don't worry about it. Car's here." He jerked a chin out towards the incoming vehicle.

The valet drove up in his dark green Audi and parked next to the curb. Panic reached out and grabbed Camden by the throat. He hadn't driven his sports car since Sam went into her coma. In fact, he distinctly remembered he'd left the Shaw's farmhouse early yesterday morning driving his azure Range Rover.

"What the hell?" he muttered, rubbing his eyes. "Hey, kid!" he shouted after the valet. "Sorry. Didn't catch your name. I drove here in this?"

The pimple-faced guy gaped at Camden like he was mental.

Maybe I am? It sure as hell feels like it. None of this makes sense. He needed to get to Sam, to the Warriors. Xavier would have an answer, even though the eccentric man scared the shit out of Camden.

"Mr. Bennett?" Confusion furrowed the young man's ginger brows. "I don't understand. You told me not to scratch it or you'd personally see to it that I was fired." The young man blanched, his freckles standing out along with the zits.

"Uh ... I did?" Camden blanched. He could be accused of many things but a condescending asshole wasn't one of them. "Man, I'm sorry."

"No worries, sir. We were extra careful with her."

"The car isn't my concern. Being a dick is never appropriate." Camden reached into his wallet a second time and pulled out a more-than-generous tip. "Take this. You didn't deserve to be spoken to like that."

The boy stared at the fifty-dollar bill in Camden's hand.

"Th-thank you."

"I gotta go." Camden walked backward to his Audi. "Thanks for keeping her safe."

He turned around after the kid waved at him and jogged the last few steps to the driver's side. Since he was doing his best to not freak the hell out, he pulled up his GPS with trembling hands, trying to gain his bearings. He stretched out his fingers, took a breath, then buckled up and hit the road. Once he reached I-75 south, he floored the gas, speeding along to the Shaw's farmhouse.

The drive did nothing to calm Camden's mind. Where were his real clothes? Where was his phone? How had he gotten his Audi? Where was his Range Rover? His whirling thoughts made him dizzy. His palms on the steering wheel were tacky with sweat.

Camden stared at the lines flashing thorough the windshield as he drove down the interstate, his heart revving along with the high-performance engine. His stomach fluttered with unease. A loaded semi-truck roared past him, blaring a horn, it was only then that Camden realized he'd drifted into the lane next to him.

"Oh, shit!" He jerked back into his lane, let the truck

pass, and turned on the blinker. He eased off to the right, onto the shoulder of the road, threw the car in park, and turned on his flashers. There had to be a reason his memory was like Swiss cheese—a perfectly logical explanation as to why he couldn't remember jackshit. He touched his forehead to the steering wheel. "Dude, get a grip."

Camden stayed like that, taking measured, even breaths. "You will not have a full-blown panic attack on the side of the highway."

After the rising tide of anxiety receded some, Cam raised his head and pulled out the silver lighter from a pocket on the inside of his jacket. He flicked the lid open and shut while staring out at the open road before him.

Think, Bennett. After several minutes, he glanced down at the metal object and frowned. *Wait. I threw this on the bed in the hotel. When did I pocket this?* And why were his initials engraved on it?

"What the actual fuck is going on?" Tears burned his eyes. "Stop!" *Get to the farm. Talk to Xavier. See what he thinks.*

If anyone could help him, it would be the Warriors of Light. His cocktail of confusion, fear, and mounting panic made his stomach clench. There had to be a reasonable explanation for what happened to him. His head swam and his headache spread from his eyes to his temples. Camden glanced in his rearview mirror. The whites of his eyes flashed red, a crushing tightness seized his chest, and extreme fatigue washed over him.

His eyes rolled back in his head and he collapsed against his seat. Less than a heartbeat later, he snapped awake, straightened up, and squared his shoulders. He looked into his rear view, adjusting it to get a better look at himself.

His eyes were no longer weary with worry; they were confident with a devious gleam. Camden lifted his chin, turned his head right then left, admiring the view of his jawline. He dipped his head down, studying his blonde eyebrows, then he licked a fingertip to smooth down the hair on one. He leaned back, not taking his focus from his reflection.

A slow, almost sensual, smile crept onto his face.

"You are fantastic, Bennett," he purred, picking up the lighter he'd dropped. He popped it open and thumbed the trigger, the flame danced in his mesmerizing green eyes. "We have work to do, young chap. Let ol' Dominic take you places you've never been."

6

HARPER

Everyone had relocated to the farmhouse when Sam went into her coma. Xavier ended up commandeering Pops's humble gym office since Camden-fucking-Bennett had taken over the one in the farmhouse. For the past week, Xavier conducted all his important business from behind the dinged-up desk, sitting in a duct-taped leather chair, battling shitty Wi-Fi coverage. He didn't have a downshift and was one of the busiest individuals I'd ever met. It was in this office that Kestler and I—along with Bear—found him sipping tea while reading over a report laid flat on the desktop.

Xavier had propped open the door and was bent over the desk, reading. His Italian indigo button-down, neat haircut, tidy goatee, and general larger-than-life energy filled every corner of the dingy office. His Guardian raven Nyx sat on her bronze perch and glared at the dog glued to my calf. I wasn't sure we'd all fit in that small space. And why Sam's dog decided to tag along with me, I didn't know, but I found his presence settling nonetheless.

Xavier glanced up when I knocked on the door jamb. His eyes darted from Kestler to me.

"How's the patient? Has Miss Fife done any further damage to her person?"

"No, sir. She's resting." Kestler settled into one of the generic guest chairs in front of him. "She asked Harper to go with Jax and me."

I sat next to her in its twin. *Fucking Bennett.* Bear threw his body on the floor, covered my feet, and sighed. His dog bed was ten feet away.

Xavier's brows shot up. "And you're going?"

"Not for him," I said. "For Sam. She's overly worried. And I don't want her doing more stupid shit if I say no."

"I see," Xavier mused. Nyx did a hop-glide and landed on his shoulder. He scratched under her beak. "Didn't you tell her about our current lack of demon activity? It's best to be vigilant but we can't be paranoid."

"Told her enough to pacify her," I said. Bear started snoring, still on my feet. I nudged my foot and got no response.

"She's concerned Cam's going to get hurt, or worse," Leigh explained. "And if he is, she wants Harper to help him."

I shrugged. "If it keeps her calm…" *I will do it.*

Sam wouldn't rest and heal if she was worried about her goddamn boyfriend. So, if finding Bennett and dragging his ass back here kept Sam calm, I'd walk through fire to do it.

"I don't see this as an issue," Xavier said. "If a demon attacks, Miss Kestler and Mr. Bozeman will be there."

Nyx croaked and chattered at her Warrior. She rifled her beak through the hair at his temple. Xavier responded to her in Spanish. I narrowed my eyes. While Xavier hadn't come right out and said it, his subtext was clear: I can go on this pathetic reconnaissance mission because there will be Warriors to keep me safe.

God-fucking-damnit.

I threw my shoulders back into the chair and crossed my arms. I was the child of two Warriors but wasn't one myself. There had never been a time in history where Warrior offspring didn't receive an anointing. Except for me. And I loathed being helpless.

Kestler nudged me with her elbow and I cast a sharp glance at her.

She mouthed, "You okay?" I ground my molars but nodded once. Xavier treated me as an equal, but his off-handed comment was a punch to the balls.

"I assume you'll be leaving soon?" Xavier asked.

"Yes, sir," Kestler said.

Xavier asked me, "What of Miss Fife? Is there anything I should know?"

"I've never dealt with demon poison and blood-magic comas, but physically, she'll improve quickly now that she's awake. However, mentally—" I rapped the arm of my chair with my knuckles and sucked my teeth. "Time will tell. Having Bennett here gives Sam one less thing to worry about." And since I didn't trust Bennett, I added, "He also knows too much. He's been living here, listening to our conversations. If he lands in the wrong hands, we might be compromised."

Xavier leaned back, the chair protesting with a loud squeak.

"Fair point," he murmured. Nyx squawked, hopped onto the desk, and fixed one bright eye on Xavier. He rubbed his lower lip in deep thought and then, as if remembering we were there, said, "You should be off, no?"

"Thank you, sir." Kestler rose to her feet. She headed for the door.

When I stood, Bear scrambled to his paws. Xavier's quiet *tsk* met my ears. I turned. Bear took a stutter-step then sat next to me. He lifted his chin as if to listen. I sensed Kestler's hesitancy when she didn't leave.

"He'll join you in a moment," Xavier said to the Warrior. "I need a private word with Mr. Tate." She sucked in a breath, but promptly obeyed. The door closed behind her.

"Andrew has been asking for you."

Not happening. "He knows where to find me. We live in the same house."

"He's not well, *hijo.*" Xavier lowered his voice. "He's losing his will to live."

Unease crept along my shoulders and slithered down my arms. Pops hadn't been the same since Ma died, with good reason. They'd been married for centuries, but more than that, they'd taken Warrior vows. There had been a blood covenant made between them. When Ma died, part of Pops did as well. From what I understood, he wouldn't be long for this world. And when he went, so did any protective boarders the man had ever erected: around churches, the farmhouse, and any properties he wanted to keep safe.

Pops had rarely offered me kindness as a child, leaving the nurturing to Ma. His training boarded on cruelty. As a result, I was a highly skilled fighter, able to recite a fuckton of Warrior history, yet useless in an actual demon battle. I'd started moving past the fact that he'd hidden the true cause of my parents' deaths. It had taken six years. But what I couldn't forgive was that, in his fear, Pops hadn't told his current Warriors about how deadly their foe truly was.

He hadn't told them that the Mage betrayed the Light for the Dark. He hadn't told them that she was a powerful being fueled by revenge. He hadn't told them the Mage had slaughtered anyone else associated with the Warrior network. She'd left Pops alive as punishment and promised to do it again should he attempt to rebuild. And he hadn't said a goddamn thing to Sam and Kestler about how the original fallen angels turned into the strongest, most ruthless demons.

But shielding people from gristly facts had always been his fatal fucking flaw.

It was that flaw that had gotten Ma killed and almost ended Sam's life.

So the fact that Pops was losing his will to live was paltry compared to his sins.

I wasn't Jesus. I didn't forgive so freely.

"And what would sitting at his bedside do?" I asked. "Fix him? Provide miraculous recovery? Bring back the lost piece of his soul that Ma took when she died?"

Xavier frowned. "I'm concerned with you making amends with the man who raised you."

Fuck that. I glared at the wizened Adviser. "With all due respect, that's none of your business."

Undeterred, he said, "Think about it, Mr. Tate. You may regret it later." Xavier held up a hand when I opened my mouth. "Unwillingness to forgive will eat your soul."

Bear pushed his weight into my leg. He huffed and his soulful eyes peered up at me. A breathy whine escaped him. I knelt on one knee and rubbed behind his ears, touching my forehead to his. That was as good as agreeing with Xavier a dog could get. I heard Xavier approach and pulled back from Bear but kept my focus on the canine.

Xavier's presence loomed over me. "I'm not telling you what to do, my dear man."

"Sure, you are. Only you've veiled it with concern for

my wellbeing." I massaged one of Bear's shoulders. He groaned and leaned into my touch.

Xavier sighed so heavily and with such weariness that I looked up. He ran a palm over his salt-and-pepper goatee. "You can't hide your hurt from me. I've been training Warriors and reading people for centuries. Andrew has made grievous errors where you, Miss Fife, and Miss Kestler are concerned, but hear me, you *will* miss him when he's gone. You'll wish he was around. You'll wish for another chance to make things right." Xavier slipped a hand into a front pocket. "I may have only known you a short time, but you love fiercely and betrayals of that love wound you deeply."

My nose and eyes burned. I averted my gaze to the floor and kept one steadying hand on Bear. Fucking emotions. *This asshole isn't holding his punches.*

When I said nothing, he released a tired sigh.

"Go look after the hapless Mr. Bennett. I suspect Miss Kestler and Mr. Bozeman are waiting."

I left the office and whistled for Bear with a slap on my thigh. He scrambled after me and trotted along, matching my pace. Excited chatter met my ears as I entered the farmhouse through the back door. Laughter led me to the Florida room outside the kitchen. Bear took tentative steps to follow me, looking twice towards the other half of the house where Sam was laid up.

"Go on," I told him. "She needs you."

The pit bull huffed before taking off to Sam's room. I jogged down the white stone tiled steps leading to the window-enclosed sunroom. Natural light bathed the space with warmth, and green plants added a touch of tranquility. DH, Bozeman, and one of Adviser Holland's Warriors were all seated on wicker furniture, playing the card game

Bullshit. I joined Kestler's side where she leaned against the wall.

"What did Adviser Gerena want with you?" Kestler asked without taking her eyes off the trio.

None of your concern. I crossed my arms and shrugged.

"We're back to deflecting, huh?" Kestler snipped. "And here I thought we were friends."

Kestler was my friend. I didn't have many. When I said nothing, she regarded me with a raised eyebrow. Fucking hell, she had gotten as nosy as Sam. I caved.

"He asked me to go see Pops."

She nodded once. "Good. You should. Adviser Shaw has asked for you several times."

I was spared having to answer when Talia Zohar, Adviser Holland's Warrior shouted, "Jackson, you cheat!" Zohar's Israeli accent thickened in outrage as she slammed one hand down on the coffee table and flipped her dark brown braid over her shoulder with the other. She leaned forward and nailed Bozeman with her golden-brown eyes. "I call *bullshit.*"

"You're finally getting the hang of it, Tal!" DH said, giggling.

"Took me long enough, no?" Zohar laughed. The lithe five-foot-seven Warrior of Light had bronze skin, dark hair, brown eyes, and plenty of swagger.

"You got me," Bozeman said. "Looks like I'm out." He tossed his cards down, but held Zohar's gaze.

A private smile tugged the corner of Bozeman's mouth. He brushed his fingers over hers. The bold woman before him blushed.

I held in a surprised chuckle and thought, *How 'bout that?* Warriors of Light had enough shit to deal with, finding some happiness with each other wasn't a bad thing.

"We need to go," I muttered to Kestler.

"I'll grab Jax and meet you out front," she said.

Bozeman wrenched his eyes off Zohar. "Y'all ready?"

"Harper!" DH shouted, her smile turning radiant. "Join us! Maybe you can beat Talia. She's on a roll."

Xavier's adopted daughter had recently made it her personal mission to try and get me to socialize. I turned her down every time, but it didn't sway her. Persistence should have been her middle name. But if I were being honest with myself, the little genius prodigy had endeared herself to me. There was something to be said about her youthful exuberance and blind optimism.

"Sorry, little bit." I pushed off the wall. "Some other time."

"Holding you to that." DH started collecting the scattered cards. "You guys going somewhere?"

"Yes," I said. "Can you look after Sam for me? Keep her comfortable?"

DH froze, a serious look crossing her petite features.

"Are you doing something dangerous? Should I be worried? Is this a covert op? Does Sam know? I don't want to slip and say something to her if it's a secret. What about you? Will you be safe? You're not a Warrior." The tiny teen flailed her arms. "Tell me nothing! They can't torture info out of me if I don't know anything."

Fucking hell. Years of disciplined training kept my face passive and body relaxed. What I really wanted to do was slam my fist into the brick wall. The reminder that I was a mere mortal was one thing. But imagining DH being tormented for answers made my clenched jaw ache.

"We're just gonna go check on Camden, D." Kestler's arm brushed mine. I caught her side-eye glance and shifted my shoulders.

"Need backup?" Zohar asked, all her playfulness gone.

"We'll be fine," I said. She studied me a little more

intently. I shook my head. "Stay here. Protect the boundary. Go relieve Kalakaua. She'll be without her partner
since Jax is coming with us."

"I will find Sajid," Zohar said with focused intensity.
"We will take over for Leilani on border patrol." She left
out the sunroom's side door.

"Is Camden in trouble?" DH asked, walking over
to me.

"Don't know," I answered. "Sam thinks so."

DH's green eyes widened and she threw her scrawny
frame at me. A split second from the collision, I lifted my
arms up and off my chest. She wrapped toothpick limbs
around me and hugged tight. Paralyzed, I looked at
Kestler. She fought off her smile. DH let me go and transferred her strangle-hold to Kestler.

"Please. Please. Please. Be careful," DH said.

Kestler rubbed the girl's back. "We'll do our best."

SORCERIE, Bennett's upscale, five-star restaurant, sat right
in front of the water on St. Pete Beach. He owned this
place with his mother, whom no one had met yet—not
even Sam. And since it was still too early to be open, the
establishment's lot was empty. A few cars were parked to
the side of the building in spaces marked for employees
only. What concerned us were the smashed up outdoor
security cameras.

This can't be good.

"Is that—" Bozeman thrust his arm between the driver
and passenger seat from the back. "That's Camden's SUV,
right?"

"Yep," Kestler agreed. "Those are his plates."

A sleek Range Rover stuck out like a sore thumb

among the mundane coupe and sedan. I pulled up next to the expensive vehicle. We filed out, shutting our doors quietly so we didn't draw attention. Bozeman circled around Bennett's vehicle, peeking inside the windows. Kestler and I went to the driver's side. My hand was on the car door when she stiffened next to me and froze statue-still. I glanced over my shoulder. Her eyes were closed and her lips parted. She inhaled.

"Kestler?" I asked.

Without opening her eyes, she stepped past me and laid her palm on the window. "There was no struggle at this point." She glanced at me and then up at Bozeman. I moved out of her way as she turned and took two steps in the direction of the restaurant. I knew Kestler had super-natural tracking abilities—a sixth sense from her inner Angel.

"He left the car of his own free will and walked over there." Kestler pointed towards the building.

"How do you know that?" Bozeman asked, a single brow lifting.

"Her Warrior gift," I murmured. "Not unlike your enhanced speed. Watch her."

Kestler was halfway across the lot when she stopped. "Something caught his attention." She spun on a booted toe and headed towards the side of the restaurant, near the dumpsters. "He went this way."

We followed, our shoes crunching on the crushed shell lot. She came to another abrupt stop and threw out an arm, signaling for us to stop. Kestler turned in another slow circle, her eyes closed, skimming her palm as if reading the air.

Bozeman leaned down an inch or two and asked me in a low tone, "This is amazing. How does her ability work?"

I tilted my head in Kestler's direction. "From what she's

told me, she sees residual outlines from recent events. Like a fucking imprint of an image."

"So, Leigh's a ghost hunter?"

I snorted. Bozeman grinned.

"Guys, follow me." Kestler waved for us to follow her as she disappeared around the building.

We jogged past a white-washed privacy fence and came to a halt just behind her. She stood at the mouth of the dumpster alley. Shredded clothes, ripped shoes, and a calf-brown purse were strewn along a strip of enclosed pavement. There was a bloody knife with fat black flies buzzing around it. The hair on the back of my neck prickled.

"Oh, fuck," I said. "Kestler, how old do you think this is?"

Kestler's hand was at her throat and she'd rocked back on her feet. Her eyes and mouth were open wide.

"I-I don't k-know. More than a few hours. Old enough that I'm not picking up a heat signature." She rubbed her palms on her jean-clad thighs.

"Man," Bozeman muttered, "this place still reeks of sulfur."

Since we weren't calling the cops and had no problem disturbing the scene, I squatted and picked up a cracked cell phone. I flipped it over and saw a recognizable surfer-brand logo on the case cover.

"This is Bennett's." I tossed the phone to Kestler. "How the fuck did he call and text you if this was lying in an alley?"

"I don't know," Kestler mused. "His voicemail came from an unknown number. Figured he called from inside the restaurant."

Bozeman picked up a navy silk shirt. "These are children and woman's clothes."

Interesting. I joined him. In fact, we'd have to clean it up.

I took the blouse from him. The front had been slit open. Whatever happened here did not include women and children. It involved demons.

Bozeman pointed a few feet away to a trail of red. He leaned down and touched his fingers to the sticky substance. "This is human."

Demon blood was black.

Kestler followed me as I walked the path of blood. It completely vanished around the dumpster. I whispered, "The fuck?" under my beath.

Kestler shook her head. "I'm trying not to panic, but all this evidence suggests that something Real Bad happened."

"Harper! Leigh!" Bozeman called from the opening of the ally. "Is this Camden's?" In the male Warrior's hand was a tan and grey boat shoe, dangling from a hooked index finger.

"Fucking Bennett," I swore. "What shit have you gotten yourself into?"

Sam had been right to worry. *Why the hell did we let Bennett go out alone?* I ran fingers through my hair. "We say nothing to Sam until we know more."

Alarm flashed in Kestler's hazel eyes. "You would lie to her? Ask *me* to lie? You remember how well that turned out for Adviser Shaw, right?"

"If we tell her right away, do you think she'll sit idly by in bed like a good little patient while her fucking boyfriend is missing, possibly kidnapped, and injured?"

She blew out a breath. I saw the argument form on her lips, then pass when she realized I was right. She grimaced. "I hate hiding things from her. She *will* ask and she *will* know that we're lying."

No doubt. "Let me worry about that." I headed back towards Bozeman.

If I withheld information, even the slightest amount, Sam would be furious—possibly even hate me. Kestler was right. I couldn't and wouldn't lie to her about Bennett. Before she'd gotten injured, I'd made Sam a promise: even if everyone else betrayed her, I would be in her corner. No questions. No matter what. Lying to her wasn't an option. But I'd have a hard fucking time keeping her in that damn bed otherwise.

Kestler and I met Bozeman at the end of the alleyway and turned a slow circle, keeping my eyes peeled for anything we missed. The one security camera overlooking the dumpster was smashed. The evidence we'd found wasn't much to go on. I scratched at the scruff on my jaw with the backs of my knuckles.

What the hell happened and what the fuck was I going to tell Sam?

7

SAM

DH was the real MVP. She'd come to my rescue and saved me from death-by-boredom. My personal pint-sized saint hooked me up with a small TV, helped me sit up in bed, and left me with the remote. Occasionally, Nigel would bring me snacks. Bear came and went, checking on me like some kind of canine house host while I stayed in my bed.

I'd just shoved a piece of Nigel's homemade pita bread, loaded with an obscene amount of tzatziki, into my mouth and mashed the "next" button for my fifth consecutive episode of *Supernatural*, when a knock sounded at my closed door.

Since I'd woke up, no one had bothered with a pesky thing like asking permission to enter my room. I didn't mind, but now I was curious. Who was behind door number one? I thumbed the pause and Dean Winchester's face froze on the screen.

I chewed fast and swallowed before saying, "Come in?"

Leilani—The Hawaiian Harpy—with her perfect golden skin, perfect white teeth, perfect face with perfect makeup, and perfect messy ponytail walked in. Even her jean shorts and plain tank top fit her like she was a model. She must have read my *what-the-hell-are-you-doing-here* expression because she held up her hands.

"I come in peace. We need to talk."

I grunted and threw her some side-eye. *"If I hit play and ignore her, will she go away?"* I asked Letty.

"Don't be rude, Brave One."

I pursed my lips and pointed to the chair next to my bed. "I'm not going anywhere." Leilani moved with more grace than should be allowed, and I huffed out a quiet snort. "What do you want?"

She lighted on the edge of the seat. "To clear the air."

I raised a brow.

"Do you remember what I said to you when we first met?" she asked.

"You said a lot of things." I shifted in bed to get a better position, preparing for a showdown. "But I've also had some trauma lately, so refresh my memory."

"You're cocky, lack impulse control, and disobey orders as you see fit."

I snapped my fingers. "That's right. I remember now." *I never forgot, little miss harpy-lady.*

Lelani steepled her fingers and pressed them to her lips before dropping them. "I know that doesn't endear me to you, but I would like for you to hear me out."

"If this is your idea of Warrior bonding ..." I snagged a carrot, dipped it in hummus, and shoved it in my mouth hole. Around that bite, I said, "You need to take some classes on how to win people over."

"And you need to stop being so damn stupid."

"This is how you 'clear the air'?" Anger climbed my spine. This chick didn't know me. I sneered. "Did you decide to come at me because I'm not at full strength? I was perfectly happy watching Dean Winchester declare that he needed to salt and burn the bones of a particularity gnarly ghost. And in case it escaped your notice, I am obeying orders by staying in this bed, you little—"

"I've spent," Lelani's interruption sliced through my words, "nearly every waking hour with either Leigh or Harper while we've been in Adviser Shaw's home. They are good people. Leigh is a damn fine Warrior and Harper —as gruff as he is—is honest and intelligent."

"Yes, they are." I tamped down a growl as ire flared in my chest. Leigh was my best friend. Harper was my—er, my whatever he was.

Leilani wiped her hands on her shorts. "The thing is, they clearly think the world of you. I watched Harper's heroic attempt to save your life. How desperate he was while you were in your coma. I've also seen how lost Leigh is without you. We had to remind her to eat. I've come to respect their opinions."

My stomach bottomed out and tears prickled behind my eyes. I looked down at my hands, one empty and one holding the remote. I'd be dead if it hadn't been for Harper. I'd be lost at sea if it weren't for Leigh. They were the two people in my life who I could depend on. Hearing Leilani speak like she knew them, like there were *her* friends, did odd things to my feelings. Shame was not an emotion I dwelled on very often. But here we were.

"I don't need you to kick me when I'm down," I said when I finally found my voice.

"Right. I'm not good at this." Leilani's cheeks reddened even through her golden skin. "What I'm trying to say, and failing to do so, is that I watched how fiercely loyal Leigh and Harper are to you." She cleared her throat. "So, I thought that perhaps I need to figure out why."

Did the Hawaiian Harpy say she wanted to know why I have friends? She'd been nothing but cold and rude to me from minute one. She openly and shamelessly flirted with Harper when we'd first met. Leilani had spent a week with my friends—my family—without me present, and she now had a crisis of conscience? I bit down a sarcastic laugh. I was *trying* to be more diplomatic on this side of my coma. Less ready-fire-aim and more think-before-I-speak.

I didn't trust her. She didn't trust me. I met her brown eyes. "Go on."

She sighed again, as if humbling herself to meet me halfway was a complete hardship.

"I've always been a bit conceited. I'm proud. A perfectionist. And I'm not used to being challenged." She glanced up at the ceiling. "And perhaps a little vain." She looked back at me. "I may have reacted that way to you because the Warrior in me recognized the exceptional Power and strength in you. Whoever your angel is, mine capitulated to yours almost immediately. And it was instant—"

"Jealousy," I finished for her. One half of my mouth lifted in a wry grin. I wasn't about to tell her that I was insanely jealous of her—my ego had limits. "You know we're never gonna have sleep overs and braid each other's hair. Doubtful we'll ever be friends."

She smiled, the corners of her eyes crinkling when she did. "That's likely true. But that doesn't mean we can't find something about each other that helps us be allies. We fight a common enemy."

She was offering an olive branch and I'd be an idiot not to take it. The Mage was an evil, powerful being. We Warriors of Light couldn't afford to let petty differences cause dissension amongst the troops. And since the Mage was human at the core, and currently unkillable, the good guys needed to stay united.

To my own surprise, I held out my hand. "Truce."

Shock flitted over Leilani's face, but she took my hand in a firm grasp. "Allies."

"Not friends."

"Never."

"Am I interrupting?" a male voice cut in.

My heart stumbled and then triple-timed. *Camden.*

He stood in my doorway. His green-gold eyes, aways holding a wee touch of pain, glittered with amusement. I wanted to jump up from my bed. To rant and rave. To beat the ever-loving shit out of him but also kiss him until he gasped for air. He was safe. He was here. So many questions ping-ponged through me.

"That's my cue," Leilani muttered. "I'll let Harper know Camden's back and in one piece." Cam moved to the side so Lani could leave, but she stopped in the doorway and looked over her shoulder at me before she left. "For what it's worth, I'm glad you survived and I'm glad you aren't dead. We need all the Warriors we can get. War is coming. I feel it."

I nodded, but my eyes were unable to leave Camden. My racing heart froze up like an overworked AC unit, and a sob escaped me before I could check it. Cam came to me at once, skirting around Leilani like she wasn't there, and took my head between his hands, his fingers burrowing in my hair. He kissed me until I was breathless, then pulled back and kissed the tip of my nose, my closed eyelids, and forehead.

My dam of tears sprang free as dread and tension whooshed out of me, opening me up for a new, crashing wave of emotion.

How *dare* he endanger himself?

"Where the hell have you been?" I pushed on his chest but held on with a fist clutching his jacket lapel. "Gallivanting off like you—"

"I'm sorry." He released my head so he could brush my wet cheeks with the back of his knuckles. "I'm sorry for making you worry, babe."

My brows shot sky high then furrowed. *Babe?* I let him go, leaned back, and gave him a second look—a more assessing study of his person.

He was dressed in a black suit so tailored to his body it looked like he'd been stitched into it. In three months of dating, he'd never worn anything like this. I mean, I wasn't going to complain because it played up his assets, but it didn't make sense. Camden eased himself down onto the bed, facing me. I ran my fingers along the underside of one lapel, traced the red outlined roses, brushed the collar of his crimson silk shirt.

"Trying something new?"

"Yep." He flashed me a devious, sexy smile. "You like it?"

He pulled my hand from his chest and brushed his lips over the pads of my fingers. My stomach swooped, and I inhaled a sharp breath. When I did, my Warrior's sense of smell caught an odd scent wafting off him: a faint hint of acrid smoke.

"You don't smell like you," I grumped.

He lifted a shoulder and took a whiff of himself. Mischief sparked in his eyes. "Are you pulling your Warrior juju on me?"

I stiffened at how casually he'd asked this question. The first mention that he knew what I was, and it was said offhand. I gaped at him. He chuckled.

With a patient smile, he reached out to reclaim my hand and said, "Sam, I've spent the past seven days in a house full of supernatural humans. Adviser Gerena explained everything the day we brought you here. Leigh, ah—" he grinned "—she gave me a crash course as to what you are."

"She told me Xavier had her go full Warrior in front of you?"

"Yes. That was an *experience*, to say the least. But it's fine. I'm fine. And now I know why you'd flake out on me sometimes." He hit me with a stunning smile, let go of my hand, and smoothed my hair back. "I acted like a horse's ass in front of Mr. Gerena, asking too many questions and refusing to listen. It was the only way he could get my attention. No time to waste, that one."

My eyes widened. "You weren't scared?"

"Well, sure. It's not every day you see someone pull out invisible weapons and start glowing." Camden ran a thumb down my neck, over my racing pulse. "Mr. Gerena offered me sanctuary and he wanted me compliant." He let out a huge sigh and sat back some. "I don't believe he trusts me."

"I wouldn't take it personally." I grabbed his wrists to keep him from pulling too far away from me. "One thing I learned about Xavier in the very short time I've known him is that he doesn't like outsiders. He cares for the Warriors and Seers under his protection. Normal humans? I think he tolerates them for the sake of his calling."

"That so?" Camden's eyes glimmered. He threaded his fingers through mine and settled our hands in his lap. He gave me a rueful smile.

"Harper seems to think there's something suspicious about me because I've only just now started seeing demons. Or that I'm a spy for this Mage—whoever that is. They don't include me in Warrior business. I'm only allowed to stay because of my connection to you."

I snorted. "Harper's paranoid." *And territorial. And confusing. And complicated. And frustrating. And my savior.* Thankfully, that all that stayed in my head. "Xavier's lived for centuries. He's seen some shit, if you know what I mean. I think they're just being cautious. Trust, but verify, and all that."

"Regardless, I've felt like quite the interloper." Camden studied the pattern on my duvet and he let out this sad little laugh. "They've developed a pretty close-knit club."

I squeezed his hand, offering him a moderate smile. "But they let you stay."

"Probably more because they don't trust me. I don't enjoy feeling ostracized." He ducked his head close to me and pressed a whisper-kiss to my forehead. "I stayed for you."

My breath hitched and my side twinged despite pain medicine and Life Elixir. "Then why did you leave? Why did it take so long for you to return? Did you care that I woke up? I was actually worried about your stupid face."

"Silly Samantha," Camden chided. "I'm back. Unharmed. You shouldn't worry like that. It's not good for your recovery."

Samantha? I scrunched my nose, but my irritation at his near twenty-four-hour absence overrode my dislike of being called by my full name. "Something could have happened to you."

"But nothing did." Camden dropped my hand and stood up only so he could sit next to me. He scooted close, hip-to-hip, looped an arm over my shoulder, and tucked me into his side. His cheek rested against my temple. "You've become my favorite person. One who I crave time with. Seeing you in that coma about killed me. I got back here as quickly as I could."

All of my thoughts went *poof*. Abracadabra. I snuggled up against his lean, hard-muscled surfer frame.

"Your worry is not needed," Camden soothed. "The only person you need to be concerned with right now is yourself. Rest and recover." He shifted and dropped a kiss on the top of my head.

Maybe he's right? Why did I worry? Here he was, back at the farmhouse unscathed—albeit dressed like a snappy Millennial hipster instead of his normal beachy college prep look, but that wasn't on trial here. Perhaps a little faith from me was in order? After recent events, my trust in all I thought I knew was rocky. This made my head spin, and a change in subject was in order—just my specialty.

"Leigh said there was an issue with your restaurant. Everything okay?" I swallowed hard when I remembered Dominic had supernaturally killed a man in Camden's kitchen. My gut clenched. "No one else died, did they?"

Cam's fingers, which had been playing with a lock of my hair, went still.

Then he laughed, like he'd brushed off his surprise, and said, "No, babe, a pipe burst in the wall."

What is with the sudden pet names? "Will you have to shut down for repairs?"

Another pause. "Not sure. Hope not. We'll lose a lot of money if we have to."

I leaned back to get a better look at his face. The wound in my side had a lot to say about such movements, and the pain robbed me of breath. A groan escaped me before I could stop it.

"Easy there, wiggle worm." Camden took my chin between his thumb and index fingers. He pressed a quick kiss to my lips. "You should rest."

"But—"

"Let me worry about the restaurant, okay?" He pulled

me back to him once more, settling me in the crook of his body, snagged the remote, and unpaused *Supernatural.* "What matters is that I'm back here with you, safe and sound."

I gnawed on my lower lip, staring straight ahead at the TV without seeing what unfolded on screen. Camden was never one to wave me off like that. In fact, he'd always volunteered information with little-to-no prodding. My bullshit-o-meter spiked. I'd gone through enough boyfriends to know when a dude was distancing himself.

Is that what he's doing? Was Camden-freaking-Bennett trying to end things with me? After helping Harper get me to safety? After staying by my side while I auditioned for *Sleeping Beauty*? After his enthusiastic greeting just now? I stiffened in his arms. He and I had never discussed long-term. Maybe now that I was awake, he had second thoughts about sticking around?

Camden tracing slow circles and swirls on my far shoulder drew me from my runaway thoughts. His fingers wove an absent-minded path, like he'd done it a million times, but the action had a soothing effect. Whatever I'd been so annoyed about, worried about, or on edge over didn't seem to matter as much. However, I wanted Camden to stay. The Mage could still go after him, like before, so I grumbled as much under my breath.

Camden chuckled. "It's nice to know you care about me."

"Of course, I care you big ol' turkey!"

He beamed at me, squeezed me to his side, then went back to his casual hold around my shoulders. "You're cute when you're indignant."

"And you're smokin' hot even when if you gave me a worry-induced ulcer." I poked him not-so-gently in the ribs.

He grabbed my hand, but his rumbling laugh made me grin. We settled back against the headboard, this time more relaxed, and went back to watching Dean and Sam on the TV. After a while, he started that same soothing pattern on my far shoulder. A humming sigh escaped me. Maybe I was overacting and things weren't as dire as I thought them to be.

"BENNETT!" Harper's furious voice bounced down the hallway from the front door. "Where the fuck are you?"

Bear's startled, deep-chested bark echoed in the foyer. My heart bottomed out. The cocoon of serenity Camden and I had been wrapped in evaporated like someone flipped on an exhaust fan. *Whoosh.* Cam leapt from the bed and was on his feet before I could catch myself. I tipped to the side and pain exploded from my ribcage. My breath hissed on my inhale.

"Dammit, Harper," I muttered.

"Shit, sorry, babe," Cam yelped as he swooped in and helped me back to a seated position.

I didn't have time to dwell on Camden's excessive pet name usage when Hurricane Harper blew into my room. The door smacked against the adjoining wall. His eyes found mine and then landed on Camden. A dark look crossed Harper's face. He glowered at Cam, making even my asshole pucker. Only Harper's years of training and discipline kept him from wrapping his fingers around Camden's throat. Leigh slipped in behind Harper. Bear darted around everyone and leapt on the bed. He snuggled against me and my hand went to the top of his head.

"Bennett, in Pop's office. Now." Harper was in full-on fire-breathing dragon mode.

Cam held up his arms, his palms raised in a pacifying gesture. "Whatever you have to ask or say, we can speak in front of Sam."

I thought Harper's jaw would break with how hard he bit down. Even Leigh looked worried.

"What happened?" I asked, turning off the TV to eliminate the unneeded noise.

"This fucker—"

"Is innocent until proven guilty," Leigh chided. Harper's lip twitched like he wanted to say something else, but Leigh turned to Camden and plowed on. "We found some evidence that suggested you were in trouble. That there was a struggle. Are you injured?"

"No, I'm fine." Camden patted over his body. "What did you find?"

"We found your broken goddamn phone and one of your fucking shoes." Harper surged forward and stopped an angel feather's distance away from Cam. "We also found a fucking bloody knife." He smacked Camden square in the chest, sending him sprawling into the chair next to my bed. Harper loomed. "Start talking. Best not lie to me."

Holy Letty's wings! What the fire fart is happening right now? I gaped at Leigh, then looked to Camden, and finally landed my eyes on Harper.

"A bloody knife." My voice sounded weak even to my ears when I echoed Harper's words.

Camden sorted himself in his seat, smoothed his palms down his chest and abdomen. He threw me a wink over his shoulder. My head snapped back. Harper silently snarled at him. Camden *never* freaking winked.

"As you can see," Cam said, "I'm quite alright. No cuts or stab wounds. I don't know what you found, but if there was a crime scene outside my establishment, I'll have to call the police. Of course, that is, if you left the area undisturbed."

Leigh paled. "Cam, you know if it was a demonic crime scene no human cop will be able to help. Xavier will be able to run DNA tests on the knife. If it is someone else's blood, then we'll call it in. However, we do have your phone and your preppy-boy boat shoe." Her brows knitted into a vee. "We were concerned—"

Harper growled.

"*I* was concerned that something happened to you," Leigh rephrased with forced patience. "I'm happy to see otherwise."

"I'm not so fucking lenient." Harper kicked the leg of Camden's chair and sending my boyfriend scrambling. "I want to know what you were doing over the past twenty-four hours."

I expected Cam to retaliate. He *had* been a brawler at one time. But he just smirked up at Harper, dipped his hand in his jacket, and withdrew his cell. "I still have my phone, and I'm not wearing any boat shoes." He pointed to his loafers at the end of the bed that he'd kicked off earlier. "But I am wildly curious about who's blood is on that knife."

The phone in Camden's hand started ringing. All eyes in the room lifted to Leigh. She had her cell out and flashed us the screen. *Camden.* "Figured this would help clear up any question about which is his. But that begs the question: who does this belong to?"

Leigh reached into the purse slung over her shoulder and withdrew yet another phone with a mangled screen. It looked identical to the one in Camden's hand.

A phone that was-but-wasn't his? A shoe that should belong to him but did not? A knife that potentially had his blood all over it, but he had no visible injuries? He wasn't even acting like his freaking self, let alone dressed in that trendy-as-all-hell suit.

I narrowed my gaze. Dominic had to be dicking Camden around again. How? Why? I thought I was the target? Had Dominic done something to Camden? Or had Dominic staged the scene at Sorcerie? Had my friends unknowingly walked into a trap? Were they okay?

My mind spun from all the different angles that Dominic's dastardly schemes could play out. Then images from fighting Enyo assaulted me. I remembered how I felt when the Mage and Dominic trapped me in my own head. I relived the feeling of being cut off from Letty. Bear pressed his weight into me. My fingers latched onto his collar, and I held on for dear life with white knuckles.

My breaths came in short, panicked bursts. Panting aggravated my wound, and agony ripped through me, pulling a groan from my very soul.

"Noooooo."

"Brave one!" Letty's alarm was palatable.

"Fuck," Harper swore. He was at my side hooking his fingers under my chin. "Sam, look at me."

I shook my head, tears blurring my vision. Letty tried pushing her warmth into my limbs, but I resisted, blocking her out in my panic. Camden, Leigh, Harper, and Jax could all be in danger. What if something had happened to them?

I cried out again as I tried to wrench my face away from Harper. His fingers gripped my jaw, forcing my head up.

Seconds ticked by.

"Sammy," he said, softer this time. His fingers were tight, but his words were gentle. "Focus those eyes on me now."

My vision started to clear, the tenderness in his voice

cutting through my pain-filled panic. I found his dark eyes. My beacon. My lighthouse in the raging shitstorm in my head.

"Breathe in through your nose," he commanded and I obeyed with a massive inhale of air. He nodded. "Good. Hold it." I did and he loosened his hold on my jaw. "Let it out slow. Steady."

"You're safe," Letty said.

The backs of Harper knuckles ran down my cheek. "That's it."

"We're here for you," Letty reminded me.

Harper ran his hand over where I still gripped Bear's leather collar. "I've got you."

"We've got you," Letty clarified.

Harper's eyes searched mine. His face had lost the severe lines and rigid toughness he used to keep people at a distance. I vaguely felt him pry my fingers off of Bear, and he rubbed my hand with his thumb. I reeled in my wildness, shoving that panicky shit into a box.

"Welcome back," Harper murmured, reading me like a book. "Alright?"

I nodded once.

"Good." He tucked my hair behind my ears, and for a scant second, I thought he'd kiss me.

What the hell? Get yourself together, Fife! Holy Heaven.

Instead of kissing me, I watched as Harper slammed the shutters on his emotions. Hulk Harper had returned, and he rounded on Camden with the force of a category five hurricane. He wrenched Camden up by the lapels and hauled him to his feet. Bear jumped up, barking, but stayed with me. Cam laughed—*laughed!*—as he imitated a ragdoll in Harper's grip.

"Harper!" Leigh shouted. "He hasn't done anything wrong."

"Temper, temper." Camden *tisked*, mocking the beast.

"Motherfucker," Harper growled. "We're finishing this goddamn conversation in the office." Harper tossed Camden sideways, shoving him towards the door. "With Xavier present. Not in front of Sam. We cannot fucking trigger true panic attack."

Panic attack? Was that what was happening?

"Kestler," Harper barked. My best friend shoulders snapped back, and she glared at him. He lifted his hand and made a *gimme* gesture. "Give me this cocksucker's phone, fake or not, and stay with Sam."

There was no room in his tone for argument. But what surprised the hell out of me was when Leigh did as he'd asked with only a low grumble.

Harper snapped his fingers at Bear. "Take care of her, yeah?" The dog flopped to the mattress, his weight pressing against my leg.

Both men left, and Leigh turned to face me. She shoved her hands on her hips, hazel eyes sparking. "What a cluster ..."

"Well, that was fun," I said with a shake in my voice.

8

DOMINIC

D ominic let Harper manhandle him down the hall. It was a cozy home with pictures of a comfortable life lining the blue walls. When the raging brute pushed Dominic inside an office, it too, had touches of a life well-lived with stacks of books on all flat surfaces, sticky notes everywhere, and trinkets lining the top of all the shelves.

How quaint? How charming? How ...dreadfully dull.

He offered no resistance when Harper shoved him into a guest chair, but did mutter, "Uncivilized fiend."

Harper stuck a finger in his face. "You're on thin ice, asshole. Watch yourself."

"Mr. Tate?" Xavier Gerena asked, his brows raised, as he crossed through the doorway. His Armani navy suit and polished exterior impressed Dominic.

But the raven perched on the Adviser's shoulder made Dominic's pulse spike. He adjusted his watch and quietly cleared his throat. An intelligent corvid woven with a sentient Heavenly being? Nyx threatened Dominic's ruse. Any Warrior Guardian did. He kept his eyes off the big, black bird.

"What's going on?" Tabitha Holland asked as she entered behind Xavier.

Tabitha was magnificent. Gorgeous. Dangerous. Dressed in jeans and emerald chiffon blouse, her wavy brown locks hanging loose around her shoulders, and her tanned skin spoke of her Italian roots? She was stunning. Too bad he couldn't have made her a Dark Warrior.

Her perceptive green eyes bounced from Harper to Dominic.

Dominic held his tongue. If he could twist it so that Harper came off as the unhinged, violent human, he would. Harper would have to explain his way out of this one. Perhaps manipulation would drive the wall-of-a-man to his breaking point. Dominic pinched his lip with his fingers.

How can I break you, Harper Tate?

"We agreed that Mr. Bennett was a guest, did we not?" Xavier settled into the seat behind the desk. Tabitha rested a hip on the edge of the desktop.

That's right. Dominic bowed his head and smirked down at his thighs. *I'm wearing a Camden suit.*

Possessing Camden allowed Dominic access onto sacred ground. How? He wasn't completely sure. Did possession allow access to protected places, or was it specifically the possession of the Bennett boy? It wasn't until Dominic arrived this afternoon and waltzed through the scared veil unscathed that he realized he could. He was giddy with his own deception.

Dominic chuckled under his breath. Camden had managed to gain the confidence of the Warriors of Light. They must have assumed he was innocent, not a carefully constructed Trojan horse. This chaos was exactly what Dominic wanted.

"He's up to some shady shit," Harper answered Xavier.

Dominic shifted to a more comfortable position in the guest's armchair, straightened his jacket, and ran a hand through Camden's blonde curls. The tricky part was making sure he passed for Camden. The boy was locked away deep within his own mind, unaware, thus allowing Dominic freedom to do as he pleased to pull off this ruse.

"Harper is concerned that I've upset Sam," Dominic said. "That I've brewed up a conspiracy."

A growl reverberated low in Harper's chest. "Don't speak for me."

"I suggest someone tell me what's going on, rather than throwing around insults." Xavier looked expectantly at Harper.

Nyx hopped off Xavier's shoulder, wandered across the desktop, and stood at the edge nearest Dominic and Harper. She glared at both of them for few heart-pounding seconds before wandering back over to her Warrior.

"While Kestler, Bozeman, and I were out looking for this asswipe, we found some shit." Harper chucked the cell phone and boat shoe on the flat surface before them. He withdrew a cloth-wrapped object, shaped oddly like a knife, and placed it next to the other items.

Dominic steepled his fingers and pressed them against his chin. He hadn't been involved with the abduction, and while he could access Camden's memories, Dominic would have to get creative with his story. He already saw some avenues he could take with his manipulations.

"We found Bennett's abandoned Rover parked at Sorcerie," Harper continued. "When we started to investigate, Kestler's tracking sense led us to the dumpsters. To the human eye it looked like a crime scene with these items

—" he pointed to the *evidence* on the desk, "—red blood, and the shredded remains of a woman and a child's clothing. Was it an abduction? Were people missing? But to our eyes, and what the demons to failed factor in, was one of their own left black blood. We also found smashed security cameras. Kestler filled in what she could with her abilities."

Dominic suppressed his annoyed hiss.

"We thought he was in trouble," Harper said, stabbing a finger in Dominic's direction. "But lo and behold, his goddam, shiny-ass Audi was sitting out front when we pulled into the drive. We found him cuddling with Sam without a fucking scratch on him."

Dominic didn't so much as flinch, but his temper simmered. *How unfortunate Enyo's minions left evidence. She's normally so thorough with choosing which underlings do her bidding.* He made a mental note to discuss the matter with his lieutenant. Her crew of inept dullards had put him in a tight predicament. Yes, it was quite the pickle. A sliver of fury flared in his chest. He resisted a sneer as he thought about the botched kidnapping. Belatedly, he realized that everyone's eyes were on him. He smoothed his jacket and tugged the hem.

"The Rover wouldn't start," he explained. "I had my mother's driver deliver me my car and I drove to him back to the beach house."

"You were MIA for almost twenty-four hours." Acid dripped from Harper's words.

Dominic propped an elbow on the chair's cushioned arm and waved a hand.

"Mother bent my ear six ways from Sunday for shirking my duties while I was here, watching over my Sam. While you may be free of a job and responsibilities to obsess over my girl, I had some major duties I had to attend to. When I got the call that Sam had woken, I tried to get here as soon as possible."

Harper's eyes narrowed. His jaw flexed. He clenched his fists so hard his knuckles turned white. Dominic smirked and raised a brow.

Aren't you fascinating, he thought. *Check, boy. Your move.*

"I want to believe you," Xavier said, interrupting their mental chess match. "But ..." He spread an arm out in front of him, palm up, motioning towards the phone, shoe, and knife. "Mr. Tate is no liar and the evidence is damning, Mr. Bennett."

The shoe was the least problematic. That could belong to anyone. The cell was dead and deactivated, but a simple recharge could cause problems for Dominic. He'd already switched cell service to the new one he'd purchased, but all of Camden's stored items would be on the old phone. And that knife? Dominic suspected it did have the Camden boy's blood on it.

He would have to steal it.

Dominic rested both elbows on the chair arms and bridged his fingers in front of his chest. Perhaps he'd lie now and nab the items later. He'd have to. The more pressing matter was that he had to throw suspicion off Camden Bennett.

"Mr. Gerena, these aren't my things," Dominic fibbed, feinting innocence. He gave an exaggerated shrug. "I really wish I knew what was happening. All this sounds like some sort of outlandish setup outside my restaurant." He lowered his voice. "What if the Mage sent demons to cast suspicion on my character? They proved that they were out to get me before Sam's coma. Maybe they've changed tactics?"

Harper's hands open and closed. Tabitha glowered.

Xavier stroked Nyx's feathered head. The damn bird stared at Dominic with her all-too-knowing, beady eyes.

"I'm not sure, Mr. Bennett," Xavier said. "Demonic activity has been low, and there have been few attacks by Lesser Demons—none by Greater Demons. The Mage seems to have gone off grid."

Yes, because our dear Samantha Fife caused unforeseen damage when she broke the blood spell cast on her.

After a contemplative moment, Xavier sighed. "We'll have to investigate this situation. I cannot demand you stay on property, Mr. Bennett, as you're free to come and go, but I encourage you to stay near, at least until we figure out what is going on."

"He's a security hazard and a risk to Sam's well-being," Harper barked. Xavier held up a hand. Harper's mouth snapped shut, the muscles in his neck straining in his effort to obey.

"As for Miss Fife," Xavier continued, "I do need her functional as soon as possible. I ask that everyone try not to upset the balance. This includes you, Mr. Bennett." Xavier leaned forward and met Dominic's eyes. The full weight of the Adviser's stare prickled along Dominic's shoulders. "Mr. Tate is in charge of her convalescence. I'm sure I do not need to give you any other warning?"

Dominic nodded. "Of course, sir. Her wellbeing is my utmost concern."

Xavier leaned back, his raven still balanced on his shoulder. "Good. I'm glad we're on the same page."

Harper didn't gloat over Xavier's executive order, but the tension in his shoulders relaxed and he nodded once at the Adviser.

This boy cares deeply for our dear Miss Fife. But just how deep does his loyalty run? I'm sure it can be tested. Exploited. Dominic also delighted in the contention between Camden and the

Tate offspring—it was delectably deep-seated and ferocious. *Perhaps I can use this, too?*

"Mr. Bennett, you are excused," Xavier's voice cut through Dominic's scheming contemplation.

Dominic ducked his head in respectful acknowledgment. "Thank you, sir."

He stood and had turned to the door but not before casting a pointed glance at the knife. *I'll have to get that somehow.* He took one step towards the exit when a rough hand on his chest stopped him. He looked down and then up at Harper. His burning blue eyes barely contained the man's rage. Dominic smirked.

Harper grabbed Dominic's shirt and yanked him close. "I don't fucking trust you, Bennett. You may have gotten a reprieve from Xavier, but I will find out what you're hiding."

"Harper," Tabitha gasped. "Don't be uncouth."

Harper released Dominic, raised his hands, and stepped back.

"If you need me," Dominic said, "I'll be with Sam and her friends. Watching TV."

A menacing rumbled came from Harper, but Dominic had already walked out of the office, creating a mental to-do list as he made his way back to Sam's room. Sow seeds of contention. Deal with damning evidence. Gain insightful knowledge. And as a bonus, make Samantha Fife an ally.

9

SAM

"*T*his *is not one of your better ideas,*" Letty said while I shuffled to the door of my room like a ninety-year-old biddy. Bear hopped off the bed, joining me.

"*I will go insane if I spend one more day in bed,*" I told my inner angel, clutching my war wound with my left hand. I poked my head out into the hall, glanced in both directions, and made sure the coast was clear. "*Ya girl can only handle so much down time.*"

Letty groaned.

And to think, she volunteered to be my angel.

At four in the morning, it appeared I'd woken before most everyone. I'd been a good little patient yesterday, played all my cards right, and earned the right to sleep alone. The Great Fife Watch had come to an end. Even Camden went to Andrew's office and crashed on a cot set up in there. But today was a new day.

Perhaps they should have left one person on duty?

If my side wasn't screaming at me, I might have smiled. Instead, I had to focus on putting one foot in front of the other, supporting myself with an arm on the wall to balance my wobbly legs. Bear ambled next to me like the support animal he was. I stopped in the front foyer, at the open entrance to Judy's formal living room, and flipped on the light. Unprepared for the swift wave of grief which crashed over me, tears sprang in my eyes.

Waterford crystal lamps, straight from Ireland, sat on top of homemade end tables. Greyscale silhouette paintings of birds and trees hung on the walls. Well-loved books were still stacked on a serving tray on top of a large white ottoman. Everything in here had her personal touch, except for rusty droplet stains marring the ultra-white carpet.

My blood?

A small sob escaped me. I winced at the sharp shot of pain and braced a hand against the jamb, scrunching up my left side.

"Jesus, Mary, Joseph, and the wise men," I muttered. This wound and my grief were going to be a problem.

"Miss Sam, whatever are you doing out of bed?" asked Nigel from behind me, his polished British accent wrapped with concern. Bear trotted up to him and shoved his head into Nigel's hand. I gathered the edges of my robe together, turned slowly, and tried to hide a wince.

"Nothing."

Nigel's eyes narrowed, probably seeing through my bullshit. "You're on a bedrest restriction."

"And yet, I'm not going back bed." I smiled. "So here we are."

I cocked my head. If he wanted to cause a stink, I had youth and being a Warrior of Light on my side, however I'd always suspected Nigel was more than an old British butler. *He'd wipe the floor with me in my sorry state.* Hell, DH could have probably taken me out at that moment. I pursed my lips.

"Whatcha gonna do about me, Nigel, ol' chap?"

Nigel glared, and my resolve almost cracked, but he said, "Since you're ambulatory, I might as well get you seated. How about a spot of tea?"

"Make it a coffee and I'll be your best friend."

He nodded, and I sagged with relief. The thought of being confined to my room any longer made me want to flip furniture.

"I gather you'd like breakfast, as well?" Nigel took me by the elbow.

I leaned on the old butler, grateful he was humoring me. "Never ever gonna turn down food."

"Come on. Slowly now."

He guided me through the living room, into the dining room, and helped me into a cushioned chair. A groan escaped me as I settled in to my seat. *Do not think about how you'd be more comfortable in your bed. Don't even do it.* Bear beelined to his bed, circled five times, and plopped down.

"But you would be," Letty piped up with her two cents.

"Just a mo' my dear." Nigel disappeared through the swinging door leading to the kitchen.

I propped my elbows on the sturdy block table and rubbed my eyes. Letting my arms flop, I studied the wood grain and traced the lines with a finger. Andrew had made this table for Judy. A lump formed in my chest. More tears burned my eyes. I cleared my throat.

Don't go there, Fife.

Instead, my dear brain bombarded me with questions. When would my strength return? How long would I have to be dependent on others? When would I be able to be a proper Warrior again? Kicking demon ass was coded so deep into my DNA that not doing so was driving me bonkers.

This blew chunks. All of it.

The grandfather clock in the corner ticked off the seconds. I studied the popcorn ceiling. The AC kicked on and a breath of cold air sluiced over me. Frustrated, I slapped my hands down on the table top. When I did, I noticed a faint red splotch that hadn't ever been there. It looked like someone had tried to clean up a spill, but the substance was stubborn. My eyes narrowed on the irregular puddle pattern.

All the air whooshed from my lungs. I jerked back from the table as if it were fire hot. Faded red splotches bled over more than half of the table. I almost died on here. Judy was dead, but I lived. My fingers closed, nails biting into my skin. I pressed a palm to my mouth.

This can't—this is my blood?

There was loud clang and heavy thump from behind the kitchen door. I reached up for one of my daggers but gasped at the fresh stab of pain.

"Shit." My heart thundered behind my ribs. "You idiot," I chastised myself. *"Since when have I ever been this jumpy?"* I asked Letty.

"Never," Letty said. *"But you've gone through some trauma. It's to be expected."*

"I don't like it." I dropped my hand, letting it *thunk* down on the tabletop. If I had this much anxiety every time I saw reminders of my dance with death, I would be a useless sack of a Warrior. We couldn't afford to have these types of breakdowns. Broken body, wonky connection to my Powers, and jumpy AF. Would I ever recover?

"You have a fierce desire to live and a resolute, iron will that's not easily changed," Letty said. *"You may have been knocked down, but you will rise. I've been watching you your whole life. You're a fighter, and even in this season of doubt, there is no other Warrior of Light I would want to be tethered to."*

If that wasn't a vote of confidence, I didn't know the

meaning of a pep-talk. I pulled in a slow, steadying breath so as to not anger my wound. Nigel stepped backwards through the swing door with a loaded tray. The smell of coffee and sugar wafted through the air. My bottomless pit stomach snarled.

"Here you are," he said, setting down the bounty. "There is more if you're still hungry. I'm familiar with Warrior appetites."

"You are a saint." I reached for a cranberry-orange scone and mulled over Letty's words. She hadn't ever let me down. If she had confidence in me, hope was not lost. A genuine angel of Heaven had my back.

Nigel poured coffee for me, nodded once, and disappeared back into the kitchen. The scone— homemade, no doubt—had the perfect amount of sweetness and tang. While I shoved bits into my mouth, a presence loomed behind me. I stiffened, swallowed my bite of pastry, and let my senses take over. The scent of something akin to an Irish countryside told me Andrew Shaw had arrived.

My exhale came out sharp and battered. Betrayal and pain hollowed out my chest. Images flashed through my mind. Andrew driving his van to Xavier's estate. Andrew not meeting my eyes during an important Warrior meeting. Andrew's face while I discovered Warrior history—history he never told Leigh and me.

The Warriors of Light had a deep, rich history. We'd fought the good fight for millennia. Merlin and King Arthur were Warriors. Moses, Gideon, and the apostles were Warriors. All the demigods, like Jason, Percy, and Hercules were all Warriors.

Overtime, as Hell advanced its Powers and abilities, so did Heaven. The need arose for organized groups to be taught by trusted mentors. Eventually, three Advisers rose to the top and were the heads of the whole damn thing.

They were Tabitha Holland, Xavier Gerena, and Andrew Shaw.

And Andrew had withheld all that, including the mass slaughter of his branch. It was vital knowledge that we found out for the first time in front of Xavier's crew.

I rose to my feet with care and turned around. Andrew's silver hair stuck up all over the place, disheveled and dingy. His typically sharp grey eyes had a glassy, lost look. Even his tall, lean frame seemed to have imploded, leaving behind a skinny, haunted man.

This man had been my world. My grandfather, really, since my own biological grandparents couldn't bother to have a relationship with me. Andrew had known me from infancy. He'd never missed a birthday or major life milestone. Hell, he'd taught me to ride and had given Max to me as a gift before I'd been a Warrior. Andrew had wiped many tears, guided me when I was lost, and had patched up more than enough wounds. He'd turned me into a Warrior of Light and harnessed all my impulsive recklessness into something good and productive.

Maybe if he'd been more honest with me, Judy wouldn't have died. Maybe I wouldn't have been injured. Maybe the Mage wouldn't have gotten the upper hand. It hadn't escaped my notice that he hadn't visited me once since I'd woken up from my coma.

But this was Andrew, and no matter how he'd screwed up—Heaven knew how many times I had—my heart forgave him in that moment. Was I still angry with him? Hell, yes. But my battered heart cracked then, seeing him standing there as if life had sucked him dry. Tears pricked my eyes. I wanted to hug him tight and cuss him out at the same time.

"My best girl," he said, opening his arms and dropping

the cordless phone he held. It landed with a dull *plunk* on the carpet.

I went to him and he enveloped me in his arms. One of his hands cradled the back of my head and the other arm banded around my shoulders. I buried my face in his chest, my anger fracturing in his secure embrace. Worry slithered in my gut. *He's to frail.*

"Oh, my dear child," he breathed out in a sigh.

He may have been my betrayer, but he was also my protector. My emotions burst open, battering down the doors of my resistance. I sobbed on my mentor's chest, dampening his shirt. My tears were fueled by fear, innocence lost, shattered reality, and physical pain as those sobs pulled at my demon-inflicted wound. Andrew held me as I wept, his hold surprisingly strong.

"I'm so sorry," he whispered, his tone contrite.

"Why didn't you come see me?" I reared back and found his eyes. "When I woke up, I mean."

"I wasn't sure you wanted me there." He brushed damp hair from my cheek.

I stepped back and he let me go. "Even when you've let me down, I always need you, old man." I touched my fingertips over my heart. "I'm pissed as hell, but I'll be damned if I don't love you."

Andrew's grey eyes watered and he gave a sad smile. "I've made many mistakes in my lengthy life, but the ones I made with you and Leigh are almost unforgivable. I should have told you what happened eighteen years ago."

I froze. *Is he really doing this right now? Right now? This morning? Lord have mercy.* Did I want to hear it? My insatiable curiosity needed to know whatever he was willing to divulge. "What do you mean?"

Andrew plucked the phone up off the floor. "I will tell you, but I had a emergent situation—"

"Miss Samantha, I found some sausages—" Nigel marched through the swing door and slammed on the brakes. The perceptive man's eyes bugged out, and he bowed his head. "Adviser Shaw."

"Mr. Hawthorne," Andrew said.

"It's good to see you up and about this morning." Nigel placed a white plate filled with sausages in front of me without looking away from Andrew. "How are you feeling? May I get you some tea?"

Andrew's mouth was a grim line. "Actually, would you please have Xavier meet me in here? I have a rather pressing matter."

What matter?

"Of course." The butler nodded and disappeared into the kitchen.

"Sammy." Andrew took my hands in his. "Our conversation is much needed and overdue, but it must wait." He raised a hand when I opened my mouth to protest. "I wasn't expecting to find you in here this morning. You have many questions, and I will answer all of them in due time, but there is a very immediate emergency."

My heart rate spiked. "Are you alright?"

A sad smile tugged his lips. "Debatable, but this isn't about me personally. I received a call that someone has vandalized my church."

"What?" My brows shot up. "How?"

"They set fire to the sanctuary."

"Are you shitting me?" My chest tightened.

"I wish I was." Andrew ran a hand over his face.

"Are they sure someone torched it on purpose?"

"Unfortunately, yes. The burn was controlled and most definitely done by someone who could manipulate the flames somehow. The fire department called in an arson expert."

Cold dread creeped over my skin. "Do you think it's supernatural?"

Andrew grabbed my hand again and squeezed. "Until we get eyes on the damage, I can't say for sure, but it certainly feels that way to me."

Andrew was old. He'd been around for centuries. If his gut told him something about the fire wasn't of this world, I believed him. But it didn't make sense. The Mage's signature was ice, not fire. Was there a new player entering the field? I hoped the hell not.

I blew out a slow breath. "But the church is still on holy ground. It's still under your wards. The perp must be human. No demon or Dark Warrior can get in."

"Sammy, you're being purposefully obtuse—"

The nerve! My mouth popped open, half-cocked argument loaded.

He pegged me with his steely grey gaze. "I'm dying."

Any argument I had withered. My heart twisted. *Breath? Breathing? What is that?*

"As my health weakens," he continued as if he hadn't dropped a massive bomb, "so do the boundaries I've placed all over the world. Not just here."

My vision blurred, head feeling fuzzy. *Need. Air.* I dragged oxygen into my lungs.

Andrew kept speaking. "...security cameras, alarm codes, and smoke detectors were disabled. Pastor Rick opened the church this morning, took one look at the sanctuary, and called the police. No one saw the fire."

The fire. Right. I nodded, trying to put the *I'm dying* aside, but hot damn.

"I need to get down there now," Andrew said, "but I'm in no condition to drive."

"Adviser Gerena shall be here in just a mo'," Nigel announced as he pushed through the door. He placed a teapot on top of a trivet and set a cup and saucer in front of Andrew.

"Thank you," Andrew said. "The police and arson investigator are waiting for me."

"I'm going with you." Nigel and Andrew looked at me like I'd lost my marbles. And maybe I had. "Please," I pleaded. "Let me have this."

Andrew's expression turned grim. "Your condition—"

"—is no worse than yours?" I grabbed his forearm. "We're both worse for wear. Besides, your wards still hold for now. Here. At the church. Please don't leave me behind."

Desperation clawed at me. While I was in no shape to go anywhere, I needed out of this house. Now. Away from the memories of a healthy Andrew and an alive Judy which filled the halls. I refused to glance at my blood stains on the table or dwell on the way everything in the house had Judy's touches on it. For the first time in my life, the farmhouse felt like a prison instead of a home.

"My dear—"

"*Please* give me this."

Andrew let out a deep sigh. "We'll see. I'll discuss it with Tabby and Xavier."

I leaned forward and kissed his cheek. There was nothing to discuss, but I'd let this play out to see what they decided. Come hell or high water, I'd be in that vehicle headed for the church house.

10

HARPER

"Pops, you ready?" I asked, lifting car keys from the small rack beside the door.

"Yes," he answered. Tabitha trailed close behind him.

We filed out onto the porch. Since Xavier had other matters to attend to today, he had asked Tabitha and me to take Pops down to the church. I hadn't wanted to leave, in case Sam relapsed, but I'd checked on her thirty minutes ago. She'd been resting with Bennett by her side.

"So, y'all decided to chose the hard way, huh?" Sam's voice dumped ice in my veins.

I whirled. "Christ."

"Shit," Tabitha muttered, pressing a hand to her heart.

Pops grunted, his expression suspiciously unsurprised.

Not many could get the jump on me, but she sure as shit had. Sam sat in a wicker rocking chair, hidden by the shadows of the porch overhang—just beyond of touch of morning sunlight. Her boyfriend stood next to her, one arm resting around her shoulders. His fingers traced a loose pattern on her skin.

I watched as Sam stood with Bennett's help. She

grimaced and pretended like her wound wasn't bothering her. With her spine straight, eyes flashing with lighting, and jaw set tight, her anger was palpable. She was gearing up to make a scene.

"You got this," Bennett whispered to Sam loud enough for me to hear. "I believe in you."

"I asked for one thing." She held up her index finger. "One. To go with you to the church and see the damage."

My anger had me closing the gap between us, the sudden advance forcing Bennett back several feet. Sam held her ground. Not even a flinch. My work boots touched the tips of her neon green running sneakers.

"Harper!" Tabitha gasped, shock evident in her tone. She hadn't seen me at my worst yet, and Sam had a knack for bringing me precariously close to that edge.

"Son," Andrew warned. "Sam."

"I'm going." She ignored Pops and trained her eyes on mine.

"Over my dead fucking body."

"Don't die on this hill, Harper," she said. "Pick a different one. My ass will be in that Tahoe."

"In what reality did you think we'd let you do this?" I grabbed her by the shoulders, anger fueling my exasperation. "How can I keep you safe when you willingly expose yourself to the enemy? They're probably lying in wait."

"I'm a Warrior of Light. Nothing in my job description suggests this gig is *safe*." She shrugged out of my hold. "The church is on sacred ground. You'll be there. Hell, let's bring Leigh, too. I refuse to cower. I'll be fine."

Heat lanced up my neck. My hands clenched and unclenched. The front porch shrank. We were the only two people alive. Sam lifted a brow—questioning my authority, challenging me. She hadn't been out of her coma that long, and I already wanted to strangle her.

Don't snap. Don't lose your shit.

I blew out a frustrated breath and glared down at her. Sam, the sly fox, had purposefully bypassed Xavier, who was busy. Pops was a push over when it came to Sam, and he'd cave to her pleading. As Advisers went, that left Tabitha. And she didn't know the lengths Sam would go to when her mind was set on something. Convincing Sam to *not* go to the church would be my battle alone.

Goddamn it.

"Spitfire, this is asinine—"

"You're gonna give yourself an ulcer worrying like you are," Sam said. "Can you back up? You're looming over me like a raging rhino."

My eyes widened, then narrowed. As if her recent injuries hadn't *already* given me a goddamn ulcer. I scrubbed a hand over my face in frustration. Unconscious Sam was easier to deal with. Awake Sam? Infinitely more difficult. I swallowed all my anger, frustration, and annoyance and shoved that shit way, way down. Awake Sam hated to be told what to do. Awake Sam had opinions. If I pushed, she'd punch back. Force wasn't going to work with her.

Gripping the back of my neck, I studied our touching toes to compose myself and took one step back. Half of her tension whooshed out of her, and her stormy blues went wide—like she was surprised I'd given her that much.

"What are you doing?" she asked.

I took her hands in mine, brought them to my bowed forehead and asked, "Why are you pushing this, Sammy?" I glanced up. "Why are you taking this risk?"

Her fingers tightened around mine before releasing one hand. She slid a thumb over the furrowed skin on my forehead. I jerked back at her soft touch, but she continued as if I hadn't moved and ran her slender fingers through the untidy hair at my temple. I closed my eyes and resisted leaning into her touch.

"Because I'm scared," she whispered so softly I almost missed her words. My eyes snapped open. That thumb of hers rubbed at my temple. "The Mage held me hostage, Harper. Trapped me in my head. Took away my Power. Cut me off from Letty. It terrified me."

Well, shit. My heart seized. Sam rarely admitted weakness, choosing to cover her fears with bravado and snark. I understood why she was asking this of us, but I didn't agree. I shook my head.

"Sam, I would do anything to help you but—"

"I'm going to the church." She dropped her hand and for some reason I missed the warmth of her palm pressed against my skin. "If I have to hot wire a damn car, I will."

"Jesus," I murmured. *She's not bluffing.* "What you're asking to do is fucking dangerous." *Steady. Force will not work with her.* I needed to tattoo that on the inside of my goddamn skull. "I don't like it."

"You don't like a lot of things," she said, the corners of her lips twitched. "And this isn't about you or my desire to drive you to the brink insanity. This is something I have to do, Harper."

I studied her face. There were stress lines around her mouth, purple circles under her haunted eyes, and a tension which I had never seen on her pretty features. She gave me a weak smile.

"Why am I always trying to talk you out of risking your life?"

"Because you care."

"Sam also needs closure," Bennet interrupted and stepped up to her. He put a hand on her in between her shoulder blades. "What she's not saying is that the inside of the farmhouse brings memories of Judy. It's hard for her to be here."

"Cam," Sam's voice turned stern. "Please go get Leigh. Tell her Harper needs her on the front porch."

"As you wish, babe."

Sam grimaced but accepted his kiss on her cheek without another word.

"I'll get the car running," Tabitha said, approaching me. "And get Andrew loaded. We'll be waiting."

I handed her the keys without looking at her.

"And for what my word's worth to you, Sam," she added, "it would be prudent to stay behind. Heal up. Recover. But I sense unrest in your soul, Warrior. I see how you struggle. See the way your experience torments you. While there is much risk for you to come with us today, perhaps this is the path to your mental freedom, yeah? However, I do hope you're not making a grave mistake."

Tabitha left the porch without waiting for a response. Sam's mouth opened, closed, and then she said, "That was unexpected."

I blew out a breath. "Pops told me once that she was the most intuitive of all of them."

"Hey, Cam said y'all needed something," Kestler said as she stepped out through the front door. She took one look at Sam and her eyes flicked to mine. "Should I have brought my bomb defusing kit? I feel like you two are going to detonate any second. And what the fluff are you doing out here, Sam?"

"Making demands." She crossed her arms. "I'm going to the church with Andrew, Harper, and Adviser Holland. And you're coming with me as my supernatural bodyguard."

"Uhhh ..." Kestler glanced between the two of us and the SUV waiting in the driveway. "Is this a good idea?"

"Hell no," I said. "But she threatened to get there on her own. Though, she doesn't know how to hot wire a car."

"The internet knows everything." Sam tipped her head side-to-side, as if weighing her choices. "Taking Max is also an option."

"Fucking A," I muttered. "She's hell-bent on this cockamamie scheme. You know her threats aren't idle."

"Oh, my lord," Kestler said, exasperated. "You're bonkers. I love you, but you're too impulsive for your own good."

Sam shrugged. Kestler's eyes widened. They had one of their non-speaking conversations. Sam held her graze straight on—determined and calm. Eventually, Kestler threw up her arms and let them drop.

"Just tell me why you're doing this," Kestler asked.

"We'll give you the *CliffsNotes* version on the road." Sam stood and shuffled for front steps. "Cam told me he's staying here to work on some paperwork for the restaurant, so come along."

This was happening. Come hell or highwater.

To my resigned dismay, I followed after her, putting a hand on her elbow to help guide her as she struggled down the first step. She jerked her arm away, gripped the railing instead, and managed to make it down to the bottom.

The SUV was parked in the circle driveway, as close to the front as possible. Pops was already settled in the front passenger seat, looking as frail and grey as ever, and for the millionth time, I wondered why either of them were going. I rubbed my hands over my face and through my hair.

I needed a fucking haircut.

Adviser Holland slammed the hatch shut in the back and came around the corner, taking the longest route to the driver's side. She checked on Pops as she went by his window. The lithe, lean-muscled woman gave me a tight smile, and she waved us over before heading to her seat.

"Did you know about her?" Sam asked.

"Tabitha?" I asked. "Yes, but only because Pops told me about her."

"Adviser Holland has a whole slew of Seer safe spaces all over Ireland and England," Kestler said. "She has more Warriors she left at home. Sajid and Talia are her alpha team."

"She didn't volunteer much information when she arrived for Ma's Warrior funeral." I went ahead of Sam and opened the passenger door for her. "She showed up and had two fully-trained Warriors with her." I held out my hand. "Let's get you loaded."

Sam ignored me and struggled to get in the SUV.

"You're in no shape to go anywhere." Kestler shook her head.

Sam bristled. "The church is on holy ground—"

"Yes," I said, my tone dropping low, "but the commute to said church is not. What if the demons are watching and they attack while we're in route? Fuck, Sam, you can barely make it down a set of porch stairs, let alone fight a Greater fucking Demon."

It was my final wild stab at talking her out of this. Sam's spine straightened and her mouth set into a determined line.

"Like riding a horse, sir. If you fall off, you get back on."

"Unless you're banged up, bleeding, or broken," I said. "All of which you are."

"Harper, the walls are caving in." Sam's voice hitched. "There are reminders here and all over this property that Judy is gone. The groans and moans of this house remind me of my screw ups. There are so many. I couldn't—she died before—"

I tipped Sam's chin up. "That wasn't your fault."

"I played a part."

Christ. She's a great martyr. I should know. With a shake of my head, I swept flyaway hairs from her face. "Are you sure you're up for this?"

"Honest truth?"

"Yes."

"No, I'm not sure," she said, her voice bright with sass. "I have a hole in my side."

I sighed and rested my forehead against hers. Sam relaxed into me. Defeat over letting her leave weighed on my soul—I pulled back, my gaze holding her eyes. *What happens if you're attacked? What if you can't call on your Power? Please, Sam, don't do this. I can't lose you.*

Sam titled her head and offered a melancholy smile. She squeezed my hand.

My own eyes widened. Had I said all that out loud?

"I can't read your thoughts, but your face is yelling," she said.

Oh, thank fuck!

"Let's get this done and over with." I let her go and shut the door.

ADVISER HOLLAND PARKED in Pops's pastoral spot next to the sanctuary. We'd made the fifteen-minute drive from the farmhouse to the church without any issues. I got out of my seat behind the driver's side as Sam unbuckled her belt.

"Easy does it," I said, holding up my arms.

"I can do—" Sam hissed as she almost fell out of the SUV. She clutched the door's armrest with one hand.

I shifted forward just as she crashed into my body. "Use me for support. Stop being stubborn." I tucked her into my side and slid an arm around her lower waist.

"Thanks," she mumbled, accepting my assistance this time without argument.

She'd lost weight during her coma. The jut of her hipbone under my fingers, the purple smudges under her eyes, and her slow movements told me just how vulnerable she'd become. She'd need rehab and strength training before she could fight demons and take on the Mage. This wound would take a while to heal. She shouldn't have been out at all.

Not this soon.

That possessive desire to keep her from harm, even from herself, bloomed in my chest. These feelings would get be me nowhere, so I said nothing. It never did any good.

Adviser Holland escorted Pops up the church's front steps. I steered Sam behind the Advisers while Kestler brought up the rear. Sam jerked against my side, and I saw Pops hesitate on the top step. An acrid, charcoal stench hit me a second later. Smoke, burned organic material, and the scent of melted plastic permeated the air. It grew stronger as we neared the doors.

All the windows to the sanctuary appeared intact. No charred wood or scorch marks marred the church's exterior. Hell, the paint job hadn't even flaked away from heat damage. The outside was pristine, and the tall white entrance doors had been propped open.

A clean-cut man with his salt-and-pepper hair cut high and tight met us at the top of the steps. He'd left his dark brown suit jacket unbuttoned and his hands plugged on his hips. Affixed to his belt was a brass badge. To his right stood a blond man with a full mustache dressed in khaki pants and a navy polo. His badge was pinned over one side of his chest and HCFR was embroidered on the other side.

"Detective Marks?" Pops stepped forward when we reached the porch. Adviser Holland pressed a steadying hand against his back.

The suit lifted his chin. "You the senior pastor?"

"Yes, sir." Pops stuck out his hand, which the detective shook. "Andrew Shaw."

"This is Arson Investigator Macy." Marks hooked a thumb at his colleague. "He's with Hillsborough County Fire Rescue and assigned to this incident."

"Arson?" Kestler squeaked.

"Yes, ma'am," said Macy.

Adviser Holland stepped up beside Pops. "How bad is it in there?"

"Mighty crispy. For the amount of damage, I'm shocked it's still structurally sound." The investigator shook his head. "Fifteen years on the job and I ain't never seen anything like it. The fire was highly controlled. Impossibly so. There should be residual hot spots, but there's not even a heat signature."

"Is it safe to go in there?" Sam asked. I didn't like the look in her eye.

Marks glared at Sam. "Even if it was, you can't. It's a crime scene, ma'am."

"Can we peek?" she asked sweetly. All too innocent for those who knew her. Both detective and investigator studied her.

"No," Macy said, frowning.

"She won't cause any issues," Pops assured them while raising a brow at Sam. "Right, Sammy?"

She shrugged. Pops frowned.

"Do you have a place we can chat?" Marks asked. "We have questions."

"We can speak in my office. Follow me." Pops and Adviser Holland started down the side of the church words the administration building. Marks and Macy followed them.

Kestler and I started to go after them when a flash of golden hair caught my eye. Both of us whipped around to see that Sam had hauled her injured ass as fast as she could right into the goddamn burned-to-shit sanctuary. She ducked under the yellow crime scene tape into the darkened hall.

"Samantha Fife!" Kestler hissed. "Get back here right now!" She used her eldest-of-five tone and made for the open sanctuary doors, hot on the heels of her best friend. "We're not supposed to go in there!"

"Fuck!" I snapped and looked towards Heaven. *Please don't let me lose my shit with her.*

I hustled over as Kestler slipped under the caution tape. She snagged Sam by the elbow and both were frozen in place by the time I reached them. It was late morning, so the initial fire scene had already been cleared, but I prayed that the women's supernatural Warrior blessing kept any lingering cops far away.

"No," Sam whispered.

Their eyes had adjusted faster than mine. As the dark interior of the building came into focus for me, a chill ran up my back.

"Goddamn," I murmured.

The sanctuary was a devastating mess of blackened walls, peeled paint, fire-eaten pews, and shattered glass from the light fixtures overhead. Insulation clung to the charred rafters in limp yellow strips. Our footsteps crunched on what used to be carpet. Debris littered the floor.

"Holy Heaven," Kestler breathed, letting Sam go and wandering off to the right. "How? Who? Why?"

It was cool and damp inside from where the sprinkler system had tried its best. While this place had been deemed sound, it was far from safe. There was otherworldly heat all over the place, and the stench of sulfur assaulted my nose. This was the work of something supernatural. Something demonic. But *how* had they pulled off this shit? That was the million-fucking-dollar question.

"I can't ..." Sam advanced halfway down the aisle before turning towards me, her face twisted with devastation. "This is—was a safe space."

She crossed her arms, looked up at the charred ceiling, and spun a slow circle. She wavered on her feet as she took in the damage. I rushed to her side, slipping an arm around her and laying my hand in the small of her back.

"You don't have to hold on to me."

"You tumbled out of the Tahoe and needed my help up the steps," I said, lifting my hand. She'd kick against the goad if I forced my support onto her. "Just looking out for you."

"I'm fine," she snipped and continued down the main aisle.

When we neared the pulpit, I stared at the spot where Ma's false casket had been set for her funeral. The memorial service we'd held here in her honor felt like a goddamn lifetime ago, not just over a week. A sharp pang twisted my heart. My nose and eyes burned.

Miss you, Ma.

"How is this possible?" Kestler asked, coming up behind us. "How is the inside destroyed and the outside pristine?" She bent down and picked up what might have been a hymnal, blew soot off the hardback cover, and ran her fingers over the damaged spine.

"My theory?" Sam said. "The Mage. Or demons."

"What?" Kestler brows shot up. "Demons can't cross the border. This is sacred ground."

"Yes," I said in a low voice, keeping my eye on Sam as she wandered. "But the man who set the boundaries is weakening every day."

Kestler grunted and set down the hymnal. Her deep sniff brought my attention to her. She pinched the bridge of her nose, bowed her head, and when she looked up, her eyes were red-rimmed.

"It's hard to think about him that way," she confessed when she saw me watching her. "That he's—he's not whole anymore."

"I know."

"Damn it!" she swore, raking her hands through her brunette hair.

My eye widened. Kestler usually kept her shit locked tight, but when she blew, it was bound to be messy. And what brewed inside had to be close to erupting.

"Not the time or place," I advised.

"Right." Her hazel eyes flashed with a cocktail of emotions, but she pulled it together.

"You good?" I asked.

"Yep." She gave me a sharp nod. "And you're right. We shouldn't be here …but while we are, I might as well do a thorough investigation. See if I can glean any details from this mess."

"Do it quickly." I patted her shoulder before heading over to Sam.

She'd hobbled up the five shallow stairs at the front of the room and was studying the burned pulpit. Her left arm was pressed tight to her side. With her right she reached out and poked at the lectern. A large chunk of burned wood fell off, exploding into dust at her feet. She yanked back, fingers curling into a fist.

"Let's not touch things," I said.

"Right. Don't disturb the crime scene and all."

"How're you feeling?" I asked. Sam turned away from the pulpit, moving away from me. I followed.

She flinched. "The actual wound itself throbs like a bitch. But I'm no stranger to pain. What worries me more is that I think this stupid thing is draining me of energy." She met my eyes. Fear swam in hers. "Whatever poison was on Enyo's blade, it's still zapping my ability to reach for my Power. It's like this vital part of me has been ripped away."

She tells me this now.

A single tear slipped out and rolled down her cheek. I wanted to wipe it away. I wanted to make this right. I wanted to slay every fucking demon and slaughter the goddamn Mage. But I couldn't without being a Warrior.

Her physical ailments, I could fix. Fuck, I'd brought her back from the brink of death—but internal, invisible Warrior issues? How did I fix that? That overwhelming desire to gather her in my arms, swoop her out of the church, and lock her away in a safety bunker returned. *You are not a primitive caveman, Tate.*

Sam wavered and stumbled. I went to her and pulled her to my chest. She could shove that independent streak of hers up her ass. "Shouldn't be up and about. You're not ready."

"Harper, that ship sailed." She slipped her arms around my waist and tipped up her chin. "We're here. I'm here."

"Obviously." I smoothed a palm over the back of her skull. "But shit, Sam, what if something *does* happen?

Kestler can hold her own, but Warriors fight in pairs for a reason."

"I thought you were on my side."

I held her tighter. "I'm trying to do right by you."

How could I tell her what Molly's murder did to me? My former fiancée's death almost killed me. She'd bled out in front of me. And for all my training to be a goddamn paramedic, I hadn't been able to save her.

I'd survived my parents' murders when I was young. Witnessed the death of my childhood friend, Teddy. Watched Molly's life leave her eyes. And now Ma's death weighed heavy on my soul. Trauma and loss had been my personal antagonists for so long that I'd learned how to press on, not letting them debilitate me. Losing Sam to Death was unacceptable. She'd been my childhood friend long before life jaded me.

"I will keep you alive even if you hate me," I said low in her ear. She pulled back quickly. My eyes bored into her hers as I hammered my point home. "You are too important to lose."

A few more, unexpected tears slid down her cheeks. I took her head between both of my hands and used my thumbs to wipe her tears. *Jesus.* A female's tears never wrenched my guts and swirled them with dread the way hers were doing now.

"Why the waterworks?" I asked carefully.

"When I'm scared, the only thing I know how to do is face it head on. But when I'm fighting ghosts I can't see, I don't know how to deal with that. I know I'm asking a lot of you and Leigh by going out today." She reached up and laid her hand over my thundering heart. "It *is* a big ask of me to depend on Leigh when I can't have her back in a fight. But I've already told you why I needed this."

"We don't know where the Mage is or what Dominic

and company are up to. This is a *massive* fucking risk, Sammy."

"I am not accustomed to feeling weak and vulnerable." She lifted the palm on my chest and gripped my wrist. "I hate not knowing how I'll react if I see a demon. I hate that part of me wants to run. I hate that I want to hide. I hate that being in the farmhouse, my place of safety and comfort, now feels like the walls are going to smother me." Her voice cracked, and more tears spilled down her cheeks. "I hate that I'm terrified. I hate that I flinch when something startles me. I hate that Camden is acting weird and that Judy is dead. I hate all these new feelings. And I don't know how to make it stop."

God-fucking-damnit!

The odd dream-vision I had while Sam was in her coma came to mind. The Mage had called me Commander. Told me that when I came into my Power, my life would be tied to Sam's. But the images of Sam being run through with demons' blades was all I could see. The terror of losing her rushed in fresh and raw. I wanted to hit my knees before her now. Beg her to go home. Beg her to be careful. Instead, I crushed her to me, like I could protect her with my normal, human body.

The lingering question was if the dream was prophesy or a premonition.

We stood there until she mumbled against my shoulder, "What if I never come back from this, Harper?" She leaned back and peered up. "What if my power is zapped? Gone. Poof. *Forever.* What kind of Warrior can I be? Would I still be a Warrior? Will Leigh have to find a new partner? What if this happened because of my stupid ass decisions? I didn't let go of Camden when I should have. I failed to save Judy. I didn't listen to Leigh. I let my impulsive tendencies get the better of me. I acted like an ass. What if —what if all of this is my punishment?"

Jesus H Christ. She was killing me. "Like I said earlier, none of this shit was your fault."

"But—"

"No," I said.

"I stormed in without backup—"

"I was there."

"Stop! Listen!" Sam shouted, flinched, and her next words rushed out as a hurried, hushed confession. "Judy was nabbed to get to me. I refused to go Dark and the Mage is pissed. That trap was for me. Me, Harper. And I walked right into it. Judy was collateral damage. The guilt gnaws at me."

"What Enyo did isn't on you."

She studied my face as if searching for any deception. Finding none, she slumped against me. I tucked her under my chin and held her until the trembling slowed. This woman had me tied up in knots. Wanting to strangle her was second only to wanting to comfort her. I knew her better than most.

"You guys!" Kestler's voice echoed across the sanctuary, breaking up our cocoon. We looked in the direction her voice and found her standing near one of the side-door entrances, staring at the floor. "You better come look at this."

Sam glanced back at me and lifted a brow.

"Are you ready?" I asked, not letting her go. At her nod, I released her.

She took a step back, smoothed down her flyaway blonde wisps, wiped her cheeks, hiked up her jeans, and straightened her layered purple tank tops. I went to the stage steps and held out my arm. She scowled and rolled her eyes, but used my assistance anyway.

The tension never left her shoulders. Her steps weren't as lithe. There was a stiffness in her gait like each step hurt. And when we met up with Kestler, I saw the way stress bracketed Sam's mouth. She wasn't herself. But she was Warrior-tough, to my utter dismay.

She'll be the death of herself, I thought. Sam would do things her way, come hell or high water.

"Whatcha got?" Sam asked with false bravado.

"This." Kestler pointed down at her feet. A large swath of burned carpet, cut at a sharp right angle, had been ripped back. It revealed a red circle painted on the concrete slab. Kestler had a good eye. It would have been easy to miss, hidden as it was under the mess.

Sam pursed her lips and furrowed her brow. "What're we looking at?"

"Not sure." Kestler squatted, pressed a forearm against her thigh, and leaned forward. She tossed aside charred bits, then shifted forward and swiped a hand through the ash. Rocking back, she wiped her palm on her jeans. Someone had painted a symbol. And not just any symbol.

"What the fuck?" I knelt next to Kestler and touched the outer rim of the crude emblem. They'd drawn a smiley face with one of the eyes winking and a knife stabbed through the top of the circle.

"You think the arsonist did this?" Kestler asked.

I shrugged. "Not goddamn clue, Kestler. Take pictures. We should tell the investigators this is here. Good catch."

"We shouldn't even be in here, let alone tampering with evidence."

I heard short, sharp pants of panicked breathing. Sam's teeth were gnashed together. She gripped her side, hunching in on herself. Her entire body shook.

"Sam, you okay?" Kestler asked.

"He's toying with me," Sam blurted. "I don't know

how Dominic did this, but he did. How did he get past the wards? Nothing demonic can get through, but he did. He did. He did. Oh, my God." Her shaking hand went to her mouth. Her eyes were wild.

"Easy now," Kestler soothed, rising to her feet and extending her arm like an olive branch to her spiraling best friend. To me she asked, "How is it possible a demon could get past the wards?"

"Not just any demon," Sam interrupted. Her Power flared to life in a golden aura around her. "This burn is precise. It's direct. It's a *message*. This is Dominic's doing." She doubled over with an anguished gasp. Her aura flashed in-and-out as she struggled.

Kestler beat me to Sam's side and grabbed Sam by the shoulder, pulling her into an embrace. With a tone she'd use to calm a scared animal, she said, "I'm sure Adviser Gerena has something supernatural to scan this place. We'll get to the bottom of this."

Sam jerked away from Kestler. "Dominic's been in my head. He knows me too well."

"But isn't the Mage in control in that partnership?" Kestler asked. "Ice is her signature."

"Dominic told me that she is stronger here on Earth. Ice would make sense. But fire?" Sam backed further away, her head wagging back and forth. "Fire is *his* signature. This," she pointed at the symbol, "is Dominic toying with me."

Sam sank down a few inches, her muscles coiling. Her breath came out in those same short gasps. In fight-or-flight, her natural inclination would be to fight instead to flee. She didn't back down easily. But right now, with the wild look about her, the thin sheen of sweat on her brow, and her sharp pants suggested she was ready to run. And I didn't want her doing that in her state.

"We believe you," I said, yanking Kestler back by grabbing a handful of shirt. With my free hand, I reached out to Sam. "You aren't wrong. This could be Dominic's symbol. This fire sure feels supernatural in nature. I sense it. I smell it."

Sam backed up even more.

Fuck. She's gonna bolt.

"Let's go sit in the Tahoe," Kestler suggested. "We can talk—"

Sam ran for the exit.

"No!" I shouted. "Fucking hell. Come on."

11

SAM

Air. I need air. I busted out of the burned sanctuary. My ribs cussed at me in protest as I ran and stumbled down the stairs. The wound in my side ripped open as if Enyo's knife were still there. I tried to slow the slam of my heart against my chest and fight the desire to draw my Warrior weapons. My hands formed fists as if wrapping around their hilts.

Helios and Sol.

My daggers.

Extensions of my being.

They whispered to me, ready for battle. Ready to help me. But there was no visible danger, no need to defend myself. The threat I felt came from within. My demons weren't literal this time. I'd been trapped in my own head, cut off from my angel, with my Power suppressed—*those* were my demons. And they came roaring to the forefront to torment me.

I barely registered Leigh's insistent calls and Harper's baritone voice swearing. I ran to the church's huge play-ground. My side screamed at me. The security fence, which kept children in and unwanted people out, might as well had been a solid wall. *I need out.* Some part of my brain remembered the security keycode. I punched it in and threw open the black steel gate. At the closest park bench, my palms hit the seat for stability before I lowered myself down.

What the fire-fart is wrong with me?

"Brave One, you have—" Letty started to say.

"If you say trauma or PTSD, I'm going to scream," I snarled, then gasped as shame washed though me. *"Oh, God. I didn't mean—I'm sorry."*

"Not to worry, Warrior mine," Letty pushed her kind warmth through me. *"Talk to me. Let's work through this."*

I knew that nothing demonic could cross a Heavenly-laid ward. But not only had Dominic gotten through it, he wreaked havoc. He gloried in causing just enough destruction to stump the humans while alarming us Warriors. While that Crimson Creep didn't have quite as strong a sulfuric scent as his brethren, that sanctuary reeked of him —faint, but in every corner. That *damn* demon. How did he do it?

"Why does it feel like my insides are having an earthquake." I took two shaky lungfuls of humid, late summer air.

"Just keep going," Letty prompted. *"Don't lock down your feelings from me."*

A horrifying thought grabbed my guts and wrung them like a sponge. My skin flashed hot and cold. Nausea bubbled in my belly. If Dominic could get in, could the Mage? She was human. But she'd never been able to cross boundaries before. If a demon could get in and cause this damage, did that mean she'd be able to waltz in and cause mayhem? How was any of this possible?

And then it hit me harder than a Greater Demon punch.

"Oh, God," I croaked, burying my face in my hands. "He's really, truly dying!"

My mentor, my Adviser, my Andrew. His decline equaled the decline of his wards. This had to be how Dominic—a *demon* for Heaven's sake—could get onto church property. I had no idea Andrew was that far gone. When he'd said he was dying, I hadn't understood. It hadn't quite registered in my pea brain. Until this very moment, I didn't grasp the depth of his slow demise.

I sat up straight, neglecting my wound's protests again. The stitches were busted anyway. Warm blood plastered my shirt to my side. How long did Andrew have left? Months? Weeks? Days? And then he'd be gone.

Forever.

My heart wrenched in two. A sob ripped from my soul. Tears coursed down my cheeks. Fear that Dominic and the Mage could roll up in here at any minute paralyzed me. My mind spun like Alice falling down the rabbit hole, like Dorothy being uprooted by a tornado.

Spiraling down. Down. Down.

Hands gripped my shoulders. My head snapped up. Harper's stout form filled my field of vision as he squatted in front of me. I reached for him, grabbing a handful of his black tee. A strangled noise rose from the back of my throat and burst forth with unladylike resolve. My chest heaved. My eyes squeezed closed. His warm palm closed over my trembling fist.

"Look at me," he commanded.

Quivering, I obeyed.

"Good girl." He gripped my wrists gently and ran his thumbs over my pulse points, gaze locked with mine. "Now *breathe* with me."

For several minutes—days, weeks even—I focused on his breaths. When he inhaled, I followed. When he held, I did the same. When he exhaled, the air in my lungs whooshed out along with his. After a while, the frayed edges of my panicked heart stopped unraveling. My free fall stopped as I landed on Harper's dependable bulwark. I felt Leigh beside me. She rubbed soothing circles on my back. I managed to shoot her a weak smile.

Harper's eyes dipped to my side and he traced his fingers over my ribs. "Show me."

The way he moved and spoke suggested I was the wild horse that needed its handlers to proceed with calm caution, so I hauled up the left side of my shirt.

"It's bloody," I confessed. "I felt something give when I ran out here."

Instead of watching Harper work, I raised my eyes to peer at the clear morning sky, preparing for his reprimand. It never came. I was met with that same quiet steadiness from moments ago. The kind of support that anchored me —kept me from shattering again and again. A flutter in my heart, that should have died long ago flickered to life.

"We're going back home right now." Harper lowered my shirt. "I have to redo some of your stitches."

"No," I said.

"Sam!" Leigh gasped, exasperated.

Harper arched a brow and his glare turned dark, dangerous—hard enough to cut diamonds. It was a look that said, *explain yourself, right the fuck now.*

"I cannot be in that house with all those memories haunting me. The pictures on the walls. My blood stains on the dining room table. And Judy—" My voice cracked. Angry, frustrated tears spilled out. I swiped at them, annoyed that I was crying. *Again.* "Why can't I pull my shit together? I just need …need …" I waved my hands only to cross them in front of my chest. "I need to get a grip."

Harper's entire expression softened. It was like my

vulnerability cracked his ragey, over-protective wall of control, and in that split second, he looked at me like he truly saw me. Saw through my shit storm of wild emotion. My impulsive choices. Harper saw *me*.

Maybe he always had.

"Then we're going back to Shield Haven," Harper said, his eyes slid to Leigh's.

She nodded. "I'll call him."

Xavier's place.

My shoulders sagged in relief as Leigh walked off a ways, cell phone pressed to her ear. She stopped beside a large slide that jutted out from the massive playhouse in the center of the park.

"Thank you," I whispered. Xavier's castle was neutral ground—mostly. His property was large enough that I could avoid most places that made me feel things.

"Promise me something." Harper tucked hair behind my ear. The quiet, softer version of this man wasn't something I was used to. The way he looked at me now reminded me that the teenage-Harper still lurked under the hardened exterior. When he had been *my* Harper.

"What's that?" I let my arms drop and rested my hands in my lap.

"Recover better." His finger tips gently grazed over my wounded side. I sucked in a sharp breath. He touched my temple. "Get yourself sorted out here." He tapped the center of my chest. "Let this heal up some."

I pulled the corner of my lower lip between my teeth. Could I make that promise? There were too many unknowns at the moment. Where was the Mage? What was Hell planning? What was Dominic's next move?

"We have good news and bad news." Leigh's voice broke through our moment. She could move like a ghost most of the time, so her footsteps crunching over gravel, announcing her arrival, had been done on purpose. I flinched at the sound anyway.

Harper's walls immediately re-bricked themselves. "Stop being a menace to everyone who's trying to help you."

"Stop being a bossy prick," I snapped back.

"Right." Leigh cleared her throat as her shadow fell over us. When we looked up at her, she continued, "Bad news first. Jax, Lani, Sajid, and Talia all have reports that Lesser Demons have lurked around the farm's border."

As if her words summoned them, a heavy demonic presence buzzed through the air. My supernatural senses flared to life, strong and snapping with energy. Their Hellish, sulfuric heat rippled along the tops of my shoulders and down my spine, summoning the Warrior inside. She rose to the challenge of potential battle, and I was on my feet in a flash, pain and fear be damned.

"Something wicked this way comes," I mused, quoting Macbeth. My hands twitched to pull Helios and Sol from their invisible scabbards on my back. Not knowing how my body would behave just yet, I waited to tap into my Power.

"I sense them, too," Leigh murmured.

"Where?" Harper scanned the playground, every bit an impenetrable wall of muscle and force. It was tragic that he wasn't a Warrior. He'd make a formidable one. All three of us searched around us without advancing a step.

"There." I tipped up my chin. "By the light post, past the playhouse—oh, shit, are they on church property?"

Leigh drew her massive white-metal sword, Fury, from the invisible sheath on her back. She held the glowing Heavenly steel in front of her, ready for battle.

A tall, purple-skinned demon with black hair stood next to his red brother—not Dominic's fire engine shade, something dusky and far more muted—and the third was a stocky, electric-teal female with yellow eyes. They were out-and-about, bold-as-brass during the day. The teal female slammed a fist against the invisible barrier. Her fist sizzled and smoked.

"The border holds," Leigh said with relief. "But Sam's right. They are much closer than they should be. It's almost like the boundary line is receding."

The tall demon jammed his black sword into the ward, sending ripples and sparks into the air. I pulled Helios and Sol from their sheaths. The boys hummed in perfect frequency with my inner Warrior and they glowed as bright as Fury. *Am I ready for this?* The question swirled in my brain like a misty ghost. It twisted up with my rising fear.

As I brought my daggers into fighting position and drew on my Power, pain burst from my ribs. Sharp beams of agony lashed out from where I'd been stabbed. My torso felt like it had been wrenched in two. I staggered, gripping my daggers. My heart pumped liquid fire, not blood, through my veins. Harper caught me. I let go of my Power.

"Not normal," I gasped to Letty.

"No, it's not," she agreed.

"Did the Mage leave more gifts for me to discover?"

I felt Letty scanning my insides. Her gentle warmth gathered around my stab wound and anesthetized the ripping agony to a more tolerable level. When she moved on, the pain ratcheted back up. I hissed.

"No trigger spells," Letty reported. *"But there are trace amounts of poison embedded in your wound. Seeing as all other Warriors before you have succumbed to Enyo's concoction, we're in unknown territory. I suspect that when you use your anointing, the poison disagrees with your nature."*

Well, hellfire and horseshit.

"Sam, fucking answer me." Harper's harsh words snapped me back to present. "What's going on?"

"My wound is contaminated." His perma-frown deepened. A quick glance at Leigh showed me that she was just as concerned. Her eyes darted to the demons and back to me.

"What about Leigh?" I asked Letty, knowing the answer. *"She'll have no Warrior partner to have her back. I'll be replaced."*

Not for the first time, nor the last, I wondered what would happen if I never got better. What if I was freaking stuck like this for the rest of my potentially long life? Perhaps, I could be an Adviser. The thought of being forced into early retirement rankled. Being a Light Warrior had become so grafted into my being that I couldn't imagine a life without the battle, the fight, the adrenaline rush mixed with Warrior Power.

"We will find a way to fix this, Brave One," Letty said. *"I vow it."*

But that wouldn't help Leigh now. I scrambled to my feet, untangling myself from Harper. All three demons stood still, eyes wide and frozen in surprise. Leigh slipped into full-scale Warrior mode. Her clothes instantly morphed into a white tunic and pants—our battle armor. Her aura pulsed and burst into a brilliant gold. Fury blazed bright white, ready for retribution. The trio scrambled back several feet but didn't leave.

"I can't let them stay here," Leigh declared.

"I can't help you, so be careful," I said.

With lightning speed, she charged at the Greater Demons. As Leigh ran towards our foe, the Heavenly glow from her sword spread over her whole body. Fierce, fast, and filled with holy rage, she was more fearsome and terrifying than usual.

The russet-colored demon slunk back. The purple

mountain retreated, leaving his black blade still wedged in to the boundary wall. Only the lone teal female held her ground, her lips puckered in a sneer, a gleam of anger in her odd yellow eyes. My Warrior's ears could hear the demons speaking to each other.

"Victoria, come," urged the purple giant. "Our Master said not to engage."

The small demon swore in her demonic tongue and prepared to meet Leigh head on. The purple demon growled, grabbed her by the hair, and pulled back. The teal harpy screamed like a banshee, flailing her body around, wielding her hands like talons. Mr. Purple ignored the slashes to his arms and face while dragging her away.

"We can take her," screeched Victoria. "She's alone! You saw Samantha Fife cannot fight."

"Fool," hissed the russet demon.

"Do not underestimate this one," the purple giant warned. "She killed Silas with a single slash."

The teal demon stopped spitting and cursing. Her chest heaved. Hatred and despair radiated from her eyes.

Who is Silas?

Leigh was within striking distance, still on sacred ground, and loaded up for a powerful swing of Fury when the demons' solid forms sputtered, like a glitching old-fashioned movie projector, and then they were gone.

"No!" Leigh shouted and pulled up just before crossing the boundary. With her unused Power, she slashed Fury down on the black sword wedged in the invisible border and sliced it in half. The severed ends burned orange and red as they clattered to the pavement. My best friend wheeled around with a roar of anger.

I knew her. And I knew that look.

She wanted demon blood on her blade and demon dust floating around her. She wanted a rugged, rough fight, just as much as I did. Instead, she let go of her Power, sheathed Fury behind her back, and she walked towards us like some Norse Valkyrie.

"Samantha!" Harper snapped my Christian name as if he'd been trying to get my attention.

"Yes!"

Harper regarded me with keen gaze. "I know you heard them. What happened?"

"They were ding dang snoops. Freaking nosey buggers. Had orders to not attack, just observe. That small female, Victoria, mentioned me by my full name." I lifted a finger. "Which never fails to creep me out."

"Sam!" Harper snapped. "Back on track."

"Right." I tilted my head towards Leigh who'd rejoined us. "The female wanted a piece of Leigh. The purple giant reminded her that Leigh killed some demon named Silas, and that took all the fight out of her. You remember any demon named Silas?"

Leigh scrunched her lips to the side and shrugged. "I've lost track of all the demons I've dispatched."

"You got closest to them. Anything you'd like to add?" Harper asked Leigh.

"Na. Except for that Victoria demon, they were your average ugly brutes."

I snorted, and she flashed me a grin when my sudden rush of adrenaline crashed. I wavered on my feet, and the overwhelming weight of my current condition washed over me. My head swam. Fuzziness overtook my vision. Two different sets of hands caught me by the biceps.

"Do what you need to and meet us at Shield Haven," Harper said to Leigh. "She's in shit shape." He pulled me from Leigh's grasp and I sagged against his sturdy frame.

Leigh reached out and squeezed my hand. "We'll bring Bear and Max. Get some rest, okay?"

I managed a weak nod. Max would find a way to get to me no matter where I was. Having my dog with me would be a bonus. My eyes fluttered shut and I sighed. Tapping into my Power shouldn't have drained me, but it left me feeling weaker and more vulnerable than before. Perhaps I should have stayed in bed recuperating? My knees buckled. Harper hissed, catching me. He bent his knees, swooped me up into his arms, and headed towards the SUV. He set me in the front seat of the Tahoe. I winced when the seatbelt buckle locked me in.

"Adviser Gerena is sending another car," I heard Leigh say to Harper when the vehicle door was closed. "I'll wait with Advisers Shaw and Holland for safety. They need to know what's going on, too."

"I don't like this," Harper said to her. I turned my face to the window. He'd reached out and gripped Leigh's shoulder. Some sort of unspoken communication passed between them when he added, "You shouldn't be without a backup, Kestler."

"I'll be fine." Leigh smiled at him. An actual, true smile. The one she reserved for the people closest to her.

I pressed my lips together hard and told the sudden prick of jealousy to die a quick death. I had a damn boyfriend. Harper was off limits to me for more than one reason. Heat climbed my neck and flashed behind my ears.

"I'm staying," Leigh said with more force. "While Advisers can protect themselves, they are retired from combat for a reason."

"Don't you dare fucking die then," was Harper's retort as he moved from the door, around the front, and thumped the hood with his fist on his way to the driver's side.

Leigh cracked open the door and leaned on the frame. "You alright?"

"Would you believe me if I said yes?"

"No." Leigh laughed. "But how 'bout the truth this time?"

"Physically?" I let out a puff of air. "I'm in pain. A little nauseous. All my energy's been sucked out of my bones."

"And mentally?"

"A tossup between hot garbage and a dumpster fire." I grimaced. "Rather not talk about that. What about you? Leaving you behind feels wrong. What if something happens?"

"I'll be fine." Leigh smiled, though it didn't reach her eyes. She dropped her voice into a teasing lilt. "I don't seek out danger like someone else I know."

"Rude." I huffed out a laugh and poked her arm. "Swear you won't do something I would do."

"Promise." She held out a pinky finger, like we'd done all our lives.

"I'll see you at Casa de Gerena." I hooked my own pinky around Leigh's and squeezed. "Be swift. Be safe."

This time her smile crinkled the corners around her eyes. "And *you* listen to Harper, okay?"

Harper cleared his throat and started the engine. I could see the smirk on his lips and his raised brow from my view of his profile.

"I didn't pinky swear to that," I said, turning back to Leigh.

"Behave," she warned before shutting the passenger door.

I watched Leigh grow smaller from where she stood in the lot as Harper backed out of the parking space and headed for the main road. All the while, my gut nagged at me that whatever happened next would hurt like a sonovabitch.

DOMINIC

D ominic found himself marvelously alone in Andrew Shaw's gym office. Aside from the Tate boy and Xavier Gerena—and possibly Tabitha Holland—no one suspected poor, polite Camden Bennett was anything but innocent. No one questioned him as he roamed the farmhouse property, free to snoop as he pleased. Only the old butler Nigel remained on the property, and he was doing whatever domestic things humans did.

Dominic's lips curled upward in a slow, malicious smile. He leaned back in the battered leather chair, his fingers tapping a slow rhythm on the worn out keyboard in front of him.

The office was outdated but well-loved. Pictures hung on walls depicting Bernard Andrew Shaw's current chosen life. Dominic had knowledge of the man from many different lifetimes. This humble farm in Florida wasn't the first place the man had made home and hearth.

It was, however, the first time in history that the head Adviser had offspring of one of the greatest Warrior couples in history: Thomas and Elaine Tate. Thomas had taken down thirty of Hell's finest Greater Demons without breaking a sweat, laughing, as if slaying demons was easy. Elaine moved like a shadow and thwarted many of Hell's plans before they could come to fruition.

Focus, Dom, ol' boy, he told himself. Hauling in a breath, he sat up and scooted the rolling chair closer to the desk. He typed in a password.

Kimberly. Shaw's deceased wife's original name. *Denied.*

He waggled his fingers before him and tried again.

Crumlin. Shaw's hometown in Ireland. *Denied.*

Dominic tapped his lips. Stilling his hand, but not removing his fingers from the keys, his gaze floated around the room. "If I were the sly Irishman, what would I set as the password?"

Several minutes and too many tries later, Dominic found himself locked out. A rare annoyed growl escaped him as he threw himself back into the chair and stared across the office. His gaze settled on an older photograph hanging with preeminence. It was the largest of the framed pictures. Shaw, Samantha Fife, and Mr. Tate were all on horseback.

However, it wasn't Andrew seated on a black mare that caught Dominic's attention. It was Samantha astride her chestnut gelding. *Max.* The very same gelding who resided in the barn today. The very same gelding who didn't have a single extra grey hair on his old red face. He was her Warrior Guardian.

Dominic's eyes grew wide. Could it be that simple?

An image of a massive red deer popped in his deep memory bank. The biggest stag he'd ever seen had stood five feet in height, and his antlers had spanned three feet wide and had been lethal in battle. Those antlers had been supernaturally capped with Heavenly metal. No one currently alive, aside from the elder Advisers Shaw, Gerena, and Holland, would remember the animal.

But Dominic did.

He'd slain the Guardian in battle centuries ago. Dominic turned back to the monitor in front of him and two-finger typed out a name long forgotten: O-I-S-I-N.

The screen flashed and he was gifted with access. "Clever old man, using your fallen Guardian's name."

Dominic began poking around the files, not finding anything of particular interest, until he double clicked on a random folder titled Vault. The computer prompted him for another password. Dominic sucked his front of his teeth. Andrew was too smart to use the same code twice. He ran his fingers over the keyboard, thinking, when the cell phone in his pocket vibrated.

"Camden speaking."

"My son," cooed a woman's voice. "Or is this my Dark One?"

Dominic smirked. He abandoned the desk chair, meandered to the front of the office, and peered out of the one-way window overlooking the gym floor. "Both are at your service, my wee duck."

"You're too good to me," she said. "Do you have anything to report?"

"I have the property to myself at the moment," Dominic said, leaning out the door of the office. He looked around and pulled the door almost shut. "I'm sleuthing."

"Oh, really?" she inquired, her tone rising. Intrigue. He heard it in her voice, clear as day.

"I'm in the gym office." Dominic wandered over to a filing cabinet and opened the top drawer. He ran his fingers over folder tab markers. "Unattended."

There was a sharp intake of breath across the line. "What are you up to, my darling demon?"

"Trying to find anything I can use. Knowledge is power, just as much as power is power. We must have both. Brains and brawn."

"What would I do without you?"

The corner of Dominic's lips tipped up and he asked, "Is there anything specific you'd have me search for, my queenling?"

"My sources tell me that bastard of an old man has made several trips to Ireland in the past six months."

Dominic took a deep breath. He could almost taste the bittersweet energy cackling through his Dark Warrior's all-consuming hate for Andrew Shaw. That energy fed and sustained him without needing to magically extract it from her.

"As you know," she continued, "Shaw has no family left on the Emerald Isle. Nothing of note, according to my demon scouts. I want to know what he's doing and why."

"Adviser Holland has her base of Warriors and Seers in Ireland," Dominic reminded her. "Might your nemesis simply have been visiting his old colleague?" He tucked the phone between his shoulder and ear, freeing his hands so he could pilfer through the files, not looking for anything in particular.

"No," she snapped. "That old bastard's up to something. I feel it."

"My wee duck, you sound positively obsessed with the man." Dominic smirked, knowing he was provoking her. He walked his fingers over the folders in front of him.

"He ruined my life!" A door slammed and her voice took on a hollow sound as if she'd stalked into a new room with marble floors. "I destroyed him once. I'll do it again; I must know what he's planning. We need the upper hand!"

Dominic's response died on his tongue. A name caught his eye and struck like a livid viper. He withdrew a manilla folder and ran his fingers over the notched tab. *Harper Tate.* Andrew Shaw had filed it under the section for Active Warriors.

Dominic's eyes widened. His nostrils flared. The Tate boy was human. *Why did you put this here, Mr. Shaw?*

"Dominic!"

"Yes?" he mused, still focused on the folder.

"Are you even listening?"

"One moment, my darling." Dominic opened the folder and thumbed through the pages. There were entries dating back to the day that Harper's parents had died.

The Tate boy's file piqued Dominic's interest more than listening to his Dark Warrior ramble on about her unending vendetta against Andrew Shaw. He tuned her out and ran his fingers down one page of typed text. Perhaps it had been mere coincidence that Mr. Tate's file had been placed where it had, but Dominic knew his adversary well enough to know that Andrew had a purpose for everything he did.

Did the old Adviser suspect that Harper would become a Warrior? Was the young champion ripe for his anointing? Could that kernel of promise be turned for Hell's benefit?

"Hmmmm," Dominic hummed. *Perhaps my dark queen should have been pursuing you, young Harper, instead of Samantha.* He took hold of the phone and straightened.

"What is it?" his Warrior demanded.

"Patience," Dominic crooned and continued to leaf through the file. "I'm following a lead but need time to do my best work."

"I don't like being kept in the dark, Dominic," she snipped. After a few moments of his silence, she huffed. "Fine. Don't waste more time. I have plans."

"Wouldn't dream of it," he said, distracted.

"What about that insufferable Fife child?" his Dark One asked, jolting him from his distraction. "When are you going to kill her? Better yet, bring her to me. I want to feel the life leave her pathetic body with my own fingers."

"My viscious Warrior," Dominic purred, sights still pinned on the folder. "Samantha Fife still has value. Your son absolutely adores the girl. I feel the depth of his affection for her. I can use those feelings. Trying to recruit Miss Fife may not have been our most prudent choice, but perhaps I can sow seeds of discord. You know this is one of my greatest talents. Miss Fife's not dealing well with our— visitation to her mindscape."

Dominic heard glass clink against marble. Everything was silent, then Aerona asked, "Sow discord how?"

"It seems that Miss Fife has a touch of post-traumatic stress. She's been trying to gain traction since she woke while also healing from the wound Enyo inflicted." Dominic tucked Harper's file under his arm, pinning it to his side. He carefully slid the cabinet drawer shut with a soft *whoosh* and padded back over to the office desk to reclaim his seat. "She's vulnerable. She's frantic about Camden's safety. She's confused."

He laid the Tate file down and jiggled the mouse. The computer screen blinked to life. Dominic could almost hear the gears in Aerona's mind as she processed this information.

"You know what she did to me."

"I know." Dominic rolled his eyes. "She damaged your magic when she ousted us from her wee mind. She humiliated you."

"I want her to pay," she snarled. "In fact, I want to break her. Death would be too merciful. I want her heart in my hands! Her blood under my fingernails!"

His Warrior's dramatics increased when he was away

from her. If they were apart too long, she'd lose her connection to her sound mind—her sanity—since his power did twist and corrupt the soul. Dominic reached for his fedora, belatedly remembering he was inhabiting Camden Bennett's body and that he wasn't wearing his favorite piece of apparel. He sighed at his forgetfulness. Lacking his hat, he straightened the lapels of his jacket and picked off a piece of lint, his plans shifting like cog wheels in head.

A deceased or hamstringed Samantha Fife was not in *his* plans.

"My Queen," he soothed, running a hand over the ridiculous blonde curls on his head—oh, how he missed his normal visage and his bloody hat. He found a teaspoon of patience for the woman on the other end of the line. "You languish without me. I feel your distress. Rest assured that I'll find out about Shaw's dealings in Ireland. The Fife girl will be handled." His eyes roved over the file in front in his free hand. "And if I stumble upon any other golden nuggets that I can mine out during research, you shall be the first to know."

"It does not escape me, Dark One, that you skated over my feelings about that brat to comment on my deteriorating constitution. But as you are concocting your delectable schemes, I'll give you a pass."

Dominic's lips pulled into a half smile. "You are most gracious."

"I'll be in touch," she said. "Have something for me the next time I call."

Dominic laid the phone on the desk top with a click. Icy prickles ran down his spine as he felt his Warrior's spike of Power—her warning. *So help me if she's slaughtering more of my brethren...* With a gusty sigh, he shoved aside the thought, leaned back, propped Camden's long legs atop the desk, and slapped Harper's file onto his thighs. And then he began to read.

The first report documented the deaths of Thomas and Elaine Tate. He skimmed the signed form declaring that the Shaws had became Harper Tate's legal guardians. Notes upon notes detailed how withdrawn the boy was as a child, how Lady Shaw had to coax him out of his shell, and how witnessing the death of his parents took a toll on him.

"Ugh," Dominic grunted. *Blah, blah, blah. How bloody boring.*

He pressed a thumb at the edge of the pages and fanned through the sheets, skimming for something more inciting, something he could *use*, when the sound of the gym's outer metal door clanged open. He heard two people chattering.

Dominic's gaze snapped to the cracked open office door at the same time he dropped his feet. The chair let out a riotous squeak when he sat up. He leaned to one side so he could slide the folder under his butt. The voices of one male and one female approaching the office grew louder. Dominic scooted into the desk, placed his hands on the keyboard, and kept a corner eye pinned on the doorway.

Through the office window, Dominic watched the Warriors arrive as he mined Camden's memory bank. Talia and Sajid. The two were laughing as Talia held onto Sajid's arm. Her eyes found Dominic's and his breath ceased. Only she couldn't have, because it was one way. Her smile vanished and she cocked her head, pointing towards the office door.

Jaw tight, spine rigid, Dominic positioned his hands on the keyboard, pretending to type. With practiced surprise, he looked up just as the couple entered.

Sajid stood in the doorway. With his black hair, wet with sweat, he looked like some ancient Egyptian god. Talia swooped in next to Sajid. He put a casual arm over her shoulders, while her ever-suspicious brown eyes regarded Dominic.

Of the two Warriors before him, he suspected Talia would be the harder to fool. But Dominic took heart that neither of these Warriors knew Camden Bennett well, and while suspicious, they might be easily hoodwinked.

His lies had to be precise.

"Hi there," he said, forcing a wide, dazzling smile— aiming for innocent. "Patrol shift over? Anything exciting happen?"

He knew damn well no demon would think of inter- fering with his plans. As long as he inhabited Camden Bennett's body, he'd ordered a cease fire of sorts, and none of his kin were to come within fifty yards of the farmhouse wards, or any Warrior-blessed place, while he was playing his part.

"All is quiet." Sajid's accent was thick, but his English was crystal clear. "Sorry to disturb you, but I wasn't aware you'd returned from your errands. You're aware Sam is with Advisers Shaw and Holland, yes? Are you authorized to be in here?"

"My dear girlfriend tasked me with recording her account of what happened in her coma." He mimed tapping a few keys as if typing into a document. "She didn't want to forget any details, so she provided them to me."

"Why not use her own computer?" Talia asked, her suspicion holding more hostility than Sajid's inquiry.

A valid question.

"Everyone is out of the house, and I don't know where her laptop is," Dominic lied. "Did you need something? A water?" Dominic pointed behind him at the small refrigerator.

"No," Talia answered, "but I think you should not be in here."

"Tally, manners," Sajid chided his partner gently. "We are guests in Adviser Shaw's home and this is Sam's boyfriend, is it not?"

"If it helps, Sam did give me the passwords needed to access this particular computer."

"I think you lie," Talia said harshly then launched into rapid fire Hebrew to Sajid—her native tongue—presumably to keep Camden Bennett from understanding her words.

What the Warrior pair didn't know was that Dominic understood a myriad of languages. Hebrew and Arabic being two of them. When she finished her short rant about Camden being where he shouldn't and lack of security, Sajid pulled her tight against his side.

"Give him the benefit of the doubt, Tally. He's done nothing wrong. Samantha asked him to be here."

Dominic kept his mouth shut and gleaned bits of information as Talia continued in her language. Apparently, Talia had spent many years pickpocketing and swindling tourists out of their ready-to-spend cash. She'd lived on the streets. She knew what an honest man looked like verses a hustler, and Camden gave her pause.

Camden had the look of a conman.

Dominic's eye twitched. This female Warrior saw too much. He did his best to portray a confused but curious calm since Camden wasn't supposed to know what she'd said. Talia shoved against Sajid, planted her fists on her hips, and turned her dark eyes, glittering with suspicion, on Dominic.

"I watch you." She pointed her index and middle

finger at her eyes, then turned her wrist to stab them towards Dominic. Without waiting, she wheeled on her heel and stormed off to the locker rooms.

Dominic huffed nervously. "Well, that went well."

"She's suspicious of most," Sajid said. "Her upbringing wasn't a gentle one."

"I see," Dominic said.

"You might want to check in with Sam. We are relocating to Adviser Gerena's estate. I'm sure she'd want you to join us.

"Of course." Dominic tried to quell his mounting unease. While no boundary had yet kept him out while possessing a human, the Spaniard was a Heaven-Blessed tinkerer. An anointed scientist. A hallowed inventor.

Xavier Gerena's wards would *not* be weak.

Dominic smiled at Sajid. "I was just finishing up in here. Maybe about ten minutes?"

"I shall keep Tally detained," the bronze-skinned Warrior said. He bowed his head and left.

"Well, that was close," Dominic chuckled.

Getting past Xavier's wards? Keeping up the Camden charade? Disobeying his Dark Warrior? Sabotaging one Samantha Fife? Digging up information on Harper Tate?

"How exhilarating!" He reopened the folder, his grin widening. "The game is afoot."

HARPER

I t took an hour and a half to drive from Pops's church in Riverview to Xavier's safehouse in Brooksville. We'd made a quick drugstore pitstop on our way because Sam had been bleeding freely. And since I'd temporarily patched her up, she'd spent the ride staring out of the window. I knew that she hadn't slept because I could see her face in the window's reflection. Her eyes were open but her stare was vacant. While I was never one to fill silence with idle chatter, Sam never shut the hell up.

"I'm not made of glass, Harper."

"Sure," I grunted and hit the turn signal to start down Casa Gerena's long driveway. "You realize you haven't spoken in almost an hour. Call it concern."

She rolled her head against the head rest to look at me. "What is there to say? I choked. What if Leigh had needed me? Or Andrew's ward hadn't held and the demons had gotten in? I *cried* instead of defending our turf. God, what's wrong with me?"

My anger spiked at how these assholes robbed her of

her confidence and Power. I slammed a fist against the wheel. Sam flinched.

"Don't be mad," she squeaked.

Fuck!

I stared out of the windshield as the tree-lined drive gave way to sprawling estate grounds. The manor borrowed bits of architecture from both castle and mansion with its grey-and-white stone walls, Gothic windows, and heavy Spanish influence. We drove past a massive dolphin fountain in the front garden, then parked under the porte-cochère at the front door.

I put the SUV in park, leaned my forearms on the wheel, and met Sam's eyes. "I fucking furious, Sammy. I know what happened to you wasn't your fault. You were set up, attacked, and wounded. I'm also pissed that you didn't listen to me when I said you weren't ready to gallivant over the whole goddamn county today."

"Right." She gave a sharp nod and reached for the door handle. "Thank you for your judgment, Mr. Perfect-McPerfectson. Wouldn't want to disrupt your *delicate sensibilities.*"

The rare feeling of my gut sinking took me by surprise. I raked a hand over my hair. "Shit, Sam, I didn't mean—"

She flung off her seatbelt, kicked open the car door, and was already scrambling out. A pained hiss escaped her.

I snagged her by the elbow. "Hold on, let me help."

The look on Sam's face was mutinous. "Fine."

She settled back into the seat and crossed her arms. I bolted from the car, jogged around the front, and joined her side. I offered her a hand, which she grasped, and then slide my other arm around her for support. She rested most of her weight against me as she slid from the cab.

"I got you," I encouraged. "Take it easy."

"You were right," she muttered.

"Excuse me?" I asked, not sure I'd heard her correctly.

"Look, I'm trying out this new thing called humility. I admit that I maybe, kinda, might have overshot my mobility ability today." Sam leaned against me as we shifted away from the vehicle. "I wasn't ready. Emotionally or physically. Things could have gone very badly at the church. So, you were right."

Any other day, in any other situation, hearing Samantha Grace Fife tell me I was right would have been cause for a goddamn celebration. Instead, it felt like a wild haymaker to the stomach. All I ever wanted was to keep her safe and for her to take the time she needed to recover. Sam met my eyes. Hers were filled with storm clouds of uncertainty.

"Where would we have been if the wards hadn't held? You saw that demon was able to stab the veil." She licked her lips nervously. "What if Leigh ended up having to fight three Greater Demons?" She raised a hand before I could defend Kestler's exemplary fighting abilities. "I know, I know, she's done it before. But that small one, the female with yellow eyes, had that look about her that she wanted to personally cut Leigh apart and eat the pieces."

"The boundary held and Kestler didn't have to use Fury," I said. "Don't borrow trouble."

With a deadpan glare she said, "That's rich coming from you."

The front door cracked opened. At that sound, Sam tensed and lifted her arm so fast I didn't have time to stop her. One of her daggers shimmered into view as she gripped the hilt. *Jesus, she's fast and trigger happy.* A woman with copper hair emerged from the shadows of the inner hall. I stopped Sam from taking any further action by laying a palm over the back of her hand that held her weapon.

"Easy, spitfire," I murmured. "Xavier said he'd have a Healer meet us when we got here. She's not a threat."

When Sam realized that the Seer before us meant no harm, she snorted. The fierce lines on her face slackened to something like embarrassment. I disarmed her, moving slowly, and took the dagger from her grip—she didn't recoil. The handle grew hot in my hand, as Warrior weapons were not meant for prolonged contact with humans. I glanced at the poor Healer who's face had drained of color.

"I'm putting this back," I told Sam and slid her weapon back home in its invisible sheath.

Proud as ever, Sam shooed my hands away, straightened, and took a few surprisingly solid steps before stumbling. I caught her as she lost her balance. She placed a hand on my forearm, steadying herself.

"I got you," I said.

"Whatever you're thinking, Harper Tate, don't you dare—"

I swept her up in my arms, as I'd done at the church, and whatever she'd been about to say or threaten got cut off with a short yelp.

"Put me down!" Sam swatted at me. "You asshole, my legs still work."

A smile twitched on my lips. Ignoring Sam's indignant protests, I asked the auburn-haired woman her name.

"Emily, sir. Adviser Gerena said you'd need the infirmary."

"No!" Sam shouted. "No more laying in beds. No more treating me like an invalid, so put me down."

Ignoring her, knowing we'd be walking unfamiliar halls, I said, "Thank you, Emily. Lead the way."

"No infirmaries, Harper!" She insisted. "Take me anywhere else."

I muttered into her ear, "Stop making a scene. Seers live here. This is their home. Pull your shit tother and let me fucking help you. You need rest, Elixir, and morphine."

Sam huffed but after a beat said, "No more pain meds, either."

I chuckled while she scowled, but she offered no more protests. With a final chin lift towards Emily, she led us through the extravagant front hall into a bustling common room. When we entered, the general chatter stopped and all eyes fell on Sam. She shuddered and ducked her head into my chest. An embarrassed groan was her only protest. I nodded to everyone as we passed through.

We reached a small room with a circular table taking up most of the space in the center. A vase filled with an elaborate display of green and powder blue hydrangeas sat atop it. To our left was a long, plain brick wall which had a secret door and was only accessible by a hidden scanner.

"Harper, I weigh a hundred and sixty pounds. I'm heavy." Sam rolled her eyes. "You should put me down."

"You can barely stand or walk up a small set of stairs," I leveled. "And you've lost weight. I got you."

Her cheeks flushed and she gritted her teeth. She muttered something that sounded like *asshole*. I stared at the stately elevators to our right.

"No stairs, miss," Emily said to Sam as she pressed a brass button to summon an elevator car. "These stop at the infirmary hall."

"See!" Sam said, as if that would change my mind.

Emily and I waited for the doors to ding open.

"Why are you treating me like an invalid?" Sam asked.

"You *are* an invalid."

"I'm not some damsel in distress. I'm like a Viking

warrior woman, or something. Bury me with my weapons and my horse!"

"You're not dead yet," I murmured into her ear.

The elevator dinged and we up to hospital ward. Rows of twin beds lined both walls of the infirmary, and an unexpected wave of grief hit me so hard I lost my breath. It hadn't been more than two weeks ago that Ma had come in here and cleaned house. She'd upgraded the ward from general disrepair to modern efficiency. I tensed, fighting my emotions.

"What's wrong?" Sam asked.

"It's fine," I muttered.

"Liar."

"Let me tend your wound." I set her down onto one of the beds and glanced at the sticky red spot on her shirt. "Get you stitched back up and on some meds."

She caught my wrist before I turned away. "No drugs, I was serious. No more."

"Why?"

She pointed to the chair next to the bed and tugged my arm. I stared at her for a moment before scooting the seat closer to her and sitting down. I leaned my forearms on my thighs and waited, watching her chew on her bottom lip. I felt Healer Emily hovering far enough away but close enough to listen.

She turned her gaze on me. They shimmered with determination, reminding me of how she always appeared in my recent nightmares, brave and bold, right before Enyo killed her. And fuck me, because I wanted to brush the few strands of hair that fell out of her ponytail away from her face now.

"My inferno of a metabolism burns through medicine in half the time it should." She grabbed my fingers, bringing the reason we were in the hospital ward into sharp focus. "My brain is foggy. It gives me a false sense that everything is okay, which in fact, we know is a load of horseshit. I think the drugs are what emboldened me to march outta the farmhouse like I hadn't just awakened from a coma and didn't have a hole in my side."

I leaned back in my seat. "That and you're naturally impulsive."

"You get me." She let go of my hand and laid her head back on the pillow.

"But you'll let me fix you up, yeah?"

She pulled up her bloody shirt. "Do your best."

"Harper, sir, would you like me to do this?" Healer Emily stepped forward. "I'm trained—"

I aimed a sharp scowl in her direction.

She raised her brows and lifted her hands in surrender. "Or I can get you the supplies you need?"

My temper spiked and I did my best to reel in it. "That would be great. Thanks."

While Emily was gone, I worked on removing the messy makeshift bandage, gently peeling away the adhesive from Sam's skin. Checking the wound, I blew out a breath.

When will she stop blowing her motherfucking stitches. And where the fuck is Emily? As if conjured, Emily appeared with a loaded medical tray in one hand and a set of clothes in the other.

"Do you require any assistance?" she asked while setting down the instruments on the bedside stable.

"No," I said with eyes on Sam's wound. "You may leave."

Snapping on a pair of latex gloves, I heard Emily's departing footsteps echo through the open infirmary. The solid doors opened and closed. Only when she was gone did I begin.

"The look she gave you could have set you on fire,"

Sam said. "Not everyone understands your bossy ass like we do. How do you function in normal society?"

A one-sided smirk tugged at my mouth. "I can be charming."

"You know, I believe that. You used to have a lot of friends." Her head lolled to the side. I felt her gaze on me as I cleaned her wound. "Something happened when you were gone. Something bad. Coupled with Andrew's betrayal, you got bitter. Angry. The boy I knew had been kind. You wanted to fix the world. Make it better. Tell me, what was it that made Harper Tate so jaded?"

"Jesus," I muttered. She might as well have stabbed me in the heart. *What was it? Losing Molly to a demon-tormented drug addict. She bled out in my arms. I was helpless. That's what it was, Sammy.* "You said no drugs. Want me to stitch this numbed or pre-modern medicine era?"

"I'll get the truth out of you one day." She tucked an arm behind her head. "Just do the damn thing."

Sam suffered in relative silence, with an occasional wince and whine. She was tough, I had to give that to her. Then, she wouldn't be Samantha fuckin' Fife if a little pain brought her to her knees. She was no stranger to it.

I finished tying the last knot and snipped the remaining thread when she blurted, "Camden's not right either."

"Oh?" I paused in redressing the wound, ice slithering down my spine.

"He called me *babe*—what even is that about? We don't use pet names. And what was he wearing? That god-awful rose ... thing. Was it a blazer? A dinner jacket? Aside from our fancy-pants date, I've never seen him wear something like that for funsies."

Sam reached out with lightning-fast reflexes and grabbed my wrist. "I sent you and Leigh looking for him when I first woke up. I begged you to do so, but then he showed up at my bedside acting like nothing was out of place. Then, *then* y'all show back up with some really weird evidence that he might have been hurt. But he looked fine. Things don't add up."

Her grip tightened. I gritted my teeth, jaw flexing.

She forgets her strength. And fuck, I didn't want to tell her that I suspected her boyfriend of being a fraud—that he wasn't what he seemed. Sam was right. We were missing facts. We had a blood-stained knife, his abandoned loafer, a fried cell phone, and Bennett's word that nothing was wrong.

He could use his liar's tongue to keep himself in Xavier's good graces, but he wasn't in mine. And the fact that Sam suspected something was amiss made all my protective hackles stand on end. He was up to something and none of it good.

I didn't want to tell Sam any of that.

She looked at me with pleading eyes, refusing pain meds so she could think clearer, and asking for honesty— hell, secret-keeping was partially why she'd ended up in a coma in the first place. I found I couldn't deny her.

That, and I'd promised that I was in her goddamned corner.

"Xavier is running tests on the knife we found. We'll know whose blood it is and if there is demonic taint on the blade. We pressed Bennett for information, but either he's innocent or a good fucking liar." She dropped her hold on my wrist like I'd burned her. Her eyes filled with tears. I regarded her with cautiousness and asked, "Are you sure you want to hear this?"

"No? Maybe? If he's in danger, I feel like—I feel like I should to help him somehow." She dropped her head back on the pillow. "I may not want drugs, but what about Life Elixir?"

"Are we changing topics?" I asked.

"Obviously."

I shook my head and rose from my chair. The inner workings of Sam's mind never ceased to surprise me. But I knew her, and this change of subject was a defensive tactic. I'd let her have this one. She'd had a hell of a day. Self-induced but, in an odd way, understandable. I got what I needed from the small fridge in the supply room, along with a bottle of water, and headed back towards my stubborn-ass patient.

"Drink up." I handed her the dosing cup of Life Elixir.

"Cheers!" Her nose wrinkled when she downed it in one swift movement. "Got a chaser for me?"

I cracked open the water and passed her the bottle. "Promise me something and please don't be difficult. Just this once."

Sam eyed me sidelong, looking me up and down. "What?"

"Fucking stay down," I said, desperation in my voice. "Don't get up and wander the fucking castle. Rest. Recover. Let others help you. As soon as I see vast improvement in your health, I swear, Sam, I'll clear you for duty."

She scrubbed at her face with one hand.

"Let Bozeman, Kalakaua, and Tabitha's Warriors worry about the demons and any potential attacks. Let your Advisers do their jobs. Your only focus should be on getting well."

"This shirt is bloody." Sam pinched and plucked at the shirt over her chest with her free hand. "I saw Emily brought fresh clothes. Be a gem and have Leigh come help me change when she arrives."

"Don't deflect," I growled. "Fucking promise me."

She chewed on her lip. Swirled her water glass. Then, with an eye roll said, "Alright. You win."

The tension in my shoulders, my gut, my jaw all relaxed in a swift exhale. *Miracles do happen.* I heard the infirmary door open and shut with a soft click.

"But," Sam said, sticking her index finger in the air as if issuing an edict, "I am not staying in this hospital ward. I can't. I won't. And I'm not going to lock myself away in my room."

"Goddamn, Sam."

"Stow me in a room with a TV with streaming services. Give me snacks, a comfy blanket, and a zillion books. I also have, like, ten seasons of *Supernatural* to catch up on. I'll be a good, little patient and recover like a champ. No more meds. No tubes, hovering, or coddling."

This woman. God, help me not strangle her. I shook my head.

"No?" she asked, eyes puppy-dog wide. "Why?"

"Pardon my interruption," Healer Emily said as she approached. She had her hands clasped in front of her. "I couldn't help but overhear your conversation." A demure smile touched her lips. "There is a common room on this floor just down that hall that, ah, fills your requirements."

Sam snapped her fingers at the Healer. "That's what I'm talking about." She then backhanded the side of my thigh. "Take me to my prison, Commander Tate."

Emily chuckled, but I sucked in a surprised breath and ducked my head.

Fucking fuck. Does she know... She can't possibly know? Sam had been in her coma when I dreamt that the Mage called me Commander and then watched Sam die on that imaginary cold, rain-soaked beach. I glanced at Sam's face. She wore a cocky smirk while looking at Emily.

I shoved down my dread and sucked it up. "If I'm a commander, that makes you my insubordinate soldier."

"You say insubordinate soldier, Harper, I call it being a maverick." She waggled her damn eyebrows at me and threw a wink at Emily. Again, the Healer chuckled. I prayed for patience.

"What you are is a stubborn imp," I said and bent to pick her up from the mattress.

"Stop that." Sam batted my hands away. "Don't do it for me."

I lifted my hands away from her in mock surrender. She sat up with a pained hiss, slipped her legs over the side of the mattress with excruciating slowness, and sat there. Despite her solid gymnast build and five-foot-six frame, with all the personality to match, her frailty was more evident now than when she'd been at the church this morning.

"I got this." She puffed out her breath upward. Her face was pale, with a sheen of sweat at her hairline.

Je-sus, woman. I itched to help, to fix. Instead, I curled my fingers into fists against my thighs. Her morning excursion and lack of meds were taking their toll on her battered body.

Emily sidled up to me and muttered, "You're really letting her do this alone?"

"Yes," I said sharper than I'd intended. Softening my tone, I added, "I'll catch her before she falls."

The Healer's lips pursed and her eyes narrowed. She disapproved, and I didn't give a flying fuck what she thought.

"No more objections about how I handle my patient?"

"No, sir." She crossed her arms and set her jaw.

I was sure that Sam's Warrior hearing had caught our muted exchange, but she ignored us. With a sharp nod, as if pick her pride up by its boot straps, she rose from the bed. Emily led the way down the hall, and step by slow step, we walked to the common room.

There were no windows, but the space was lit with soft yellow light from ornate lamps mounted along the walls and situated on side tables. To the left and right of us, heavy, floor-to-ceiling bookshelves with rolling ladders lined the walls. Along the opposite wall from the entrance was a fire place with a large-screen TV mounted above it. A warm brown leather couch, love seat, and recliner filled the center of the room on top of a massive Persian rug.

"Xavier doesn't do small, does he?" Sam asked as she examined a painting depicting a war in the clouds between angels and demons.

"He takes great pride in his manor, miss," Emily said. "Can I get you anything to eat?"

"Oh my god, yes. You'd be my hero." Sam shuffled over to the couch. I followed her and held out an arm. She glared at me, but grabbed on anyway.

"Mr. Tate, how about yourself?" the Healer asked.

"I'm fine." I held myself steady as Sam grabbed onto me and braced her other arm on the couch.

"Very well."

"I might have overdone it." Sam lowered herself down before peering up at me. There was rare vulnerability in her eyes. "Will you stay? Just for a little bit?"

My gut clenched. My heart twisted. I was so fucked when she looked at me that way—the way she did when we were kids and I had hung her moon. Hell, she had been my most favorite person back then, too. And I hadn't always been a bitter, jaded asshole.

"Please?" Sam scooted towards the middle cushion and patted the end seat.

Ah, fuck it.

"Let Emily here help you change. I'll be just outside when you're ready."

Outside the common room, I leaned against the wall and let my head thump backward. There would have to be a meeting when everyone was back at Xavier's manor. We needed to discuss what happened at the church. Was the fire an isolated incident? Kestler would report on the random trio of demons. I would have to bring up Sam's observations about Camden. I also needed to relocate the Kestler family—*again*—and figure out how to get Sam's parents and little brother to a safe place since the wards Pops placed to protect them were all failing. So much to do.

The opening door drew me from my thoughts. Emily let me know Sam had changed and she'd return with food. I went inside and settled beside Sam at the end of the couch. She immediately scooted up next to me, giving me no choice but to put my arm around her, cradling her against me. It was a natural movement, one I'd done a million times when we were younger. Back when we didn't have as many wounds and scars on our souls, when life was far simpler. And damn, did it feel nice to have her safe, still, and listening to me.

Sam sighed and gave me her weight. I stroked the blonde hair along her temple, rested my own head back against the couch, and studied the ornate mantle of the fireplace. A feeling of vulnerability crept up on me, ramping up my anxiety over the whole shitstorm that had been unleashed since she'd almost died on me. There were things I wanted to say. Things that would have crossed a line between us.

You scare me so fucking much. The thought of you dying rips me up inside. I can't lose you. I hate seeing you in pain. I hate that I can't fix this. You're like the sun. I love your warmth, but it burns at times.

But I had no right to say these things—I had no claim on her. Not after the damage I'd caused and the miles and years of bad fucking blood between us. Were we working towards middle ground? Sure. The fences were mending, but spouting sentiments like that would spook the shit right out of her. Right?

As if she were reading my damn thoughts, she asked out of nowhere, "Tell me what happened when you left six years ago. Where did you go? Who did you meet? How did you make money? Tell me the normal, human things you did."

My eyes tightened. My fingers stilled. Molly's face popped in my head with her long blonde hair, wide green eyes, and dressed in that sundress I loved.

"You should rest," I deflected.

"You were eighteen, Harper." Sam glanced up. "That red truck of yours was ancient. Did you get stuck somewhere? Did you drive until you ran out of gas on purpose? I'm not asking to delve deep into your dark secrets. I'm just asking for a distraction from, you know, my own dark thoughts." She settled back into the crook of my side. "And Emily is taking forever. I'm starving. Distract me."

God, Tate, overreact much? I am so goddamn reactive. I sighed. Her head on my chest rose and fell with my breath. I could let down my walls a little. Knowing Sam, she'd try to breach them, but she deserved some honesty.

My fingers resumed stroking her hair. "Drove up 75, crossed over to 95 via I-10, and then headed north until some asshole's tool box fell off the back of his truck. Smashed the fuck out of my bumper. Ended up breaking down just outside of Savannah. I was stranded for a few hours when a Georgia DOT officer stopped. He took pity on me and called a tow ride for me on his own dime."

"That was nice of him."

"Like you said, I was eighteen, out of state, and broke as fuck."

Sam looked up at me, gnashed her teeth, and reached for her side. I leaned back into the leather cushioned arm of the couch. With one arm open to her, I grabbed a throw pillow to settle on my thigh.

"Lay down."

"Uh, what?" Her brows furrowed.

"Don't argue. Just do it." I patted the pillow. "I'll tell you what happens next in the story. Including how I got a job."

"This oughta be good." She scooted down with my help, and before she laid down her head, she gathered her hair in one hand so it didn't get stuck under her.

The flash of blonde against my leg brought that goddamn scene from my recurring nightmare roaring back. I saw Sam stabbed by several black swords. Demons laughing. The Mage's black aura pulsing, red eyes flashing. I clenched my teeth, halting the growl that threatened to escape. My heart raced and terror climbed my throat.

"Hello, silence is not golden, Harp." She poked my knee. "You promised me a story."

The fuck?

"Harp?"

"Thought I'd give it a spin. Always wanted to try it out."

"Pick a different one."

She tapped her chin with her index finger. "You're right. Didn't feel natural."

"Will you settle the fuck down so I can tell you this damn story?"

Her answer was to gently hunker closer into the couch, get as comfortable as her side would let her, and tuck her arms into her chest. She snuggled her head deeper into the pillow. A smile tugged the corner of my mouth and I let my fingers trace gentle patterns on her arm.

"Where was I?" I asked, knowing damn well where I was in my history.

"Some jackwagon didn't secure his toolbox properly—he was probably going Mach Jesus on the interstate—and it fell out. Jacked up your truck when you ran over it. You broke down. A friendly road ranger called you a tow. I was paying attention, Harper Tate."

"Smartass." I squeezed her bicep. "Anyway, this tow guy took me to an auto parts shop just outside of Savannah."

"Why did you have him take you there and not a shop?"

"Didn't have the guts to tell him I couldn't afford jack-shit and let him go."

"Ha!" The brat chuckled. "That tracks."

"*Anyway*," I punctuated, "there I was laying on the hot-as-hell asphalt looking at my truck's undercarriage—racking my brain how I'm going to fix the fucker without funds or Pops's garage—when this burly mountain of a man wearing an orange Buddy Smith's Auto polo toes me in the ribs. Fucking steel-toes, too. Turned out he was the DOT officer's brother-in-law. Rick had called ahead and told Bud about me. Told him I looked like a kid that needed a break."

"Lucky you." Her words were slow and low. My chin dipped down and I saw her eyes were closed.

"Yeah, it was." I smoothed my hand over the side of her head. Like an appeased feline, she nestled deeper and something tugged hard in my chest. *She's safe.* We sat in this peaceful silence and I watched her side rise and fall.

"What happened next?"

The question jolted me out of my quiet lull. "Thought you were asleep."

"Uh-un. I've got you pinned to rights, and you're gonna give me the deets."

"It's like that, huh?"

"Yeah."

"Alright. Bud got me into his store and proceeded to play fifty fucking questions with me. He wanted to know what I knew about vehicles, how to fix them, my work history, how I dealt with people. Grilled me for a good thirty minutes—put me through the goddamn ringer. Turned out that was a job interview. When he stopped asking questions, we sat there in silence until he grunted, offered me his massive hand, and asked if I wanted a job."

Sam huffed a soft laugh. "What a roller coast of events."

"That's just the beginning. We got my truck around back to his private garage, he offered me the apartment above the garage, and chucked an orange polo at me. Said training started immediately. Worked there a little over a year. Busted my ass. Got several promotions. Saved every fucking penny I earned."

It was where I met Molls. Where I busted her brother's nose. Where I learned to stand on my own two feet. Despite what I knew of the world and the dangers that lurked, I wouldn't have given up my time working for Bud. It had been the break I'd needed.

I didn't have to practice with weapons, adhere to a rigid schedule, and or contend with Pops and his cold, ruthless training. Bud had allowed me room to grow, forge a new version of Harper Tate.

A gentle knock at the common room entrance pulled

me out of memory lane. I peered over my shoulder to see Emily holding a service tray filled with food in both hands. She bustled into the room and beeline towards the coffee table.

"Apologies for the delay," she chirped.

I glanced down at the Warrior on my lap since she'd gone quiet and still. Her breath had deepened and become more even. *Finally.* I caught Emily's eyes and pointed down at Sam, then pressed that finger to my lips.

"Ah, poor girl," the Healer whispered. "She needs her rest."

Emily set down her tray with a quiet click and started unloading charcuterie-type foods—salami, crackers, olives, and cheese—as well as two bowls of what appeared to be French onion soup onto the table. My stomach snarled. Emily's eyes crinkled at the edges and a close-lipped smile graced her face. She handed me a steaming bowl and hot pad.

"Thank you," I whisper, accepting the crock of soup. "And yes, she's had a long day."

While I dug into my food like a savage, Emily retrieved a blanket from the neighboring loveseat. She flapped it open and slid it over Sam.

"The remote is in that drawer." Emily pointed at the side table next to me. "I trust you know how to work it." At my nod she continued, "I'll check back in in an hour. Need anything else?"

"No, we're good."

———

THE SOUND OF DISHES CLINKING, followed by greedy licking noises, jarred me awake. My eyes shot open.

Where am—oh, yeah. I blew out a breath and focused on the source of the racket. Bear had stretched his nose as close to the edge a plate as he could get to search for leftovers. He'd tilted his muzzle sideways trying to lick at a block of cheese.

"Hey, man," I said. "Not for you."

The pit bull pulled back in surprise. Warm brown eyes darted from mine to the cheese. When he looked back at me, I swear he let out a defeated sigh. Abandoning the coffee table, he hopped up in the recliner next to the couch and plopped down with a grunt. In the the commotion, Sam hadn't flinched, continuing with soft snores.

"Sorry! Sorry!" Kestler's voice shouted from out in the hall. Her lithe frame appeared in the doorway, brunette hair flying like she'd hauled ass. "I tried to stop him, but he caught your scents and took off."

I pointed down at Sam. "Didn't bother her, but it startled the shit outta me."

A breathy laugh escaped Kestler. "Sorry. And yeah, even when she's not in magically induced comas, Sam sleeps like the dead."

With the least amount of jostling I could manage, I stood, cradling Sam's head. Once on my feet, I laid her back against the now flat pillow. In rest, the lines of pain and worry had ebbed. She looked peaceful, her breaths steady and sure. There were no wires, tubes, or medical equipment attached to her.

Beautiful.

I tore my gaze off her and onto Bear. The dog seemed to raise a brow at me.

Shit. Shit. Shit. Where the fuck had that thought come from? And what a dangerous slope to fall down. I busied myself looking for a pen and paper. Kestler joined me a moment later.

"Got Sam's phone on you?" I asked.

"Yeah." She pulled the cell from her back pocket. "Figured she'd want it just in case Camden called or something."

"Good." I found what I was looking for in the bottom drawer of the coffee table, and gestured for her to hand the phone to me. I jotted down a quick note for Sam:

> *Call me the minute you wake up.*
> *Don't wander the halls.*
> *Don't do any stupid shit. Got me?*
> *—Harper*

I passed it off to Kestler to read. She perused it, rolled her eyes, and handed it back to me.

"Your bedside manner rivals Mother Teresa's."

One side of my mouth tipped up, and I grunted a short, muted laugh before arranging the note and phone directly in Sam's eye-line. At Sam's side, I took her pulse, watched her breath, and moved the blanket up over Sam's shoulder. Her dreams must have been good because she sighed and relaxed any remaining tension in her fair face.

"Sleeping Sam is much more animated than Coma Sam," Kestler said behind me. "I'll take it."

I tipped my chin up in agreement and went over to Bear. Squatting in front of him, I scratched behind his ears. He groaned as it if was the best fucking thing to get an ear massage. When I let go, he met my eyes.

"Watch over her, yeah?"

He fake-sneezed so I took that as an agreement.

I joined Kestler and steered her out of the room into the hall. "Everyone's here now?"

"Yeah, I was sent to find you. The Advisers want a meeting to discuss recent events."

Why do I need to be there? I'm not a Warrior. Who was I to argue with the authorities? I had nothing better to do. It was do something productive or sit and watch Sam like a fucking hawk.

"Do you remember where the war room is?" I led Kestler down the corridor to the elevators, knowing damn well she did. Her solid sense of direction came from her phenomenal tracking skills.

Kestler scoffed and mashed the *down* button with more force than necessary. "You question my sense of direction? Me? I want to be offended, but I can't tell if you're just trying to needle me, Tate."

"Don't get your feathers ruffled. It was just a question."

She pursed her lips and I hid my smirk. We stepped into the car, the door slid shut, and we descended. Silence permeated the small space. I leaned against the handrail, crossed my legs in front of me, and let my head rest against the cool metal wall. However, tension crept into Kestler's shoulders, down her neck, and along her back. Her lips twitched like she was speaking to herself. I suspected she was working up the courage to ask me something.

"Christ Almighty," I grunted after another few seconds. "Out with it, Kestler."

She crossed her arms and huffed. "You moved my family to the hospitality house at the church, right?"

"Yes."

"How did they keep that a secret from me?"

"I told them to."

Her body jolted like I'd punched her.

"They didn't say anything because I asked them not to. It was for their safety."

She glared and took a step towards me. Kestler could kick my ass if she wanted to put some Power into it, and tinkering with her family—even for the greater good—was a great way to get my ass kicked. *Perhaps a different angle, then.*

"Have you forgotten your first and only run-in with the Mage, Kestler?" If her back got any tighter, it would snap. I pushed off the wall in case she wanted to deck me. "You showed up at the farmhouse half mad and out of your goddamn mind, saying that the Mage knew where your family lived. Later, when you were calm and resting, Sam came to me. Asked me to put your family somewhere safe."

Kestler's brows shot up.

"I stashed them where I thought they'd be safe." The stubble on my chin rasped against my palm when I ran a hand over my jaw. "Being safe and lying to you was better than your family being dead and gone for good."

Anger danced across her face.

"I did what I fucking had to with a limited about of time and information. Your parents understood." Her mouth opened and I held up a hand, silencing her. "I didn't say anything to you, because if you were compromised again, you wouldn't know where they now resided. I told no one." A ragged breath escaped me. "Except Ma."

Her arms dropped and she turned away from me. With her head ducked, she took in a rocky lungful of air. The elevator dinged. The doors slid open. Neither of us moved.

Then, "Harper!" she gasped. Her chin snapped up and her wild hazel eyes found mine in the elevator mirror. Those intelligent wheels in her head churned. "The borders are failing at the church. What—what are we going to do? They—Oh god, what about Sam's family? Do you think the Mage will go after them?"

"I'll deal with it. You have bigger issues at hand." My plan involved a conversation with Xavier. I couldn't move forward without his approval. "Let me do my job and you do yours. And I swear to fuck, they will be fine. But for their safety, I'm still not telling you shit."

If she blanched any further, she'd be a ghost. The freckles over her nose stood out in stark relief. I found the spot between her shoulder blades and gently shoved her forward before the doors closed on us.

"Trust, Kestler," I murmured. "Now put your game face on for this meeting. You got this."

14

DOMINIC

Dominic let out an undignified snarl as he jerked his hand back from the ward, shaking out his burning fingers. His digits weren't charred, but they would have been if he'd been in his demon form. Since he inhabited Camden's body, the veil wouldn't harm his human bits, but it still scorched him with holy fire.

It *hurt*.

Dominic studied the intricate layers woven with complex threads. This veil had teeth, and those teeth promised retribution to anything Hellish that tampered with it.

"Xavier, you're a paranoid old man," Dominic muttered with a grin. He smoothed the front of his jacket. "Not that I expect anything less from a divine weapons master."

Determined to get onto the castle grounds, Dominic picked up a predatory pace along the boundary. If he couldn't figure out how to get in, his elaborate ruse would go up in flames. Weaseling his way into Warrior relationships, gathering information, and planting seeds of discord required him to maintain a constant presence in the Warriors' ranks. Not to mention making sure that Samantha Fife wasn't suspicious.

He bared his teeth and let out a low growl. A glimmer in the veil caught his eye. He stopped, pursed his lips, and narrowed his gaze. He cocked his head so he could peer flush along the ward. As it stretched out a hundred yards down, it appeared to become less dense further along.

Dominic followed the barrier, occasionally tapping his pinky against the transparent wall, hissing when it burned him inside. He walked until a town came into view. The precious wooden sign nestled in a well-manicured flowerbed read *Shield Haven*. Xavier's strong veil blanketed the entire community, but it had thinned to a normal level instead of the demonic equivalent of a tungsten metal wall.

"Curious," he mused, tilting his head.

Did Xavier think this area didn't need as much protection, or had the Adviser expended all his energy laying down the veil where the Seers resided? He pressed a palm against the membranous ward and his hand passed through without so much as a single singe.

A wicked grin split his face.

Dominic turned down the sidewalk and meandered along the street of this quaint, central Florida town. People came and went from shops along the strip. The buildings had that down-home, grass-roots vibe of southern, small-town USA. The people, the street, and the general area were clean and tidy. Children ran about in a park to his left. He studied them and deemed none had the smell of Power— he doubted that any of them would be Warriors.

As he strolled along, he pulled Camden's phone from his jacket pocket and thumbed the quick-call to Sam's phone. The line rang and rang before going to voicemail.

"Babe," he started, "I'm so sorry to leave you a message like this, but I can't stay with you at Xavier's manor. I so wanted to. But my mother is pressuring me to come back to work. I really have neglected my duties. It's much too far to commute back and forth from Sorcerie." Dominic smiled, willing humor into Camden's voice. "I'll be careful. I can see the supernatural now, remember? I'll get with you later."

Dominic ended the call and ducked into a sweets shop. He pushed the aviator sunglasses up on his head and peered into the ice cream freezer. *Blasted human hunger.* It would do him no good to starve Camden. He wanted the boy alive, after all.

"Welcome to Betty's, sir, what can I get you?" The petite Seer, with pastel pink hair, smiled at Dominic from behind the counter. She didn't look a day over eighteen.

Camden Bennett was a handsome human specimen with his blond curls, green-gold eyes, and surfer-lean body. Dominic would use these excellent resources to his own advantage. He returned her smile—a brilliant, flirty one. The girl's cheeks reddened, and she ducked her head. When she recovered and looked back at him. He threw in a wink for good measure as he read her name tag.

"How about you surprise me, Linny?" he asked, his eyes twinkling.

"How do you—? Oh!" She touched the badge on her shirt and turned a brighter pink. A shy smile appeared. "What do you, um, like?"

Dominic watched her reorganize the ice cream scoops in the dipper well three times.

"What do I like?" Dominic put his hands in his pockets, stepped closer to the counter, and leaned forward. "Perhaps an adorable, pink-haired maiden who serves sweets to the masses?"

Linny giggled, her hand flying to her mouth to cover it up.

Dominic rifled through Camden's mind for the boy's favorite flavor. "I'll have a waffle cone with mint chocolate chip. Two scoops."

"S-sure thing," she stammered and got to work.

Dominic meandered over to the cash register on his left, turned around, and rested his hip against the green counter top. "Linny, I'm passing through, but need to spend a few nights here. Can you tell me where I should stay?"

Linny joined him at the sales counter and handed him his cone. "My best friend's parents own a B&B at the edge of town. We're in off season since it's summer-time in Florida and all, so you should be able to book a room without any issues. Do you want me to call ahead?" She lifted a cordless phone.

Dominic met Linny's eyes. He winked. She blushed. Human eyes were called windows to the soul for a reason. In that one look, her read her desires and fears in mere seconds.

You are starved for male attention, aren't you little one?

Just as he'd suspected.

His lips lifted in a slow, sensual way as he reached over the counter—hesitating just so—and gently touched her hair. He rolled a lock between his fingertips. Her breath hitched. Her heart sped.

"That would be lovely, sweet Linny," he said in a low voice filled with promise.

She sputtered and fumbled with the phone. It clattered onto the counter. They both looked down, and when her eyes returned to his, he inhaled. *Might as well feed the demon and the Bennett boy.* He consumed her giddy nervousness, her uncertainty, her insecurities. He took only enough to satiate himself.

"How much do I owe you?" he asked, letting go of her hair, his feast over.

Words failed Linny for a moment. She took a large breath, laid a hand over her heart, and found solid ground once the full force of Dominic's demonic gaze no longer bore down on her.

"On the house." She swallowed. "As a 'Welcome to Shield Haven' gift."

"You're a peach."

After Linny called the B&B and booked his stay for him, Dominic used her rough-sketch directions scribbled on scrap paper to find his lodgings. On his way, he made another phone call.

"Dominic," Aerona snipped. "Where are you? I expected you over an hour ago."

"I'm on a bit of a field trip. Sammy and the gang relocated to Xavier Gerena's estate north of the farmhouse." He rounded a corner, checked his directions, and turned down a side street. "The place is crawling with Seers. The mad scientist has been a sneaky, sneaky bastard plopping his estate in the middle of Florida. Unlike his contemporary, this veil is impeccable. Strongest I've seen, even for him. It seems he's only gotten better in his old age."

"You mean to tell me," she seethed with lethal ice in her voice, "that Xavier Gerena has been hidden under my nose in plain sight?"

Damage control, ol' chap, before she loses that temper on your brethren.

"My wee duck, you know Gerena's talents," he soothed. "Weapons and wards."

She snarled, was silent for a beat, and with more decorum asked, "Did you get the information I wanted?"

Dominic strolled up a grey-and-white brick path leading to a large, pale-yellow home. The building had white-framed windows. The rocking chairs on the porch screamed warm country chic.

How quaint. He sneered in distaste. *This will have to do. Here's to roughing it.* A luxury hotel would have been his preference, but those were hard to come by in the middle of nowhere. He headed down the quaint walkway.

"Dominic!" Aerona snapped.

He rolled his eyes at her impatience. "Perhaps, my terrifyingly beautiful Dark One, I have incomplete knowledge. Would you like a half-report?"

"Yes!" She took a slow breath. "I don't mean to be short with you. I detest not having my Power, my magic. I only have it when I'm in my throne room and feel hollow when I leave. The loss has worked its way into all parts of my life. I need you back here and I need my son running that blasted restaurant. His staff are grating on my nerves. It won't do to kill one of them."

Dominic reached for the hat that wasn't on his head—Camden didn't wear them, after all—so he cracked his neck and shifted his shoulders.

"Patience, my wee duck. Give me two more days. Two measly days."

"Fine," she grumbled. "But tell me your 'half report' about Shaw's dealings in Ireland."

"Of course. A moment, please." Dominic veer away from the B&B's front porch, strolled down a side path that led to a small garden, and stepped up into a white-washed gazebo. After glancing around, he said, "The ever-secretive Shaw always flies into Dublin, and no matter the time of day or night, he rents a car from the airport under the name Bernard Murray—his given name, his first."

His Warrior scoffed. "How many aliases does he have?"

"More than you know, my Queen." *He's an old slippery bugger.* "Shaw then drives north to County Tyrone and spends the night. Never more than one and never in the same place. The details on where he goes the next day are murky, and the paper trail ends. He leaves Northern Ireland, fills up a tank of petrol, and then disappears."

She said nothing. His cue to go on.

"Shaw is careful to avoid common roads, towns, and *most* places where his visage can be caught on camera. He's virtually a ghost."

Dominic waited. He heard what sounded like glass shattering against stainless steel. *Such lovely violence.* With a smirk he continued, "But this is the twenty-first century. I found several tourist photos near Ballycroy National Park containing the Adviser Andrew Shaw. He is ever paranoid. I also found pictures of him around Black Valley in Kerry."

"What the hell is that old coot up to?"

"I put out—what do you call them—*feelers*. Your dear son has joined several Irish pages, groups, and clubs. He's asked some innocuous, probing questions. Have I ever told you how I adore social media? The back-biting. The unasked-for opinions. The viciousness. The chaos. It makes my mouth water. Really too bad demons can't feed off digital negativity. We'd grow fat."

"Get your mind off your stomach," she snapped. There was a rustling over the phone, and in a muffled voice she yelled, "Yes, you dolt, I threw it at the wall. Get me a new glass of wine and clean that mess up before it stains." Another rustling and she spoke clear again. "Is that all you have for me?"

"No, my darling." Dominic studied Camden's well-groomed nails. "You may want to take a heavy swig of that wine and brace yourself."

Now was as good a time as any to break the news of Harper Tate's identity. Ambrose, that idiot, had been tasked with watching and stalking the Tates eighteen years ago. It would have been his job to report they had a son. The Mage's rage would be incandescent.

Ambrose might not survive the fallout of this aftermath. In his brethren's defense, Andrew Shaw had been much sharper, more cunning, and every bit a shrewd Irishman back then. No one in Hell knew of the boy until Dominic discovered the adult version a little over a week ago.

"Remember when we went to the Tates' house to stop the rise of any potential threats to you, my Dark queen? You slew Thomas in cold-blooded, spectacular fashion. But killing Elaine grieved you so—"

"You walk a dangerous line, Dominic." Her tone came out alarmingly calm. "There better be a reason you brought this up."

"They had a son."

"She had a *child*?" There was a shout, a thud, and another shattering of glass. Glasses. Several. Like a tinkling rain of glass shards onto tile.

"How long have you known?" she roared.

"I only recently discovered this myself." Dominic sat on one of the built-in wooden benches.

"How recently?" She punctuated each word precisely.

"Do you want to know about her offspring?" Dominic baited, knowing she would bite.

A deep, frustrated sigh was his only answer.

"Excellent," he said, tugging up on his pants and crossing a leg over his knee. "Let me tell you a story."

THE FOLLOWING MORNING, Dominic traced his steps back to where he'd stowed Camden's Audi. The ward around the castle grounds crackled with that same inhuman, powerful energy. He trudged into the Florida wild, clearing away brush, scrub, and trees which he'd strategically placed to obscure the car's whereabouts.

He disarmed the alarm and had just cracked open the driver's side when Camden's phone rang. Dominic grinned when he saw the caller ID.

Show time. "Good morning, beautiful."

"I don't like this plan of yours," Sam said without preamble.

Dominic tipped his head back and bit back a grin. He *knew* she'd disagree with the voice message he'd left last night, calling late enough that no one would answer. Sam plowed on before he could say anything.

"There's some weird ass shit going on right now and you could be in danger. I know, I sound like a broken record. But, like, the demons and the Mage *know* what you mean to me. They know who you are. They've already come for you once. I can't—no, I won't risk you like that. Come to Xavier's place. I have to see with my own two eyeballs that you're alright."

"Sam," Dominic crooned. "You know how my mother can be. Renard and Jackie can only handle so much of her. My restaurant cannot wait."

"They're adults. They can deal. The building is still standing."

"But aren't you an adult as well?" Dominic asked. "Can you not understand that I am needed somewhere else? I can ill afford to cater to your paranoia, babe. We've seen neither hide nor hair of this Mage. Maybe I'm out of danger."

Sam's sharp intake made Dominic smirk.

"That's not fair, Cam." Her voice cracked with hurt, like she'd been stung by his words. "I only want to keep you safe."

"Perhaps being around you is what's bringing the danger to me."

"Stop! What are you doing? This isn't like you. Why are you being so hot and cold? You're gonna give me whiplash."

Dominic slid into the Audi. "I'm reevaluating some things."

Silence stretched. And then, "Are you—are you reevaluating me?

Dominic waited.

"Camden, do you not want to be with me anymore? Do you want to breakup with me?" Her voice cracked. "Say something. Anything. I'm dying here."

"My feelings for you haven't changed, babe," Dominic said. "I adore you, but—"

If it were Camden speaking for himself, that would be the truth. Dominic had rummaged through the boy's brain enough to know that Camden thought he might even love the ever-charming Samantha Fife. Which made this particular betrayal so much sweeter.

"You *are* breaking up with me!" Her words came out like rushing water. "Over the damn phone?"

"Let's call it a pause."

"Can we talk about this?" Panic hedged her voice.

"I need time to think."

"But why now? After you stuck by my comatose ass? You leave me *now*?" She almost sounded offended. "I-I don't recognize this Camden. How do you just turn off your feelings? This isn't you."

Dominic didn't even need to gaslight her; she did such a fantastic job on her own. He bit his lip, reveling in her spiral.

Sam gasped. "You've been thinking of this ever since I was attacked, haven't you? When you first saw demons. That's why you've been flaking on me, isn't it? That's why you weren't there when I woke up and why you took your sweet ass time to come see me."

Now for the coup de grâce.

"I'm sorry, Sam." He walked his fingers along the dash- board. "You're right. I guess I'm trying to cope with seeing the supernatural. *You're* a supernatural. Stronger, more powerful than weak, little me." He silenced her incoherent objections by plowing on. "I don't know where I stand in your world. Would I even be in this situation if I didn't know you? And it doesn't help that Harper is so hostile."

"What?" The question was short and sharp.

"He didn't tell you?" Dominic traced the interlocking rings of the Audi logo in the center of the steering wheel. "He threatened me on numerous occasions. Even tried to keep me from seeing you. Xavier and Leigh had to step in and call him off. I mean, you saw how he manhandled me. Called me a *cocksucker*. That's mild compared to the insults he's hurled against my character. He's a bully. Sometimes I fear for my life around him."

Silence.

Doubt.

Discord.

Dominic smiled and bit a knuckle.

"Is he why you won't stay?" Tears clogged her voice. "Or is it me?"

She's playing her part so perfectly. A small amount of disappointment pulled at his gut that he had to break this Warrior's spirit. He did actually admire her. Adored her. A small part of him wished he'd hitched his wagon to her and made *Sam* his Dark Warrior. But she'd never turn. And he was partial to his current Warrior.

"A little of both," he said. "Babe, I do care about you, but Harper makes me nervous and you're so far out of Camden's—my league."

The Bennett boy might love Sam, but he'd never be able to hold onto her. Dominic figured that out in five minutes, although his host had yet to arrive at that conclusion. But Camden would. Eventually.

"I *need* to be at the restaurant. People are depending on me. My mother gets angrier with me the longer I'm away. You haven't met her yet, and maybe that's a small blessing —she can be so brutal. But, babe, I've got to try to move forward. Please just give me time?"

"Take it." She gave a mighty sniff and her breath shuddered. "Since I'm trying out this new thing where I consider other people's feelings and all, I'll respect your decision. But I don't like it. I don't agree. I want things to be different. Distance from me may or may not make you safer. Your mom doesn't scare me. And I've met Renard and Jackie. They are hella capable of running your restaurant. But I won't force you to stay."

So dramatic. I love it. Dominic almost chuckled. "Just until I get things sorted out, you know?"

"Whatever you need," she acquiesced. "Just be safe. If anything remotely demonic comes for you, please call me. Please."

Begging? Delightful. "I swear it."

"Bye, Cam."

"Bye, Sam." Dominic caught a faint sob right before he

ended the call. He started the Audi's engine and drove away from Xavier's blasted impenetrable ward.

An hour later, he pulled up to the Bennett's beach-front estate. Instead of entering the home, he headed around back, through the property gate, and trudged across the sandy beach. A shimmering veil appeared. One made from the dark magic of Hell. Dominic raised his hand and pushed his palm against it. With a crack, he vanished from the beach and appeared in the dingy, damp hall leading to the Mage's throne room—his domain.

"Ahhh, that's more like it." He breathed in, snapped his fingers, and a fedora appeared in his upturned palm. With a grin, he settled it on his head and sauntered down the passage to plot his next move.

15

SAM

"*S*amantha, *you have used that thing on me in the same spot for twenty-three strokes. You are going to rub off my hide,*" my Guardian complained, jolting me to the present.

I'd parked my horse in the middle of Xavier's immaculate barn aisle—wide enough to fit two heavy-duty trucks. The groundskeepers kept the elaborate place so clean one could eat off the concrete floor. Okay, maybe not *that* clean but more than the average stable. Even the rafters were free of cobwebs, and the floors were clear of rogue hay pieces.

It was Sunday. Fourteen days ago, I'd watched Judy die. Seven days ago, I'd woken up from a coma. Three days ago, Camden had broken up with me.

"*Ah, damn.*" I changed the pattern I used to sweep the body brush against his copper coat. "*Sorry, Max. I was thinking.*"

"*We know,*" Letty said.

"*You have been quite sullen and broody, my human,*" said Max. "*Which isn't like you.*"

"You know," I said to both. *"I want to be mad at him. Who breaks up with me? ME! No one. I do the breaking of hearts. But here we are. I don't know how to deal with this on top of all the other shit."*

Paddle fans, mounted in between strategically-hung chandeliers, whipped the humid Florida air overhead. And like the castle we resided in, the stables borrowed bits of Xavier's Spanish heritage, with black iron accents, fancy iron lamps, dark polished wood, and white walls.

And yet, still no spiderwebs to be seen.

"Your wound is healing faster now that you're awake," Letty said. I assumed it was her attempt to change the subject.

"You bipeds get so bogged down with emotions." Max shook his head and the clip on his lead rope jangled on the lower ring of his halter. *"And I'm acutely aware of how lost in thought you were. Tell me, do I still have hair in that spot you cleaned so thoroughly?"*

"I said sorry!" I pursed my lips. *"And don't get me started on Harper."*

That little common room on the hospital ward floor had become my personal haven. I'd refused to lay in one of those infirmary beds. They triggered memories of Judy. Addressing her loss was a hard *no* for me, and my commandeered space in Casa de Xavier had everything I needed for recovery.

Who knew Xavier had such a lovely spicy book selection? Hello, libido. Perhaps it was Emily who'd stocked the room with smut? It shocked the hell out of me when I'd woken up yesterday and saw Leigh, of all people, reading one of them. What was the world coming to?

But still no Harper.

Healer Emily took orders from him regarding my recovery, yet he was nowhere to be found. He'd been so gentle with me and now nothing. A barbed seed of unease settled in my chest. The feelings of betrayal from when he'd left the farmhouse when I was fourteen rose to the surface. On the heels of Camden's bizarre, painful call, I couldn't handle this.

For the umpteenth time I thought, *Is Harper avoiding me? On purpose?*

"Perhaps he's busy?" Letty said. *"Xavier seems to depend on him more than any other. You* know *he cares. He wouldn't have gone to the lengths he did if he intended to leave. He promised to be there for you and he hasn't broken that pact yet."*

I hadn't asked for her sage opinion, though my heart did this weird twisty thing when I mulled over her words. Harper had swooped me into his arms like I weighed nothing. He'd spoken with kindness—at least for him, anyway —and stroked my hair. He'd given me honesty. He'd acted like the boy I'd loved as a child, only now he had a *lot* more life trauma on board.

And that's enough of that *line of thinking, Fife.*

With a final sweep over Max's hindquarters, I tossed the dandy brush back into the grooming box and took out a hoof pick. I'd cleaned out one hoof and stood when the barn tilted. A lance of pain ripped through me. I braced a hand on Max's round ribcage, closed my eyes, and bent at the waist.

Pulling in a steadying breath, I grumbled to Letty, *"Thought you said my wound was healing?"*

"It is healing," she pushed right back. *"As in actively under construction."*

My lips twisted at her chiding. I didn't mean to be grumpy, not to her. At the sound of nails clicking on concrete and the shuffle of shoes, I picked up my head up and opened one eye. A dark silver fox, with his bushy, white-tipped tail held high, trotted over. He circled Max and me once, licked my knee, and sat on his haunches next to my leg.

"Hey, Fred," I mumbled. The small Guardian's Warrior would be close behind.

Talia walked into the deep shade of the barn, looked right and then left. Her eyes landed on us. She was in khaki cargo pants and an olive-green slouchy tee. Her dark hair was braided in a loose plait and fell over the front of her shoulder.

Tally was new to me, but I'd liked her from the second I met her this past week. She had all the jokes and knew how to take them. She also knew her English was imprecise and couldn't be bothered to care. That was the kind of energy I appreciated. Her Warrior partner, Sajid, had perfect English and perfect discipline. They were coffee and cream.

Like Leigh and me.

"She's in here!" Talia called to someone over her shoulder. "Call off the search wolves."

I chuckled. *Dogs, Tally, dogs.* Same difference. She jogged over to us, speaking in a steady stream of Hebrew, with a palm pressed to her chest as if something had scared the beejezus out of her. I stood up, shifted so my shoulder propped against Max's side for support, and cocked a hip. *Act normal.* At least the barn stopped spinning.

"You are in hot trouble," Tally warned. Fred trotted over to his Warrior and stared up at her. Probably conversing about me.

"Maybe she didn't see me doubled over in pain?"

"Not likely, human mine," Max said. *"That Warrior sees all."*

"Couldn't you lie to me to spare my dignity, or something?"

"I am a horse."

"You were looking for me?" I asked Tally.

She rolled her eyes in a way that made me proud. "*Everyone* is looking for you."

DH's silhouette appeared at the side entrance to the barn along with Bear. The pit bull caught sight of Fred, sprinted after him, and the two bolted in a dancing twist of brindle and silver. DH nodded once and pulled out her phone as she headed on over. She spoke as she walked, her bright smile absent from her face.

"Yeah, hi. She's in the barn." DH paused, listening. "Yep. Understood. Tally's with me."

When she hung up, I lifted a brow and crossed my arms, still using Max to hold some of my weight. Fatigue and slivers of pain warred with my stubborn grit to stay vertical. Maybe, just maybe, the barn trip *and* grooming Max had been too much. In my defense, I hadn't had fresh air or freedom since Wednesday.

"Dee, my favorite human, what can I do for you?" I asked.

"You left your nest without telling anyone," DH said, shoving her phone in a back pocket. "People are in a tizzy. Healer Emily said you were missing."

"Missing." I waved a hand. "I'm not missing. Clearly, I'm here. Wanted to see Max."

A woman could only sit and read smut for so long. When clicking through my comfort shows provided no comfort, and nothing new caught my fancy, I knew I had to fly the coop.

"Next time you try crazy stunt," Talia said, "leave note."

She scratching Max under his short mane. He groaned and let out one of those gusty, relaxed horse breaths.

"Traitor."

"Daddo's concerned. Harper's enraged. Poor Emily took the brunt of their ire."

This time, regret hauled off and sucker punched me. I'd have to make it up to Emily and knew just the thing. I'd discovered good ol' Em's guilty pleasure was chocolate sandwich cookies. The red velvet flavor.

"Dee, I'm broken. How far did y'all think I'd get? I haven't been gone that long. What are we talkin'? Thirty minutes?"

"One hour," Talia offered with a shrug. "I told them same thing. They insist you left."

"Well, shit." I tossed the hoof pick into the grooming box.

My cell phone sat on the end table in the common room. I didn't have a watch. Without meaning to, my jaunt to the stables had turned into an accidental Houdini act. But like, did they know me at all?

I pushed off Max and waited to make sure the stall walls didn't start wavering. I was pleased that the wave of pain and dizziness had passed. I'd told Harper no more coddling. That I'd stay put. But I was a freaking Warrior of Light, all blood and guts. Steel and glory.

And a horse girl at heart who missed her pony.

"No one thought to look for me in the barn?" Legitimate question, in my opinion.

But that seed of guilt burrowed deeper in my chest. That new awareness of other people's feelings that I'd been trying to foster told me that perhaps I should have texted someone, left a note, sent up a flare.

The wrath of Harper and Xavier? Nope, no thank you. Maybe I could avoid them? Ugh. I *so* owed Emily.

Talia and DH glanced at each other and back at me. The Warrior grinned, but the pixie bit her lip and worried her tennis shoe in the divider between the concrete slabs. Where Tally seemed cavalier, DH looked doggone guilty.

"Why you think we here?" Tally asked with a wink and raised her palm. "I knew."

"You called Harper?" I asked DH.

"Yeah." She shifted her shoulders. I hadn't meant to make her squirm.

I pulled the young genius into a hug. "You know I'm not mad, right?"

"You're not?" The pixie met my eyes.

While I felt bottom-basement bad that I'd worried people, and Emily definitely took a verbal beating, frustration over Harper's own disappearance took root.

"Na, you're good, girl." I gave her a squeeze. "Call him back."

"You play with fire, *meshuggener*." Talia stopped massaging Max and met my eyes over his back with a smirk. "The bull is big mad. I'm not missing these firebooms."

Meshuggener, the bull, and firebooms? Oh, my.

With that, Talia swooped and snagged a finishing brush from the grooming box. As soon as she ran the soft bristles over Max's thin hide, he shifted his weight and hiked a hip. For good measure, he cocked the opposite rear hoof.

"This one has an honest touch," my traitorous horse told me.

DH tapped my arm and handed over the cell. I put it to my ear and waited for Harper to answer. DH joined Talia in taking over grooming tasks. Both of them appeared intent on making sure Max's coat went from old penny to bright copper while they listened in.

"Are you on your way back?" he asked without preamble, but a fare amount of gentleness.

"Tell me, Harper dearest, how hard did *you* actually look for me?"

"Sam." His voice cooled. "You're——"

"No," I snapped. "Don't be all nice to DH but immediately throw shade when you find the caller to be me. You've been ghosting me. Avoiding me. I did what had to. Now, pray tell, how the hell did you not know I'd be in the barn? What about Leigh? Where is she? She would have known where I was——"

"Stop," he commanded. To my surprise, I did. At my silence, he continued, "Kestler went with Bozeman to speak with your former employer. Since Kestler tendered both of your resignations while you were in a coma, you both had paychecks waiting for you. She is picking them up."

Milton's Feed and Tack. Thinking about that cozy shop I held dear triggered a barge of grisly images. Ambrose ripped into Judy's neck. The light in her eyes sputtered out. Enyo's knife sliding into me. Instant tears pricked my eyelids. I clenched my teeth.

"I haven't been ignoring you," Harper said, pulling me from my tumble down flashback lane. "I've been giving you space. Come back up to the manor. We'll talk. My promise stands, Sam." He lowered his voice and made my tummy flip. "I'm in your corner."

Most of me believed him, but a small part whispered from the deep recesses of my mind: *Camden left you. Harper's done it before. What if he leaves again?*

My heart tripped over itself and I winced before reminding myself that Harper's first departure had nothing to do with me—that had been between him and Andrew.

I shut down the dark thoughts and blinded them with truth. The lies scattered like roaches exposed to light. Everyone kept telling me that what I was going through was *trauma,* but I sure as shit didn't like how uninvited insecurity crept in without notice.

"I was tired of lounging around all day," I said. "I'm wasting away. There will be no Warrior left if I keep this up."

"What you call lazy is what normal people call recovering," he said.

I bristled. "Being sidelined sucks."

"Imagine," he rumbled low, "not having the Power to do anything, and instead, your sole task is to keep one stubborn ass Warrior, who *can* fight against Hell, stationary long enough to heal a hole in her side."

A muscle in my neck twitched as I froze. Harper never spoke about his lack of Warrior Power, but when he did, it hit like a sobering wave. *And proves that I'm still a selfish twit— just like Leigh said.* It begged the question as to why anyone tolerated me. I knew Harper wouldn't want me to comment on his admission, so I thought a change in subject would be just the ticket. Since everyone was hell-bent on keeping me from even going to the barn, maybe I'd pay attention to strategy and tactics. For once.

"If I promise to be on maximum security lock down," I said, "will everyone stop leaving me in the dark about demon activity and the movements of the Mage?"

Look at me, the negotiator.

"We'll talk when you come up to the house. I'm in Xavier's office outside the war room."

"That's not an answer."

"Goddamn it, Sam," Harper growled. "You're not in any condition to be in the fucking barn doing God-knows-the-fuck-what. *Please,* come back now." Harper never asked. He commanded. The genuine concern in his voice robbed me of all sass.

"Okay," I whispered.

"I'll have Nigel meet you outside."

"No need. Tally and DH aren't gonna leave me to my own devices."

"They sure as hell won't."

That tug of fatigue and pain from before came back and my drooped shoulders. Talia and DH's laughter filtered to me while they brushed Max.

At least they can move about without an evil stab wound hindering them. I pressed the heel of my palm to my forehead. There was muffled conversation from Harper's end of the line. My amped up Warrior's hearing caught snippets of Xavier's Spanish-accented words in the back ground. Reports. Demons. Whereabouts.

Harper's voice sounded too loud when he finally spoke into the receiver. "We have a Warrior meeting this afternoon. Xavier's agreed to let you join in if—and only fucking *if*—you keep your shit together."

"Deal. See you in five minutes."

I hung up before he could change his mind and moved to stand in front of Max. I rubbed under his forelock. The horse had fallen asleep and his lower lip drooped. Even his mental space in my mind had gone silent.

"You good?" DH asked.

"Yeah." I extended her phone out to her. "Thanks, Dee."

The little genius appraised me with sparking green eyes. "We gonna have World War Three when we get back?"

"No, but I think I just scarified my last bit of independence to Harper Tate."

Talia joined us after putting the brushes away. "At least your dictator is nice to look at, yeah?"

I choked on a laugh as I reached for Max's lead rope. She winked. I snorted.

"Tally, you and I would make a wonderfully chaotic Warrior team."

"Oh dear, Daddo's goatee would go even more grey than it already is," DH said with a giggle.

"But," Talia waggled a finger at us, "we would have most fun."

"No doubt," I agreed and mentally prodded my Guardian.

"Maximums Prime. Wakey, wakey. I gotta to be an obedient, dutiful Warrior."

He moaned in protest but offered no resistance as I put him in his stall. After latching the door, I met my dynamic duo of allies at the barn's side entrance.

"You think you can carry my ass if I pass out from overdoing it today? My side is yelling profanities at me."

Talia flashed me a brilliant smile. "If needed."

Back at the manner and standing at the beginning of Warrior ally, I took in the long corridor ending at a massive set of wooden doors depicting Angels and Demons fighting. I felt Tally and DH step up on either side of me, and I let out a deep breath. I knew that a brass placard read *Warrior of Light Operation Command* to the left of the room. Behind those ginormous doors was a massive library of Warrior and human history.

That was the room where I learned Leigh and I came from a rich history of Light Warriors filled with triumph and defeat. It was also in that room where Andrew's betrayal of my trust had run me through like a hot blade.

All of it felt like a lifetime ago instead of days. I'd first arrived at Casa de Xavier, filled with wonder and cocky swagger, but a demonic invasion of my innermost being had produced a humbler Samantha Fife. Xavier's office was to the left of Operation Command and where I needed to be about five minutes ago. I licked my lips and swallowed down a raging case of apprehension.

"I'm gonna hurl," I muttered.

"You'll be fine," Letty coaxed and her signature warmth flowed through me. *"I'm with you."*

"We'll see you later," DH said.

I glanced at my allies. Tally gave me one firm nod of what I assumed was solidarity, before leaving the way we came in. Now I was alone. All by myself. Preparing to face the music.

"Right." I clapped once. "Here goes nothing."

Halfway down the hall Letty shouted, *"Wait!"*

"Holy frick!" I stumbled forward but pulled up hard. *"What the fire fart, Letty?"*

"I have to show you something."

"Now?"

"Yes, take a seat."

"I'm late to a meeting where we'll be discussing my recent disappearance."

"They can wait," she insisted. *"Heaven itself has declared that you must see this."*

I eyeballed the corridor around me. Looking for a chair or bench.

"Sit, Brave One. What I must do for you to witness this will require me to put you in a trance."

"A trance?" I said slowly. "Why not?" I threw up my arms and let them flop back to my sides. I groped the wall with a hand and used it to lower myself onto my ass. *"Alright, angel lady, hit me with whatever Heaven wants me show me."*

Letty's warmth seeped back into my blood stream. Only she didn't stop at a gentle reminder, it kept going. My eyelids felt heavy. My head rocked back against the partition behind me. And before my next breath, I stood before Letty in that white void of nothing in my mind.

Her crystal blue eyes softened when she saw me. A small smile graced her perfect features. She wore the same a tunic and pants that matched my battle whites. Her wide-spread, opalescent wings settled to a relaxed position.

"Brave One," she said and opened her arms to me.

I hugged her without hesitation. "How am I in this space again? Can you do this anytime?"

"No." Letty let me go and laid a hand on my cheek. I almost blushed from the way she looked at me with so much pride. "I can only bring you here if you've been rendered unconscious or Heaven allows it."

I wished something more intelligent came out of me, but "Oh," was as good as it got.

"Come." She looped her arm with mine. I had no choice but to follow.

"So why the 911?"

"We don't question when we get an order from on High." Letty hauled me along as she sped up.

"Gotcha." I looked at her side-long. "Of course we don't."

"What I'm about to show you is part of Heaven's history. Not many are granted this Blessing."

I jogged a few steps to keep up with Letty's brisk walk. "How does this work?"

"Nothing can hurt you in here, but watch that last step into the vision. It can be turbulent." Letty stopped, her wings flaring. Grace and elegance in motion.

I, on the other hand, lumbered to a halt like an ox.

"Now, are you ready?"

"I—sure." I shrugged. "I'm game."

"Excellent. I knew you would be." She grabbed me by the sides of my shoulders and her eyes swept over me in an appraising way. "It is an honor to be given a vision of Heaven."

"Not that I'm not grateful, but what are you showing me?"

Letty smiled. "Watch closely. Learn what you can. Remember what you see."

"Alright." My brows furrowed. "How do I press play?"

"You don't."

Letty spun me around, putting my back to her, then shoved me with force. I lurched forward, jogging a few steps so I didn't eat the ground—not any ground, gold. Streets of freaking gold stretched out in front of and behind me. White buildings stood far out in every direction.

However, black scorch marks marred their pristine exteriors. The stained-glass windows had been blasted outward and littered the golden bricks below with rainbow-colored shards. Smoke billowed out of the ruined gemstone rooftops and the reek of burned wood filled my nostrils.

The sky was grey with floating ash. Behind me, a massive golden temple rose up high and undisturbed. It glinted and gleamed with light that came from within. There was no sun here: light burst forth from the temple illuminating everything. But the sprawling city was war-torn.

What happened here?

At the sound of thundering feet, I looked back up the main road. A herd of hundreds of angels came barreling towards me. None of them flew, though they all had wings. They also had flaming swords, ripped white tunics, and those snowy wings were stained with golden splotches. *Angel blood.*

Eyes wide, I wheeled around and sprinted in the direction they were headed, my heart slamming against my ribs. Being run over by stampeding celestial beings was not high up on my bucket list. But the Heavenly Hosts caught up to me—and passed through my body as if I were *Casper the Friendly Ghost*. I stopped running, annoyed with myself. Letty had assured that nothing could harm me while in this memory. I patted my chest, my stomach, my legs, and shivered.

"Well, that was fun," I grumbled, and did the only logical thing I could think of—I followed them.

At the city's edge, the resplendent road and sparkling white walls stopped short, and before me stretched a massive field filled with angels. Slain bodies were strown everywhere. Golden ichor was mixed with dirt. Feathers had been trampled into battle-torn grass. A massive pile of weapons created a small hill next to a raging fire. The throng of celestials I'd followed sprinted to the aid of their kind, all of them scattering in different directions.

I focused on the fire where a line of angels with black wings stood trembling. Fear glazed their perfect features. Burned meat mixed with the tang of something supernatural assaulted my sense of smell. My gut told me that this was what angel blood smelled like.

Beside the leaping flames, at the front of the black-winged angel line, a white-winged angel raised her blazing sword and slashed down. It sliced through the male's wings, right where they attached to his back. A shriek of sheer agony ripped across the battle field, drowning out the post-war noise.

"Holy—" I gasped. My skin crawled. My chest bottomed out. Dread washed over me.

Two white-winged angels picked up the discarded set of black wings and threw them in the fire. A third white-winger grabbed the now de-winged, sobbing angel and shoved him along into another line. Golden blood flowed from his back, staining his tunic that had started to fade to grey.

Tears stung my eyes. Burned my nose.

Trying my best to ignore the screams of another angel being de-winged, I focused on the second line of defeated angels. At the front was Letty, of all people, and she stood with fury on her face. Her wavy brown hair flowed around her head and shoulders. Her aura glowed a brilliant opalescent white. As each shorn angel stepped up, she tore open their tunic and branded them on the chest with a symbol I didn't know. A final angel then shoved that disgraced angel over the edge of Heaven.

"Holy Heaven!" I bent forward and put my hands on my knees, sucking in breaths like air was a scarce commodity.

Heaven declared it necessary that wee little me witness The Fall of Lucifer and his merry band of traitors.

Why?

I blinked and studied the field with new insight. The Fallen's eyes, while filled with a measure of fear, they held malice and hate. They didn't tremble in terror, they vibrated with rage. I walked through the field with my new lens.

The slain white-winged angels' bodies had grotesque mutilations carved into their corpses. The marks were symbols that looked vaguely like a language. Some of the angels' eyes had been gouged out, and other atrocities had been done to them. I hoped they had been dead, not dying, when this was done to them.

If I hadn't been in a memory, I probably would have puked. The images were burned into my brain, never to be forgotten. Once I was closer to vision-Letty, I heard her speak to each Fallen angel before they were cast out.

"For the crime of treason and six counts of defilement on your brethren, you are hereby banished." The gold branding iron in her right hand sizzled when she pressed it to the Fallen's skin. She'd nod at the angel next to her, and they tossed the Fallen angel out of Heaven.

"For unholy acts in the most Holy of places and murdering your kin in their beds, you are hereby banished."

Rip. Sizzle. Toss.

"For spying and relaying information to Lucifer while in service under the Archangel Michael, as well as butchering sacred animals, you are hereby banished."

Rip. Sizzle. Toss.

This continued until none remained. I crumbled to the ground, my knees weak with grief. I wanted to cry. No, I wanted to sob. Tears, snot, hiccups—the works. The betrayal and cruelty of The Fallen's crimes broke me.

"To the faithful, the loyal, and those who remain, gather around!" Letty's voice echoed across the battle field and echoed far into the distance, as if her voice were magnified. "Those not present, be still and listen."

In the sky above, two male angels circled. One descended and landed with a ground-shaking thud. He had to stand close to seven feet tall, and had enormous white wings which spanned twice his height. He had dark tan skin, close-cropped blond hair, and his eyes shifted colors—brown, blue, green, grey—never staying the same. His arms, legs, and everything about him screamed Sword of God. But the most menacing feature of this terrifying angel was a nasty wound that ran diagonally across his face.

"Michael has arrived," Letty's voice boomed. "He will carry out final sentencing."

Oh shit.

This was *the* Archangel.

There were no other angels that outranked him. He took his directions from God Himself. Even in this mere memory, Michael's power shook me to my core.

His ginormous hand clutched a golden chain and in one swift movement, he gave a full-bodied tug against it, hard enough that the angel attached to the other end—the one still in the sky—plummeted downward. The falling angel roared, landing in a tangled heap of black wings, grey tunic, and gleaming metal.

The black-winged angel rose to his feet as regally as he could considering a collar of glowing gold circled his neck. He dusted off his body and casually flicked grass off one side of his chest. He ran a hand though his mussed brown hair, tousling it in a way that I could only describe as sexy, then straightened his tunic.

He couldn't have been any taller than six foot, had muscle packed in all the right places, and enough arrogant swagger that I rocked back on my heels. His molten-brown bedroom eyes scanned the battle field, and he rubbed his square jaw.

"Lucifer," Michael growled, sending a shudder of terror through me. His voice boomed louder than Letty's had. Every square inch of Heaven would have heard him. "Son of Morning, Archangel of God, what do you plead?

Good God, Fife, I cringed, *you just checked out the devil.*

Lucifer speared his captor with a glare of deepest loathing. "Michael, you brutish barbarian, you know my answer."

Lucifer's tone, relaxed posture, and flippant manner did not lend itself to an angel that was being charged with the greatest count of treason in the history of eternity. He had the balls to wink at Letty. To her credit, she didn't react—I would have given him a middle-finger salute.

"What do you plead?" Michael jerked on Lucifer's chain, leaving no room for continued shenanigans.

This time, the fallen angel's lip lifted in a menacing snarl as he spat out, "Guilty."

Michael bowed his head and his jaw clenched. In a quieter voice he said, "Brother, there is forgiveness if—"

"I. Am. Guilty," Lucifer clarified, his voice thundering. "In every way, in every time line, and every sense of the word. I do *not* repent."

Lucifer spat at his brother's sandaled feet. Michael's eyes gleamed a kaleidoscope of colors, and a lion's growl rumbled in his chest.

"I will not kowtow to the vermin we call humans," Lucifer continued. "I do not regret sparking their fall into sin. They are insignificant beasts. A plague. A nuisance. Furthermore, I will not prostrate myself before our Father like some weak, sniveling coward. I was created for more than mere servitude. My legion, and those others who willingly followed me, did so because they felt the same. I will take my punishment. Do your worst, *brother*."

I watched this scene unfold with eyes wide and mouth gaping. My tiny, infantile, human brain desperately tried to grasp the enormity of this betrayal. Letty had told me to watch, listen, and remember. Well, I could never, ever forget. Not as long as I lived.

"For the highest levels of treason," Michael said in his amplified voice, "Lucifer, you are hereby banished from the Heavenly places, stripped of the title of Archangel, and sentenced to eternity without your wings."

My stomach turned. My fingers curled around the edges the shirt I wore. My entire body trembled.

Lucifer paled for a single heartbeat before his cocky smirk returned. He landed his sinfully chocolate brown eyes on Letty.

"No fateful kiss goodbye, love?"

This time Letty did react. She launched a dagger at his head.

He lean out of the blade's path, deftly dodging injury. "Star-crossed, really. It's *criminal* you'll never know what sharing a bed with me is like. It would have changed your allegiance."

Letty's chest filled with indignance and her lip lifted in disgust.

"Enough," Michael thundered.

I ducked because, well, it felt like the best thing to do if I wanted to hide.

In one lighting-fast motion, Michael unsheathed his flaming greatsword and brought it down on the juncture of Lucifer's back and his wings, slicing through bone, tendon, and muscle like warm butter.

When his great black wings hit the ground, a burst of power exploded outward. The shockwave bowled over angels and rocked the very foundation of Heaven, splitting the ground. And before Lucifer's scream became audible, Michael kicked the disgraced Fallen down into the rift and he plummeted from view.

I woke from my vision screaming, grabbing at my shirt, chest, shorts. I patted my head, my body. Pain lanced through me from my wound. And no matter how much I tried to breathe in, I couldn't get enough air. In blind panic, I thrashed. My side throbbed. Hands landed on me, gathering me to sit upright.

"Purse your lips and breathe slowly through your mouth." Harper's insistent voice was low and hoarse. He lightly cupped a calloused hand over my lips. "Breathe from your belly." He'd cradled me with his free arm and murmured soothing words. "That's it, Sammy."

The storm ebbed. Sweat dampened my hair, my neck, my tee. Behind his palm, I asked, "Am I okay?"

"Yeah, spitfire, you're alright." He dropped his hand and gently tipped up my chin. His sapphire eyes burned with intensity, but they held a softness. He stroked my cheek with the back of his knuckles. His brand of kindness. I launched into his arms. He caught me and fell back on to his own ass, never letting me go. He gathered me into his lap, and we sat that way until I no longer trembled.

"Now," he reared back and brushed hair from my face, "wanna tell me what the fuck that was that about?"

16

SAM

"I had a vision." Harper shifted to help us get up, and a pained hiss escaped me.

His hand brushed my side. "Let me see."

I waved away his touch. "Didn't do anything to cause damage this time. It's residual evil mojo in the wound. I'm fine."

He looked as if he wanted to argue but did not. He flipped his hand over in a "go on" gesture. "You had a vision?"

"I was almost to the office when Letty announced that Heaven decided to bestow this *honor* on me." The heeby-jeebies skittered over my skin and I shivered. "Why they wanted me to watch Lucifer be stripped of his angelhood, I don't know why, but here we are."

"Sounds like a blast." Harper slipped a strong arm around my waist, and I leaned into his solid body. He smelled like sandalwood and clove, just like normal. *Ah, nostalgia.* His support enveloped me in a comfortable safety.

"You and I have very different definitions of fun." We walked the long hallway together with me gimping along.

"To answer your question, no. Letty just popped up outta nowhere, and *boom*, I'm walking the streets of gold."

"Hmmm," Harper mused.

"That's it? I tell you I witnessed Michael—who is freaking terrifying, b-t-dubs—de-winging Lucifer, and you just grunt? Did I mention the flaming sword? Mike's blade was literally on fire. And—" I clucked my tongue and slashed a hand down through the air. "No more wings."

Harper shook his head, but I swear that a smile tugged on his lips.

Xavier's office looked much like the one he kept above Xavier's Antique Emporium in town. Warm wood, chocolate leather, heavy furniture, and old-world charm filled the space. Nyx, Goddess of the Night, croaked at me when we entered. She rotated her head left, then right, hopped off her perch and walked the length of the desktop.

"Good morning, Miss Fife," Xavier said without looking up from the paper in his hands. "So glad you could join us. You've had an eventful day already, yes?"

I heard him, but my sights zeroed in on Andrew seated in a guest chair in front of Xavier's desk. His grey eyes had lost their mischievous gleam. His skin seemed to cling to his bones. A bittersweet wave of emotions hit me. We'd cleared the air, but a sharp twist wrenched my heart. There was still a loss of trust between us, and it still smarted. He offered a smile, which I returned.

Without dropping Andrew's gaze, I answered Xavier. "I like to keep things fresh. Unpredictable. Adventurous."

"Menace," Harper whispered into my ear as he eased me into the leather loveseat in the corner. A shiver ran through me, and I forgot to be offended. Maybe it was my imagination, but Harper's insults were losing their edge.

From a side bar, Xavier poured a glass of water. "Why

don't you take it from the top, Miss Fife, and tell us about this vision."

Friggin' bat ears on this one. "You heard all that?"

He handed the glass to Harper, who knelt in front of me and pressed it into my grasp. "Take small sips."

"Yes," Xavier said. "And I'm rather curious."

The office door banged open. Leigh stood in the entrance. Her eyes found mine. "Samantha Grace!"

I smiled at her. "Hi. That's me."

"I could kill you!" Leigh hurried over.

"But you won't."

"I was gone for a few hours." She pulled me into a gripping hug. Either she didn't see or didn't care that I winced. "Nigel told me you went to the barn and didn't tell anyone."

"It's not like I left the property," I grumbled. They were all overreacting. *Honestly.* "All that doesn't matter. We have a more pressing issue. Heaven granted me a vision. I hyperventilated afterward. Harper found me. It was an ordeal. I was just getting ready to tell the room about what I saw. Cozy up, bestie, it's story time."

I patted the seat next to me.

"Vision?" Leigh brows furrowed. "What—"

"Best let Miss Fife explain, Miss Kestler," Xavier said. "I'm sure all will come to light."

I nodded at Xavier and plunged right ahead, detailing what I had seen. The images of war-torn Heaven with angelic bodies, golden blood, smoke, and fire made me want to hurl. Nothing had been able to hurt me, but my senses had been on full alert. I told them everything, keeping the bit when Lucifer flirted with Letty to myself— that had a private quality to it that even I didn't want to delve into.

Once I finished speaking, four sets of eyes stared at me. I looked at each of them.

"It is rare that a Warrior is gifted with such things," Andrew said, breaking the silence.

"That's what Letty said to me."

"Why do you think Heaven wanted Sam to see this specifically?" Leigh asked, her eyes bouncing from me to Andrew to Xavier.

Xavier handed Nyx a cracker. "That, Miss Kestler, remains to be seen. We cannot pretend to understand the ways of Heaven. However, I do think we need to acknowledge that it could be cautionary. No one has heard from Lucifer in millennia. I'm old, and I've never seen him." Xavier glanced at Andrew.

"Nor I," Andrew agreed. "And I'm slightly older."

Leigh, Andrew, and Xavier started conjuring theories about my vision without my input—what it could have meant and how we should apply that knowledge. None of their theories suggested that it had been a good thing. They spoke of gloom and doom, as if *I* were on Heaven's naughty list. I tuned them out and studied the water ripples in my glass.

The weight of Harper's gaze bore down on me. He stood by my side—silent, strong, and brooding. When his hand slid down my neck and rested between my shoulder blades, I flinched. His thumb made firm, soothing strokes against my muscles. A reminder that he was in my corner. I relaxed at his small touch and chose to ignore the negativity flying around. Instead, I turned inward because I had an angel that had some *'splaining* to do.

"Soooo you and Lucifer ..."

"I never returned Lucifer's affections." She actually *tisked* me.

"It sounded like there was something there," I said.

"All one-sided, I assure you, and not for his lack of trying." Her sheer exasperation washed through me. *"Relationships between angels aren't forbidden, but neither are they encouraged. He wanted me to be his Fallen Queen. You saw that, even in the end, he never stopped trying. I was the only one he ever propositioned."*

"I mean, he was smokin' hawt." I pictured his smoldering eyes, cut jaw, tousled brown hair, and golden skin. He was most beautiful. Flawless. The Morning Star. *"No judgment if you* had *accepted. I applaud your restraint."*

"You're incorrigible," Letty grumped.

While I said I wouldn't judge, Letty's admission that she'd never slept with the enemy loosened a knot in my chest that had appeared when I'd witnessed the scene. *He wanted me to be his Fallen Queen.* Letty's words echoed in my head. The vision and my angel's confession gave me much to mull over in my down time.

"You okay?" Leigh peeked at me then squeezed my knee.

I winked at her. "Never better."

Before Leigh could respond, Andrew said, "There is the possibility that Sammy was given this vision as a gift."

Finally, we can agree on something.

What Heaven had given me felt more informative than cautionary. Like I was a bystander watching a Heavenly documentary.

"She survived a massive psychological attack," Andrew continued. "Also, no Warrior has been able to fight through Enyo's poison and live to tell the tale until now."

Yes, yes, my sheer stubborn will and refusal to let the bad guys win was admirable and all. But it also was my fatal flaw. I almost died. According to Harper and Leigh, my heart had stopped a couple times.

The conversation took a more positive turn, and they launched into alternative possibilities. Unexpected tears burned my eyelids at Andrew's support. My rattled confidence had encouraged my recent insecurities to run wild. My people weren't doubting me, they were exploring different theories about this vision. These people cared about me; they didn't want to think the worst. Their conversation buzzed in the background. I felt Letty's warmth seep into my frazzled brain, my shaking hands, my rattled confidence.

"Do you have any theories?" I asked Letty. *"Was Heaven trying to warn me or discipline me?"*

"I was not told why they chose to give you this vision, but in all my existence, they are only given to elite Warriors—ones with strong fortitude. And they are rare. I think you know in your heart that you were gifted this for a good purpose."

Gifted.

My heart swelled. *"What do I do with the knowledge?"*

"All will become clear in time."

Right. A non-answer. But one thing was already clear to me. I needed to do better. I had to get well—physically and mentally. I had to listen to Harper. I was no use to Leigh or my Warrior peers in this state of bullshit. I would rise and punch Hell in the balls. They would not win.

"I think," I cut in, silencing everyone, "since I'm the one that had this vision, it's my responsibility to decipher the whys and whats. Kinda? Maybe?"

Leigh flinched. "Sam, we didn't mean—"

"I know, but y'all are here discussing *my* vision—a vision Heaven gifted to me—like it was a bad thing. A warning. A slap on the hand to keep me in check. But I gotta say, I think y'all are wrong." I glanced at Andrew. His slight nod and ghost smile gave me the confidence to continue. *He's still rooting for me.*

"While I *am* a wild card that makes questionable choices, choices that led to my current predicament, I've been doing some soul searching. Since I'm of no use to anyone in the field right now, I reckon this is my puzzle to figure out."

Xavier's eyes danced with enigmatic fire. Andrew's gaunt face relaxed and he smiled. Leigh's grip tightened on my fingers. And Harper? Still silent as ever, hand pressed into my back like a steadying force. I tilted my head back, peering up at the man who was my cornerstone.

"After the Warrior meeting, I'll behave. For real this time." I made an X motion with my finger over my chest. *Cross my heart, y'all.* "No more unapproved field trips. No more complaining. I'll take Life Elixir, burrow into the common room, and follow your roadmap to recovery. I'll take it seriously."

Harper's sapphire eyes widened, his lips parted, and his nostrils flared. Relief. The look that passed over his stoney expression told me that my words assuaged some of his anxiety. My heart tripped over itself. I kept forgetting how much Harper cared. He hid it well. He was a gruff, stoic prick, but I'd was starting understanding this version of him better on this side of my *incident*. My promise eased his inner turmoil.

As quick as it slipped, his hardened mask snapped back into place. "Glad to hear it."

"Do I detect a sense of humor, Harper?"

"No," he grunted.

I grinned. "Forced stall rest might make me go insane from boredom, but I'mma do it."

His mouth twitched, fighting not to smile. "You're already batshit crazy."

"Maybe I'll make a full recovery." I lifted my shoulder in an exaggerated shrug. "You never know."

"I'll believe it when I see it," was his sardonic retort.

"Wise decision, Miss Fife," Xavier said, breaking up

our banter. "We have fifteen minutes before everyone is to gather for the meeting. Can you see your way over to the war room, please?"

I saluted him and got up from the couch by myself. Leigh, Harper, and I all filed out of Xavier's office and headed next door. At the massive set of carved wooden doors, I balked.

Leigh said nothing, but her raised brow asked all the questions: *Are you okay? Really. Don't lie.*

I clenched my teeth. My heart raced. My palms felt clammy. I wiped them on my jeans then adjusted my orange tee shirt. *I need to be in this meeting.* I puffed out a breath as if bracing for a heavy lift and raised a *stop* hand to her.

"Don't rush me. I'm building my courage."

"If you aren't ready—" she stepped towards me and rested a hand atop my shoulder "—we don't have to be here."

Collect your shit, Fife. All of it.

I was still a Warrior. I still had a job to do. Injured or whole. In a coma or awake. Trauma or not. I never backed down from the hard things. And that wouldn't change today.

"Let's do this," I said, firming up my resolve. "*Carpe Diem. Seize the day, boys!*" I strode forward, grabbing my bestie with me. "Seize the moment, bestie."

"Really? Quoting *Dead Poets Society* right now?" she asked as I dragged her over the threshold into the museum-library-war-room.

"Felt appropriate." I shrugged.

The inner sanctum of Xavier's command center was a hallowed hall of Warrior history contained inside a command center. Two stories high, it was packed with books, scrolls, priceless artifacts, and odd Xavier-made trinkets. The last time I was in here, I'd wanted to touch everything. This time was no different. There was a pedestal with a long ruby cushion, and on top sat some sort of glowing rod. Leigh snatched my hand before I could trail it along the metal.

"No touching," she hissed.

Someone cleared their throat and pulled my attention to the long wood table stretching down the center of the room. Harper, Tally, Sajid, Leilani, Jax, and DH were all staring at Leigh and me.

Probably, mostly at me.

"Way to make an entrance," Leigh muttered and slipped by me. She gave one of my belt loops a gentle tug. I followed and landed in the empty chair between Harper and Leigh.

A barrage of mental images bombarded me: Xavier's power point presentation, our haunting Warrior of Light history, a brutal slaughter by Dark Warriors, Andrew's tortured expression. That feeling of not being able to get enough air.

I closed my eyes and used the breathing technique Harper had taught me. But the memories didn't stop, and they morphed into other things. Dominic sitting in a lounge chair in my mind, putting duct tape over my mouth, controlling my environment. The Mage arriving, throwing magic around, freezing me out in my own head. Cheryl's implanted memories surfaced.

My body flashed hot then cold. A buzzing rose in my ears.

"Sam." Harper's voice was a command. It stopped the assault and battery in my broken brain.

Does Harper know he grounds me?

"Everything alright, Miss Fife?" Xavier said, taking his seat. I nodded once.

Tabitha joined her Warriors, propped her elbows on the table top, and steepled her fingers. She rested her chin on top of them. Andrew pulled out the free chair next to Leigh and nodded at me.

Andrew looked like the walk from office to war room taxed the hell out of him, like he had one foot in the grave. I suppose he did. My chest tightened. I ignored the punch to my gut. He'd been married to Judy in the Warrior way, which was more binding than a legal marriage. That lifeline had been severed because I'd failed to save Judy. Part of me wondered if he held that against me.

Don't let them see you're one wrong word away from a breaking, I coached myself with a head shake to dispel the waking nightmares. *It's show time, bitches.*

"Sorry, sir, but I *am* a bit slower these days." I beamed at everyone. "But, now that you have my full attention, do go on."

Xavier's brown irises turned red on the very outer edges. His energy aura changed from enigmatic to dangerous in a breath. My internal warning systems sounded off. I struggled with the concept of respect on a good day. I stepped out of line often. But no one intimidated me quite like Xavier did without a single word, and I knew I'd taken one step too far.

"S-sorry, I'm just gonna—" I pinched my fingers and ran the tips over my lips, then tossed away the non-existent key.

"That is wise," Xavier said.

I let out a short, sharp breath when he directed his attention elsewhere. The whole exchange earned me a dark scowl from Leilani. We were frenemies after all. She hated my flare. I hated her ass-kissing. Because I couldn't help it, I winked at her. Her scowl turned into a silent snarl. Jax, ever the embodiment of blond sunshine, grinned and gently tugged on Leilani's ponytail. She bristled, turning her petite nose up and looking at Xavier.

Sajid watched me, too. His white button down made his bronze skin pop. He'd rolled up the sleeves to his elbows, accentuating the muscle in his forearms. Between his dark curly hair which swept the top of his collar, his heavy five o'clock stubble, and his dark eyes, Sajid was drool-worthy.

I didn't fan myself, but I definitely needed to lay off the romance novels.

Tally caught my attention. Her smirk and sparkling eyes silently said, *he's deadly eye candy, ain't he?* I chuckled. Harper's heavy arm landed around the back of my chair.

He leaned over and spoke into my ear. "Thought you said you'd behave."

Whoops. Mind your eyes, ol' girl. They give you away.

"Now that Miss Fife has given me permission to start —" Xavier withdrew a fancy silver pen from the inside of his navy blazer. He twisted the barrel and poised it over a notebook. "Mr. Aziz and Miss Zohar, what do you have to report?"

Sajid Aziz and Talia Zohar. Roger that. Knowing the names of your allies felt important. Tally rapped Sajid with the back of her knuckles.

He nodded at her and said, "We covered quite of bit of ground during our hunt and ran into a few hordes of Lesser Demons. Easily dispatched. We did not find any Greater Demons."

"And the farmhouse?" Tabitha asked.

"No change." Sajid glanced at Andrew. "The borders still hold, though they are frail. Talia and I also checked on Adviser Shaw's church. That boundary continues to shrink."

Shit. My heart climbed my throat. The church's veils

were specifically laid by my mentor. This news didn't bode well. Everyone shifted in their seats. Andrew bowed his silver head. Xavier jotted down a couple notes.

"Before anyone asks," Xavier said, "I cannot simply plop down my own wards in front of failing ones. It takes time and a fair amount of my energy—neither a luxury we can afford—to lay down a boarder of that magnitude." Without looking up or missing a beat, he said, "Miss Kalakaua, report."

"Same as Adviser Holland's team. Nothing of significance. There was a higher concentration of Lesser Demons south, along the Gulf Coast, but nothing that wasn't easily dealt with."

Xavier's pen scratched as he wrote. Still looking down, he asked, "Mr. Bozeman, have you or my darling daughter discovered anything about the odd fire or sigil painted on the floor of Andrew's church?"

My breath hitched. *Sigil, my ass.*

These Warriors with their bat hearing heard my balk. Jax's kind blue eyes met mine, and the big, blond Warrior's cheeks flushed. He rubbed the back of his neck. I'd been a raving lunatic when I freaked out over that damned smiley face painted on the floor of the church.

It *still* freaked me out.

It was Dominic's doing, but I didn't know how that was possible.

Jax's held my eyes with his. "We scoured over the texts and internet about it and hadn't found anything— until right before this meeting." He looked away from me to Xavier and slid a sheet of paper towards his Adviser.

Xavier's eyes roved over the page in a cursory read-through. "The Infernal Zealots, eh? According to this, they are an obscure international sect of radical Satanists. They operate in the shadows and have been known to cause mayhem to local churches."

I chewed my lip. It was some crazy group of normal humans who thought Hell was something to celebrate? *Idiots.* Demons didn't care about hero worship. And given my recent vision, Lucifer hadn't liked humans either.

"Andrew or Tabitha, have you heard of this group?" Xavier arched an aristocratic brow.

"No," Tabitha said, her tone all business, "but I've got a gentlman in Ireland of questionable repute. He's my ears on the street since he refuses to stay at my safe house. I'll have him look underground."

"I used to have a running journal of all extremist groups. Judy——" Andrew's jaw flexed from where he'd clenched his teeth. He blinked away tears. "Judy stopped keeping tabs eighteen years ago when I severed all Warrior ties." Almost before my eyes, I watched my chosen grandfather grow another century older. He'd walked away from the Warriors of Light to give the survivors safety from the Mage's wrath.

But at what cost? The hits kept coming for him.

Xavier turned the page of the legal pad to a fresh sheet. "Why is information on this group so hard to find? And how did they have such a controlled burn on the inside of the sanctuary?"

"I reckon they wanted to stay hidden, sir," Jax said.

"Keep digging," Xavier instructed. "Have Delaney continue assisting you. There is no one better at research than my daughter."

Jax gave a firm nod, and his eyes slid to me again. *Is that pity? I hope to hell not.* I stretched my neck. Jax was a perceptive sonofabitch, he could probably smell my confusion—if that were even possible. The incident didn't feel like the work of humans. I chewed on my lower lip.

Do I say something? Is that out of line?

"Next order of business," Xavier said, moving on and making the decision for me. "I finished analyzing the evidence found outside Mr. Bennett's restaurant."

My blood froze. Camden's name sent a blow to my already wounded heart. Any air I had in my lungs vanished. I vaguely felt Leigh's hand on my shoulder.

"The internal bits of the phone were, ah, crispy," he continued. "Nothing could be pulled from it. There wasn't evidence to prove the shoe had any connection to Mr. Bennett. However, the blood on the knife was his. Any thoughts or theories on how this could happen?"

By the grace of Powers that Be, I remained upright in my seat. With my eyes squeezed shut, I gripped the arms of my chair. People spoke, answering Xavier, but my ears heard none of it. It all became a rumbling buzz of sounds.

I told myself I wouldn't shed a single tear over Camden, but to have it brought up so casually stole my breath. None of them knew we'd broken up. Hell, I hadn't even told Leigh. I'd stewed on this shit for three days. Camden could make his own choices—stupid idiotic choices—but breaking up with me didn't stop me from worrying.

"You're a ghost. Need to get out of here?" Harper said, speaking into my ear. I hadn't felt the solitary tear slide down my cheek until he discreetly brushed it away.

"Nothing," I muttered. *Deflect, deflect, deflect.* I cleared my throat.

"Bullshit," he rumbled.

"So, what is the working theory about the blood on the knife?" I asked the group.

Harper raised a single finger in the air, gaining Xavier's attention. "Can we take a breather?" At Xavier's nod, Harper helped me up.

"I'm *fine*," I hissed low.

"I'm coming with," Leigh said, springing to her feet.

Once in the hall, my best friend and my *whatever* Harper was stood before me. Leigh rubbed my arm from shoulder to bicep. Harper's mask was a stoic wall of impenetrable emotion.

"Sam, what's going on?" Leigh asked. "You knew we were running tests on the stuff we found."

I pressed my lips together. Truthfully, I don't know why I didn't tell them about Camden. *You're embarrassed.* I couldn't remember the last time someone broke up with *me*, never mind someone I was trying to keep safe. I didn't want to be angry at Camden, but I was. I was freaking furious.

He knew what I was now. He saw the dangers of my life. And he still left.

"Camden broke up with me," I mumbled in a rush.

"What?" Harper barked.

"She said Camden broke up with her," Leigh said, aghast.

"Blast your stupid Warrior hearing," I snipped.

"When?" Harper's eyes burned a little darker blue. "Why didn't you tell us?"

"You hate his guts. Thought you'd be happy." I crossed my arms, wincing when the movement pulled at my wound just right. Through my gritted teeth, I hissed, "Thursday."

Leigh rubbed my shoulder. "I'm sorry. You okay?"

"Yes. Fine. His timing couldn't have been more perfect." My nostrils flared in my brief spike of anger, but that rage evaporated, leaving behind my wounded heart. "It freaking sucks monkey balls."

The tears that sprang up and clogged my voice were because his actions had been the final blow to my destroyed confidence. And for the first time since Camden dumped me three days ago, the flood gates opened up. I buried my face in my hands, pissed at myself for crying.

Leigh grabbed my wrists, prying my palms from my face. "I've never seen you cry over—" Her hazel eyes flicked to Harper for a scant second. "I've seen you cry over exactly one guy in our entire twenty years. I know Camden was different, but the waterworks don't make sense. What's wrong?"

"I'mma freaking mess in here." I tapped the side of my head. "I cry at random times, and in the next second, I'm throwing books at the wall. I have nightmares. I'm on edge. I flinch all the time. And that's really dangerous for a Warrior, you know? I drew my weapon on Healer Emily the other day! A Seer! She was terrified. All she did was walk into the common room and startle me." I threw up my arms, grunted at the pull in my side, and blinked away fresh tears. "I'm broken. I'm so annoying with these leaky feelings."

"Honey," Leigh's voice drawled long and slow, "that's called trauma. And you need to deal with it. You can't bury it." She pushed me away and held me at arm's length.

I glanced over at Harper. Instead of stoic intensity, there was compassion in the soft expression on his face, in the gentleness of how he looked at me. As ashamed as I was to admit that there was more wrong with me than I wanted, it felt good to get that out—like letting air to a wound that needed to dry out.

"You're my bestie first and foremost, right?" she asked. I nodded and she moved to my side, looping her arm around my waist. "Then I'm in this with you. If you're benched then so am I. You're going to get sick of me. Let's get you somewhere far away from Warrior business."

"I'll let Xavier know. Stay put." Harper headed back into the meeting and returned in less than a minute.

After making our way upstairs, the three of us gathered back in my common room soon after. Leigh had settled in one of the plush leather chairs, legs tucked under her, while she sipped on a cup of cocoa. Bear had wedged himself close to me on the couch.

Safe. I feel safe in here.

And damn it all if that realization didn't suck. I was a Warrior who'd been putting on a brave front. My eyes stung. Harper crouched down in front of me, framed my head in his hands, and looked at me square in the face.

"I swear on my own goddamn life that you'll be back to wreaking your own brand of havoc on the world. But I need your full cooperation. I need you all fucking in. Are you in this with me?"

That was downright verbose for Harper, and the urgency behind his words stirred something in my heart. His thumbs brushed my temples, waiting for my answer. I averted my eyes because he held my head. I sighed, long and harsh.

"Trust him." Letty's voice was a whisper.

"I do," was my auto response.

"Trust him like you trust Leigh."

Trusting Harper on the level my angel spoke of brushed up against something intimate. It meant opening up old wounds. No matter how much I fought it, friend-Harper would always be linked to the boy who had owned my heart. I couldn't separate the two as a teen, and I probably couldn't separate them now.

I gnawed on my lower lip. My head and my heart waged war. What if he went away again? What if he died trying to protect me? What if I never got better and he looked at me like the weakling I currently was for years to come? My heart tilted like a damn ship tossed about in a damn hurricane.

But Warrior me had to get better. Because I wasn't me without the Warrior, and I was useless to her right now. The only way to heal was to wade through the bullshit emotions and rest my battered body. As daunting and humiliating as it might've been, nothing was keeping me down. There were demons to slaughter. A Mage to neutralize. Humanity to protect. Despite feeling vulnerable and fragile, I was *alive* to fight another day. Mostly due to the man in front of me. But I had to be smart about it.

"Sam?" Harper said, breaking me out of my internal diatribe.

"Yeah?"

He tapped my temple. "Where'd you go?"

"Nowhere. I'm right here." I met Harper's eyes. "How 'bout we retry Operation Fife Recovery, Dr. Tate?"

17

SAM

My daggers, Helios and Sol, warmed in my hands, ready for violence. I held them low and flared out from my body, blades pointed down while I studied my opponent. Leigh struck fast and hard, trying to distract me with fancy sword work. She sliced downward. I blocked her hit by crossing my weapons in front of me. She kicked at my leg, throwing me off balance.

"No!" I shouted as my heart raced. Sweat trickled down my neck, her speed winding me.

She grinned and pulled her sword back. The sound of screeching steel echoed off the rough, cavernous walls. She whirled and stabbed forward, aiming for my healed left side. Reflex and muscle memory took over. I leaned to the right, dodging her blade, and slammed Helios down while swinging Sol up beneath it. With her weapon scissored between my daggers, I wrenched them, and her blade clattered to the ground.

"Victory!" I declared.

Leigh smirked. "Because I took it easy on you, and

you're still drawing on your Power. Drop it, and then we'll see who's the Big Bad Warrior."

She bent over and retrieved her practice sword. While I was better, I wasn't at full Warrior capacity, and I'd been using my Power to fight her with a dang *practice* sword. Had she fought me with Fury, I wouldn't have parted her from her weapon so easily. Grumbling, I severed the connection to the divine. My blades dimmed. Fatigue washed over me.

I pointed Helios at her while she re-racked her sword. "Best friend mine, I've been trying beat you since Harper cleared me for sparring a week ago. Let me have this moment." I whipped my daggers in a circle to sheath them in their invisible scabbards on my back. "I earned my win today."

Leigh rolled her eyes. "She's cocky, to boot."

"Watch out, Hellspawn." I raised my arms in victory over my head. "I'm back, bitches!"

"Samantha Grace," Leigh hissed.

"What?" I lowered my arms and grinned. If she busted her ovaries over my cussing instead of worrying she'd hurt me while sparring, I considered it a win.

"Can we not with the swearing?"

I snorted. "You never correct Harper's pirate mouth."

"No, I don't."

"Why not?" I asked, catching the towel she chucked at me and wiping the sweat from my face.

She gave me a deadpan glare. "Are *you* willing to tell Harper to stop swearing?"

"He'd probably tell me to 'fuck off' or something."

"Sam!"

"Muhahahaha!" I cackled and bolted towards the stairs.

It had been a long month of sitting and recovering. I'd ticked off each day from my superhero calendar with a permanent marker. There was no longer a hole in my side, and I'd been granted permission to have my daggers back.

More importantly, my Powers were back without hindrance.

During my convalescence, I'd almost decapitated Xavier once by accident. He'd spooked me, since he moves like a damn ninja, while I'd been reading a creepy murder novel. He had entered the common room and was standing over me when he'd cleared his throat. Before Letty could stop me, I'd had Helios pressed to Xavier's throat.

My dear, sweet, loving Adviser had called it a trauma response and took my daggers away until Harper deemed me healed. It hadn't been one of my finer moments. There had been screaming, begging, arguing, and tears. At that point, Xavier recruited Nigel to teach me meditation and breathing techniques.

It had been a long, tedious month, but well needed.

I climbed the stairs from Xavier's gym to the kitchen, a spring in my step from the thrill of sparring. Humming, I checked the coffee pot, filled two cups of coffee, and tossed waffles into the toaster. Leigh joined me in the industrial kitchen.

"Your menace levels are rising back to normal." She took the cup I offered her.

I rested my hip against the dark marble counter. "You love me, impulsiveness and all."

"You're lucky I do."

The toaster dinged. I set down my mug, grabbed a couple plates, and snatched the waffles one-by-one. I dropped them onto the dishes and blew on my fingers. Leigh snagged blueberry jam for me and maple syrup for herself from the fridge.

Breakfast of champions, baby.

"Thank you." Leigh took her plate.

"I got you, boo."

Leigh sat down at a four-seater table next to the long window wall overlooking the castle grounds, and doused her waffles with syrup. The sun was starting to peek up from the horizon, but everything outside was quiet. A rooster crowed in the distance. I grabbed the remote, flicked on the TV, and joined her.

Since I'd slept like garbage during the past month, I'd learned two things. First, I could now navigate Casa de Xavier without an escort. And secondly, Nigel liked to have an hour of relative peace at four in the morning while he drank his tea, ate his scones, and watched the morning news. I'd sat with him often, and Leigh started joining us after the second week.

"Where's our favorite butler this morning?" Leigh asked. "It's Monday. I thought he'd be busy cooking for the masses." She took a polite bite of her waffle.

"He switched days off to match Miss Betty's schedule." I waggled my eyebrows. Nigel had been spending more and more time with Shield Haven's sweet shop owner. "She's closed on Mondays."

Leigh swallowed and held her fist in front of her mouth. "He—what?"

I grinned "Our boy is sweet on the candy lady."

"Well, if that isn't the most precious thing I've heard, I'm not a Warrior."

"We have an urgent news alert that just came in," said the anchorman on the TV, snatching our attention. The newscaster wore a pressed suit, conservative tie, and trimmed beard. "We've been reporting on the mysterious string of arson fires in Hillsborough, Pinellas, and Polk counties. So far, four churches, two synagogues, two mosques, and a Thai temple have all been set ablaze. And last night arsonists attacked another place of worship. Russell Belcher is on the scene. Russell, tell us what's going on."

Leigh's head whipped in my direction, her brows arching high. I met her knowing gaze. Whoever had set Andrew's church ablaze had been busy while I was recovering. I'd watched the reports every morning with Nigel. The Warriors were looking into it, but as we weren't law enforcement, it had been a slow-going investigation. I snatched up the remote and mashed the volume button.

"—burning only the inner sanctuary and leaving the outside intact," said Russell. "In all instances, the security systems have been disabled. These fires continue to confound authorities. The biggest mystery is how blazes are being controlled so they leave the exteriors of the buildings unharmed. Detectives suspect an anti-religious group. This image, their calling card, appears at all the crime scenes."

A familiar red circle with a winking smiley face flashed on the center of the screen. My heart leapt into my throat. My blood ran cold. I rubbed my mouth. These fires were demonic, and that face was a taunt. My gut told me that they were Dominic's work—somehow, someway. But now that stupid sigil no longer tortured me. It *infuriated* me. These assholes were playing games, just because they could. Anger licked up my neck like flames.

Since I hadn't attended a Warrior meeting once I'd promised to recover obediently, I asked, "Is Jax still point Warrior for this investigation?"

"Yeah, DH does the research, and Jax does the leg work. Lani goes with him to hunt down any leads they find." Leigh ran her thumb over the handle of her coffee cup. "It's always the same. Burned inside, pristine outside, that smiley face, and no leads."

Russell must have been listening to us because he interrupted with, "We have a developing situation. I'm told that a body has been found in the rubble."

The mug I'd lifted slipped from my fingers and shattered on the tile. Hot coffee splattered my skin. My chair screeched as I shoved against the table and stood. Leigh leapt up and ran for kitchen towels. Russell? He kept talking, but I heard nothing he said.

"Sam, are you okay?" Leigh threw the towels on the floor and tapped them with her foot to soak up the liquid.

"I'm going to kill him."

Leigh paused her shoddy mopping job. "Who?"

"Dominic. This is his doing." I pointed to the flatscreen.

"Sam," Leigh said, her tone placating, "you have no evidence of this. And we haven't seen Dominic since before you went into your coma."

"Easy," Letty soothed. *"She doesn't understand why you have that inclination. She wasn't in your head while he was there. Don't snap at her. Explain what you know. She is your Warrior Partner."*

I froze, releasing my hold on my Power. Letty didn't interfere with my day-to-day actions unless she felt like I needed her immediate counsel—or when I unintentionally drew on my Power like I just had. Most of the time, I was certain she liked my fire and spontaneity, but right now, she was right. Leigh deserved to know my thoughts without me losing my shit.

I blew out a big breath and squatted to pick up the broken pieces of my mug. I felt Leigh's eyes on me as I cleaned up my mess and threw the bits into the trash. I made a ritual of pick up the ceramic shards, taking soothing breaths, and focusing my thoughts.

Thank you, Nigel, for your woo-woo breathing techniques.

With my back to Leigh, I made a fresh cup of joe and

stared down into the steaming brown liquid. "I *know* this is Dominic. He stalked me, went after my boy—ex-boyfriend —to get to me, and he camped out in my head. That bastard stole my voice *inside* my own damn mind."

"What?" Leigh gasped.

I hadn't told anyone the nitty gritty of what Dominic said and did while having my psyche on lockdown. My body went still, and my breath came out hard while I remembered what happened in my coma. I rubbed at the knot forming in my chest before finding my words.

"He yammered on about the political structure of Hell —the Infernal Order—that holds Hell together, then launched into this story about what happened to The Fallen when they were booted from Heaven. Their skin changed, eyes blackened, and natures twisted. But in their torment and, they found a sort of freedom. They started to breed. They fed on human energy. They grew strong. They thrived. When Heaven found out that the demons weren't wasting in eternal punishment, the Warriors of Light were created to slaughter them. And the poor demons were only trying to make do with the cards they were given."

"I can only assume that last bit is sarcasm," Leigh interjected. "Or are you sympathizing with demons?"

A harsh laugh burst from me. "Dominic has a silver tongue." I turned and found Leigh watching me with a tilted head. "He used his words to spin a web of woe, trying to get me to believe that bull crap. But he also tried to convince me that becoming a Dark Warrior was a benevolent thing because the host human has to invite them in, whereas Light Warriors never get a chance to 'consent'—they have their anointing thrust on them without asking."

"How does this tie into whoever is burning the places of worship?"

"Letty warned me that Dominic will manipulate and twist anything to get his way. No one and nothing is off the table when it comes to Dominic." I tossed a glance towards the TV. "Someone is dead because of this arsonist. Dominic murdered Camden's prep cook, Javi, for funsies, remember? Did it without lifting a finger."

Leigh's gaze slid from me to the window wall. The sun had risen past the horizon and lit the property in gold and orange. She chewed her lower lip.

I joined Leigh at the table. "Light Warriors defend humanity at all costs."

"We haven't spotted any Greater Demons since that day we went to Adviser Shaw's church. How would we even go about proving Dominic's involvement?"

How indeed?

Going out and investigating wasn't on the table. Harper would lose his ever-loving mind—actually, they all would. This was an active murder-arson scene. I pinched my lip with my fingers, deep in thought. Xavier was the most competent adult I knew. He managed hundreds of Seers, an estate, and us Warriors. He owned a ding-dang town. He had clout and charisma out his ass.

"How deep do ya think Xavier's connections are with the local political powers?"

"Oh." Leigh lifted a finger and gave me a sidelong look. "Do I even want to know how you arrived at that question?"

"Listen. If there is anyone who can insert themselves into an active investigation, it would be Xavier."

"You want him to roll up to the crime scene, and what, exactly?"

"I don't know. That's for him to figure out." I headed for the door. Over my shoulder I asked, "Yo, you comin'?"

"Yes. Someone has to keep you in line." She tossed the

coffee-drenched towels down a laundry shoot and jogged to join me.

We found Xavier in his office next to the war room. Once we entered the open door, Nyx's bright eyes followed my every movement. She flapped her wings once, puffed her feathers, and positioned herself to keep me in her sights. I met her bird-glare with one of my own. She croaked and settled.

"Miss Fife. Miss Kestler." Xavier checked his watch and ran a hand through his salt-and-pepper hair. "To what do I owe your company at six fourty-five in the morning?"

I rounded his desk to stand next to him and tapped the newspaper that lay open on his desk. "We just heard what happened."

He leaned back in his chair, an amused glint in his eyes. "Enlighten me as to what you're specifically referring to?"

"Another fire. Someone died this time."

His jaw flexed.

Yes.

"This has Dominic written all over it." I tapped the paper again.

Xavier studied my face before glancing down at the paper spread before him. The front-page story of the *Tampa Times* was about the arsonist. He lifted his cup and saucer and sipped his beverage. I swore he did it to hide his skepticism.

"We have to intervene." I wasn't nuts. I was thinking with clarity. "You have the tools to prove it, as long as the crime scene is fresh."

"And how, Miss Fife, do you propose I do this?" His tone held a sense of curious amusement.

Keep your cool, Fife. You want to be taken seriously.

"I know that a man of your stature has connections high up the food chain. Why not use them? When Judy—

when all *that* went down—there wasn't even a peep from the media. No cops. No public spectacle." I squared my shoulders and boldly met his gaze. "Of all people, you have the power, the means, and the clout to cover up any shenanigans. If there is anyone who can gain access to this type of crime scene to use their fancy Warrior equipment, it's you, sir. These fires aren't from the Infernal Zealots or whatever group wants five seconds of fame."

"They aren't?" His words were a command: *Tell me why you think that, Miss Fife.*

"There is no way a human can control fires like these. Hell, I don't even know how a demon can do it, but if there's one who can, it's Dominic. He likes to play games. He's playing chess with us."

A knock on the door interrupted us. Harper's bulk filled the entrance as he leaned one shoulder against the jamb. His hair was damp, and his jaw was heavily stubbled like he hadn't bothered to shave for a couple days. Clad in jeans and a grey Tom Petty shirt, he appeared calm and collected. His eyes met mine. After a moment, his gaze slid to Leigh, then to Xavier. His cheek flexed.

"You called?" Harper said to Xavier. Bear ambled up beside Harper and sat at his feet.

I narrowed my eyes at the brindle traitor. He'd been spending more and more time with Harper. I felt like the spare human. I'd been the one that nursed his mangey self back to health. *And this is the thanks I get?*

Rude.

"Yes." Xavier leaned back in his dark leather desk chair. "And now that Miss Fife saved me the need to call on her or Miss Kestler, we can start. Sit."

None of us dared disobey that direct order because he spoke in a way which held no argument. Harper sat beside me on the couch, and Bear wedged his bean burrito body between us. He laid his blocky head on my thigh. With his relaxed sigh, all my crankiness evaporated. I stroked his velvet ears. Xavier tapped the paper in front of him, just as I had.

"Miss Fife was telling me her theories about the arson, and reminded me that I'm in a unique position to use my city and state connections for personal gain." He quirked an eyebrow at me. "How morally grey of you." A smirk ghosted his mouth, which he covered by running a palm over his goatee. His eyes freaking twinkled. "But I happen to agree with her."

Excuse me, what? I jerked upright, dislodging Bear. He grumbled in protest and burrowed his shoulder deeper into the cushion.

"I was hoping Mr. Tate would accompany me to the most recent crime scene." Xavier stroked Nyx's glossy head. She leaned into his touch.

"Yes, sir," Harper said.

"So you knew? About this morning?" Leigh asked.

Xavier nodded.

They were going alone? Just the two of them? No Warrior? I understood keeping me sidelined since I hadn't been cleared for field work, but going without backup sounded risky. Dread clawed my guts.

"Is Jax going with you?" I asked.

"No need," Xavier said with a flick of his hand.

"But—" I pressed my lips together. *Why Harper?*

Xavier had Powers, Harper did not. It was stupid of me to worry about Harper. He'd proven he could handle trouble. Anxiety hooked its talons into my chest. I could not lose any more of my people—especially Harper. I steadied my breathing.

"Leigh can go with you," I said. "She picks up on things others miss. What if your fancy-dancy demon

scanner misses clues? What if your connections don't guarantee backstage passes to the crime scene? What if something doesn't work and—"

"All solid points, Miss Fife," Xavier gently interrupted.
He tapped Nyx's beak and then his shoulder. With a flap
of her iridescent wings, she settled on his shoulder. "Miss
Kestler, can you be ready in twenty minutes?"

"Absolutely. I'll be right back."

Those anxiety talons retracted from my chest a touch,
and I took my first full, easy breath. I trusted Leigh with
my life. She would keep Harper safe. I felt the man
studying my profile, but I didn't trust myself to look at him.

Not much later, I found myself waiting inside the
manor's massive entrance hall. Leigh had gone to get the
car. Xavier was speaking privately with Nigel near the
door. And I stood there grumbling to myself that I couldn't
be the one on this mission. Movement caught my eye as
Harper joined the party. He'd exchanged his tee for a
button-down dress shirt that he'd tucked into dark jeans.
He'd ditched the sneakers for Oxford dress shoes.

Damn. Don't check him out, Fife. Don't do it. Inappropriate.

"I know why you volunteered Kestler," Harper said,
diverting my wayward thoughts.

I picked at the frayed hem of my shirt. He hooked a
knuckle under my chin and tipped it up. I expected anger
or annoyance, but only saw the Harper of old. The one I
used to hero-worship as a kid. The one who did what it
took to keep me safe. He let go of my chin and brushed
along my hairline, tucking strands behind my ear.

*Why is he so hot? Why does his touch feel like home? Why do I
still have this stupid crush? Gah, these feelings!* Everything was
clear as mud when it came to Harper.

Shoving my Harper-thoughts away, I shrugged. "She's
a great tracker."

"Mmhmm."

"You and Xavier are very buddy-buddy. Why does he keep dragging you around everywhere? He grooming you for something?" I waggled my eyebrows.

He gave me a subtle smile. "Not sure. It started after Ma died and Pops started to decline."

"Xavier always puts you in charge."

"He does."

"How do you feel about that?"

"Does it matter?"

A month ago, that retort would have been a slap, would have felt like a shut-down. But older, wiser Sam recognized it for what it was and didn't take offense. Harper would do as he was told if he believed it protected the people he cared about.

I placed a palm over his heart. "I wish I could go."

"Soon." He put his hand over mine and squeezed. "You'll be able to wreak havoc and fuck up demons very soon."

I chuckled, then met his gaze. Laugh lines framed his eyes.

"Mr. Tate, we're ready." Xavier's head popped around the front door then disappeared.

Harper lifted his chin to acknowledge him but didn't look away from me. "Be good."

"I'll try." I shrugged. "But you know me."

He took my head in his hands and leaned down. I froze. Butterflies took nosedives in my belly.

What is he doing? Harper pressed his lips to my forehead and then to the corner of my mouth. He was out the door before I remembered how to breathe. *What the hell just happened?* I touched two fingertips to where his lips had been so close to mine. The line between platonic Harper and daydream Harper blurred. He'd been millimeters from a full-on kiss. *What the hell do I do with that?*

I ended up in the common room where the Seers were playing games, reading books, and chatting amongst themselves. Did I think about Harper's actions for an hour after he'd been gone? Yes. Did I worry about the fires and how they tied to Dominic? Yes. Did I text Leigh every ten minutes to check in? Also yes.

I read her most recent reply: *Stop distracting me. I need to focus.*

"Fine," I huffed.

I wandered around the common room, trying not to overthink all the ways things could go wrong, when I noticed Andrew sitting in a leather chair next to a window. His face was gaunt and his eyes were haunted. He'd lost significant weight and looked fragile in that chair—looked like a shell of his former self.

My heart stumbled. I'd never seen him less than self-possessed and sure of himself. He'd been such a strong force of good and love in my life. He'd given me everything I needed to succeed. I loved him like my own flesh and blood. Any betrayal I felt from his mishandling of my Warrior training or his lies paled in comparison to all the good he'd done for me.

Tears burned my eyes. It was as if all his centuries had caught up with him all at once, leaving him a defeated and old. *I'm going to lose him.* My nostrils flared. I blew out a breath and went to him, dropping into the chair catty-corner to where he was seated.

A small smile lifted his lips. "Good morning, my best girl. How are you?"

"I should ask you that myself. Whatcha thinkin' over here by yourself?"

Andrew didn't answer me for a long while. Several

emotions passed over his face, and when he did answer, his tone was wistful.

"Time passes so swiftly, Sammy. I'm old and tired, but I swear I can reach out and touch memories from a hundred years ago." He leaned over and took my hand. His long fingers were bony and frail. "I'm dying, and I can't stop it. I don't know how long I have left."

Shit. The tears fell now.

"Oh, my child, do not fret." He smiled and squeezed my hand. "I'm not gone yet. I don't fear death. I'm not scared. Death is not the end of oneself, you know. I'll live on in you. In Leigh. In anyone who remembers me or reads my works."

I shook my head, not trusting myself to speak.

"You've made me so proud." For a moment, the spark of life lit his grey eyes, that mischievous glint of Irish charm shining through. "Even when you're reckless and wild, you're the best Warrior I've ever trained."

I swiped at my cheeks. "Damn. You got all the problem children then, huh?"

We both laughed. Rather, I choked around my emotions, and he chuckled deep in his chest.

"Come here." He stood and opened his arms. I walked right into them. The ridges of his spine against my palms while I clung to him, absorbing all the quiet strength and love he could give. He pulled back and kissed my temple, like he always did.

"What's on the books for you today?" I asked.

"Tabitha, DH, and I are going to the farmhouse. We need to clear out all documents, books, and journals I've collected over the years. The border I set will fall any day now, and we can't let that information fall into enemy hands."

"What? How's it gonna fall? You aren't gone yet."

"I can feel it, girl." He tapped his fingertips over his heart. "Any sanctuary I've built in my long life will fall once I'm gone. I dismantled most of them around the world so I could focus on maintaining the ones around the farmhouse and my church property. But now—" he smoothed the front of his shirt "—I have to stop funneling fixes to the holes in those veils."

I ran my nails over my scalp. "That's some heavy stuff there, Andrew."

"I know."

"I'd offer to help—"

He patted the side of my head in a fatherly gesture. "No, no, child. I imagine Xavier and Harper have you on lockdown."

"I'm *trying* to be good and follow orders." I lifted my shoulders and let them fall with dramatic flair. "Honestly, it's a struggle."

"Don't yield too much ground. You are still Samantha Fife. While I'm not encouraging mutiny," he raised a warning hand when I opened my mouth, "I'm saying remember who you are. Remember what makes you such a fantastic Warrior."

He gave me one more Andrew-hug and left me in the common room. I reclaimed my chair and leaned my head back, sunlight spilling over my face. I closed my eyes, reveling in the warmth as I mulled over Andrew's words.

I'd been about to ask Letty her thoughts on Andrew when my phone went off. Thinking it was Leigh finally calling with an update, I glanced at the caller ID. A shockwave rolled through my body. My breath hitched. My heart bottomed out. Any quiet contentment I'd garnered for myself washed away with one single name showing on the screen.

Camden Bennett was calling.

CAMDEN

"Y ou've got some nerve, Cam." Sam's voice zinged like a bolt of lightning.

Camden looked around his office in Sorcerie. His mind reeled. His body buzzed. He pulled in a ragged breath and raised a trembling hand. Dried blood—*blood!*—had crusted in his nail beds and cracked over his skin. It had turned a rusty brown. He rubbed the palm of that hand down his red splattered polo.

"Sam, oh God, I think I—" *Killed someone?* Dread roiled his stomach. He scanned the room, searching for any clues. "W-why wouldn't I call you?"

"You broke up with me, shithead, over the damn phone." She was seething.

"I—what?" He sat up straight. "When? Why?" He cleared his throat. It felt like sandpaper. "Listen, something is wrong. Very wrong. I don't remember anything." He ripped his fingers through his blond curls and winced. "I broke up with you? Why can't I remember?"

"This is bullshit," Sam muttered before heaving a sigh. "But I'll bite. What's the last thing you remember?"

He heard her disdain, her resentment, her pain. He must had been a real dick and the damage ran deep. She'd just extended an olive branch—a tiny one—and he could work with that. He racked his recent memory, but there was a huge black hole.

Camden licked his lips, his nerves tattered. "I *can't* remember."

"Unbelievable."

Gut punch.

"I'm missing time, Sam." Cam closed his eyes, clawing for calm. "A huge chunk of fucking time."

"Where are you?"

"At my restaurant." He waggled the mouse, waking up his computer, hoping it would give him a clue. "But I don't know how I got here."

"Maybe you should see a doctor? Why are you calling me, of all people?"

Shit. Sam had been the first person on his mind. He stared down at the blood on his hand and shirt. *Why* did *I call her?*

"Are you in trouble?" Sam asked. "Of the demonic persuasion?"

"Maybe? I don't know." He glanced around his office again, hoping an answer—any answer—would pop out.

An angry scoff filled his ear. Camden clenched his teeth. *Why can't I remember breaking up with her? Why did I do that? Why am I at my restaurant? And what's with the blood?*

"Can we talk?" His voice cracked.

"Isn't that what we're doing?" Her tone was icy.

"In person."

"No, I don't think that would be a good idea."

Cam closed his eyes and pinched the bridge of his nose. "Okay, fair enough."

There was a knock at his door, and before he could

invite the visitor in, Jackie O'Rourke, his sous chef, was halfway inside. Her blonde hair was tied back in a pony-tail. She wore her white chef's coat and black non-slip shoes. And she took one look at Camden, and her mouth pulled down in a tight frown. Her eyes narrowed with concern.

"What in the world are you doing here?" She crossed her arms.

"I have to go," Cam said to Sam. He hung up and let the phone clack onto the desktop. "I honestly don't know Jackie. Have I been acting *weird* lately?" He ran his hand through his hair again.

"Yeah, you've been a real cocky son of a bitch. Renard and I were going to give you some space and let you work out your shit, but if you didn't come around in the next couple weeks, we were going to intervene. You've been giving us Mother Bennett vibes."

"Shit." Camden ducked his head and rubbed the back of his neck. "I've been Aerona-level crazy?"

"More like the junior varsity team."

"Small mercies, then." Cam checked his watch. Dried blood darkened the groove around the face. "You're in early for your normal shift."

"Big seafood order coming in. The last time they delivered and I wasn't here, they left us with a couple bags of spoiled scallops."

"Ah." *Real eloquent there, Bennett.*

"Kiddo," Jackie said, hauling him back to the present. "I'm not going to comment on why you look like you've stepped out of a horror movie, but please get cleaned up before anyone else sees you." She gestured to the door with a nod. "If you hurry, I'll make you something for lunch."

He stood, nodded, and stepped around Jackie. Dizzi-ness washed over him. He swayed on his feet, his pulse pounding in his temples. Camden grabbed the door jamb. He fell into a black oblivion.

A wicked grin split Dominic's lips. He enjoyed letting his human toy out of lockdown just long enough to discover the damage he had done. It was interesting to him that the first person the boy had called had been Samantha.

"Cam? Are you aright?" Jackie said behind him. She placed a hand in between his shoulder blades.

Dominic whirled on the woman, drew his body to its full height, and grabbed her wrists. His grin morphed into a malicious smile. She struggled in his grasp, pulling away from him.

"C-Camden, w-what are you doing?" She trembled in his grip. "Let go, you're hurting me."

"You weren't supposed to be here." Dominic put both of her wrists in his right hand. With his left hand, he stroked the back of his index finger down her cheek. "You shouldn't have come so early."

Her eyes went hard as rock. She aimed a kick at him at his crotch. He blocked it with supernatural quickness. His hold on her wrists tightened until she yelped. He glared at her with malice.

"What am I going to do with you, Jacquelin Eloise O'Rouke?" Dominic crooned, his smile salacious. "I can't let you walk out of here, no matter how loyal you are to the Camden boy. You saw some incriminating evidence."

Jackie blanched white. "What are you—"

Dominic spun the sous chef around, pressing her back to his chest. He cradled her head in his arms, securing a rear headlock. He buried his nose in her hair and inhaled her fear, helplessness, and desperation, feasting on her frantic emotions.

"Little lamb," he lowered his voice to a whisper, "you shouldn't have snooped."

Dominic snapped her neck.

He dropped Jackie's body. It thumped on the floor, her head twisted the wrong way. He studied the corpse.

"Pity. You weren't in my plan. But you tasted delectable."

Dominic smoothed his shirt, straightened his belt, and righted his blood-caked watch. He headed to the bathroom and studied Camden in the mirror. There was gore everywhere on his person.

The preacher's life had been so easy to snuff out, but humans bled so damn easily.

In this body, Dominic's power was limited. However, the feeding he'd taken from the now chef gave him the juice to remedy this mess. With a snap of his fingers and a wave down the front of himself, the rust and red stains disappeared. His skin cleared, and his shirt became pristine white.

"Better," he told his reflection.

It really was a shame that he had to rid himself of the evidence of his kill, but he always preferred cleanliness. He rolled down his sleeves, plucked up his suit jacket from the back of a dining room chair, and slipped it on. A smirk touched his lips at the scent of smoke on the dark cloth.

Burning the sanctuary with the dying preacher inside had been a masterful escalation.

Why'd he do it?

Because he could. Because the preacher's fear fed his demonic hungers. Because it was certain to gain Samantha Fife's attention. Whistling a cheerful tune, Dominic buttoned his coat and meandered through the restaurant.

"This is really a gorgeous place," he said to the empty dining room. "The color scheme, with its blues and greens, makes me think of the ocean. And the furniture?" He gave the room a chef's kiss. "Exquisite. White. Upscale beach vibes, as the kids say. Charming, really. It would be a shame if something happened to it."

At the large, well-stocked bar, Dominic poured himself two fingers of Woodford Reserve and swirled the bourbon in a glass tumbler, humming Amazing Grace. The sunlight steaming through the skylights caught the liquid, and amber sparkles glittered on the bar top. Dominic sipped, savoring the deep smoky flavor.

He continued his methodical tour of the restaurant, passing through the waiting area at the front. He stopped and planted his hands on his hips when the empty floor-to-ceiling bird cage caught his attention. Camden's hyacinth macaws had *not* appreciated Dominic's presence. Animals, intuitive beasts, could sense a possessed human. They'd raised a robust ruckus whenever he came around, so Dominic had sent the birds to a sanctuary, claiming it was for only a short period while they were *renovating* the restaurant.

In the kitchen, while continuing to hum Amazing Grace, he turned on every burner and fired up the grill. Drawing on Power from his O'Rourke snack, he snapped his fingers, turned his palm upward, and flames danced in hand. He didn't need the additional heat and gas to burn the place to a crisp, but it would expedite the process and destroy *evidence*.

He smirked and threw balls of fire around the space.

"Cheers."

Dominic strode through the other rooms, igniting them. He welcomed the heat on his skin and the acrid scent of burning carpet and fine furniture. He could wield ice magic, courtesy of his Dark Warrior's twisted Powers, but fire was his favorite form of destruction. He exited the building through the main entrance.

"Now for the *pièce de résistance*." Several of his Greater Demon kin appeared, eager expressions on their faces. "You lot love a good, calamitous show, don't you?"

They rumbled their agreement.

"Excellent."

Dominic clapped his hands, rubbed them together, then pulled them apart. A fireball the size of a dinner plate ignited between his palms. He shot the flames into the foyer of the restaurant, pouring on the Power.

A rousing cheer rose from the six demons. They liked watching Dominic deploy his innate prowess, and he liked putting on a show. What he didn't expect when he launched that fireball was the sting of cold, bitter Winter to stir in his chest. A thin film of ice to crust over his hand. He waved his fingers, crumbing the ice.

His eyes blazed with knowing satisfaction.

"Ambrose," Dominic acknowledged the midnight-black hulk who appeared at his side.

"My liege?"

"Make sure this place is complete ash. Do not leave until then." Dominic had other plans than watching this inferno. In a lower tone filled with calm malice he said, "Do not fail me."

Ambrose, though he dwarfed his superior, bowed his head. "I won't, sir."

"That remains to be seen." Dominic looked up with a side-long glance at the monstrosity next to him. "Did you come from the Shaw property?"

"Yes, sir."

"Was there anyone there?" Dominic watched the fire engulf the building. He heard sirens wailing in the distance.

"A few. The elderly one arrived a few minutes ago."

"How'd he look?" Dominic asked.

"One foot in the grave, sir."

"Was anyone with him?"

"Tabitha Holland and that daughter of Xavier Gerena's. Delaney, I think?"

Dominic pursed his lips. "Did you test the border?"

"I did." Ambrose met Dominic's eyes. "It's crumbling like dry clay."

Dominic inhaled, a rush of exhilaration washing over him. "Watch the fire. Be ready when you're summoned. Don't fumble this one, Ambrose."

"You have my word."

Dominic turned on a loafered toe and sauntered away from the inferno, his footsteps crunching on seashell gravel, the roaring fire music to his ears. Killing the chef and destroying the building hadn't been in his plan, he'd only meant to torture the Camden-boy by letting him come out to play. The destruction of life and property had been icing on the cake. He felt *good.*

Time for his next move. He drew his cell phone and hit the speed dial for Aerona Bennett. She answered on the first ring.

"You should call your insurance company." Dominic's voice poured like warm honey. "There's been an *accident* at Sorcerie."

"What happened?"

She sounds amused, at least. Dominic's shoulders shrugged as if she could see him. "It'll be on the news soon."

"Dominic, do not play coy with me." He imagined her arched white eyebrow.

"Settle your feathers, wee duck. We have other things to discuss. I felt the pulse of your icy Power a moment ago. Is it back, my Dark One?"

"Mmmm," she purred. "I see it sparkling, ready for use. That insufferable brat broke my magic when she expelled me from her mind, but my Power has returned."

"Fantastic." Dominic slipped into the driver's side of Camden's green Audi. "You may want to answer the calls you'll be receiving. The police get so prickly when important buildings burn to the ground. They'll be in a tizzy when they discover the corpse of your recently deceased sous chef in the ruins. She may have been murdered."

"Dominic! I thought you intended to be discrete while inhabiting the body of my son."

"All work and no play makes for a miserable existence, my sweet." Dominic slid on Camden's aviator sunglasses.

"This'll be a nightmare to deal with, you conniving demon." Her words sounded harsh, but there was a hint of admiration there as well. "What were you thinking?"

"It will be advantageous for us, my sweet." Dominic adjusted the rearview mirror before starting the car. He pulled out of the lot. "I'll meet you at your beach abode. We have wickedness and villainy to carry out."

SAM

My pacing was going to wear out the expensive rug covering the gleaming hardwood. After Cam had hung up, I'd stormed up to my assigned room—since Healer Emily had booted me from my common room last week—and had sat on my massive bed while my overactive imagination took over. But now, I couldn't sit still.

Why did Cam call me? What the hell is he thinking?

Pace. Pace. Pace.

He'd acted like he remembered nothing.

How do you forget breaking up with your girlfriend? And that jackwagon had hung up on me. Phone in one hand, I fiddled with the small stud in my earlobe with the other. Frustration warred with empathy. He might be on my shitlist, but he'd also sounded so confused. So lost.

Another pass.

I chewed on a thumbnail. He'd sounded so panicked—terrified, even.

Of what? Well, he'd hung up before he could tell me anything, didn't he? Granted, I hadn't given him the chance to explain. No, I'd been a jaded twit. Though he'd torched our relationship, concern for him didn't go away. He shouldn't suffer if he was scared.

What are you worried about, Cam?

Should I call him back? Would he even answer? "To call or not to call? That is the question."

I tapped the cell phone against my thigh. If Camden were in danger—real, actual, lose-his-life-danger—I needed to be the bigger person. After all, I'd turned over a new leaf in the maturity department.

I lifted my phone. Facial recognition unlocked it, and the background photo of Max's chestnut face stared back at me. I rubbed my lips together.

"Put your brave pants on, Fife."

While gathering my wits, Cam's caller ID popped up. I started, and my body flushed hot then cold.

Speaking of the devil. I swept my thumb across the glass to answer.

"Camden." I closed my eyes. "Two phone calls in one day. I'm gonna get the wrong impression and think you still have feelings for me."

"Sam," his voice rasped.

"I don't give second chances, Camden."

Unless your name is Harper. The feel his lips pressing against the side of my mouth in an almost-kiss flashed through me. My eyes popped open. *Holy Heaven.*

"Just listen," Camden ground out. "I swear God, I don't remember ending things with us. I don't remember a goddamn thing. I think—oh, fuck—this is gonna sound absolutely batshit nuts, but I think I'm cursed or hexed or something."

Anxiety's grip—a constant nag these days—tightened around my lungs.

"When I called you earlier," Cam continued. "I was at my restaurant. Jackie showed up, and she was going to make me something to eat. I walked to the door, and now?" A keening, terrified sob escaped him. "Sam, I'm at my beach house! I have no fucking clue how I got here."

My heartbeat thudded in my ears. My hand trembled.

I'm cursed or hexed or something, he'd said.

I stared without seeing at the armoire.

"I don't even know how the hell I got in my office to begin with," Camden said, undeterred by my silence. "My hands were covered in blood! Did I hurt someone? Oh, God. Oh, God. Oh, God. What if—what if I did? What did I do?"

"Covered in blood." I blinked. Every gut instinct I ever had paled in comparison to the neon warning that flashed in my brain.

"Yes!" His anguished wail sizzled through the airwaves.

My belly swooped.

"And just now, before I called you, I could have sworn I felt like I wasn't *alone.* Like, on the inside."

I'm cursed or hexed or something.

My teeth clenched. *"Letty, could he be—? I thought you told me it's hard to—is Camden possessed?"*

"Evidence suggests so, but we can't know unless you see him in person."

"I thought you told me that possession is nearly impossible?"

"I believe the key word was 'nearly'. It is possible. It has been done and will be done again. But—blessed be—that boy would have had to have ingested quite a bit of the same demon's blood most of his life. It takes time to prepare a human vessel to contain that much uninvited demonic chaos."

I pressed my knuckles to my mouth, struggling to steady my breathing and calm my racing heart. Camden had grown up with his grandfather. Had Archie Bennett been up to nefarious things—like preparing his grandson to house a demon? That didn't track with me because Cam always spoke fondly of the man. But Cam had lived with his mother as a toddler, before she'd gone AWOL.

What if Aerona …

"Sam? Are you there?" Camden asked, urgent and low.

"Yes." His question jerked me from my thoughts. "Give a girl a minute. You just hit me with some seriously heavy stuff."

A shaky exhale was his answer.

"Letty, give me a crash course in demonic possession."

"Depending on the amount of blood exchanged, the strength and class of the demon, and how susceptible the target human is, a possession can overtake someone so completely that the human does not sense it. The demon can make the human go dormant."

All the supernatural alarm bells went off in my head.

Since the moment I'd awakened from my coma, Camden had been acting strangely. He wore clothes that I'd never seen him in. He had smelled different, had moved different, and had spoken in a different cadence.

He'd called me *babe*.

All the dots were there, and I was only now drawing the lines.

Camden Bennett, my Cam, would never have broken up with me over the phone. Hell, I was confident enough in reading people to bet that the man had no intentions of leaving me. But if he were possessed—

Dominic.

That crimson, manipulative, hat-wearing, smooth-talking bastard. He'd already proven that he'd screw with Camden to get at me. I'd *kissed* Cam while he was possessed by Dominic.

I pulled in a deep, soul-soothing breath to keep from panicking.

The arsons, the winky-face appearing at every crime scene, and the peculiar burn patterns were all Dominic's calling cards. This had to be how he was got past the inherent divine protection of these sacred places.

What if wearing a human-suit muted Dominic's demonic attributes? What if it provided cover for him so he could enter any church, mosque, synagogue, or temple? Or perhaps it allowed him to waltz through the weakened borders maintained by a dying Adviser.

Tears spilled down my cheeks.

Dominic wasn't doing these injustices with just *any* body. No. He'd chosen a very specific human. One I'd happened to care about. My chest ached and my neck hairs prickled.

Camden had broken up with me after we'd moved to Xavier's place. And of the three Advisers, Xavier was now the biggest, baddest, and strongest of the trio, so his wards were probably impenetrable to a possessed human. Dominic was playing chess with our lives.

"Motherfucker," I hissed.

"What?" Cam gasped.

"You're at home?"

"Yes."

"Letty, will my wound be a problem? If I get in a supernatural fight, is my body fit for battle?"

"What are you planning, Brave One?"

"Just check, please."

A warm sensation, like a trickle of water, started at my head, pooled in my left ribs, and ebbed out through my toes.

"I don't detect anything that will hinder you."

I pressed my lips together and squeezed my eyes shut,

trying to stave off more hot tears. Cam was a kind, respectful, innocent man who'd gotten caught in the crossfire between Heaven and Hell.

Why? And where the fire fart does the Mage fit into this?

"Cam, stay put." My nerves were trip-wire tight. "Fight, Cam. Fight like hell to keep control of yourself."

"You believe me," he said, relief rushing through the line.

"Yes, I do." I cleared my throat. "Send me your address and a picture of your house. I'm coming for you."

I hung up. Max could get anywhere quickly while in Guardian mode and with a solid destination in mind.

"Brave one, I don't know your thoughts, but I can sense your motives, and I must protest this," Letty said.

"I'm a Warrior of Light. Humans come first, right?"

"That is true, but you shouldn't go without your Warrior Partner. We don't know what will happen. If he is possessed, you can't cure him, and you can't kill him."

That internal wire stretched tighter. Xavier, Harper, and Leigh were out trying to gain access to the crime scene. Andrew, Tabitha, and DH were at the farm house. Leilani and Jax were making their rounds in Shield Haven. Where Sajid and Tally were was anyone's guess. But Camden was in danger.

"There's no time."

The gravity of what I was about to do washed over me, and it felt like something took my brain from my body, like I was looking down at myself. I stumbled over to the closet and rested my forehead against the cool wood, trying to breathe through whatever was happening.

Heat shot through my body but my fingers felt like ice. Nausea bubbled in my gut. That bitch called Anxiety wrapped its way around my confidence like a boa constrictor and squeezed. With my eyes pinched shut, I let the feelings of inadequacy wash over me, breathed my way through the swirling chaos, and came out feeling shaky.

Shaky, but grounded.

I dressed myself in jeans and a tank top, shoved my feet into boots, redid my messy bun, and then ninja-ed my way through the castle, cell phone in hand. Xavier had surveillance cameras up, but I'd be off property before anyone could stop me. Guilt tugged at my heartstrings. Harper and Leigh would come back to a Sam-less mansion. I didn't have time to weigh the pros and cons of this. From what Camden told me, Dominic could take over at any time, and then where would he go?

"Shut it down, Fife. Camden needs Warrior Sam."

My phone dinged. It was a message from Camden with an address and picture of his house. I typed out a thank you to him, and while I was at it, shot Leigh a text letting her know where I was going. Was this classic Samantha Fife? Absolutely. And I'd probably get in trouble. But a human's life was at stake. Wasn't that why I was anointed? To protect humanity? I slipped out the front door, thankfully not running into anyone.

"Max." I prodded the Thoroughbred in his mental space in my mind. *"I need my Guardian. Be ready to—"*

Before I finished the thought, Max, in full Guardian armor with glowing hooves, stood before me. *"I am always prepared, Warrior mine."*

I placed a hand on the white armor plate protecting his forehead. I never questioned how Guardians moved like they did, never mulled over how they got from point A to point B, and I wasn't going to start today. I swung up onto his back, mentally showed him the path to take, and we were off, slipping through time and space.

What will I find when I get there? Will Camden be himself or will it be Dominic? If that Crimson Creep is in control, how do I handle that? I can't kill Camen. How the hell do I de-possess some-one? God, please just let it be Cam.

Questions flitted through my mind as my anxiousness and worry ramped up. Mere moments had passed when Max stopped in front of a massive beach house made of white stone featuring huge window panes without curtains. The paved, curved driveway, attached garage, and mani-cured front garden reeked of excess. This was Aerona Bennet's mansion, and Camden lived in it.

"Here goes nothing." I slipped off Max and kissed his large cheek "Don't know what I'm going to find in here, bud, so stay on guard."

"Be safe. Be swift. There is an odd feeling in this place." Max blew a soft, warm breath on my neck.

He walked away and his image melted into a dense crop of palms and palmettos. Only the gleam of his eyes told me where he was in the foliage's shadows. Whatever inhabited a Guardian animal, it gave them some serious camouflage abilities.

I turned back to the mansion and let out a slow breath while calling on my anointing. Heat from the activated Power spread from my heart outward. There was no pain, not even a tingling from where Enyo had stabbed me. I wasn't in full Warrior mode, but the lack of agony was encouraging. I steeled myself for whoever—Dominic or Camden—waited for me inside this house.

"Alright, Letty," I said under my breath. "Let's do this."

I did a quick supernatural scan for immediate danger. Finding none, I trotted up the front steps. *What will I find on the other side of this fancy contemporary door?* The fluttering in my chest returned as my soul felt like it left my body— lurking at the edges. *If something happens, will I be able to defend myself?* My stomach knotted. Another hot-to-cold flash shocked my system. My heart climbed my throat. I clenched my teeth against the rising tide of anxiety and nausea.

These episodes, man. I was not a fan. This time, Letty's soothing warmth wove its way through my rocky feelings.

Once I could breathe normally again, I raised a finger and pressed the doorbell, which echoed through the house. Holy Heaven. I hadn't seen Camden since he'd broken up with me. Seeing him again, with him missing time and possibly possessed, I didn't know what to expect. I squared my shoulders and huffed a breath for courage.

Camden opened the front door.

His sage button-down was rolled up at the sleeves and untucked from his khaki pants. The sandy beard dusting his jaw and weariness in his bloodshot green-gold eyes suggested it had been a long day for him. He ran his hand through his blond curls, disheveling them even further. His face appeared gaunt, and his fit, surfer frame seemed leaner. But he stood on his stoop, looking so handsome but, oh, so haunted.

"You actually came." Cam's eyes widened and then his body sagged in apparent relief.

My heart—my poor heart—tripped over itself as I remembered how he'd broken up with me by phone. He'd ended it like I hadn't mattered to him as much as he did to me. Never mind, that it most likely Dominic's devious scheme. And while it might not have been Cam's words, it had been his voice to do the deed. However, I pushed past those feelings because this wasn't about me right now.

"Oh, Cam," I said. "What happened to you?"

"I don't know, but you're a sight for sore eyes." He stepped back into the house and pushed the door wider. "Come in."

"Be careful," Letty warned. *"If he's possessed, the demon inside will hear everything you say. Don't give anything away."*

The demon. I knew damn well which demon inhabited Camden. The man before me held himself like Cam. Gone was the swagger and posture from the last time I'd seen him. While Dominic lurked beneath his skin, in that moment, I knew in my gut I was interacting with the man, not the demon.

Crossing the threshold felt a lot like entering a gladiator arena, even though it was a contemporary modern designer's holy grail of open concept living space. The kitchen, seating area, and dining room all flowed together. The white tile floor and red accent colors gave the home a cold, aloof feel. A ripple of unease ran up my spine.

"Do you want a drink? Beer? Wine? Something stronger?" Camden asked as he stepped up to a service bar and poured himself a finger's worth of amber liquor. His hands trembled as he tossed the alcohol back in a single gulp. "I don't know how much time I have before—"

He shook his head and shivered.

"Before you're not you anymore?" A sad smile touched my lips.

I crossed the room, set down his glass for him, then grabbed his arm and pulled him over to the couch in the center of the room. He didn't resist. We settled near each other while he leaned forward, elbows pressed to his knees, and buried his face in hands. My feelings warred inside me. I wanted to touch him and offer some sort of comfort, but my gut might as well have been flashing me a huge caution flag.

"What can I do if he goes all possessed on me?" I asked Letty.

It occurred to me that I was asking her this a little late. She'd already told me I couldn't save him.

"The demon's strength will be muted, but the boy will be stronger than normal. You may be able to fight him off. The best course of action is to speak to the humanity, not the supernatural."

"Right. Easy peasy."

At Camden's anguished groan, my heart cracked in a million pieces. "Cam, tell me what's going on. Start at the beginning."

And tell me he did.

He told me about waking up in a hotel room he hadn't booked, getting his Audi from a valet when he hadn't remembered driving the car, and dressing in clothes he'd never wear. He had no recollection of when I'd woken up from my coma, only that he'd been trying to make it back to my side at the farm house. The last thing he remembered before this morning was driving on I-75.

This morning. A life time ago.

"Sam, I had *blood* on my hands." Camden raked his fingers down his chest, as if he could claw out his heart. "Then things went black again, and I found myself at home."

Well, damn.

I gingerly patted the back of his back shoulder. "When you called me from your office, you hung up because someone came into the room. Maybe they can help shed light on what happened?"

"Jackie!" Cam sprang to his feet, strode across the room, and picked up his cell.

He tapped the screen and pressed his phone to his ear while picking up a determined pace. I could hear the faint ringing roll over into a voice message. Hope slipped from his face. He pulled the cell from his head to look at it. He called again. His brows furrowed.

"Maybe she's busy?" Cam checked his watch. "They should be prepping for tonight."

"Possibly." And maybe it wasn't the right time to have asked, but I had to know. "Do you really not remember breaking up with me?"

"No." Camden deflated and plunked his phone on the counter behind him. He crossed the room to kneel in front of me. He met my eyes. And in that moment I knew …

This was *my* Camden. My heart triple-timed.

"You're the only bright spot in my life." He brushed the backs of his knuckles down the column of my neck.

I stiffened.

He jerked his arm back, grief etched on his face. "You're like light in the darkness. I adore you, and your snark, and your bravery. I had no plans to leave you. And I would *never* have done it by phone." His voice caught in his throat. "I was in knots while you were in your coma. I'm devastated I wasn't there when you woke up."

Tears—freaking tears—spilled over. My brain believed him but my heart resisted. He'd hurt me. Harper kissed me. My feelings were still a big ball of tangled yarn. But Camden was scared, possessed, and in need of compassion. I reached up and brushed his temple with my fingers. When he leaned into my touch, and before I could stop myself, I slipped those fingers into his curls.

"You're really not alone in here are you?"

"No." He leaned into my touch. "And I'm fucking terrified. How does this happen?"

His eyes met mine once more, searching for answers, when I saw it—the shift of shadows in their green depths.

"Is that the demon?" I asked my resident angel.

"I'm afraid so."

Holy Heaven. I covered my mouth with a hand. More damn tears fell. *"Is Cam fighting, then? Or is Dominic toying with him? Do you know?"*

"I wish I knew, Brave One." Letty sounded somber.

Camden gently gripped my wrist, a sad half-smile tipping his mouth. "That bad, huh? Tell me how this happens, Sam. I need to know."

"From what I understand," I pulled out of his grasp, "you had to have ingested demon blood for a long time, like, long before we ever met. And not from some random demons. It had to come from one source." I tapped his chest. "The one—the one inside you. But that demon has also been partaking of your own blood. A bit vampiric, if you ask me, but over time, you become a habitable host. They can gain entry as easy as inhaling."

Camden paled. His Adam's apple bobbed. He didn't deserve this.

"I don't know all the specifics of the how, Cam, but I swear on all that's holy, I will do what I can to purge you of what's inside."

The shadows shifted again, and the outer rings of his irises glinted red.

I leapt to my feet, scrambled, and called on my Power. *Get away! Run!* ricocheted in my head. Pure instinct had me hurdling over the back of the couch. With my heart slamming against my ribs, I pressed a hand to my sternum and spun back in his direction.

"Shit, Sam, what happened?" He'd half-stood in my retreat and was patting down at his chest. When he looked up, he was utterly confused. "Am I changing or something?"

I pointed to my eyes. "Red. Shadows. Shifting."

I would defend myself if Dominic was ready to take back complete control and come at me. But whatever I did to protect myself would hurt Cam. The tears returned. Camden gaped at me and backed up, not looking as he went, and he clipped a hip on the kitchen island. While trying to keep his balance, he windmilled his arms and back handed a large vase filled with flowers.

He couldn't catch the glass vessel and it toppled over,

crashing and shattering on the tile. Glass, flowers, and water went everywhere.

"Shit!" Camden swore.

He pulled a hidden trash can from inside a cabinet and started tossing large shards of glass and flowers into the bin. I ran over, grabbed the dish towel hanging on the stove and tossed it to him. Snatching up a paper towels, I joined him.

After a silent moment of clean up, Cam rocked back on his heels. "What do I do?"

I chewed my lip, shook my head, and tossed a mangled flower into the trash. He came to me and tipped up my chin with gentle fingers. I didn't want to meet his eyes— didn't want to see evidence that he was possessed. My stomach roiled.

"I'm sorry," I whispered. "I'm so sorry that this happened to you. You're a good guy."

"Sam, you're not blame. This was going to happen one way or another." Cam lifted his arms and hands an exasperated shrug. "I'm the one who's apparently been drinking demon blood."

I gave him a sad smile. He was right. But the facts didn't make me feel better. Cam was just a man, trying to be a good son—a good man. I couldn't look at him anymore, so I twisted out of his grip and continued sopping up flower water.

I really needed to get out of here.

How?

If I made a run for the door, it could trigger Dominic to take over. *Am I even fit enough to fight?* Letty had told me I was physically healed. But what about mentally? Camden was an innocent, but he was dangerous. Holy, holy Heaven. What had I gotten myself into? I checked the tears that threatened to escape. *Idiot.*

"Don't shut me out." Cam's voice broke through my torment. "I'm hanging on by a thread here."

I blinked to clear my eyes and cleared my throat. Forcing a calm that I didn't feel, I smiled at Camden. "Let's finish cleaning this up. Careful of the glass shards. They're sharp."

HARPER

"Oh no," Kestler muttered. She stood beside me in the shade, at the edge of the active investigation inside Bethal Baptist Church. The sanctuary smelled of charred wood, melted plastic, and burnt flesh.

Xavier had indeed pulled all the strings he could to get our asses in here. Some bullshit about being a consultant. I don't know how he got Kestler and me clearance, but he did. He was currently conversing with an investigator over the charred, unrecognizable body of the deceased. My stomach roiled at the scent.

However, it was Kestler's dismayed tone that captured my full attention.

"What?"

"I really don't want to tell you." She kept her eyes on her phone.

That lifted the hairs on my neck. "Spit it the fuck out, Kestler."

She didn't say a word. Just handed over her cell.

Sam: *Cam's in trouble. I'm doing a welfare*

check at his home. Taking Max. Address: 1389 Gulfway in St. Pete.

"Fuck!" *She left the manor.* "Fucking, fuck!"

My chest hollowed out. A kaleidoscope of emotion took me from rage to disbelief and right into betrayal. This was another broken promise from her. How could she? Why would she? My knuckles turned white from where I gripped Kestler's phone. *Because she's Samantha Fife, and we left her un-fucking-attended.* I punched speed dial for Sam. It rang and rang.

"Sam, answer your fucking phone," I growled into her voicemail, then hung up. I dialed again. No answer. I pounded out a text message: **Why did you leave the goddamn property?**

I drummed my fingertips against my thigh. My molars ground together. CSI techs and cops scurried about like ants. The press were cordoned off so they wouldn't snoop where they didn't belong. I stared at the cops speaking with Xavier.

"I'll take that before you crush it." Kestler pulled her phone from my grasp. I reached in my pocket and found my keys. I headed for the exit.

"I'm going to get her."

"What?" Kestler's face was etched with worry. "Wait! Harper! Do you want back up? She might need back up of the Warriorly persuasion."

Fuck. My jaw flexed as I bit down. She wasn't wrong but ... "Xavier needs you here."

"Then see if Jax—" Kestler's hand settled on my shoulder.

"No."

My feet were already headed to the black Tahoe in front of the church. Kestler grabbed the back of my shirt. I twisted around, ripping away from her, and she drilled me with a hard glare. A snarl rumbled up from my chest. She let out an unimpressed huff. I took a breath. Then another. I grabbed the back of my neck and squeezed.

"I don't have time to waste calling in the goddamn calvary, and Jax's on patrol."

"Fine. Take Thad. He'll get you there faster than a car."

My eyes widened. "He's your Guard—"

"Don't argue, just do. Let me help."

I rubbed the scruff on my jaw. Using a Warrior's Guardian felt like a violation. Hannah, the old black mare, was one thing because she was Warriorless, but Thad was an active protector of Kestler. However, Sam was in danger, and that made things crystal fucking clear to me.

"Call him."

Within seconds, her dapple-grey gelding appeared from under a crop of dense trees near the church, specter-like with a smoky outline. His hazy form solidified as he walked over to us. In Guardian form, only those with Sight would notice a random horse. Kestler pressed her palm to Thad's forehead.

"You're sure about this?" I asked.

"Go get our girl, Harper."

Enough said. I moved to Thad's side, pausing long enough to grip Kestler's shoulder and give it a *thank you* squeeze, then vaulted onto the horse's back. I peered down at Kestler.

"Be careful." She bumped my thigh with her first then walked to the front of her horse. With his head in her hands, she whispered to him. "Go to Max. Bring Sam home."

I nodded at Kestler when she released Thad and muttered to the Andalusian beneath me, "Let's go, kid."

When I arrived at the Bennett mansion, I dismounted

and scanned my surroundings. Sam had told Kestler she'd ridden Max here, so he had to be here somewhere. The wise old horse had likely camouflaged himself. He wouldn't be easy to find.

"Max," I whispered, treading quietly over the crushed shell pathway. "Where are you at, man?"

From within the shadows of a crop of trees, his chestnut hide shimmered into view before blending back in the black. He wasn't raising hell, so I took that as a good omen that Sam wasn't in dire straits. The woman was going to give me an ulcer. *What the actual fuck were you thinking, Sam?*

"Wait with Max," I said to Thad and watched him join his barn mate.

Keeping my senses sharp and body poised for action, I passively scanned my surroundings while heading up to the front door. With every step, the inner caveman urged me to bust in and demand Sam come with me—to demand answers. Instead, I knocked like a fucking civilized human being. As I did, I heard Sam's panicked voice.

"Oh God, there's so much blood."

That inner caveman turned into a beast. I tried the knob. *Locked.* In a smooth move, I drew my Glock from the concealed holster at the small of my back and smashed the butt against the frosted glass. I snaked my arm through the hole and turned the deadbolt latch. The door cracked open as I shoved my way in. Sam and Bennett's heads snapped in my direction. Bennett winced, looking tormented and haunted. Sam froze, her mouth agape.

I couldn't get my heart to stop hammering, my breath to steady. I briefly closed my eyes and pinched the bridge of my nose. When I reopened my eyes, I saw Sam had a kitchen towel wrapped around Bennett's hand. Blood droplets dotted the white tile at their feet. That helpless floundering in my heart hardened and settled on anger.

"Samantha, what the actual fuck?"

She didn't move her body, but her eyes shifted back and forth between Bennett and me.

"I needed to talk to Cam."

"You're phone works just fine," I snapped. "You texted Kestler with it. What on God's green earth possessed you to come in person? What if—" I shook my head. "This was fucking stupid and so fucking dangerous."

Her gaze flicked to the shithead next to her.

"I hope you said everything you needed, because we're leaving." I could hardly keep my rage in check.

"Let me explain," Sam said in a rush.

Jesus H. Christ. This woman. I cocked my head and raised a brow. Rage was easier for me to grab onto than my sheer terror that something could have happened to her. Her leaving without back up had scared the shit out of me. Her broken promise made my heart twinge.

I glared at her. *How could you, Sammy?*

She flinched. Part of me wanted to back off. Fuck, my intention wasn't to intimidate. I just wanted to get her back to safety. We had no way of knowing what lingering effects her poisoning, her stabbing, or her coma could still have. I'd cleared her to start rehab, not to fucking swoop in like a goddamn hero.

"He's scared, with good reason." She removed the towel wrapped around Bennett's hand and inspected his palm. She glanced up at his face before looking back at me. "If you woke up one day and couldn't remember anything about where you were or why you were dressed a certain way and found dried blood on your hands, wouldn't you call someone you trusted? Someone who might know about what's happening. I took a chance to help a friend."

"A friend." My throat burned. My skin crawled. This cocksucker didn't deserve her compassion or empathy. I stalked towards them. "Does a friend make you cry? Break your heart? Treat you like trash that can be taken out without a second thought?"

"Harper, stop being a prick," she snapped. "He's possessed."

Blood roared in my ears. "The fuck are you talking about?"

"He's missing time and memory because a demon took over his body!" She turned towards me while Bennett slunk backwards with his head bowed sheepishly. Sam's indignation burned bright in her eyes as took a bold step in my direction. "You'd leave him to suffer that alone?"

Shit. That fear-rage combo had me moving again. I invaded her space, my chest bumping up against her shoulder, as I turned her and gently tipped her chin up so she had nowhere to look but at me. *Easy, Tate, don't bite her head off.* That would be the quickest way to get her to shut down.

"You thought that—what? That you'd be able to preform an exorcism?" I waited, but she said nothing as resignation dawned on her face. I shook by the shoulders. "Help me out here, Sammy. I'm trying to understand without losing my fucking shit."

Those stormy blue eyes of hers swirled with emotion as she whispered to me, "He sounded so scared. I had to do something."

In my peripheral vision, Bennett stepped closer. "Harper, I asked her to—"

"You, shut the fuck up." I took a step towards him, but Sam gripped my shirt. I stopped, glancing down at her. The tight shake of her head kept me in place, so I pointed at him, directing the force of my fury through that finger.

"If you were so scared, you should have called Xavier. You have his number."

Bennett's chin tipped up in defiance. "Perhaps—"

"What were *you* thinking, Bennett?" I growled. "That Sam could help you? For all you knew, she could have still been injured. Instead, you risked her life. Every second Sam spent with you today has endangered her. Did you think of that?"

Bennett jerked. "I—well, damn."

"Yeah, that's what I thought."

I felt my shirt pull taunt as Sam's grip tighten.

"Sorry, man." He shook head, sounding genuine. "I freaked. Wasn't thinking anything through."

"That much is evident."

"Harper," Sam whispered.

I laid a palm over her hand, hauled in a breath, and worked to settle the enraged beast inside before I could meet her eyes. "We're leaving."

"What about Cam?" She worried her bottom lip between her teeth.

Damn it. I gently removed my shirt from her grip, but held onto her hand.

"I'll have Xavier call him." To Bennet I snapped, "I don't give a shit what happens to you, but this possession is a bigger issue, and you've now become *our* problem. Lock yourself up and throw away the key. Xavier will help you."

With that, I headed out the front door, compliant Sam in tow, as my anger boiled. Dark thoughts swirled. I pulled her over to the horses, and then fired off a text to Kestler to let her know we were headed back to Xavier's manor. Luckily in one piece. We mounted without saying a word.

Sam broke the silence before we moved out. "Harper, I know you're furious, but I—"

I lifted a rigid hand and glared. *Not fucking now.*

Her cheeks scrunched. "Right." She stroked Max's neck. "Take us to Casa de Xavier, buddy."

On the ride home, I spent every minute mentally cussing out Bennet for being an idiot, berating Sam for being reckless, and talking myself off the motherfucking ledge. My grip on Thad's reins tightened. My jaw ached from clenching my teeth. It had taken all my effort to stay silent and not say something I'd regret. I'd fucking *trusted* Sam to stay put. My mistake. One I wouldn't make again.

When we hit the one-lane delivery road leading to Xavier's barn, Max and Thad slowed to a comfortable jog, the sound of their shoes echoing on the pavement. Thad wagged his head back and forth when I didn't loosen my reins. I scrubbed a hand down my face and felt Sam's gaze on me, but she didn't say anything.

So goddamn reckless.

As we dismounted outside the barn, Xavier's stable manager stepped out of the covered side entrance. His hands were stuffed in his pockets. "Leigh called. Told me what's up. I'll take care of the boys for you."

Still not trusting myself to say anything, I slid off Thad and muttered to him, "Thank you, kid."

Thad dropped his Guardian connection. The stable manager slipped a leather halter over the grey horse's ears and reached under his jaw to snap the brass throat latch. Sam handed over Max's reins and took a step towards the mansion.

I grabbed her arm. "Barn office. Now."

"Don't tell me what to do." Sam wrenched away from me, and her eyes flashed with lightning.

I shook my head once. "Don't fucking push me."

Her nostrils flared. And just when I thought she'd dig in her heels and fight me, she huffed and stormed towards the barn door. I strode after her, following her into the office. She sat her ass on the desk with her arms crossed her arms, worrying the inside corner of her mouth. I slammed the door shut. She flinched.

"Do you realize how stupid—" I hissed a breath through my teeth. "I'm so fucking furious with you, Sam. Why did you leave? How can I trust you?"

"Don't scold me like I'm a child." She hopped up. "I have a father. And an Adviser. Of which you are neither. Now can we speak to each other like—"

"You know what, Sam, fuck you. I saw Enyo stab you." She flinched again, but I was on a fucking roll, anger fueling my every breath. "I kept you from bleeding out. I stitched you back together every time that demon's poison dissolved the threads while you were in that coma. I stabilized you every time you seized." I slapped my chest. "Me. Because I care so goddamn much about you that I can't fucking lose you!"

All the fight drained out of Sam. Her features softened. She stepped towards me. My body tensed. Bile climbed my throat. I buried my face in my shaking hands, then raked them through my hair. Words hemorrhaged out of me.

"Jesus, I *thought* you'd stopped fighting me. I thought I could trust you. I thought we had moved past this kind of bullshit. I was wrong. You're just as impulsive and selfish—"

Sam's palm covered my mouth. She stepped so close I had to grab her shoulders to steady us. She took her hand away, stood on her tip toes, and pressed her lips to mine. Electricity crackled in my chest. *Oh, fuck.* She broke the kiss and rocked back on her heels. Her eyes met mine, and they held a humility she so rarely showed.

"I'm sorry I betrayed your trust." She placed a hand on my chest, over my heart. "I'm very sorry I scared you." Her blue-grey eyes brimmed with tears. "Harper, what *you* think of me matters. Your disappointment in me is—well, I hate it. But I gotta own up to my stupid, stupid choices. How do I fix this? Fix us?"

I rubbed my thumb over my lower lip. Her warmth. Her words. Her sincerity. *Fuck me.* They consumed all my fear, rage, and better judgment. *She cares. She gets it.*

"And I'm sorry that—"

"Shut up." I grabbed her by the ass and hauled her back against my body. Her arms wrapped around my waist. Her nails dug into my skin through my shirt. Her eyes flared, pupils dilating. She meant so damn much to me in every stage of our lives, and having her almost die? That changed everything. "You drive me bugfucking nuts."

But I need you anyway.

I slid my hands up her back to bury them in her hair. I tilted my head, brought my mouth to hers, and kissed the shit out of her. On her surprised gasp, I plunged my tongue into her mouth. She melted against me, a small sigh escaping her, like I was her safe haven, so I deepened the kiss.

I'd been so goddamn careful not to take this step with her. Somewhere along the way, my desire for her had bloomed and hovered at the fringes of my mind. But I'd held back. I'd refused to acknowledge those feelings.

But, as usual, whatever line I drew, Sam danced right over it.

And my restraint was fucking shot.

21

SAM

Harper kissed like a desperate man with nothing to lose. It was heat and tongues and teeth. It wasn't gentle. It wasn't rough. I was freaking Goldilocks who'd found the perfect porridge, perfect seat, and perfect bed.

Harper spun us without breaking the kiss. He walked forward a couple steps, pushed me back against the office wall, and then slid his solid thigh between my legs. *Oh, God.* I shuddered when his calloused hands slipped from my hair, stroked the column of my neck, brushed along my shoulders, and coasted down to rest on my hips. His grip tightened.

Holy shit.

Fourteen-year-old Sam had died and went to Valhalla, Elysium, and Heaven. Twenty-year-old Sam wanted Harper's hands every-damn-where. Maybe I'd read one too many sports romance novels during my month of rehab, but really it was the Harper-effect. My massive crush had never gone away—it only went dormant.

His rough palm slipped under the hem of my shirt and pressed in the middle of my back, drawing me closer.

Harper broke our kiss and gazed down at me. His sapphire irises burned so dark that his eyes blazed black, scorching my soul.

Don't stop.

Harper's possessive growl rumbled deep in his chest. He lowered his face towards my neck, and in a silent demand, he nudged at my jaw with his nose. *Lord, yes!* I tipped my head back to rest against the wall. He peppered kisses and nips along my neck. And all on his own, he found that sensitive spot at the small juncture of my ear and neck.

My brain fried. Complete mush.

The gritty, powerful theme song from *Wonder Woman* rang from the phone in my back pocket. At the same time, an obnoxious, loud siren tone blared from Harper's cell. Harper pushed away and drew out his phone. I leaned against the wall, stunned, and ignored whoever called me. The loss of Harper's body heat, coupled with the cold AC, made me shiver like I'd been splashed by icy water.

"Xavier," Harper answered, walking across the room like he hadn't just kissed me into oblivion.

Goose bumps rippled over my arms. My face was on fire. My heart galloped like a thoroughbred on the back-stretch. I blew out a rocky breath, pushed off the wall, and straightened my clothes. I pulled out my ponytail, finger-combed my hair, and put it back up in a messy top knot.

I'd kissed a *lot* of boys in my twenty years. Some of them were bad, some were decent, and others were swoon-worthy. Hell, I'd even rounded a base or two with the guys in that last category. But none of them—and I mean *none*—compared to Harper.

I was so screwed.

When I'd kissed him, I had only wanted him to feel my sincerity. Everything he'd said prior to that had been real and raw. His words struck like punches. My apology had needed a grand gesture, one that wasn't flippant. When he'd stormed into Camden's house *for me,* I'd been on edge and unsure how to leave. He'd rushed in to save me from my foolishness *again.* And I'd never been happier to see Harper in my life.

My phone went off again and this time I grabbed it. "Hi! What's up?"

"Have you been running?" Leigh asked. "You sound out of breath."

"Something like that," I muttered, glancing at Harper. His back was to me, still on his call with Xavier. He gripped the back of his neck that looked a little redder than normal.

"Whatever," she snipped. "We have a problem."

Unease prickled along my spine. "Dare I ask?"

"The farmhouse is under attack."

"What?" Dread slithered into my gut, squashing any remaining sexy feelings I had. "Are you for real?"

I glanced at Harper again. He dropped his arm and his head lifted. Tension made his shoulders stiff.

"DH called. She could barely speak between tears and fear. It's bad, Sam. I'm just around the corner from there."

Damn. Damn. Damn.

"Advisers Shaw and Holland are trapped there with her," she continued. "Tally and Sajid are either there or on their way. Jax and Lani are in route, too."

Andrew had told me this morning that they were going to pull the records and bring them to Xavier's estate. The Warrior in me jumped to attention. All thoughts of what just happened between Harper and me got shoved to the back burner.

"Have the borders——" I cleared my throat. "Is Andrew still alive?"

"I think so, but I don't know much. DH didn't let me ask anything before she hung up."

I covered my mouth and looked over at Harper. His back was still to me.

"We need you, Sam." Leigh's voice was soft. "If you're ready for this."

My guts felt like ice. The last time I'd been in a battle, I got my ass handed to me and wound up in a coma. When I'd seen Dominic lurking in Camden today, my body responded to the threat, but could I face a full-scale attack? Would I be able to perform in battle?

"You had no backup, Brave One. This time is different. You'll have your Warrior Partner and two other pairs," Letty said, pushing her soothing warmth past my insecurities. *"I feel you're ready."*

"But I haven't gone into full battle mode. What if something malfunctions? What if there's pain? What if the Mage turned me into some kind of sleeper agent and going full warrior turns me against my team or something?"

"Peace, Brave One." A stronger push of her magic soothed me. *"You're no stranger to pain. Your body is completely healed."*

"Sam, did you hear me?" Leigh asked.

"No. Sorry." I blinked and looked up to meet Harper's intense stare. No longer on his call, his expression was grave and his jaw flexed. I diverted my gaze to the wood floor. "What did you say?"

"Are you ready for this?"

Show time.

Willing bravado I didn't truly feel, I said, "Born ready, baby."

"See you soon." She hung up.

I slowly dropped my arm while Harper moved in front of me. He tipped up my head with a knuckle under my chin, holding my gaze with eyes narrowed. Whatever he saw in me made his expression soften. With a light touch, he used that same hand to brush a lock of my hair behind my ear and then cradled my jaw.

Harper searched my face, sighed, and said, "Xavier said the farmhouse is—"

"—under attack," I finished for him.

He gestured to the phone still in my hand. "Spoke to Kestler?"

I nodded.

"She needs you." Stress lined his face.

"Yes." I reached up to grab hold of his wrist. "You don't want me to go."

"Right."

Letty's soothing juju coursing through me must have been working, because I started to feel braver and far surer of myself than I had a few minutes ago. The fire of my anointing crackled to life in my belly. That emboldened feeling snaked up my spine, swirled around my limbs, and flooded my bloodstream. I gave Harper's wrist a gentle squeeze then let go to rest my palm against the side of his neck.

"I won't leave my fellow Warriors to fight without me."

Harper's mouth twitched. A scowl creased his forehead. His nostrils flared.

"If anything happens to DH, I'll never forgive myself," I whispered.

He released a long breath.

"I can't let *Leigh* fight alone."

He grunted.

"Harper. I won't be flying solo. This isn't like going into Cam's house without backup. This isn't me riding to the feed store to save Judy like the Lone Ranger. My track record in making wise choices is admittedly kinda shitty, but this, fighting along with my fellow Warriors for the greater good, this is what I do." I felt his pulse pounding against my palm. "You know that."

With one more grunt, he grabbed my hand and tugged me to the door. "We'll take the horses."

As we walked, Power swelled in me. My grip in his became steadfast. A glimmer of the Warrior I'd been before this mess rekindled. There was no pain. There was no room for wavering. However, there was still a small part of me that doubted I could walk into battle. But I'd always been a fake-it-til-ya-make-it kind of girl, and right now, I was in full force.

"Brave one, I will do everything in my power to see you through this. I will not lose you."

Letty couldn't promise that I'd survive, but she could promise to make sure I had all my faculties about me. She could give me a solid fighting chance. And maybe it was my newfound paranoia driving me, but I made a pit stop in Xavier's armory and grabbed Azira—my former Warrior bow and her ever-returning arrows. She'd be my backup, even if I preferred my daggers. Because Helios and Sol were already stored in their invisible sheaths between my shoulder blades, I had to wear Azira the old fashioned way —slung over my back.

Harper, who always carried his Glock, threw on a chest holster for his gun. He also slid a spare magazine of bullets into a slot on one of the straps. Without missing a beat, he picked up a normal sword and belted it around his hips.

That's hot.

"Focus," Letty murmured.

"Yes, Angel Lady."

Once Harper and I finished arming ourselves, we looked at one another. I saw the battle raging in his dark irises, so I laid a palm on his cheek. He closed his eyes.

Harper's desire to keep me safe warred with what he knew to be true: an invasion at the farmhouse was an all-hands-on-deck emergency, and everyone needed Samantha Fife, the Warrior of Light powerhouse-bulldozer.

He reached up, squeezed my hand, and dropped it. We arrived at the barn to find Thad gone. I assumed Leigh had summoned him. Harper and I mounted Hannah and Max, urged them into Guardian mode, and were off.

The ride over was swift and short with little time to speak. We entered Andrew's property from the rear acreage. My Warrior's hearing picked up the distant sounds of battle, however our immediate surroundings were eerily silent—as if all nature had been scared off. My heart thrummed like a hummingbird. I could do this. I would do this. My fellow Warriors needed me. Storm clouds, which had gathered as we traveled, darkened. As we wound our way along, thunder clapped, and moments later, the Florida sky delivered a torrential downpour.

"This feels like fucking deja vu," Harper muttered.

"What?" I quirked a brow.

"Nothing." He reached for my forearm, giving it a squeeze. "Do me one favor, if Enyo is here, don't fight her alone."

I blanched. "No worries there." I had zero desire to face the she-devil and her poison-laced sword anytime soon.

Our Guardians trotted swiftly toward the sounds of battle. Rain fell. Lightning flashed. Steel screeched against steel. Angry shouts rose above the rain. Those distant sounds of battle grew louder. We came to a clearing in the trees and saw two Warriors of Light locked in a fight with several Greater Demons.

Sajid shouted, and a massive black hawk dive-bombed a demon coming up on his right. The bird struck its foe's face and sunk glowing talons into the demon's eyes. Sajid slashed his broad scimitar at a grey-skinned demon. Talia fought at his back, her double-bladed staff flashing. Sajid attacked, Tally defended. A cohesive unit.

A muddy purple demon barreled toward Talia. Her eyes were on another demon. Sajid had his sword buried in another's chest.

My Power sizzled through my limbs. I whipped out Azira and shot the purple brute. The gleaming arrowhead impaled his throat, knocked him backwards, and black blood spurted from his wound. Seconds later, his body burst into flame, and his ashes disintegrated into the mud.

Bastards.

Talia's perceptive Warrior eyes found me. She gave a sharp nod, then whistled three notes. Her Guardian fox, Fred, streaked from the trees, weaving through the legs of the demons, nipping and scratching as he darted by—a quicksilver blur. Sly and clever, he twisted through the enemies, leaving stumbling and confused demons in his wake.

Chaos erupted amongst the demonic ranks, and they turned on each other, shoving, pushing, letting fists fly. I shot arrow after arrow, picking off the outliers while fox and hawk wreaked their havoc. Tally and Sajid gained ground, slicing outward through black blood.

After the last demon in this wave crumbled, Sajid turned to us, tipped his head, and raised his curved sword in salute. Tally lifted her staff and free arm above her, pumping them in victory. I waved back.

"You're glowing," Harper murmured.

My golden aura burned bright, pulsing and alive. My clothes had transformed into white pants, a tunic, and boots. My Warrior Whites—my Heavenly armor. Holy fire sizzled through my body. I welcomed the heat that never burned, celestial light refracting outward through me. I freaking loved this feeling. Despite the rain and the seriousness of our situation, a smile tugged at my cheeks. I felt like *me* again.

"So I am." I grinned at him. "No pain either."

His tense shoulders eased, like I'd answered his unspoken question. "Good. I'm gonna go find Nigel and DH. Get them to safety." He leaned over, grabbed my forearm, and pressed a kiss to my forehead. "Stay alive."

I watched Hannah carry him into the storm-tossed trees.

"Find Leigh," Letty prodded.

"On it." I urged Max forward.

We navigated through the property we knew by heart, searching for any signs of life, be it friend or foe. The deluge of rain lessened to a soft, persistent shower. As Max took us towards the farmhouse, a shout followed by a scream had us changing course on a dime. He galloped towards the barn-side of the property. We stopped just before a clearing of trees where another battle raged. I spotted Jax instantly, but Leilani wasn't anywhere to be seen. He fought from the back of his palomino Guardian, Ana.

With an angry shout, Jax swung his mighty Warrior's axe as Ana charged forward. Tabarzina cleaved through a Lesser Demon, and the force of his blow carried it into a second. They both caught flame and burned into a poof of demon dust despite the rain.

The mare spun on her haunches. Jax loaded his arm for another swing. His eyes blazed with an unearthly light, and his backslash split three more demons open like they were firewood. Ana aimed a powerful kick at a scrawny blue one, nailing him in the teeth with her white-metal shoes. His face caved like crushed tin. All the broken and bleeding demons Jax and Ana had hit burst into dust.

Another scream ripped through the rain.

The palomino mare spun again and raced towards the source of the scream. Demons jumped into her path becoming a wall of flesh. Ana half-reared, narrowly avoiding a collision.

"Go!" I urged Max with my mind. He sprang into a gallop. In my peripheral vision, Jax's axe cut down his swarm of Lesser Demons.

I finally spotted my favorite Hawaiian Harpy. Her whip sword cracked and flashed, driving back a female demon. A dark green male slipped past York's deadly hooves and hauled Lani off her Guardian's back. Demons surged at the blood bay horse. He let out a ghastly equine squeal. As Lani hit the ground, she jerked her sword hand hard enough to sever the female demon's head from her neck. Her green attacker leapt for her. She tried to blocked him with a stiff arm from the ground.

"I've got Leilani," I said to Max. *"You help York."*

"If you're sure …" Max's reluctance washed through me.

"Definitely not." I clucked my tongue. Max galloped in Lani's direction and when we got close enough, I vaulted from Max's back, pulled out Helios and Sol, and slashed Lani's attacker in an X across his back. He exploded into demon dust.

Lani kipped-up to her feet.

"'Bout time you got here."

"You're welcome," I snapped. She wore a small smirk, but there was a glint of gratitude in her brown eyes.

A chestnut blur zoomed by, closely followed by a bay. Teeth and hooves flashed as Max and York circled around us, their Guardian strength and speed driving away droves of demons. But even with the two horses buffering us, enemies still slipped in through the gaps. I spotted one charging at Lani's back. I stepped around her, and the yellow demon ran into Sol's glowing blade.

I turned back to her. "They just keep—"

Lani pushed down on my shoulder. "Duck!"

I dropped, heard the metallic lash of her whip sword, and then the squelch of ripping flesh. Warm droplets of demon blood splattered on my neck, mingling with cold rain.

"Let's get back to Jax." Lani held out her hand and helped me up.

"Great idea."

We fought together in a pull-push dance, stabbing and slashing at the demons who got past Max and York's barrier. Fifteen yards away, I noticed Jax fighting from the ground. He'd either fallen or dismounted, but that didn't slow his use of Tabarzina. Lesser Demons fell in waves of five or six with a single blow from his axe. His glowing eyes found us fighting our way to him.

He whistled and Ana, who'd just caved in a demon's rib cage, swung her golden head towards Lani and me. She galloped over to join York and Max. Working together, the three horses closed the gaps in our defenses, allowing us to maneuver over to Jax safely. Once we were back-to-back with Jax, the Guardians opened their protective ring to include him, giving us a moment to regroup.

"Thanks," Jax said, his voice atypically gruff. "Drove of Lesser Demons broke a huge hole through the border. They just kept coming and got between Lani and me."

"Call me the cavalry." I grinned.

"I hadn't ever seen you in a real fight," Leilani said. "You're every bit as good as Adviser Gerena said. I'm happy to do battle with you anytime."

I pressed a dramatic left palm to my chest and shook her proffered hand with my right.

"Find your Warrior partner!" Letty demanded. *"She needs you."*

"I gotta go find Leigh," I said, rushing to Max.

"I last saw her out front of the farmhouse," Jax said.

"Ready for this to break?" I asked, twirling a finger in the air to the indicate circling horses.

At both of their nods, I said to Max in my mind, *"Get us to the farmhouse,"* and waited at the edge of the ring for him to streak by. When he passed by, I grabbed his mane and swung aboard. With my weight settled over his center of balance, he veered out of the equine barrier, and we were galloping to the farmhouse lawn.

The scene in front of us brought Max to a stop. My thoughts froze.

From Thad's back, Leigh fought that tiny teal female we'd seen at the church ages ago. Tabitha, clad in her Warrior whites, battled a burgundy demon from the ground while using the big grey horse as cover. Behind them and closer to the farmhouse, Xavier freaking Gerena and Andrew freaking Shaw were locked in their own intense duel against none other than Enyo and Ambrose.

I remembered that midnight demon's horrid breath, his brute strength, the way he'd savaged Judy's neck with his own damn teeth.

"Stay present," Letty's kind, but firm, command broke through my flashback.

I shook my head, clearing my thoughts. *Focus, Fife.* Harper reminded me to steer clear of Enyo, but there were still three others that needed to be taken care of.

The dark red demon—an unknown factor and a solid fighter—dodged around Fury as Leigh took a slash at him. He spun to his right, narrowly avoiding Tabitha's morning star and grabbed her wrist, wrenched back her arm, and ripped the weapon away. With lethal speed, he pulled out a dagger and sliced her forearm. The Adviser snatched her hand back, cradling it to her chest. Red bloomed over her white tunic.

Where was Harper? *He should be here. Around here. Somewhere.* Worry stirred my gut.

That sweeping feeling of not being in control tugged at me.

Oh, crap.

My hands trembled. I shivered, even though my cheeks felt hot. My mind pulled away from my own body. I froze as the battle raged on. I couldn't feel the rain on my skin. Dizziness had me gripping Max's mane to stay on as anxiety wrapped tendrils of dread around my throat.

No. No. No.

I couldn't pull my eyes away from the fight. I couldn't move. I needed to join my people. Had to fight with them. But all I *could* do was frantically try to find my breath.

In. Out.

In. Out.

In. Out.

"Letty, help."

22

SAM

"**B**rave One." Letty pushed her warmth outward from my core.

My hands shook. My chest heaved. The skin on my forearms pebbled with goose bumps.

"*I can't.*"

"*You* can. *I will lend you my strength.*" That heat of hers met my anxiety and shoved against it. "*Leigh and the Advisers need you.*"

"*But I'm damaged.*"

"*Perhaps. But you're not alone.*"

Letty's gentle reassurance turned into something more determined. The numbness of my soul ebbed. I zoomed back into my body. The intense wave of nausea passed, even though my stomach was still rocky.

"*You're not just any Warrior. They need you, Samantha Fife—the maverick. They need the one who doesn't play by the rules.*"

The maverick.

Letty's warmth, my Power, Max's steadiness, and Helios's and Sol's duet all hummed through my blood, emboldening me. I lifted my chin, squared my shoulders, and unsheathed my weapons.

I *could* do this.

Me.

No one else. My fellow Warriors were fighting their own battles. They were doing what they'd been blessed to do: defend and protect. And no matter how I felt inside, my best friend needed me, damn it. I refocused on the scene before me. Leigh, Thad, and Tabitha were closest. Andrew and Xavier were a hundred yards farther away, near the farmhouse.

Tabitha ran and jumped as Leigh reached down with her left hand. In a launch-and-grab move, the Adviser leaped up and settled on Thad's back behind Leigh, right before the burgundy demon could attack another time.

Thad quickly swung his hunches into the demon, making him stumble back. Leigh slashed Fury down at the teal female with her right hand. However, with the added weight of a second rider, Thad's movements were slowed. The two demons came at Tabitha, Leigh, and Guardian from both sides.

"*Max!*"

My horse burst into a gallop like he'd sprung from the starting gate. As we neared the fight, Max telegraphed his plan.

"*The Duck and Spin?*" I asked, sitting up and preparing to bail on impact.

"*The Duck and Spin!*"

He plowed into the male demon, dipped his shoulder, and spun so his hindquarters clobbered him. The maneuver predictably unseated me. I rolled over his quarters and landed on my feet.

"Adviser Holland!" I shouted and pointed at Max.

Relief and comprehension passed over her elven-like face, and she nodded.

"Get Tabitha out of here," I told my Guardian. *"I'll help Leigh."*

"I am not leaving you."

"She shouldn't be fighting. And I don't know where Harper is! Find him. Please."

"Fine." Max's displeasure washed over me as he swung himself toward where Leigh was battling. *"But I loathe it."* With his sights locked on the enemy, he pinned his ears and charged.

I didn't have time to see the outcome, because the burgundy demon recovered from his collision. He jumped to his feet, shouted at me in his hellish language, and whipped a dagger at me. I ducked to the side. The blade *wzzit* past my head. Adrenaline spiked alongside my Power. My aura pulsed a brighter gold.

"Enough of that!" I shouted at him.

The demon cocked his head and smiled. Another small black knife appeared in his hand.

"Letty, who is this prick? Whatcha got on him?"

"I believe this is Nero. He's known for—well." Letty shuddered inside my soul. *"He desecrates the bodies of his victims."*

"Desecrates ... how?" My skin prickled at her silence. *"On second thought, I don't wanna know."*

"He is quick with daggers. Prefers to throw them. Not good at actual hand-to-hand combat."

"But I am." I unsheathed Helios and Sol.

"Samantha Fife," Nero said, switching to English. "I will kill you, paint your blood on my body, and piss on your—"

"Okay! There will be none of *that!*" I sunk into my fighting stance. Power thrummed inside me. My blades warmed at my touch and flared bright white. "You wanna dance? Let's go."

I ran at him. He flung his knife. I swerved left, and his blade passed by harmlessly. He had two more daggers out and ready when I arrived. I slammed Sol down on his weapons. With a strong push-kick, I sent him stumbling backwards. He windmilled his arms, trying to remain on his feet, and he somehow found his balance.

"Victoria!" he shouted over his shoulder while backing up.

The teal demon's gaze landed on me. The rain had softened enough that I could see the hatred and malice glinting from her freakish yellow eyes.

"She's Enyo's protégée," Letty said. *"Rather vicious, but not as cunning as her mentor."*

The mere mention of Enyo caused my heart to lurch. The grip on my blades slipped in a moment of weakness. I over-corrected and my knuckles popped when I tightened my fingers on their hilts.

My eyes darted to where the navy-skinned demon dueled against Xavier and Andrew. *"She's too—I can't —she—"*

"Focus on what's in front of you!" Letty's tone slashed through me.

"Yes, ma'am." My attention snapped toward Victoria.

She took a step in my direction, and Leigh slashed her sword down her back. The petite Greater Demon stumbled forward with shoulder blades drawn towards her spine in obvious pain. Victoria brushed off the minor wound and darted out of Fury's range. Since Tabitha was still behind Leigh, her reactions were slowed and hindered, allowing Victoria to escape without taking more damage. She joined Nero's side, and with their attention solely on me, a trickle of anxiety wove through my lungs. My breath went shallow. I gritted my teeth.

"You will not fall today." Letty's signature warmth turned into something with more heat. Something stronger. Something more celestial than ever before. *"We do this together."*

Girded with her assurance, I found a teaspoon of courage and called to them, "What are you waiting for? Fight me!"

What was I doing? *Oh God. Oh God. Oh God.*

My heartbeat hammered against my sternum as the demons sank into action with their weapons in hand—Nero with his knife and Victoria with her sword. Past them, I caught Tabitha changing horses.

"Max, find Harper!" I pleaded to my horse as the demons attacked. I blocked Victoria's sword with Sol and parried Nero's knife with Helios.

"As you wish," he said. It sounded more high-pitch horse squeal than logical Guardian—a sure sign he disagreed. But before my two dance partners could counter-attack, Max and Tabitha slipped away unnoticed by the demons.

Victoria and Nero came at me again. I ducked, rolled out of the way, and dropped into a crouch with Helios and Sol poised to defend. The glowing white tip of Fury burst through Nero's chest. His body went in and out of focus, and a breath later he vanished—evidence that the Mage's profane blood magic protected him.

I glanced up. Leigh still sat atop Thad about ten yards away. She nodded once while wearing a grim, closed-mouth smile. My badass bestie had just *thrown* her long sword. Only Divine Intervention could have given her that kind of insane accuracy to find its intended target.

Hope kindled in my soul.

"Nero!" Victoria's unhinged wail pierced the air. "You idiot!"

She tossed her weapon aside, launched her small body, and collided with mine like a ten-ton truck. I jammed Helios into her thigh before we both hit the ground. She howled and bit my neck where a small patch of flesh was exposed.

"You bitch!" I dug my heels into the mud and thrust my hips up, trying to throw off this nasty piece of work, but couldn't find solid purchase in the rain-soaked earth. She punched me in the ribs. On the left side.

All breath left my lungs.

While my body was healed and the pain was minor, the action was enough to stun me. It robbed me of that small bit of hope that had flared to life when Leigh banished Nero.

Victoria's legs pinned to my waist, one hand trapped my dominant arm, and her other went for my left. I brought up Sol and sliced the right side of her ribs. She screamed. Pain exploded when she slammed her head into my face. White stars danced across my vision. A warm gush of blood filled my nostrils.

She ripped one arm free, reared back, and went for my eyes. I let go of my dagger and grabbed her wrist. We struggled, locked in this impasse. *Where's Leigh?* I thought, frantic. My ribs ached, my nose throbbed, my neck stung. *I'm going to die.*

A flash of white light sliced through the teal demon's neck, and all of Victoria's fight vanished. She loomed above me, motionless, her strange, yellow eyes frozen in surprise. Then her head tumbled off her shoulders. Both body and head flickered and blinked out of sight. Leigh reached down, grabbed the front of my tunic, and hauled me up. Thad was nowhere to be seen.

"Thanks for the save." I swallowed. *She's your best friend. She's not judging you, Fife.*

"Always." She gave me a small salute by lifting Fury halfway. "You good? Xavier and Andrew need our help."

Lightning flashed and thunder boomed, rattling my bones. The sky reopened, unleashing a new deluge of rain. I stiffened, my muscles locking up as terror seized my heart. I was *not* good.

Ambrose had already broken my body once before— he'd been the first Greater Demon I'd fought. He'd killed Judy. Enyo would have stolen my life if Harper hadn't intervened. She was the one demon Harper had told me to stay away from. And here I was getting ready to go round two with the both of them. At once.

So, no, I wasn't freaking *good*.

"Brave one," Letty murmured, irrupting my spiraling thoughts. *"Go forth and fight."* Her angelic heat roiled through me, burning away all the self-doubt and fear. *"I am with you, always."*

Emboldened with borrowed fortitude, I said to Leigh, "Yes. Yes, I'm good."

Her eyes narrowed. "Not sure I believe you."

"I'm sure not I believe myself, but we are Warriors. They need our help now."

She nodded, then tilted her head in the farmhouse's direction. "Then let's do this."

As we sprinted towards our Advisers, I reached for my Guardian. *"Max! Report!"*

"I am with Harper. We are safe." His answer eased one knot of worry in my gut. *"The old human, the child, and the wounded Adviser are gathered here. Thaddeus and I are standing guard."*

Leigh and I arrived at the driveway in time to see Andrew aim a weak stab with his rapier towards Ambrose's chest. The demon grabbed my Adviser's wrist. He slammed the hilt of his short sword against Andrew's hand, causing him to drop the rapier. With his free arm, Ambrose punched Andrew in the head, in the chest, in his side.

Those brutal blows against Andrew's already weakened constitution made him stagger. He barely kept his balance. Ambrose punches hit like freight trains; those strikes had rocked me to my core. Fear reared its ugly head in my heart. Clutching his side, Andrew raised a shaky hand—as if that would block another attack.

Shit! I can't lose Andrew like this. Not by this *demon.* He'd already taken Judy from me.

Ambrose chuckled—a deep, menacing boom. It raised the hairs on my neck. His laugh mocked me, taunted me, haunted me.

"Come on." Leigh tugged my arm since I'd stopped.

"Wait," I whispered, trying to get my breathing to mellow. "I need …a moment."

"Any last words, Old One?" Ambrose asked, looming over Andrew.

"No!" I shouted at Ambrose and at my boiling anxiety.

"Go!" Letty spurred me on.

This time I grabbed Leigh. "Let's go."

As we ran, I absorbed Letty's sharp push of Heavenly heat, ignored my desire to flee, and dug into my Power. With a burst of speed, I slid in front of the demon, Helios and Sol lifted in a defensive X, and roared. The demon slammed down his midnight fists just as I brought up my weapons. The white-hot blades sliced his flesh. His wounds sizzled and smoked, even in the rain. He bellowed in pain and backpedaled, curling in on his injured arms. When he lifted his head, shock flared in his black eyes before they narrowed in malice.

"Samantha Fife." A foul grin split his face.

To Ambrose I bared my teeth at him. "The one and only."

Leigh paused, glanced at me then Xavier battling alone.

"Go. I got this one," I murmured to her. She needed no more encouragement and sprinted away into a different fray.

"We meet again." Ambrose rose to his full height.

"I'm ready for you this time." I lifted my daggers and shifted into fighting position. "Brought some new friends with me. Whatcha think of them?"

"I think you're dead," he growled. "My master doesn't care if you live or die this time."

"Sammy, don't taunt him," came Andrew's quiet request.

I nodded once but didn't take my eyes off my opponent. Farther behind me, I heard the clang of steel, the grunts of an intense skirmish, and snippets of speech from Xavier. Wind blew the rain sideways. I was all that stood between this mountain of a monster and Andrew's imminent demise-by-demon.

"Fight me." I held my ground. "Not him."

"Andrew Shaw will perish by my hand, just like his wife."

The balls on this guy. Rage lit like kindling in my heart. "Then it'll be over my dead body."

"It's your death wish, little Warrior."

Before we could begin our battle, an opalescent portal opened next to us. The temperature plunged. The rain turned to snow. Grey mist swirled in the supernatural window. A hooded figure emerged. While I'd been distracted, Ambrose had given me a wide berth so he could kneel, head bowed.

"What do we have here?" The Mage's frigid tone made my skin crawl.

Panic seized me. My breath came out in ragged, misty puffs. My heartbeat *wooshed* in my ears. A cold sweat broke out between my shoulder blades, and acid boiled in my belly. I wanted to puke. To run. To hide. I couldn't do any of that.

The Mage lifted its arm, revealing white flesh swirled with glowing red tattoos. They made a "come here" gesture. Another hooded figure stepped from the portal. The Mage then flicked its wrist and snapped their fingers. The portal spun shut, vanishing into the Aether.

"Oh my, my," the Mage mused, taking in the scene. "There's far too much commotion here. That won't do." They swooped that same arm in a large circle in front of its body and pushed their palm upwards towards the sky.

As if on command, lightning flashed. Thunder cracked. A terrible shearing sound echoed behind me, and the fighting sounds stopped. *No way. The Mage can't—are they* dead? I risked a quick glance over my shoulder. A crystal-clear wall of ice encircled Leigh and Xavier. She pounded on the barrier with Fury while he tried to pull her back by the waist.

Enyo lurked behind me. Ambrose stood in front of me. The Mage was to my left with some hooded, unknown being by its side. My only backup was a weak and wounded Andrew at my back. I was surrounded. Panic weaved its way into my heart like some necrotic black disease.

"Ah, that's much better." The Mage sighed and turned its hooded head towards me. "Samantha, Samantha, Samantha. What will I do with you? You who thwarted my power. Wounded me. *Crippled* me."

The Mage's eerie voice invoked images of me fighting

Enyo, being stabbed, having my mind invaded, and being trapped in a coma. I shook my head, but the mental fog clung. My muscles went rigid. Even Letty's warmth couldn't calm the storm inside.

"Letting your Advisers battle for you? That hardly seems noble," the Mage drawled. "Letting worn out elders go up against two of my strongest? *Tsk. Tsk. Tsk.* Samantha, you should be ashamed."

My teeth chattered. My eyes burned. I wanted to cry.

"Lost your voice?" the Mage taunted.

This is a trap. The whole attack on the farmhouse property was a damn trap. And we'd all fallen for it. I wavered on my feet. *Breathe, Fife.*

"Where is all that bravado?"

My mind whirled. My fingers ached from where I gripped my daggers so hard to keep from shaking.

"Speak, child!"

No. I don't think I will. My teeth clenched. I snapped up my chin. The rain turned to sleet. Small pellets of icy sludge slid down my neck. The Mage glided forward—like they didn't walk on normal feet.

I expanded my Warrior senses, trying to locate my people beyond the immediate battlefield. I pushed my senses a little further and, on my periphery, found Harper. But not Max. *Where is Max?*

"Such defiance," the Mage crooned, circling me. I turned with them, blades up. The Mage closed the circle. Both tattooed hands clasped the edges of their hood and lowered its cowl. "You must learn manners."

"Oh, my God," I gasped.

I'd never gotten to discuss my theories with Xavier, but I knew this was Cheryl Talbot. The woman who'd betrayed all the Warriors of Light. Andrew. Xavier. Tabitha. Betrayed Harper's parents—*murdered* them. The one whose memories had been permanently implanted in me.

My body went taut as a bowstring. The cords in my neck strained. Crimson tattoos writhed on the Mage's porcelain face. She pulled her straight, white hair from the robe, and it cascaded down her back. Her eyes glowed red.

Holy Heaven.

"Let me introduce myself," she said.

With a wave of her hand, her appearance transformed into a human face. Her white tresses turned deep auburn. Her features shifted to a woman's softness. Her brilliant green-gold eyes tugged at my heart, my head.

I *knew* those eyes.

"*How?*" I breathed. "You said you killed her."

She gave me a patronizing laugh. "I assure you, Cheryl is quite dead. The spineless, pitiful waif she was." The Mage smiled. "She died the day I took back my life. When I took back my Power. When I became my true self."

"She—Cheryl—*you* were pregnant. W-what happened to the child?"

The Mage waved her arm. "Show her."

The second robed figure revealed himself by lowering his hood. Camden's eyes burned red.

"No." My nose itched and burned with unshed tears. I felt my heart crack in two. Camden was *Cheryl's* son. The one she was pregnant with in my memory. Cheryl and Aerona were one and the same. "How—how did we not know? You two are practically identical."

"Blood magic is quite potent, Samatha. It was easy to blur the resemblance between myself and my offspring."

Tears tumbled down my cheeks unbidden. "Possession isn't easy …"

She smiled. "No. He's been fed drops of Dominic's blood since birth. There was that period of time he lived with his grandfather, but it is of no consequence. I'd already laid the foundation. He's the perfect vessel to use as I wish."

"*That poor boy,*" Letty gasped.

I reeled back. "But he's your son!"

"He's a tool," the Mage clarified. Her bluntness made me wince.

From her position several feet away from me, she lifted a hand and ran a knuckle downward. I felt an icy trail from cheek to jaw. My body trembled with equal parts anger and terror.

"*Absolutely not!*" Letty's celestial Power pulsed hard, coalescing with my own. "*That loathsome woman shall not touch her.*"

My golden aura flared out from my body, almost like a set of wings trying to unfurl. It pushed back the Mage's frigid magic, keeping it from touching me. Comfort and warmth flooded my system, burning away my insecurities.

The Mage jerked her hand back and gaped at me. "How did you do that?"

"*But seriously, how* did *you do that?*" I asked Letty in my mind.

"*I may not be an Archangel,*" Letty said, "*but I am Michael's right hand. That affords me more Power than most all of Heaven's armies combined.*"

"The better question is ..." the Mage continued as if I hadn't just dispelled her magic touch. She glided a half circle around me, and on instinct, I turned with her, loathing that it put Ambrose at my back. "Why did your beloved Adviser never tell you about me and my potential offspring? I told you he kept too many secrets."

Andrew, who also kept his sight on the enemy, stood in front of me. Possessed Camden followed his mother and stopped next to her. I had a clear view of Leigh and

Xavier, walled off from us by an icy barrier. Enyo stood beside them with her hip cocked, her poison-coated sword lax at her side. She wore a smirk.

Surrounded.

Trapped.

Dead.

How am I going to get us out of here? I frantically ran through scenarios, not able to focus on a single one. *I can't—*

"You can," Letty said firmly. Fire in my bones snapped me back to the present.

"—warned you, old man," the Mage seethed. "I told you I would destroy you. Take away your legacy. Undermine your legitimacy. I slaughtered your precious Warriors, and I left you alive to *suffer.* You had one rule—one—never anoint another Warrior, but you never learn."

Andrew sighed. The weariness there tugged at my heart.

"Ah, Cheryl—"

"Cheryl. Is. Dead!" the Mage screeched. Ice shot across the wet ground at her feet. "It's Aerona. My new name, given to me at my rebirth."

I flinched against the bite in her voice and the air.

"You forbade me to create new Warriors after you destroyed nearly the entire Light network and sent me, Xavier, and Tabitha underground, but we answer to a Power so much higher than you."

Andrew's answer was firm. Unwavering. Aerona's eyes glowed bright red. My breaths came out in steamy puffs. My teeth chattered. Celestial fire pulsed from within me, and the cold vanished.

"I'll never ignore my Heavenly calling to anoint Warriors. Hell cannot stop me, *Cheryl.*"

The falling sleet turned to snow and whipped around

in vicious whorls. Frigid wind blew across the lawn. I felt none of it and tightened my grip on my daggers.

Andrew's voice rose above the wind. "You're still human, so I cannot kill you, but you will not win."

That cadence. That defiance. I knew it like the back of my hand. *Oh. My. Mercy. Andrew's taunting her!*

"What are you doing?" I shouted.

Andrew half-turned and opened up his side to me. A flicker of his bygone glory glimmered in his eyes, reminding me of his former strength. A smirk tipped his lips. Worry ripped through me.

The Mage let out an angry scream. "Dominic!"

Camden sauntered forward and aimed a wink at me. Dread clutched my gut. Cheryl—Aerona—whatever the hell she called herself—stroked Cam's curls. His eyes glowed a brighter red. She beamed. "It is time."

Aerona's dark Power lashed out and grabbed my wrist. Artic cold raced up my arm, fighting against my internal Heavenly heat, and her iron-like grip latched on. Time slowed. I became sluggish. Like I was trying to swim through an ice field. Whatever hocus pocus juju Aerona wielded, it held me captive. I could only watch in horror as Cam easily stepped forward, drew Dominic's wide black scimitar, and speared Andrew through the stomach. Andrew crumpled.

"Noooooooo!" Agony lanced my heart.

"I said, you will not touch her!" Letty's angry voice echoed in my mind. Her Power ignited with a heat so fierce that I could hardly stand it.

I felt Aerona's hold falter and yanked back control. Time snapped back to normal. Her touch disappeared. Helios and Sol lit up like beacons. I leapt forward, passing Andrew's fallen form, leading with my blades, but the Mage blinked away. She reappeared next to Enyo, her human glamor gone. The snow around us turned back to rain.

"You little bitch, you burned me!" she screeched, lifting her porcelain white palms. They were blackened and smoking. The acrid scent of burnt flesh met my Warrior-enhanced nose. "What are you?"

I don't care. Was my heart still beating?

"How are you able to thwart me? Rob me?" The red glow in her etched porcelain skin flickered. "You're nothing but an arrogant, insignificant girl!"

Andrew. Andrew. Andrew. I chanted in my head. *Be alive. Be alive. Be alive.*

Dominic's roar of laughter rose up and clashed against his Dark Warrior's anger. But he sounded like Camden, looked like Camden. Amusement danced in those familiar green-gold eyes. He backed up several feet and saluted me.

Aerona snapped her fingers. Nothing happened. "What did you do to my Power, girl?"

Andrew still didn't move. I gripped the hilts of my daggers. My knuckles cracked. The desire to check on him warred with my Warrior-instincts to stay ready for battle. And without Letty helping me, I wouldn't have been able to do any of it.

"This is not the end." Aerona rushed forward, grabbed Dominic's sword arm, and swiped her fingers through Andrew's blood on the blade. Her dull red tattoos flickered and then burned brighter. "You will pay for this!"

With a final snarl at me, she opened a portal and stumbled through. It snapped closed. Enyo's body flickered and blinked out of sight. I felt Ambrose's presence behind me disappear. The ice wall dropped, and Leigh stumbled forward where she'd been pounding against it. Xavier caught her. And only a possessed Camden remained behind.

My ex-boyfriend stepped closer to Andrew's crumpled form as Leigh ran at us. His eyes glinted supernatural red, and his aura burned with Dominic's burnished bronze. A smirk graced his familiar, handsome face.

He murdered Andrew.

Fire raced through my arteries. Pulsed in my veins. Climbed my spine.

"Brave One, no," Letty warned.

"Sam!" Leigh shouted.

What I felt was beyond rage. Beyond hurt. Something broke in me. I raised my weapons and slipped into that fighter's stance my beloved Adviser had taught me.

He murdered Andrew.

"Samantha Fife," Letty commanded. *"Hold your weapons."*

Hot tears poured down my cheeks.

He murdered Andrew.

Letty tried to throttle my Power. I felt that tug in every fiber of my being, but I lunged at Camden.

"Spitfire!" Harper's gruff baritone cut through the falling rain, cut through my internal inferno, cut through everything. "He's human!"

Somewhere in the roar of righteous anger, Harper's words sank in. *Camden* was human. I was Warrior. I wasn't allowed to kill him. But I'd already committed to the strike; I couldn't back out. Camden was too close. I was too fast.

By the grace of Heaven, I shifted my body enough to change my blade's trajectory. Dominic winked, and right as Helios slashed Camden across the thighs instead of his neck, I saw a flash of green-gold instead of red in his eyes. Blood spilled over Cam's jeans. My chest heaved. I'd almost murdered a human. A human I cared about.

Camden started chuckling.

Not Camden.

Dominic.

"Would love to stay and chat, but it seems that my host's body no longer agrees with me."

At that, Camden's thighs started smoking and hissing.

"Until we meet again, my dear," Dominic said in a disembodied voice. He pinched the brim of his non-existent hat and tipped his head.

The unnatural glow in Cam's eyes went out. His irises became their normal color, shock written on his face. Cam wheezed like someone had grabbed his lungs and squeezed out the air. He hacked and struggled for breath while crimson smoke streamed from his mouth, his nose, his ears. The red vapor pooled at Cam's feet, collected itself, and rose up into a misty, humanoid shape. When Cam no longer smoked, that red cloud chuckled, then zoomed off like a swarm of bees.

Camden's body rag-dolled to the ground.

The entire property seemed to exhale, relieved to be free of evil. The rain fell softly.

"Check him!" I yelled at Leigh, pointing to Cam, as I hit my knees in the mud next to Andrew.

Harper appeared and sank down at Andrew's head. He cradled the wounded Adviser's upper body in his lap, comforting the man he called Pops. Harper pressed his hands to Andrew's abdomen. It did nothing to stanch the flow of blood. I slid my right palm over Harper's left hand, spreading my fingers over his. We pressed down in unison.

It was pointless.

"Andrew, Andrew, Andrew," I lamented, smoothing his rain-darkened hair from his forehead. "Why did you taunt her?"

"My brave Warrior," Andrew said. Blood spurted from his lips.

"Hold on, okay?" I took his hand in mine, kissed his

knuckles, and started to rise. "I'll get you some Elixir from the house."

"Sam," Harper murmured. "There is none here. We used the last on you."

I sank back down. "Can't you heal him like you did me?"

"His wound is ..." He winced. "He doesn't have much time left."

Harper's words punched me in the chest.

"Don't say that," I choked.

Harper's jaw locked. Grief swam in his eyes. He shook his head.

"My girl." Andrew grabbed the sleeve of my tunic with feeble strength. "Come. Listen quick."

I leaned close. My tears mingled with the softly falling rain.

You can't be dying. Don't die. Please.

"I made a mess of things," Andrew said. "I'm sorry. I betrayed you. Trust me now. You will evolve. Everyone will. Change is coming. The Warriors of Light will not be the same."

"What?" I asked.

He tried pulling me closer. He was so weak, I let him. I felt his mouth against my ear as he spoke in a whisper only my Warrior's hearing could pick up. "Harper will need you. Stay with him. No matter what. No matter how prickly he gets, don't let him go. You're the only one who can reach him."

"I will." What else could I say to a dying man?

Andrew released me, and his free hand flopped over his heart. "You're my ray of sunshine. I love you, Sammy."

"I love you, too." I leaned back, hollowed out and numb. Like someone had taken my heart from my chest.

"Help me." Andrew touched the base of his throat. His

Warrior's key appeared on a silver chain around his neck. "Take it."

No. My stomach clenched. *I can't.*

"You can," Letty reminded me for the millionth time. Her gentleness smoothed the jagged edges of my battered heart.

Choking back a sob, I reached behind Andrew's neck and undid the clasp. Harper's heavy gaze weighed on us—watching, waiting. I pulled the necklace free and lifted it so all three of us could see it.

My Warrior's key was a simple skeleton key, but Andrew's was elegant and ornate. The bow of his was a set of wings spread open, and there was a scrolling inlay of golden swirls in the metal.

"My son," Andrew rasped. Harper's jaw tensed, and his eyes dropped to the man in his arms. Andrew's free hand grabbed at Harper's pant leg. "You struggled so much. Was never the right time. Didn't want to burden you. But—" He winced and coughed up blood. "But this is yours. Leadership key."

"The—what?" Harper asked.

Andrew pushed my fist holding his Warrior's key at Harper. "It's yours now."

Harper wrapped gentle fingers around the key. He took it and slipped it into his shirt's front pocket instead of putting it on.

"You're the next leader. This—" Andrew struggled to breathe, and his eyelids fluttered as if too heavy to stay open. "You're the Head Keeper of Light now. Was always meant for you. Was hard on you. Knew what was to come."

"Pops, what are you saying?" Harper asked.

"You are my successor." Though faint, his voice was sure. No wavering. "You *will* lead."

"I lived a long time. Too long, really. I'm tired."

"Pops!" Harper tightened his hold on Andrew's body. "Fuck!"

A smile graced Andrew's lips. "Proud of you, my son. Proud of the man you've become. You're my boy."

Harper cleared his throat and wiped his nose on his shoulder sleeve. Tears streaked down my cheeks.

"Son," Andrew gasped.

"I'm here." Harper grasped Andrew's flailing hand.

"Take care of Sammy. Stick with her."

Harper met my gaze. "Yes, sir."

"Good man," Andrew sighed.

We looked down. Andrew's chest rose and fell. Then it did not. His body went limp and heavy in Harper's arms—his grip lax in our hands—and the light of life left his grey eyes.

"Ah, Pops," Harper whispered. He ran his fingers over Andrew's lids, closing them. "Goodbye, old man."

My breath came out as a garbled mess. I covered my mouth and cried, unable to take my eyes off Andrew's lifeless body. We sat that way for seconds? Minutes? An hour? I lost all track of time.

"Um, y'all …" Leigh said, making me jump.

I glanced at her over my shoulder. Camden was on the ground—still breathing—with Xavier and Leigh's hands on his wounds, but their gazes were lifted to the sky. I followed their line of vision. A blazing ball of amethyst light raced from Heaven. The center was dark purple, softening out to pale lavender at the edges. Harper looked up, too. Confusion tightened the skin around his eyes.

"The hell is that?" I asked.

"It's Harper's time, Brave One," Letty said. *"You may want to give him some space."*

"What? Why?" I watched as that sphere of energy sped towards us, its trajectory headed straight—

"Oh, fuck!" Harper let go of Andrew and shoved himself away. He sprawled out in an un-Harper-like in a heap on the wet grass.

That ball of purple light swept down and slammed into Harper's chest.

"Holy crap," I whispered.

Harper Tate was getting an angelic upgrade.

23

HARPER

My body hurled through a purple-tinged void—twisting and flailing. No control. No idea or sense of up or down. Panic gripped my throat. The loss of autonomy made my heart thunder. The darkness shifted to a light shade of lavender. I stopped falling as my back hit some invisible floor. My head smacked against it.

"Ah, fuck." Groaning, I rolled to my knees, rose on shaky legs, and shuffled in a slow circle. Every direction was empty lilac space. I ran a hand over my mouth. "What the hell? Where am—"

"We are in your own consciousness," a deep voice said.

Motherfucker! I jumped and spun, searching for the source of speech.

An angel—at least seven feet tall with massive white wings, kaleidoscope-colored eyes that changed from brown to blue to green, and he had a nasty jagged scar running down the left side of his face—appeared next to me, radiating pure celestial power. He was clad in leather gladiator's armor. Everything from his strong aura to his stern expression, down to his rigid posture demanded obedience.

I felt a threat that said: *fuck around and find out.* I couldn't swallow.

Do not fidget.

The angel tucked those wings in tight to his body, grasped his hands behind his back, and tipped his head to the side. He regarded me like I was some sort of fascinating specimen. It was a clinical inspection—one I'd failed.

It took a second, but when I found my balls, I asked, "Who are you?"

"I am called by many names." His voice boomed in the light purple space. "The Great Captain. Leader of the Heavenly Host. The Helping Warrior. Mikha'el." One side of his mouth lifted in what looked like an attempt at smiling. "However, I suspect you would know me best as Michael, the Archangel."

My heart bottomed out into my stomach. I roughly scrubbed my mouth with my palm. Fucking *Michael* stood before me with his hands tucked behind his back—*smiling*—and spoke to me as if we'd known each other my whole life. It seemed as if he was trying to aim for casual, not intimidation.

I cleared my throat. "What's happening, and why are you here? Sir."

"You are a smart man, Commander. You know why I am here." He dropped a massive hand to rest on the hilt of his sword. "Bernard Andrew Shaw has passed into rest, and you now possess the Leadership key. This is your Anointing."

"M-my anointing." *Don't fucking stutter! Get your shit together, asshole.* I took a cleansing breath that did little to calm my nerves. "I'm a Warrior of Light?"

This time Michael gave me a full smile, which did little to soften his angelic authority. "You have yearned for this your entire life. How does it feel to finally receive your gift?"

From the accounts I'd read on Warrior conversion, all of them said they'd felt safe, supported, and comforted. Pops and Xavier confirmed their anointings were peaceful, smooth transitions. Sam said she'd felt like it had been a warm embrace. While I wasn't exactly scared of Michael —he wouldn't hurt a human and I suspected he was damping just how powerful he was. But I still felt like shitting my pants.

"Unsettling," I answered after a beat and crossed my arms to keep the shakes at bay. Michael frowned. *At me? Or what I said?* "Look, you're *the* Archangel, and we're having a conversation like you've invited me to have a beer."

"Ah, yes," the Archangel mused. "An unfortunate side effect of who I am—Sword of God, the Bringer of Justice. I deliver punishment or provide reprieve without emotional bias. I can see how that would be uncomfortable."

Uncomfortable? Right. "With all due respect, can you get to the fuc—" I cleared my throat. "What does the Leadership Key have to do with me?"

"No need for the forced reverence, Kingling." Michael lifted his scarred brow. "I am well aware of your proclivity for *ebullient* word choices and refreshing bluntness." He turned those ever-changing eyes on me, a hint of humor gleaming in them. "We are bonded now. Angel to Warrior. I wish to be your most trusted confidante."

"Jesus," I muttered.

Having this all-powerful being tell me he wanted to be friends was a real mindfuck. I ran a hand over my face again and dropped my arms. Michael continued to regard me with that dispassionate expression. It dawned on me a second later that he might not actually know how to interact with a human.

"You are not just *any* Warrior. You're the anointed leader for the Warriors of Light. This means that you alone have the authority to operate outside of Warrior law."

I titled my head and stared at him. It took a moment for his words to filter through my pea brain. There were many *rules* when it came to being a Warrior of Light, but there was only one *law*. The gravity of what he said finally hit its mark and my eyes widened.

"Fuck me sideways." I stumbled backward a few steps. "Are you telling me I have the authority to kill humans?"

"Affirmative."

"Christ." My skin felt too tight to contain my body. "Pops didn't have this right."

"Correct. You are the first. No one has ever had an Archangel as their conduit."

I shook my head as if that would clear my thoughts. I'd become a paramedic to *save* people. I did my damnedest to keep humans from dying. But ending a life—

"Heaven allows the Warriors to evolve and change. They must, in order to stay ahead of Hell's deviousness. This is the natural progression."

"You have the wrong man." I felt dizzy. "I want to *save* people, not kill them."

"I do *not* have the wrong man." Michael bristled, his glare burning into me. "I would never align myself with someone who glorifies violent behavior."

I raked a hand over my hair. "This is fucking nuts."

"Your objective to preserve live is precisely why you are best suited for this position. Your sense of justice is in balance with your compassion." He dampened his aura and air rushed back into my lungs. "Think, Kingling. Are there not humans who have been influenced by darkness? Those who have allowed evil inside? Those who have been corrupted beyond saving? It is those *humans* who pose a threat to all mankind. Heaven cannot sit idly by and allow them to slaughter more innocents."

Cheryl Talbot.

She'd turned too many humans into Dark Warriors and orchestrated mass murder on the Warriors of Light. She'd slaughtered my parents. On her authority, her demon had killed Judy. She'd manipulated and altered her son—grooming him to become something he'd never consented to. Possessed Camden murdered Pops. My lip curled. My hands tightened into fists. The thought of slitting the Mage's throat flashed through my mind.

"I see you have realized your purpose. And I am here to help you embrace it." Michael laid a heavy palm on my shoulder. "You will not turn into a blood thirsty murderer, Kingling, but will be the sword which Heaven uses to carve out Earth's cancer."

I inhaled and let it out slowly. *What the fuck do I say to that?*

Michael's solid form started fading around the edges. "You are waking." That hint of a smile reappeared. "No matter what happens now, I am with you."

In a flash of brilliant amethyst light, Michael was gone and I was falling again through the void.

I woke with a desperate gasp and sat bolt upright. Wet grass soaked my ass through my jeans. Drizzling rain peppered my skin. A cacophony of a few different voices assaulted my ears, and I couldn't identify who was speaking. Damp earth, blood, sweat, and a million other scents met my nose. I blinked, and everything around me snapped into vivid, colorful focus.

Sam was on her knees in front of me. I looked over her

shoulder to see Kestler and Xavier approach Pops's unmoving body. Grief sucker punched me right in the goddamn sternum. *He's gone.* The urge to cry choked me. I bowed my head and pressed my index finger and thumb to my eyes. *Don't cry now. You won't stop.*

"Harper?" Sam whispered.

I lifted my chin and met her eyes. Wet droplets clung to her lashes. Her face was red. *From crying?* Her blonde hair was dark and plastered to her head. Her Warrior whites clung to her athletic form.

"Are you okay?" she asked.

How have I never noticed there are gold flecks in the center of her eyes?

"Harper?" Her tone rose in pitch.

She's fucking gorgeous.

"*Kingling!*" Michael's curt tone cut through my fixated thoughts.

"*Yes!*" I snapped to attention.

"*Focus on bringing your Powers to heel. Breathe. Find your center. Control.*"

"*How?*"

"*Start with her, Commander,*" Michael growled in my mind. "*She will help ground you while you acclimate to your Power, but do not get caught up on the wrong details.*"

"*Right.*"

Sam seized the wet fabric of my shirt and heaved me closer to her body. I grabbed her biceps to steady us. She stared at me for a long moment, as if memorizing the details of my face, then slammed her lips against mine. It was a punishing, desperate kiss laden with anguish.

I slipped a hand under her wet ponytail and held the nape of her neck. A few seconds later, she pulled back by a few inches, far enough that I could see her clearly. Whether she knew it or not, the woman held all the pieces of my shattered heart. I rubbed my thumb against the damp skin of her neck.

"Harper," she gasped, pressing her forehead to mine. "You're alive. Holy shit, you're alive."

My brow furrowed. "Was I dead?"

"I thought you were!" Sam swayed back and held me at arm's length. Pop's blood was still smeared on her arms. "You stopped breathing. You had no pulse." She hastily wiped her cheeks. "I thought you died!"

My heart stopped? "How long was I out?"

"That's your question?" Her eyes bugged. "You were *out* long enough to give me a damn heart attack."

"I'm sorry?"

Her gaze narrowed, danger crackling like lightning in their stormy depths. She released my shirt only to punch me repeatedly in the shoulder, each blow landing on a word. "You. Asshole! You. Aren't. Allow. To. Die. Without. My. *Permission!*"

"Ow. Fuck!" I grabbed her flying fist. "Spitfire, don't beat the shit out of me." I tugged her to me and wrapped an arm around her lower back, holding her in place. "Shhh, I'm here. I'm not dead."

She struggled in my arms for a few seconds, then softened.

"Andrew's gone," she mumbled into my chest.

"I know," I answered, tucking my face against the top of Sam's head.

Kestler approached and squatted next to us. The sorrow on her face mirrored what was in my heart. *Don't you dare break, Kestler.* If she did, I wouldn't be able to keep my shit on lockdown.

To distract myself, I scanned her with trained paramedic eyes. "You hurt? Any more demons lurking around?"

"Not physically," she said, her voice cracking. "All the demons disappeared after—after Adviser Shaw ... you know."

Pops's dying breath. Pops's blood filling the grooves around my nail beds. Pops telling me he was proud of me. Pops asking me to take care of Sam. *Christ Almighty.* A hard knot formed in my throat. My nose burned. I lost the fight and wet warmth mingled with cold rain on my cheeks. *God damn tears.*

I coughed to find my voice. "Injury report? Did we lose anyone else?"

Kestler lifted her chin and squared her shoulders. "Camden is unconscious, but he's alive. Xavier is checking on everyone else."

"Good." I nodded once before gently pushing Sam away from my body. I brushed back the hair plastered to her cheeks. Traces of blood tracked from her nostrils down to her throat. "You okay?"

With her eyes wide and glassy and her body trembling, she let out a shuddering breath. "I'm, like, *totally* fine."

I choked back a bark of laughter and pressed a kiss to her forehead before standing. I pulled her up with me, tucked her under my arm, and tried to ignore the Power of an Archangel thrumming through my bloodstream. A slight tremor of something akin to battle lust rippled through me—electric and strong. Sam must have felt me twitch because she propped her chin up against my pec and peered at me with those perceptive eyes of hers.

"Are *you* okay?" she asked.

Because my senses were heightened and every sound, shift, scent amplified my drive to fight, my muscles were taunt and ready to take quick action. Telling her I felt like fucking up a slew of demons by ripping out their hearts with my bare hands, and crushing said fucking hearts between my fingers might freak her out. Then again this was Sam. She never did anything the normal way. But I didn't feel like explaining this delightful feeling of bees buzzing through my goddamn arteries and veins. It could wait.

"Yeah," I said, shaking out my free arm. "This Power is new to me. That's all."

"Control, Kingling," Michael said. *"You must learn to harness this. Channel it. Do not allow it have mastery over you."*

I grunted.

"You sure?" she probed.

I squeezed her against me before taking the few steps over to Pops's body. He appeared almost as if he was sleeping, at peace and resting, save for the gaping wound in his abdomen. His chest didn't rise and fall with breath. There would be no steady beat of a pulse.

Pops might have been a relentless bastard. He might have ridden my ass like a slave driver and been just shy of cruel, but he did it all for a purpose. He knew I would have to be tougher than the average Warrior. The reality of my new mantle sharpened into clarity what I'd have to do.

Pops knew I'd have to kill the Mage.

Damn you, old man, why didn't you tell me about the Leadership key? Why didn't you tell me I even had *a destiny to fulfill?*

Of course, Pops wouldn't have divulged that information. How could he? How would one even start that conversation? I sighed and raised my eyes to the sky. The rain had slowed to a fine mist, and feeble beams of light now peeked out from behind ominous clouds.

"Your former Adviser has been received in Heaven," Michael said in our moment of silence. *"He is at rest. He is with his bride."*

At least there was that.

"Come." I tugged Sam with me. "We'll honor Pops

properly when we're done sorting through the shit show of today. Go find Xavier and see if he needs help."

Either she was in shock or numb because Pops was gone—possibly both—because she grabbed Kestler's hand and they walked off to do what I said. I watched them disappear around the side of the farmhouse before cautiously approaching Bennett's side. Sam didn't need to deal with this motherfucker right now.

I squatted, resting my forearms on my thighs. Makeshift bandages covered the wounds on his thighs, dyed red from blood which soaked through. Xavier and Kestler must tended to his wounds while Sam and I had been with Pops. Bennett groaned and shifted. He rolled his head towards me. His eyes were open but vacant.

"What do you have to say for yourself, fucker?" I reached forward and nudged his shoulder.

Bennett answered with a moan. Yeah, the lights were on, but nobody was home.

"Fuck knows what we're going to do with you, but I'm not leaving your ass here. Sam wouldn't want you to suffer. No matter how much I think you deserve it."

I pulled out my cell from my back pocket to make a quick call to Xavier, and sensed, rather than saw, Nigel and DH walk up behind me. I stood and walked towards them, thumbing the speaker so they could hear. Nigel wore a sad smile. DH's green eyes were wide and searching.

"Harper," Xavier answered on the second ring. "I assume you've undergone some, ah, upgrades."

"You could say that." I looked out at the farmhouse yard, still processing the whole afternoon. "A lot to take in."

"I thought that to be the case. Miss Fife was worried. I was not. I suspect we'll need to pick up your training in the very near future."

Considering it was taking all my effort to not let my senses overwhelm me now, he wasn't wrong. But it wasn't the time or place. I pressed fingers to Bennett's neck. He had a thready pulse. His thigh wound leaked. Sam had almost killed him. Thank Heaven I had gotten to her in time.

"Later," I said to Xavier. "We've got enough to deal with. Starting with Bennett." *Preferably before Sam comes back.* "He's in bad shape. We'll take Nigel's SUV to the manor."

"We have holding cells. Have Nigel show you. Healer Emily can help set it up to provide medical attention."

"Thanks. Kestler has Sam. They're both a mess, but Sam's shell-shocked."

"I saw. Just sent them home with their Guardians."

I jolted. *Home?* Of course, we couldn't stay at the farmhouse. It was no longer protected. *Is Safe Haven our new home?* If it weren't for Xavier, I would be fucking homeless. I was already parentless—including Ma and Pops. I raked my fingers over my scalp.

"Miss Fife had to face some of her fears today," Xavier continued as if he hadn't just verbally sucker punched me in the heart. "And we *all* lost Andrew."

I closed my eyes and pinched the bridge of my nose. *Hold your shit together.* "Where are you?"

"Seeing to my other charges. Miss Kalakaua and Mr. Bozeman are rather beat up from defending their part of the property."

"But they're okay?" We didn't have any Life Elixer on property.

"Nothing traumatic. Am I on speaker?"

"Yes, sir."

"Delaney," Xavier said, fatherly concern lacing throughout his tired Spanish accent.

"Daddo." The pixie girl shuffled forward. Shivers

racked her small body. Her teeth chattered. My own clothes were drenched. I had nothing to offer her in way of warmth.

"You're whole?" he asked. "Not hurt?"

"Not a scratch. Nigel kept me hidden. But Daddo," her voice cracked and her always-bright face scrunched in helplessness. "I saw what happened to Adviser Shaw—"

"I know, *mi hija*." Xavier said.

My resolve fucking cracked and a few tears leaked out. My barely controlled Power made my hands shake. It was just too hard to lose yet another person I loved. No matter how strained the relationship had been with Pops, it fucking sucked. And yet, somehow, Sam was still breathing. That thought alone kept me from crumbling.

"Yes, focus on the good. Easy now," Michael encouraged. *"Warriors who die in battle are exalted in Heaven. Your Andrew Shaw died an honorable death."*

I blew out a breath. *"That—were you trying to offer comfort?"*

"Yes. He no longer suffers. How would that not bring solace?"

Jesus. This relationship was going to come with a steep learning curve on both sides. I tuned back into the human conversation.

"Go with Harper," Xavier instructed his daughter. "I'll return soon."

"Yes, sir," she said.

"Mr. Tate, we'll meet tonight."

"Yep." We quicky tied up the call, and turning to Nigel, I gestured to DH with my chin. "Can you find her some dry clothes and a blanket in the house, then can you bring the Tahoe around?"

"Of course." He looped an arm around DH's small frame and guided her away.

Once they were gone, I nudged my booted toe against

Bennett's ribs. "You're getting a one-way ticket to a cell at Casa Gerena, fucker." I bent down and hefted him into a fireman's carry with an ease that I never would have been able to accomplish an hour ago. "Until we get some fucking answers on how much of a dangerous liability you may be, you're considered a threat. And definitely not to be fucking trusted."

SAM

Xavier performed Andrew's Warrior send-off the night he'd died. I remembered standing in between Leigh and Harper, holding their hands as if my life depended on it. Leigh's tears flowed freely, but Harper was a stoic statue. He declined to speak, even when Xavier asked him if he wanted to say a few words. I wasn't any better. The only energy I managed to muster was to watch the flames and smoke as they reached for Heaven, taking Andrew's ashes with them. My world had been shattered, but all I felt was numbness that night.

Five days later, Xavier performed a public funeral for Andrew at a church which hadn't been crispy-fried by a demon-possessed man. He'd managed to put together a massive "celebration of life" ceremony, and hundreds upon hundreds of people came out.

I hadn't wanted to be around the tears and grief of people who didn't know the real Andrew. I hadn't wanted to attend a faux-funeral and relive the wrenching loss I felt inside. I hadn't wanted to suffer through well-meaning platitudes: *Sorry for your loss. Praying for you. It will get better. God called him home. He's no longer suffering.*

Vomit.

But I ended up going in the end, though it was under protest. Leigh had to nag me until I relented. That, and she played upon my Harper sympathies. Harper, who hadn't been so lucky when it came to dodging the masses, was the sole surviving son of Andrew and Judy. For appearances, he had to be there. It was expected.

So, I went for Harper.

Newly Warriored, with a side order of emotional trauma? Recipe for catastrophe. He'd already suffered too much loss in his twenty-four years, and now he was bound to freaking Michael, the Archangel. Harper was a Warrior on steroids with a shit storm of grief. He could explode if someone looked at him with a teaspoon of too much pity.

My instincts had proven correct. While he'd avoided everyone that the whole week, including me, on the day of, he took hold of my hand and held on for dear life during the service. During the reception, he parked a chair right next to me and sat down like a sack of potatoes—weariness etched deep in his soul. He'd glued me to his side but barely said a word that whole day.

And three days later, he was *still* holing himself away.

I'd vowed to myself that would give him space—I really did—but my impatience reached its pinnacle. I was worried about him but also a little angry. We needed to have a little chat. And that was why I was marching my ass down the hall at Casa de Xavier to Harper's room.

"I've given him time," I told Letty. *"If sulking isn't healthy for me, it's not healthy for him either."*

"Mmmm, I'm surprised you left him alone this long."

"This is the new and improved Sam, remember?"

I swore I heard her laugh in the outskirts of my consciousness.

"Samantha Grace," Leigh said, catching me by the arm just when I got to the first step leading up to Harper's floor. "Where're you going?

I whirled in her direction, hand pressed to my chest. "Leigh Payton, you scared the daylights out of me."

"That's what you get for not paying attention. I just know you're up to no good, but we're supposed to meet up with our folks in a few minutes. Your deviousness will have to wait."

The protections Andrew had laid around his church and the Fife and Kestler homes dissolved when he died. Xavier had insisted our families move into his massive mansion. Leigh's parents agreed rather quickly, seeing as they'd been in hiding ever since Harper relocated them the church's safe house. Peter and Renee Kestler knew keeping their kids safe required them to move again.

However, my mother had not been such an easy sell. Dr. Sarabeth Fife was chief of surgery at Tampa Presbyterian Hospital. She was president of the HOA in their ritzy neighborhood. She sat on so many boards and made so many executive decisions it made my head spin. She'd never been one to take orders without explanation.

She was at the top of the food chain, professionally and personally. Enter Xavier with his demands veiled as requests, not offering any reasons for the upheaval to their lives other than 'It's for your safety,' and things about went nuclear. She even went so far as to demand that Xavier pop up wards around their house and her hospital. It took my dad pulling rank for my mother to relent. Adam Fife was the only person she ever surrendered to, and he *never* abused that power.

"Ah, that's today?" I cleared my throat and glanced up the stairs.

"Yes," Leigh snipped with narrowed eyes. "Don't play coy with me, missy. Got a text from Mama. They're fifteen minutes out."

"Soooo," I drawled, "enough time for me to nip upstairs and beg Harper to let me in?"

Leigh's expression flattened. "Parents first. Frustrating male second."

"Damn," I muttered.

"Sam," Leigh said, her tone chiding. "You promised your mama you'd be waiting for them when they got here."

I held up my hands to stop her. "I'll be there. But I—"

"Seriously?" Leigh pursed her lips and tipped her wrist to catch the time. "This chat you need to have with Harper will definitely take more than a few minutes. It's been over week. What's another hour?"

"Bah!" I threw a hand out in front of my body, but she was right, and I knew it. "Lead the way."

"Cut the sarcasm." She poked me in the ribs. I took one last glance at the stairs before letting Leigh steer me away.

In the common room, I plopped my ass in a leather lounge chair. "Listen, if my mother starts in on me about—"

"Sarabeth is a good mom, Samantha Fife," Leigh scolded.

I blew out a breath. "She is. She's the best, but I've never had my human life rub shoulders with my Warrior life. It might be uncomfortable, I'm just sayin'."

"You'll be fine," Leigh said.

"Says you. She and I are too much alike, bestie."

"Well, then it's a good thing Xavier has such a massive home. We'll put you on one end and Dr. Fife on the other. You can only meet in the middle with supervision."

I tucked my chin, a smile grabbing my lips. A few minutes later, the flash of brake lights in the front windows lifted my head. I cracked my neck, stretched each arm across my chest, and stood.

"Show time," I mumbled.

"Behave," Leigh said. I gave her a *who me* shrug. She rolled her eyes.

The Kestlers entered first with their brood. They all greeted me like I was one of them. Their loudness, their love for me, their *muchness* had emotion clogging my chest. So by the time my family entered, my breath hitched from refusing to cry.

Dad held my baby brother in his arms. Jared had been a surprise to all of us since the parentals had had trouble having a second child. He was four. Behind my professorial father, my mother appeared. Where dad was tall, dark, and handsome, my mother was willowy and light. Her blonde hair was done up in a French twist, and her navy pencil dress hugged her perfect figure.

"Mom!" And I was running.

I slammed into the lean woman, wrapping my arms around her, and held on strong.

"Missed you, too, babygirl," Mama soothed, embracing me the same way.

After all family members were welcomed, hugged, and settled into their new rooms, I made a getaway while my mother and Mrs. Kestler discussed the gilded Artesonado ceilings, mar-a-lago interior walls, and soft arch hallways. And hey, while Xavier's home was a lovely mix of his roots and his current station, I was on a mission.

For the second time that day, I climbed the steps toward Harper's room. He had the same fingerprint scanner outside of his door as we all did. I contemplated pressing my thumb to the pad to see if he'd added me as an approved visitor—I was in Xavier's security system after all—but didn't want to barge in. Unexpected shyness swept through me. His fiery kiss, his almost-death, and how he'd clung to me during the funeral tangled my head and heart. A flush of heat warmed my cheeks.

That wasn't why I was here, but I couldn't help but wonder where we stood. We needed to talk. About feelings. About a million things. I inhaled the deepest breath I'd taken all day and rapped my knuckles against the door.

No answer.

I pursed my lips and tapped out a cheerful staccato with both hands.

Still no answer.

I narrowed my eyes.

"Perhaps," Letty interjected, *"he isn't here?"*

"Oh." I stopped, fist suspended in midair. *"Well, there's always that."*

Dropping my arm, I stepped forward and pressed my ear to the wood. Nothing. I tapped into my Power, a zing of heat raced up my spine. My hearing sharpened. Masculine humming came from inside. I chuckled. Something about Harper humming a tune was so ... normal. Comforting?

"Harper Garrett Tate!" I pounded against the door. "Do not ignore me! Open up!" I leaned my ear back to the barrier. His humming stopped. "Harper, I know you're in there. Don't pretend—"

The door opened. I stumbled forward, caught myself, and straightened upright. Harper stood in the wide-open doorway, clad only in black linen track pants. I got a good eyeful of his chiseled chest, broad shoulders, and washboard abs. My mouth fell open. He used two fingers to close my mouth and tip up my chin. He wore an amused smirk.

"Eyes up here, Spitfire."

His hair was damp, and he smelled like clean soap and spice. He might have just showered, but he hadn't shaved. Dark facial hair stubbled his jaw.

Holy shit balls.

He raised a brow when I said nothing. "Is someone bleeding? Dying?"

"What?"

"With the way you were shouting out here, I thought you had an emergency."

Is he—was he— "Was that a joke?"

One side of his mouth quirked up. *Is that mischievousness?* My eyes flicked to the tattoo on his left pectoral, and I step closer. Without thinking, I reached out to touch the tribal-looking sun inked into his skin. He gently captured my fingers before they connected.

"Sorry." I tried to take back my hand, but he held on.

"Don't be."

"A sun?" I asked.

"For brighter days." He lowered my hand without letting go. "And a reminder for each person I've lost."

Well, blow me sideways. I took a closer look as he tapped to certain symbolic sunbeams flaring out from the clear round center: Thomas, his father. Elaine, his mother. Teddy, his teenage best friend. Molly, his ... someone?

Who was Molly?

I hissed in a painful breath. Judy and Andrew's names were etched there, the edges of his skin red, raised, and angry around the script. Their names were fresh. No wonder he didn't want me touching it.

"Harper, I—that—"

He squeezed my hand and shook his head. I watched

his Adam's apple bob when he swallowed. "Why were you trying to break down my door?"

"Right." I tugged my hand free and straightened the hem of my shirt. "I want to talk about why you've been doing your best impression of a mute recluse."

"I'm using words now."

"Don't be a turd."

"A turd, huh?" That barely-there smile reappeared.

My stupid heart did that little flutter it always did when Harper softened and reminded me of how we'd been before life happened. He gestured with his head to invite me in and left me at the door. I stepped in, and he disappeared into the bathroom.

"Okay, then."

I wandered around his extravagant room. His which looked like mine, but rather than being light and airy, his was dim and cozy. It gave speakeasy vibes with warm, dark wood, iron furniture, brass light fixtures, and various shades of gold bedding.

I ran my fingertips over the back of his leather couch situated in front of the fireplace. Bookshelves filled with very old books flanked the cold walnut-and-stone hearth. I turned a half circle and spotted a well-loved, well-used guitar on a stand next to a plush leather chair.

It was the only thing in the place not supplied by Xavier. I smiled and went to it, reaching out to stroke the cool wood. The guitar was just as I remembered. Memories of listening to Harper play it, his baritone singing songs, and how at peace he looked when he did so came rushing back to me. I picked up the instrument and slung the strap over my neck.

"Did you learn to play in the past six years?" Harper asked.

I jumped, clutched his guitar to my chest, and spun to

face him. I'd been so absorbed walking down memory lane, I hadn't heard him. That, or maybe his new Warrior Powers amplified his natural ninja skills.

Harper had slipped on a white cotton shirt. A stark contrast to his black pants and bare feet. He looked equal parts dangerous and delicious.

None of that, Fife. You are on a mission.

He gestured to me. "I tried to teach you several times, but you never had the patience."

"I still don't. It's not in my skill set." I removed the instrument and handed it over. He took it in both hands. Belatedly, guilt settled between my shoulder blades. "She called to me. I just wanted to see if we remembered each other. Sorry for touching your stuff."

"That curiosity of yours—"

"Yeah, I know." I waved a hand. "It'll kill me. We've already established I have several cat lives left to go."

One deep chuckle came from his chest, and he shook his head. Since I was never one to beat around the bush, I plowed right ahead with why I'd interrupted his day.

"You've been aloof. Broody. Pulling away." *From me.*

His knuckles turned white from gripping the neck of his guitar. His stubbled jaw flexed. It was only then that I realized why his sudden distance bugged me. Why it burrowed under my skin more than anyone else.

"It's like you've left again, but your body's still here."

A haunted shadow passed over his face, and his shoulders drooped. Dark eyes snapped to mine. That impenetrable wall he usually sported to guard his soul was completely down. I sucked in a breath. The surrendering of his defenselessness made me feel vulnerable. Raw. The Harper in front of me was the one from our past. The one who was softer, gentler.

"Don't look at me that way, Spitfire."

"Like what?"

"Like I hung the stars for you. That I'm the hero of this story." He let out a sigh, the weariness sounding as deep as the ocean, as he slipped the guitar strap over his head. A barrier separating him from me. "That was a long ass time ago and a fuckton of hard road. I'm not that guy, Sammy. Not anymore."

He was wrong.

Sure, he had much sharper edges and unhealed wounds now, was gruff and hard, but over the last month, I'd watched how he interacted with Leigh. How he became the protective brother figure for DH. How he supported the Seers who lived here under Xavier's protection. Hell, how he even pitched in to help Nigel. The old Harper still lived inside him in the way he calmly and quietly filled in as leader of the Warriors—just like when we were kids and he was the leader of his group of friends.

And there was the way he dealt with me. Always blunt, but ever steadfast. I might've had doubts about where we stood emotionally, but he had my back, my best interests, and my well-being at heart.

He still cared. He still hoped.

He'd become a damn paramedic to help people. In the past, he'd been much freer with his words and affection, but Harper had *always* shown his love best with action. And the past couple months had been no different.

He needed to be reminded.

I closed the space between us. He reared back, but I laid my palm over his heart.

"You may be more of an asshole now, battered and bruised and cussing like a sailor, but you're still you in here." I smiled at him, deciding, in that moment, to let us start new.

Start over.

Ah, maturity. Look at little Samantha Fife growing up.

Harper's neck went tight, but I kept my palm splayed on his chest.

"You're going through some stuff, yeah? And becoming a Warrior? I know a little something about that, too." I waggled my head side-to-side. "Okay, so I'm not partnered with an Archangel. But having all that Power brimming inside, your Warrior senses going on high alert without permission, and having this voice inside your head that wasn't there before? I know how that feels." I tapped his pectoral. "Hell, you haven't even gotten your Guardian. Now *that's* a trip when they first speak to you in your own brain."

Harper slipped off his guitar and put it on its stand. He settled in that plush armchair, scrubbing a hand over his face. Still putting space between us, still not saying a word. Like this whole week.

Son of a gun! What's gonna break him out of this?

"What about losing Andrew?" A pang stabbed at my own heart. I didn't wanna go there, but I could and would if it reached the mute man before me. "We watched him die. You keeping that on lockdown, too?"

"Jesus," he grumbled.

I raised my shoulders and let them drop. "I miss him."

"I spent six long years hating that man." Harper looked so dejected. "Now he's gone, and I actually miss the bastard."

"First Judy, then Andrew—" My voice cracked. "Harper, they both died on my watch." Wetness trailed down my cheeks because my eyes had spontaneously started leaking tears.

"It sure fucks you up." His voice was quiet as he leaned forward and ducked his head to catch my eyes. "I know a little something about that."

A sad, watery smile tugged the corners of my mouth. "You're like a pro."

"Yeah, I am."

Harper snagged my wrist and pulled me until I fell into his solid body. He let me scramble upright, but kept me caged against him. I righted myself, straddling his waist with my legs and my hand braced against his chest. Before I had the chance to overthink this position, his hands framed my face, and he brushed his thumbs over the tear tracks on my cheeks.

"Pops's last request was about you. To look out for you." He held me with his warm, calloused hands. "I'm doing a shit job of it, huh, Spitfire?"

"Yeah, kinda. Actually, no." His brows shot up, and I snorted. "Like, you've been there for me when I needed you, but just—"

"Not emotionally present," he finished, echoing my earlier sentiment.

"Yeah. That."

"Because—" He blew out a breath, the wheels of emotion turning behind his eyes. He dropped his hold on my head and hooked an index finger into one of the belt loops of my jean shorts—anchoring me—while he tapped his sternum with his free hand. "Because it's been a long fucking time since I've let anyone in. The last time—the last time was my fiancée, Molly."

I jerked in surprise and my mouth popped open. My brows furrowed. *Fiancée! Engaged? Last time?* I shook my head before I realized I was doing it, connecting the dots. Harper had tattooed her name on his chest. He'd loved her. Lost her. Equal parts heartbreak and jealousy warred for my attention. But this moment wasn't about me.

My mouth formed a silent, "*How?*"

"She was murdered. A tweaker, being manipulated by

a demon, hopped into our backyard. He shot her. I was too late. She died in my arms."

Harper delivered this new information without emotion, like he was reading a newspaper instead of recalling a lived experience. I ran my nails through the short hair at his temple. He shocked me by leaning into my touch.

"After Molls, I bricked up that door. Can't get hurt if I don't let anyone in."

"Sounds really lonely."

"Yeah, it really fucking is." He slid his palm up my back, under the fall of my hair, and rested it against my neck. "Pops was right. I promise I won't shut you out any more. You're the most important person I have left, and we need each other. Forgive me."

Well, damn.

I barked a laugh. "I came barging in prepared to do battle with an angry tiger. Instead, I found a calm lion. That you, Aslan?"

Harper smirked, then leaned back into his chair. He dragged me with him, using a touch of his Power. I gasped and stiffened, sprawling over him. He nuzzled—freakin' nuzzled—his nose into my neck.

"Don't fight it, Sammy." He pressed a kiss to that hollow below my ear, sizzling against my skin. "There's a shitstorm brewing. We're gearing up for war. Just be with me. Let me hold you."

Double damn.

How could I say no? Apparently, once I stopped trying to reconcile the old and new versions of Harper, and chose to roll with the punches, I became putty in his hands. I snuggled against him. He felt like a safe harbor to a sea-battered ship. A lighthouse in the raging storm of grief and fear. He was warm and smelled like his usual clean sandalwood-and-spice scent.

After a beat, I admitted, "I'm worried."

He shifted to search my face. "Explain."

"You're going to have to kill the Mage. Since you've told me, it's one of the many things I think about when I fall asleep. How will you do it? And Dominic is her right-hand demon. Who knows what new mayhem he'll stir up? How he'll thwart us next? And Camden. Oh my God—" I shoved off Harper so fast I almost fell backward, save for him banding a forearm around my back.

"Camden! Shit! I keep blocking that whole scene from my mind. But Dream Sam won't let me forget. Do you know how many times I've woken up from nightmares of him stabbing Andrew? I *know* it was Dominic wearing a Camden suit, but it was Cam's face." Revulsion and remorse shredded my guts. "How did I not know he was possessed? How did I not put two-and-two together? Maybe I *did* know. Something was way off about him, but I ignored my gut. I'd just woken up from a coma. I couldn't trust—"

"Stop it." His voice cracked like a whip. "That's not your fault. How could you have known? Dominic tapped into Bennett's personal thoughts. He knew how to play the part. *You* didn't hijack his body like his goddamn mother did. She's responsible." He shook his head and looked up towards the ceiling before lowering his gaze to me. "Not to speak ill of the dead, but Pops can shoulder some of the blame for this, too. He should have told you and Kestler what you both could be facing."

"Where is Camden?" I'd been too afraid to ask this question before now. My blade hadn't killed him, but what happened to him after his de-possession, I didn't know.

Truth be told, I'd hadn't wanted to see him. Hadn't wanted to ask about him. I wasn't ready.

"He's in—"

"Wait, I don't wanna know!"

"—one of the holding cells."

"Oh," whooshed out of me. "He's in a cell?" He raised a dark brow. "Like a prisoner? Has he asked for me? Is he okay? Should I go see him? Why's he in a cell? Is he dangerous? Can—"

Harper's mouth was on mine in a flash, his fingers slipping into my hair at the same time. The man kissed me breathless, fightless, speechless—all the lesses. But he ended it before it could escalate. My chest heaved. He rubbed the back of my head.

"I'll take you to see him when you're ready."

I let out a shaky laugh. "Like time is gonna make *that* any better."

Harper huffed a laugh and slipped his arms around my waist. He adjusted us into a more comfortable seat.

"You're awfully touchy-feely today, Tate."

How would we even work out as a couple? Could Harper ever be with me? Could I be with him? Did he view me as a lost little girl, wild child young adult, or a Warrior woman?

"Quit that," Harper growled.

"You interrupted my spiral."

"I know. Let this, whatever it may be, settle between us. We'll figure it out as we go."

"Okay. Yeah." I tried to forced myself to relax. "Easy peasy."

Harper's deep answering laugh made me think he did indeed hang the stars in my universe.

HARPER

Since Sam and I were ripping fucking Band-Aids off our souls, and since keeping her at arm's length now seemed fucking stupid in hindsight, I figured it was time for another confession. One that I wasn't sure how she'd take. One I wasn't sure I had the balls to say out loud.

Having Sam this close soothed the savage aspects of my Power. Michael brought his duty to uphold justice and bring about balance to this partnership, but it was a double-edged sword. I inherited his righteous retribution, too.

I wanted to break Camden because it wore the face of Pops's murderer. I wanted to hunt down the Mage and slaughter her. I wanted to lay waste to every demon. I wanted to roar, and fight, and wage war against Hell and anyone who stood with it. Human or supernatural, this new part of me didn't give a flying fuck, only that they must be brought to heel. Or die.

And it terrified shit out of me.

But Sam muted the cacophony of violence in my head. I'd spent time with Xavier, Kestler, and all the other

Warriors here, but none of them did for me what Sam's presence does. Having her in my space, her voice, her touch—it all soothed me.

It was just so damn peaceful with her here.

"Your ears might as well be smoking from how hard you're thinking," Sam fanned her hand next to my head. "What's cooking in there. Is it burning?"

I tucked fine blonde flyaways behind her ear. "I don't want to fuck up what I need to say." I turned inward and asked Michale. *"Why is being with her easy but also so damn hard?"*

"My ideas are naught but theory at this point."

"Try me."

"Very well," he rumbled. *"Leticia, Samantha's angel, is my second-in-command. Her Power compliments my own. We have been partners for millennia, during peace and war. We have been each other's closest council. Her Power calls to mine."*

"Okay. And?"

"You have been comrades with Samantha since you were children. She knows you about as well as any other. You trust her with your life, and she most certainly trusts you with hers. That kind of bond is the foundation on which strong Warrior Partners are made."

I huffed out a sigh, and Sam tilted her head. I shook mine, and said to Michael, *"Kestler is her Partner. Not me."*

"Perhaps," Michael mused, his tone sounding like I was a complete simpleton. *"You have feelings for Samantha that run deeper and more primal than you're willing to admit to yourself. Love is the most powerful force in the cosmos. Intimacy between souls is hard to find, and I believe you have that with her."*

My head snapped up, and I looked wide-eyed at Sam. Her brows rose.

"Harper, you're actually kinda worrying me now. What's going on?"

Did I love Sam? Did I crave true intimacy with her?

"Fuck," I muttered. My heart pounded against my sternum.

I wanted to deny it—deny what Michael hypothesized. But, goddamnit, I couldn't. Shit, that was a massive divide to cross. When had this happened? What shifted? When?

"Sam, I—" I swallowed. "I don't want to … Look, I don't understand parts about my new nature, but you—" I squeezed the back of my neck. "But you …"

"Uh oh." She gave a lopsided grin. "His hard drive is overheating."

While I gathered my shit to speak again, the blare of my phone's siren-style alarm robbed me of my nerve for this discussion. Sam tried scrambling off my lab, but I held her in place with one hand, while snagging my cell off the side table with the other.

"Holy Heaven." Sam gripped the front of her shirt. "You gotta change that ring tone."

"Yeah, probably." Xavier's name flashed on the ID. *God, the man has shit timing.* I pressed the *answer* button.

"You're late," Xavier said without preamble.

I brought us both to our feet. Sam let out a squeak, but I kept her upright and gave her a quick kiss on the forehead before answering. This conversation was far from over, but Xavier's interruption gave me an excuse to postpone it.

"I am." I glanced at my watch then looked back and held Sam's gaze. "Got tied up with something important. Be there in five."

After hanging up and stowing away my phone, I smoothed Sam's hair behind her ears and cradled her head. "Come with me?"

Confusion furrowed her brow. "Where?"

"Xavier and I have been testing weapons. He's had to dive into his vault since everything works well in my hands, but nothing has claimed me. I was supposed to meet him ten minutes ago. Walk with me?"

"He's got *more* weapons in a vault?" Sam took my proffered hand. "Is it, like a super special Warrior storage unit? He's already got a bat cave."

"One way to find out."

"Oh, I'm all over this." She laced her fingers with mine and dragged me to the door. "Let's see what Warrior Batman has in his arsenal."

I tried to ignore how Sam kept her hand in mine even as we descended into Xavier's training gym. At the last step she stopped me with a gentle tug. I faced her.

"Yes?"

"Are we cool? I meant for the malfunctioning hard drive comment to lighten the mood. You were going to give yourself an aneurism. I thought it might make you crack a smile."

Christ, I really am an asshole. I squeezed her hand. "Yeah, we're good. I prefer you with me anyway."

Sam's face lit up, and her smile shifted to devious. "You're *sure* you don't want to talk about *anything?*"

I snorted. "There is shit we need to discuss, but it'll have to wait."

"I did not take you for a coward, Kingling," Michael said. *"Embracing vulnerable feelings is not a weakness."*

"What are you? My therapist?" I snapped at him.

"If I need to be."

Fucking A. I blew out a breath, tugged at Sam, and strode into the cavernous gym. We crossed over the black mats of the large sparing area, by a training area with various pieces of equipment and targets, and stopped near Xavier's blacksmithing forge. Nyx croaked and stalked a lizard scurrying around a bucket.

"Ah, Miss Fife," Xavier said when he turned around.

He glanced at me before returning his attention to Sam. "You'll be joining us today, then?"

"She is," I answered.

Sam swatted me. "I know how to use my words, oh mighty Warrior." To Xavier she said, "Harper mentioned you were pulling more toys from storage to find him a weapon. I'll be his sparring partner."

Xavier's lips twitched, but otherwise hid any amusement. "Very well."

He beckoned us to follow with a finger crook and led us to a massive wood-and-leather trunk at the edge of the training mats. He squatted in front, spun the number combo on the lock, and with a click, the mechanism popped the lid up. It squeaked when he opened it all the way.

"How are these different from those?" Sam asked, pointing at the weapons in the trunk and then waving her hand at the wall of weapons displayed behind us.

"They are heavier. Older." Xavier pulled a war hammer from its depths. "Made by Warriors of old. They have minds of their own."

"Right." Sam hit me with a *what the fuck is this old coot talking about* look. A smile tugged at my mouth, and I resisted a laugh. She winked at me. "Are they sentient?"

Xavier gestured to Sam with the hammer. "When you partnered with your daggers, you felt that connection immediately. They spoke to you on a preternatural level. When you moved, they moved. A part of your being."

"Yeah, that was pretty awesome." She reached for the hammer, grasped the handle, and hissed. Her eyes shot wide as she jerked her hand away, holding that fist to her chest. "What the fire fart was that?"

"The ancient ones are more aggressive, aren't they?"

Xavier's sly smirk suggested he'd been expecting her reaction. *Cheeky bastard.* Sam bristled and swiped the weapon from him.

"I'll be right back," Xavier said, turning away. "Give it a test drive, Miss Fife. It's good to be proficient in all types of weapons."

I watched while she obeyed him, willing to let her satisfy her curiosity first. Xavier and I had already exhausted hundreds of weapons, and I doubted the older ones would prove differently. Sam swung the war hammer right to left, up and down, and overhead. But her jaw stayed clenched the whole time, as if holding onto the weapon took all her concentration.

"Gah!" She transferred the hammer to her off hand and shook out her right. "This thing gives off violent energy. What kinda weapons were they making back in the day? Good Lord."

"That bad?" I asked.

"You grab one and find out, Mr. We-can't-find-you-a-weapon."

I chuckled and reached into the chest. The second my fingers wrapped around the handle of a three-foot-long morningstar, the fucker telepathically latched onto my limb with invisible teeth. Heat lanced through me from hand to shoulder. I, too, hissed. It didn't hurt, but the sensation sucked ass.

"Playing musical weapons is getting old." I let go of the damn thing and massaged my left forearm.

"Try something else." Xavier reappeared with an envelope in hand. He leaned against a support column and crossed his arms. Nyx glided above the sparring area, then settled on her Warrior's shoulder. "I wouldn't have chosen that one for you anyway."

"I'm getting real tired of being a goddamn test subject, Xavier." I reached for a short-arm scythe. This one didn't bite so hard, but it felt like it had plans that would clash with mine. Like Sam, I took a warm-up swing and had to grip it tighter. The hooked blade wanted to arc wide.

"Jesus. This isn't it either." I placed it back into the chest. "Just give me the sword or halberd I tried yesterday."

"Thank Heaven," Sam mumbled, depositing the feisty hammer into the chest. "Wasn't looking forward to sparing with that. It's a mean bastard. Helios and Sol were offended I even picked him up."

I nudged the chest with a foot. "These medieval assholes are cranky and opinionated."

"I'll make you something," Xavier said with a chuckle. "But no promises it will connect with you."

He unfolded his arms and tapped the envelope against his thigh. Nyx shuffled her beak through the grey hairs at his temple. She let out an opinionated croak, and Xavier nodded.

"Andrew left you a letter in my office above the Emporium in Shield Haven." He pushed himself off the stone column with his shoulders. "I didn't expect to be giving it to you so soon.

Xavier handed me the letter, showing Sam and I the front: *To Harper, upon my death.* The blood drained from Sam's face. I slipped my arm over her shoulders. She settled in against my side. But a prick of pain and regret needled my heart at Pops' tidy script. Xavier's eyes were haunted when he passed me the envelope. We all felt Pops' loss as a silent moment of mourning passed between us.

I took the packet from Xavier and pulled out several slips of paper: a letter, something like a family tree, a map, and a list of instructions. I handed everything but the letter to Sam and started reading.

My dear son,

As cliché as I may be for saying it, if you're reading this, I have entered into Eternity, and the Leadership key has passed to you. Know that, although you are not my biological son, you are mine in every way. I held you at arm's length and never coddled you because I knew what was in store for you. It was my sacred duty to prepare you for what was to come.

Harper, it is my deepest regret that I will never see you become a Warrior of Light, but I believe you're the strongest, brightest, and most versatile fighter I've ever had the privilege of training.

I cannot imagine the battle you're dealing with inside yourself right now. Receiving an anointing from a normal infantry angel is an adjustment all Warriors go through, but to have the Archangel of all angels merge with you? That's bound to be a graver struggle. I'm assuming that you've been partnered with Michael—the prophecies all pointed to you, at the very least.

The battle lust is normal, but it will be tenfold for you. I'll repeat this since you're as stubborn as your father. The struggle to adjust to your anointing is perfectly normal. You aren't going insane. You aren't weak. Son, you'll try to shoulder this alone as some form of lone wolf machismo, but hear me now: Warriors of Light always flourish when they work together. Let Xavier, Sammy, and Leigh help you acclimate.

Included in this envelope is a portion of the lineage for one Timothy Patrick Quinn, who lives in Ireland. (He's a distant cousin of our Sam.) You and Xavier need to find him. He knew that I would be calling on him when the time came, but as recent events changed my plans, he may have gone underground. It is absolutely vital that you find him. I've also included instructions which should allow you to locate Mr. Quinn.

I have a vault in my homeland that is deeply warded. These wards will survive my death. I provided a map to show you how to find this vault. You must take Timothy and Sam with you. The doors will only open with their blood. You'll learn why after reviewing Mr. Quinn's lineage. Inside my vault, you will find your true Warrior weapon. I'm sure Xavier has exhausted his efforts to find one for you by now. There are other items in there that will be of great interest to you, too.

Keep Sam close, keep her safe, and don't make the same mistakes I did with her. I never intended to hurt her. It was a grievous error in judgment and fear of the past which led me to withhold information from both her and Leigh. I now realize they are two of the most loyal individuals I've ever mentored. They could and should be trusted with any sensitive information. As you now possess the Leadership key, you'll find that sometimes you'll have to make judgment calls which may prove costly. It is a duty I hope I prepared you for.

May Heaven be with you,

Your Pops

I tightened my grip on the paper. My eyes burned. Pops rarely gave me any encouragement, let alone be as candid as he'd been in the letter. He was gone. The man who'd raised me and did what he could to prepare me for this Warrior life was just … fucking gone.

"Harper, lemme see this." She grabbed at the letter but I lifted it out of her reach. She elbowed me. "Asshole. What does it say? Why are you being cagey?"

I cleared my throat. "Looks like we're going to Ireland."

"We?" Sam asked.

"Yeah," I grunted.

"We. You and me."

Xavier beckoned me to pass him the letter. Sandwiched between two fingers, I passed the sheet over. "Just give me a sword and a knife for now."

Her eyes widened. "By ourselves?"

Fuck. How do I travel with her alone? "Yep."

"What about Leigh? I can't leave her partnerless. The Mage? Dominic?" She pulled away from me. "Wait. Why aren't we finding you a weapon? You need one. A good one."

"I'll get it in Ireland."

"Why Ireland? What did Andrew say?" She poked me in the shoulder.

I eyeballed her. "Answers."

"We're *all* going." Xavier handed the letter back over to me. "We all seem to have our directives. You must find that vault and retrieve your weapon. Tabitha and I must locate a Warrior named Timothy. Miss Fife will help you keep your wits about you. And I suspect that Miss Kestler will not acquiesce to staying behind. I won't leave Delaney. Nigel goes where I go." Miss Kalakua and Mr. Bozeman will remain behind to watch over my affairs in my absence, keep my Seers safe, and deal with any issues that arise."

A fucking international field trip.

"For the love of Letty's wings!" Sam threw up an arm and let it drop. "Let me read that damn letter."

"No." I shoved the paper in my pocket.

Sam's spine snapped straight, and her nostrils flared. She didn't need to see his written words right now. I raised a hand, stopping whatever she was about to say.

"Later. Promise. We have a bigger issue." I met Xavier's eyes. "I told her about—" I tilted my head towards a door in the corner of the gym.

"Ah, Mr. Bennett," Xavier said, his tone contemplative. "Have you considered your options?"

"Our options," I clarified.

"No, these are *your* options, Mr. Tate," Xavier said. "You hold the Leadership key, and you've been granted Powers that none have had before you. Myself included. His fate is in your hands."

"Oh," Sam breathed out. "Oh, shit."

Her breaths grew short. Her eyes grew wide. Her head

shook in apparent disbelief. I grabbed her by the shoulders before she could freak all the way out. When she fought my hold, I firmly took her chin in my thumb and index. We locked eyes, both of us knowing she could break free if she wished, but I had her attention.

"Trust me?"

She grabbed my wrist, took a juddering breath, and nodded.

"Do you want to see him?"

Sam made a keening noise. I let go of her chin and reached for her waist. She let me pull her closer.

"Perhaps we should have this conversation later." I glanced at Xavier, then down at Sam. "With less company."

Sam stiffened. *Ah, there's the fire.* I didn't let her go even when she tried to wiggle away from me again. I held her gaze.

"Easy," I murmured. "This is my call, not his." When the fight left her body, I asked again, "Do you want to see him?"

"No," she groaned, then gasped, "Yes!" Sam rubbed her chest. "Shit, I don't know."

"Whatever. Xavier is right, it's too soon for you. You're not in a place—"

"Harper Garrett Tate," she snarled. "I know what you're doing. And I'll be damned if it's working. I gotta face him sometime. Might as well be now."

I dropped my voice. "You don't have to do this." She peered up at me. I squeezed her side.

Sam rolled her eyes, but there was hurt and fear in their blue-grey depths. I watched as she walled up her emotions and reached for that false bravado she used so often to shield her heart.

"I *do* have to. Let's go see my murderous ex."

"His actions may not have been entirely own, Miss Fife," Xavier interjected. "We don't know all of what Dominic may have done to or through him."

"True." A war raged in her eyes which brimmed with unshed tears. She let out a ragged breath. "But Dominic wore his face to kill someone I love. Pardon me if it's going to take a hot minute to work through that."

HARPER

Xavier escorted us through a nondescript door and down a wing accessible to authorized personnel only. Sam said nothing as we followed him, which didn't bode well since she never stopped talking unless something was eating at her. I felt her hand slip into mine—her tension palpable—and gave her fingers a gentle squeeze.

When Xavier stopped at another metal door, Sam's tension had risen to a crescendo. Light spilled from a tall rectangular window embedded in the door. The hallway beyond it had white walls, floor, and ceiling. I tried to block her view of the window.

"You don't have to," I murmured down at Sam.

"Yes, I do."

I quirked a brow, thinking *are you sure?* She gave me one firm nod, as if answering *absolutely*.

"Miss Fife," Xavier said, "I want to warn you that Mr. Bennett is not of sound mind. Whatever happened to him put him in a catatonic state."

Sam caught her lip between her teeth. Her grip tightened. She cleared her throat. "Show me."

"Very well," he said.

He pressed his index finger to the security pad next to the door jamb. The lock clicked open, and a door slid into a pocket in the wall. We stepped inside.

The hallway was lined with brightly lit twelve-by-twelve cells, separated from the center walk by thick panes of glass. Each cell had a seamless glass door with a fingerprint scanner, a twin bed, a sink, and a small bathroom shielded by a concrete modesty barrier.

What the fuck does Xavier need six observation cells for? I thought while following the man. He stopped at the first one, allowing us to pass him.

"He's in three," Xavier said for Sam's benefit.

I'd already seen Bennett a few times this week. With each visit, Xavier ran through my options on what to do with the man. Michael agreed with the old Adviser and told me he'd support my choice. Bennett's fate was mine to decide.

And I fucking hated it.

"Oh my God." Sam brushed past me and ran the last few yards to the only occupied cell at the very end. Her palm slapped the glass as she pressed herself against the pane and whispered, "Camden."

My heart beat tripled timed. The way his name fell from her lips, the desperate glance she threw at me, and the way her defenses crumbled like dust hit me square in goddamn the chest. She would be fucking shattered if anything happened to him. In that moment, the final piece of the puzzle snapped into place for me.

I'd *needed* to see her response to Bennett before I could choose what to do with him.

As I joined her, my eyes shifted from Sam to the man sitting upright on the bed. His back was pressed to the wall and his legs were stretched out before him. Healer Emily had cleaned him up, tended his wounds, and put him in a green scrub top and simple gym shorts. His heavily bandaged thighs were a stark reminder that Sam had fucking filleted his legs open.

They'd repaired his physical body, but healing from having a demon ripped from his mind and soul proved to be the more difficult task. Bennett didn't blink or acknowledge his ex-girlfriend. He stared into nothingness. Even when Sam called his name a second time, her tone choked with emotion, he didn't move.

"I'm going in," Sam demanded, spinning toward us.

"Like fuck you are," I growled.

"That's not wise, Miss Fife," Xavier said, bringing up the rear.

"Why not? He's practically a vegetable," she snapped.

"We don't know the extent of his condition. He seems to be going through the motions of eating and existing, but only with help from the healers." Xavier gripped one of her shoulders. "He's had a couple outbursts. Gave one of my Healers a concussion when he threw her against the wall. He turned feral with fear when Harper entered."

"Holy Heaven." Sam's eyes welled with tears. She broke away from Xavier, spun to face the glass again, and rested her forehead on the pane. "I did that. He's like this because I purged Dominic from his body. Letty told me so. I almost killed him!"

I stepped up behind her so her back pressed against my chest, and banded an arm around her for support. "You did what you had to. He was fucked either way, Spitfire. Being possessed by a demon is no life."

"He killed Andrew," she whispered.

"Dominic did that," I said, matching her low tone.

Sam shook her head and tears ran down her cheeks.

Then she struggled against my hold. I loosened my arm enough for her to turn and face me.

Her face tipped up, and I saw thunder clouds brewing in her eyes.

"I *know* Dominic wore Cam's face when he murdered Andrew. And then I see Cam like this, and I feel guilty. Cam was good to me, Harper. He only ever wanted to keep me safe—as stupidly human and mundane as that may sound. Camden always tried to treat me right."

I framed her face with my hands, my fingers splaying through her hair, and brushed her temples with my thumbs. Her thoughts were written on her face, in her tense muscles, in her trembling. Sam wanted to flee, so I gave her the avenue to do so.

"I need to talk to Xavier about him." I released her and smoothed a wrinkle in her shirt at her shoulder. "You might not want to hear that."

She turned back to the cell. From her reflection, I could see her casting guilt-ridden eyes at Bennett. Concern the prick didn't deserve. Her hand pressed against the glass. Her forehead gently butted against the barrier. I placed my hand in the small of her back. She leaned into me.

"There is no shame in walking away."

"Does it make me a horrible person?"

"No."

"Miss Fife," Xavier said, "why don't I have someone come get you? Let the team know we'll be leaving for Ireland in the next week."

Her shoulders heaved with one, two, three breaths. She nodded. "That, I can do."

Xavier hit a button on the wall at the end of the hallway.

"Sir?" Nigel's crisp accent came through the speaker.

"Please come to the holding cells and collect Miss Fife."

"Of course, sir. Be right down."

Nigel appeared a few minutes later. I promised to see her soon, kissed her forehead, and let the old butler ushered her out. Turning back, I stood outside Bennett's cell with my arms crossed over my chest and heaved a great sigh.

His lips moved as he muttered to himself, but his eyes were vacant. He slept, woke up, and used the shitter. He eventually allowed the healers to change his bandages once he'd been sedated. One of the questions that had nagged at me all week resurfaced.

Is he faking this?

Xavier joined my side. He also took a deep breath, then pressed his thumb to the pad on the door. A beep chirped, and he typed in a four-digit code. The transparent door unlocked.

"After you, Mr. Tate."

I entered the cell and went to Bennett's bedside. His green gaze slid to us, and he blinked once. When he reopened his eyes, there might as well have been a not-fucking-occupied sign on his chest. With two fingers, I reached over and pushed on his forehead. His head moved back from the pressure.

No resistance.

"Why's he like this?" I asked, bending down to study him. "I get that he was possessed. I get that Sam abruptly severed that connection. But this? Is the mind-numbing shit a normal side effect?"

"Among the unfortunate souls I've encountered post-possession, he is by far the worst." Xavier also studied the cockroach in front of us, but his expression held more empathy than mine probably did. "From my tests and scans, the best I can determine is that part of his soul is missing. Missing or dead, I cannot determine."

Jesus H. Christ.

"Then he's fucked if that piece is dead." I rubbed at the scruff on my chin. "And if it's missing, where the fuck is it?"

Xavier's shoulders shifted, and his nostrils flared. "I suspect, due to the sharing of blood, that it might be with Dominic."

"Motherfucker." I slammed a fist onto the mattress.

Bennett didn't so much as flinch.

"Precisely." Xavier straightened a cufflink, one of the small tells indicating his worry. "What that particular demon would be capable of doing with just a sliver of human soul ..."

"Catastrophic," Michael completed the thought.

I growled. Anger at Bennett, at Dominic, at the whole fucking fucked up situation flared hot and bright in my chest. Heat burst out from my heart, racing along my rib cage, my limbs, and into my fingertips. They glowed a soft amethyst.

"Mr. Tate," Xavier warned, peering at me from the corner of his eye.

Taking several steps back, I bowed my head, struggling to keep my shit together. This anger wasn't completely mine, part of it was coming from my anointing.

I need Sam.

"Reign in your temper. Now." Michael's curt command cut through the building fog of rage in my mind. *"Before you do something you regret."*

Head still bowed, I drew in as much air into my lungs as I could manage and held it to a count of eight. With measured slowness, I let that breath out as steady as I could muster. The purple light faded from my hands. My racing heart slowed. The desire to go to war ebbed. The hot anger in my veins cooled.

"Better," Michael said. *"You must remember that your Power is on a hairpin trigger until you adjust to it."*

"Is the battle lust still an issue, Mr. Tate?"

"It would seem so," I said through gritted teeth. I rocked my head, stretched out my neck, and forced the remaining flickers of Power dissipate. *Sonovabitch. That is uncomfortable.*

"Mmm," Xavier mused, his lips pursed. "I know you don't like to discuss it, but is there anything that helps? Have you found something that grounds you?"

"Sam," I barked, my voice echoing in the small space.

Xavier's brows shot up. Bennett flinched. I ground my molars together and roughly scrubbed a palm over my facial scruff.

"Miss Fife grounds you?"

"Yes, goddamn it. That's what I just said." I raked a hand through my short hair. "And I feel like shit because of it. She isn't some emotional support animal. She's a trained Warrior of Light and a grown-ass woman. But her presence soothes me. She helps me center my emotions. Michael gave me some reasons."

"I might be able to guess a few of those reasons."

"Can we focus on Bennett and get this over with? Jesus."

"Certainly."

"Do we know if this asshole remembers what happened?"

"Maybe? If Mr. Bennett weren't non-verbal right now, perhaps we'd know for certain. Historically, the others did."

I sucked my teeth. "Remind me, why his sentencing mine to deal with?"

"Because you—"

"That was rhetorical." My skin prickled. "I'm judge, jury, and executioner since I have the Leadership key and an archangel tied to my fucking soul." I spread my legs wide, planted my fists on my hips, and scrutinized Bennett. My first official ruling as whatever-I-was would be to decide the fate of Sam's ex-boyfriend.

Motherfucker.

"What are my options here," I prompted, knowing damn well what they were.

"As I see it, Mr. Tate, you have three."

I nodded, studying Bennett.

"You can leave him as he is, but he's vulnerable in this state, especially with a piece of his soul missing. His mind is apparently broken. However, he can't stay here. I will not endanger those in my care while I'm off gallivanting in another country. If you go this route, he'll have to be in an assisted living facility with no defense."

If he woke up, went berserk, and hurt people, their blood would be on my hands. If he stayed catatonic and we stowed him elsewhere, the Mage—his own goddamn mother—could come for him. That brought undo risk to more innocents. Dominic wasn't to be underestimated. What if that demon got to Bennett again and used the useless man to fuck with Sam even more?

No. We couldn't leave him here or turn him out.

"The second," Xavier continued, "and the one which might be the most merciful, would be to end his existence."

My head snapped in Xavier's direction. "Jesus Christ."

Xavier shrugged. "We can't know the threat he might pose in the future. There are too many variables that make him dangerous. And if, by some miracle—"

My lungs seized. "Fucking hell, Xavier, you're talking about killing a man. I'm a goddamn paramedic. I *save* lives."

"It would be the cleanest option. You now have the Power to make these judgment calls. I cannot presume to know what it's like to be in your position. I'm only offering you my educated options. And there is the chance that as the offspring of a Warrior of Dark he will become one himself—just like a Light Warrior's child always becomes a Warrior of Light."

"That would be really fucking bad."

Bennett going Dark made me shudder. He knew too much. He had seen our inner workings. But murdering him felt wrong deep in my gut. I wanted to kill Dark Warriors and The Mage, not her pathetic son.

"*Kingling,*" Michael said, "*your anointing allows for the execution of those who pose threats to humans, Seers, and Warriors of Light. Ending this one's life* could *be considered an act of mercy and protection against the* what if.*"*

My stomach turned over, and my knees weakened. I squatted, resting my forearms over my thighs, and letting my hands hang limp between my knees. Of all the things for Xavier to suggest, and for Michael to fucking agree to, murder was not something I would have expected. Another spark of battle-lust struck me from the inside like a bolt of lightning. I flinched. Bennett killed a Warrior of Light. Not just any Warrior. He'd killed Pops.

Andrew Shaw.

Our leader.

Demon blood ran in Bennett's veins. He was tainted. *Smell it. Feel it. Deserves death.* There was a piece of me—an ancient, deep, and angry part of my soul—that had visions of stabbing Bennett in the throat. Of watching his life's blood spill from him. It would be a justified kill.

Sam's face swam before my clouded vision. She was crouched next to her dead ex-boyfriend. Her blue-grey eyes lifted to me, filled with outrage and disbelief. Her apple cheeks were streaked with tears. Her nose was red from crying.

"How could you?" her vision asked—no, demanded.

My Spitfire.

I blinked.

Sam.

I shook my head.

She'd be devastated.

Not just devastated, she would *hate* me. If I killed Bennett, who couldn't even defend himself, she'd despise me forever. Sure, she'd resented me in the past, but this would move past that into unforgivable territory. I couldn't do it. I fucking wouldn't.

I rose up from where I'd crouched and looked at Bennett. Then I pinned Xavier with my deepest, ugliest, nastiest glare. The infamous scowl that'd made many before him crumble. The ancient Adviser, not prone to intimidation, leaned away from me. He squared his shoulders and pursed his lips.

"No," I growled. "I'm not murdering a defenseless human. Loathe the bastard? Yeah. But I'd rather kill him when he can defend himself."

Xavier smoothed a hand down the buttons of his dress shirt. "Very well."

"And the third option?"

He grimaced, then tilted his head, his eyes boring into me, as if trying to convince me that this wasn't the best one. I raised my brows in a battle of wills. *You said three, old man? It's my choice.*

With a sigh, he said, "As you know, I'm a tinkerer of Heavenly tools. I have a near-infinite number of artifacts

I've invented but never used. After the last encounter with an exorcised human, I created an item which unifies the mind. I created it by imbuing it with sacred Power."

"Is that possible?" I asked Michael.

"Only for Xavier Gerena. His angel, Cyrus, is Heaven's finest innovator and armorer. Cyrus's talents and abilities pass through to his Warrior."

I nodded, mulling over Michael's answer. To Xavier, I asked, "What is this *item*?"

Xavier reached into his pants pocket and drew a black velvet drawstring pouch, smaller than his palm. He untied the delicate knot and pulled out a small object. He held it up in his long fingers, allowing me to get a better view.

The ring he showed off had a thick silver band which wrapped around in the shape of angel wings. The wings were white—Heavenly metal white. I plucked it from his hand and weighed it in my palm. It had heft to it, even though it appeared light and weightless. The craftsmanship he'd used to weave together silver and white metal was seamless. The wings were elegant, intricate, and precise.

"Unifies the mind, huh?" Holding the ring aloft, I rotated it left and right. Even in the harsh fluorescent light, I couldn't find a single flaw. "So this ring will—what?—heal him?"

"Not heal." Xavier lifted an index finger. "It's a bandage for his deeper issues. As long as he wears the ring, the Power in it will stave off the effects of missing part of his soul. It fills in the gap and prevents anything *else* from returning."

I gave the ring a small toss and caught it in my palm. "The downside? Because I fucking know this doesn't come without cost."

"Quite correct, Mr. Tate." Xavier inclined his head and tucked his arms behind his back. "As long as Mr.

Bennett wears it, it will grant him a measure of Warrior ability. He'll be swifter, have sharper senses, and possess greater strength than the average human."

"Hmm," I mused. "Anything else?"

"Since the woman I made this ring for took her own life before I could get it on her finger, I don't know all the long-term effects. The Power will never fade, and as long as it is worn, the bearer will be blessed by its properties. But if they were to be separated after a lengthy use…"

"We won't know what will happen," I finished for him.

Xavier looked wearier than I'd ever seen him. The lines in his weathered face showed his grief and concern. I opened my mouth to speak, but closed it. What was there to say? I hadn't lived as long as he had. I didn't know what battles he'd fought.

Movement in the corner of my eye brought my attention back to the bastard in the bed. Bennett's fingers twitched on the sheets as if he were trying to claw at something. His mouth had dropped open in what looked like a silent scream. Horror and fear filled his previously blank eyes. I recognized his building panic attack before Xavier could react.

"Fuck!" I slipped the ring in my pocket and launched myself at Bennett. To Xavier I shouted, "Get Emily! Need diazepam. Now."

"*¡Mierda!*" Xavier swore. *"Dios Mio,* they're getting more frequent."

"Glad Sam isn't here to see this," I muttered.

"Mmmm, quite." Xavier strode to the intercom with hurried steps.

Bennett thrashed and screamed. His head came perilously close to slamming against the metal frame of the headboard. I snagged a flailing arm and almost lost my grip when he tried to rip it away.

"Enough of this," I growled.

A sliver of heat shot down my spine as Power boosted my strength. Bennett was no match for that, and I held him down long enough to get the restraints attached to the bed on his wrists and over his chest. Standing straight, I tipped my head back and wearily rubbed my eyes. My free hand went to my front pocket, and I felt the circle of Xavier's heavy ring.

"I could ease his suffering," I said to Michael. *"Without killing him."*

"It is a valid option. The ring contains powerful Light properties."

"But it comes with an unknown price."

"You have your options, Kingling. Make your choice and be swift about it. You do not have the luxury of time."

Bennett continued to whimper and twitch. Tears streaked down his temples. The sheets and blanket had gotten tangled up in his legs. The bandaging over his thighs bloomed with blood where his wound had opened. Emily would be irate. Bennett's suffering tugged at the healer in me.

I dug in my pocket and pulled out that ring. White metal wings flashed in the light. Xavier had made it for a woman, so the only finger it fit was Bennett's pinkie. I jammed it on him and stepped back.

The haunted shadows on his face ebbed. Whatever nightmare he'd been fighting must have stopped because his whole body relaxed and oozed onto the mattress. The tears subsided, and his mouth slackened. The dullness in his eyes brightened from his pupils out, turning his iris back to their normal color. His gaze met mine, his expression clear and whole.

"Are you, you?" I asked.

"Yes," he croaked.

"Do you know what happened to you? What I did just now?"

His fingers dug into the sheets where they were buckled down.

"Yeah." His voice was raw.

"Good." I approached the bed. "Don't make me regret this, asshole. That ring on your finger? It never comes off. Not when you shower. Not when you shit. Not when you fuck. 'Never' means not even for a second. It's the only thing keeping you from being catatonic. Got me?"

Bennett glanced at his hand. "Got it. Where am I?"

"Safe. What do you remember?"

The color drained from his face. "He kept me awake, locked inside my own mind when he … Is he gone?"

"Yeah, man." I started undoing his restraints. "Dominic's gone, and he can't get back in as long as you wear that ring."

"And Sam?"

"*That* is more complicated." My jaw clenched. I didn't want to discuss her with him.

"She hates me, right?" He rubbed at the ring with his thumb. "I'd hate me, too."

"Lucky for you, Sam has a soft spot for you." I peeked under his bandage and grimaced. I rapped my knuckles against the bed frame. "Stay away for a while. Give her time to work through this shit. Maybe she'll surprise you."

"Right." His body locked up as what was clearly pain ripped through him.

"I'll call the healers. They'll help with the pain."

"Water?" he rasped. "Maybe a lobotomy? A redo at my joke of a life?"

Aerona Bennett, formerly known as Cheryl Talbot, had been close friends with my mother. Cheryl had betrayed Thomas and Elaine Tate. She'd killed my parents. Cheryl had also twisted and manipulated her son—betraying him in many ways. And as much as it chapped my ass to admit it, Bennett and I had a lot in common. Including a compli-cated relationship with Sam.

"If you find out how to get a redo," I said after a moment, "let me know. I've got my own shit I want to do differently."

27

SAM

"You haven't said anything in ten whole minutes," Leigh punctured our little cocoon of silence on the patio of Bulwark Bistro. She took a long drink from her blueberry mocktail. "I'm concerned."

I picked at my chili cheese fries, staring at the swirl of fake cheese, red sauce, and chunks of meat as they softened the once hot, crispy potatoes. The bistro down in Shield Haven had some of the best fries. Their variety of toppings would take me at least three months to get through.

Leaning back in my metal chair, I watched early-for-the-season Snowbirds come and go out of the shops along Main Street. I heaved out a massive sigh.

"Sorry." I popped a soggy fry in my mouth. "Just thinking."

"Penny for your thoughts?"

It was a lovely afternoon, cooler than normal for the end of September in Florida. A breeze ruffled the canopy shade overhead. Mister fans around the courtyard made sitting outside tolerable. I *should* have been happy. The restaurant had filled with more patrons since we'd arrived for lunch, but I didn't give them too much notice.

I swallowed. "Did you know Xavier was holding Cam in a cell in the safe house? Full on observatory-like, like he's a science experiment."

Leigh lowered her fork. "Yeah. But I haven't done see him."

"I did. Yesterday. It got me all torn up last night. I had these horrible nightmares and gave up trying to sleep around four this morning. Nigel was awake, as usual, so I had him take me back down there." My stomach twisted. I shoved my fries away. "Camden's gone. Xavier and Harper won't tell me where he is or what's happened to him."

"Maybe—" Leigh smoothed her palms over the white tablecloth "—maybe it's for the best?"

My lips pursed. "Considering how everything went down between us, time and space might be better for me. I just worry about what Harper might have done to him."

Leigh reached over our small table and flicked me on the forehead. "Do you trust Harper?"

"Absolutely."

She smiled that all-knowing smile she got when she knew she was right. "Then trust that he did right by Camden."

Thinking of Harper led my thoughts to that moment where he'd pulled me into his lap yesterday. Heat race up my neck and behind my ears. I'd spent six years despising Harper, but he supported, saved, and defended me. We'd made our amends. He'd proven himself true.

Then he went and kissed the fire out of me. Stirred my blood. I touched my fingers to my lips.

God, is this real?

Leigh's hazel eyes narrowed on me. "What was that?"

My arm dropped like dead weight. I'd never told her about the stolen moments. It hadn't been on purpose.

Someone revoke my best friend card. Between the battle at the farmhouse, Andrew's death and funeral, our families' arrivals at Casa de Xavier, and my worry over Camden, I hadn't found the time to tell her.

"Samantha Grace Fife, you better spill whatever's got you turning bright red!" Leigh demanded. "What did you do?"

I glanced around, leaned forward with an elbow propped on the tabletop, and spilled my guts to the bestie. Her eyes slowly widened. Her mouth gradually gaped open the more I divulged. And when I told her about yesterday's moment in Harper's room, she straight up shoved me. My arm slipped, and I scrambled to keep upright.

"You jerk! How dare you keep that from me!"

I shrugged. "Timing wasn't right?"

"Not good enough," she growled and punched my shoulder. "I saw you kiss him when he Warriored up, but I thought it was a heat-of-the-moment, impulsive Sam thing. But there was more behind it the whole dang time."

"Um, yeah?" My scalp prickled. I scratched my head.

"You're the worst." She picked up her fork and speared a tomato. "So what does Harper say about your smoochy-smooching?"

Wasn't that the million-dollar question? He'd tried to tell me something, but freaked the hell out. Total brain-meltdown. I ducked my head and dragged a fry through the cheesy concoction. I wish he'd gotten it out, however bumbling it would have been.

Another deep sigh escaped me. "Have you met Harper? He's allergic to discussing his feelings."

"True." Leigh pointed her cutlery at me. "And yet

every time I see him these days, he's got you glued to his side."

I lifted my hands, palms up, and spread my arms. "He said not to stress it. Let it happen. Whatever *that* means. It's confusing and frustrating. And yet, I'm not mad about it because it really feels like he's softened to me. Like he's no longer locking me out, emotionally speaking."

"Taciturn as ever. He'll have to talk about it eventually."

"Right. On his *own* time. Men!" I shoved soggy potatoes in my mouth.

Leigh chuckled. "He says similar things about you." I glared at her. She grinned, her mouth sharpening into mischievous delight. "Sooooo, how was it?"

My cheeks heated. "How was what?"

"The Harper make-out sesh, duh." She looked at me like I was dense. "I'm pretty sure you've been daydreaming about that since you were, what? Thirteen?"

I snorted. "Twelve."

"Oh my gosh, Sam." She threw a crumpled napkin at me. "Don't you dare leave me hanging!"

"Harper didn't just kiss me." I lifted my eyes, studying the supports of the overhang to keep from meeting Leigh's prying stare. "He's ruined me. No one—not a single other male—has made feel what Harper did."

"So glad you haven't lost your flare for the drama," Leigh said dryly.

"There you are." A shadow appeared over our table. "I've been searching all over for you two."

Leilani stood above us, looking like a gorgeous Hawaiian model in her cut off jean shorts, flowy open-back tank top, and OluKai *slippahs*. Her black hair was pulled into her signature messy ponytail, and her face was done in her perfect minimalist makeup style.

Did she overhear us? I hoped to hell not. We might have found some middle ground, but I didn't want my frienemy listening to me spill my mushy girl-feelings about a man I've had a massive crush on since childhood.

I looked up at her. "Who's looking and why?"

"Adviser Gerena sent me to round up the Warriors. He wants a meeting with everyone before we fly out tomorrow morning. I left Sajid at the manor settling a fight between a couple teens." She hooked a thumb over her shoulder. "Found Talia teaching a group of Seer children how to pickpocket. And Jax helping some elderly couple take their groceries into their home. He's waiting for me."

Sajid the diplomat, Leilani the ass-kisser, Talia the rogue, and Jax the gentleman. *If that isn't keeping in character, I don't know what is.*

I checked my phone to see a few missed Lani texts. "Sorry."

Leigh also woke up her cell, tapped the screen a few times, and blanched. "Oh, dang."

Recognizing *that* tone—the one that suggested Big Things were happening—I demanded, "What is it?"

Lani cocked her head. "Everything okay?"

"Not sure I'd say 'okay' but it's definitely an interesting turn of events." She turned her phone around. "Read."

Leilani shifted a few feet to loom over my shoulder. An article from the Tampa Times filled the screen. It was timestamped from an hour ago.

Hillsborough Hellraiser Arrested
Alex Jacquet, leader of regional Satanic cult called the Infernal Zealots, has been taken into custody for the recent string of arsons targeting local places of worship. Authorities found Jacquet's DNA on evidence collected from the most recent crime scene, linking him to the fires and murder of Reverand Harrison Weaver. Witnesses say

Jacquet vocally welcomed the arrest and boasted of his horrific crimes as he was loaded into the police vehicle ...

I looked up at Leigh. "Well now, that wasn't on my Warrior Bingo card."

Leilani reached over my shoulder and used a finger to scroll further down in the article. "Those crimes were committed by Dominic while possessing your precious ex-boyfriend. How did this Jacquet guy get caught up in this ..."

I bristled at Lani's unspoken implications with the *"precious ex"* comment. Just like that, the Hawaiian Harpy was back—frienemy status firmly in place. I opened my mouth to tell her as much when Leigh grabbed and squeezed my wrist. She gave me a sharp look.

With a much brighter tone, she said, "We shouldn't keep Advisers Gerena and Holland waiting." She stood, fished in her purse, and threw some cash on the table. "It's almost two, and your food's cold, anyway."

"Guess you're right." I shoved away from the table, the chair legs scraping over the concrete. It took all my recently-learned decorum, and the fear of Leigh's retribution, to keep from saying a single sassy comeback and follow Leilani off the patio. The three of us weaved our way out of the cafe. We filed out onto the sidewalk.

"Jax is waiting for me and I'm not your babysitter." Leilani turned on her white tennis shoes, and strode off down the path. Over her shoulder she called, "Don't keep Adviser Gerena waiting."

I rolled my eyes. "God, she's so bitchy."

"Sam!" Leigh backhanded my shoulder gently. "She is a fellow Warrior. And a good one at that. Mind your manners."

"Whatever." I tilted my head in the same direction as

Lani. "Let's not give her more ammo to *besmirch* my good name."

Leigh shoved me forward. "You're ridiculous."

As we headed towards the paved pedestrian path that connected Shield Haven to Xavier's manor, we passed Xavier's antique shop. Harper jogged down the front steps. He wore his normal black tee, work-worn jeans, and scuffed-up brown boots.

To my horror, my girl hormones noticed the way that shirt stretched over his chest and around his biceps. The way his jeans settled on his hips. That he wore his dark scruff longer. And sometime between now and yesterday, he'd gotten a haircut. Super short on the sides, inch long on top.

Cut it out. This isn't one of your romance novels. Lordy.

Harper lifted his chin when he saw us. When his sights landed on me, there was a softening in his hard-ass demeanor. My heart triple-timed for a moment.

Get it together, girl.

"Just heard from Xavier," Harper called out to us. "You two headed back?"

"Yep!" Leigh grinned at me, like she'd read my mind. I didn't like the mischievous glint in her hazel eyes. Only my bestest friend could embarrass me about the massive flame I carried for Harper.

"Whatever you're thinking, don't." I pointed a threatening finger at her.

"Wouldn't dream of it." She lifted her hands, Cheshire smile on her face as she backed up a few steps.

Harper continued his jog over and joined my side. He placed his hand on the small of my back. "I'll come with you."

"And I'll give you two some space." Leigh cackled and

twirled face-forward before giving us a small lead. "I don't want your love-bug cooties."

I sighed and rolled my eyes. There would be no such thing as privacy with her bat ears. Harper chuckled and my heart leapt when he twined his fingers with mine. He gently tugged my arm.

"Come along, Spitfire."

I followed him and after a moment asked, "What's with the nickname anyway?"

"Fits you." He shrugged. "You earned it. Sammy seems inadequate now."

"I'm kinda partial to Sammy. But I like Spitfire, too."

"I'll still call you Sammy." He let go of my hand and pushed me in front of him as a pack of middle-aged women spilled out of the only bar in town.

One lady wore a sparkly pink tiara and a white sash with rhinestones, which spelled out 'BRIDE' across her chest. And in the shuffle of trying to bob and weave around the gaggle of tipsy ladies, we caught up to Leigh. As we crossed in front of a wide alleyway, something red flashed in my peripheral vision. I stopped, looked down the corridor, and took two curious steps between the buildings.

"What was that?" I asked Letty.

"I think you know. But how?"

The hair on my neck prickled.

"You feel that?" Leigh asked from beside me. "It's almost demonic, but how—"

Whatever she was going to say next died in her mouth because Harper let out a low growl. His unique lavender aura pulsed out like a beacon. A sure sign his Power had been triggered. I called on my own, and a gentle buzz of heat zinged down my spine. My hearing perked up. My Warrior eyes sharpened.

With my superpowers turned up, I saw a certain crimson-flesh demon dart across the way and disappear behind a dumpster. I bolted down the passage with Harper and Leigh hot on my heels. I tackled Dominic to the ground. He didn't fight as we went down, his hat tumbling away, and I won the battle position by straddling his stomach,

He'd used Camden.

He'd been inside my head.

He'd *murdered* Andrew!

The asshole laughed. Freaking laughed! Like this was a game. I reached for Helios. The hilt warmed to my touch as it materialized. I brought the dagger over my head, and the conniving demon went utterly still. His black eyes met mine. I paused, which seemed to be his objective, and I hated him even more for it.

"You can kill me." A hint of a smile twitched in the corner his mouth. "But know that I possess the missing piece of Camden Bennett's soul."

My stomach bottomed out and dread sluiced through me. I lowered my blade, stunned into inaction.

"It was quite a shock to me, as well. That nugget is a living thing, and it is grafted to me so long as I walk the Earth. If you kill me, you kill a part of him. I'll eventually return, but the boy? Not sure how that would work."

His words were ice water on an open nerve.

I called for more Power. Grabbing his hair with one hand, I slammed his head against the concrete. Once, twice, three times before Helios clattered to the pavement and both my fists pummeled his guts, his sides, his face. He threw up his arms, blocking me where he could. He needed to hurt. To bleed. I wanted to disfigure him. *Ruin* him. Rage and heartache brought forth angry tears. I continued to wail on him while Dominic continued to laugh and wheeze.

"Sam!" Leigh shouted. "Stop!"

"Sammy, that's enough." Harper's voice cut through my frenzy.

My body jerked at the panic in their voices. I finally felt Letty's calming warmth flow through me. I quickly glanced over at Leigh and Harper. They stood off to the side six feet away. Leigh had Fury her right hand and her left was extended towards me. Her hazel eyes were wide with shock. Harper's purple aura flickered as he tried to rein in his Power, but his expression was furrowed in concern.

Chest heaving with exertion, I scrambled off Dominic, snatching up Helios as I went. With a growl, I reached down, yanked Dominic to his feet with one hand, and threw him against a dumpster. I crowded him and pressed my forearm against the demon's windpipe with Helios's sharp tip pressed against his stomach. He grinned and black demon blood coated his white teeth.

"You," he whisper-wheezed, "are a delight."

"And you're a piece of shit," I snarled. "How'd you get past the wards?"

"Hey, guys!" DH's voice rang out clear and bright. Almost of its own accord, my head whipped in her direction. To my horror, Xavier's daughter came trotting down the alley. "Everything alright? I saw—Oh. Oh, my gosh."

She stopped abruptly a few yards away from us. My world came to a screeching halt. *Why is she here? She's supposed to be attending online class today.*

"Fucking hell." Harper's gaze darted between me and DH, his aura still flickering with his indecision. DH or me. His jaw flexed.

"Get her out of here!" I shouted, making the choice for him.

"I got her," Leigh said. "Stay with Sam." At Harper's nod, Leigh whirled to meet DH halfway.

With renewed intensity, Harper stepped up beside

Dominic and me. "Answer her question, demon. How'd you get past the protection on this town?"

Dominic's chest shook with laugher and my attention snapped back to him. I met his eyes, glared at him, and added a touch more weight against my arm at his throat while increasing the pressure of Helios against his belly. He hissed as the blade met his skin, bringing with it the smell of burning flesh.

"You can kill me," he goaded. "But I wonder what would happen to your dear, sweet Camden if you did."

"Is Dominic telling the truth?" I asked Letty. *"If I send him back to hell, will I kill a part of Cam?"*

"I suppose given the conditions, that could happen," Letty said. My skin crawled. She continued, *"Camden is the Mage's direct blood descendant, and she's connected to Dominic in Power. Dominic has been consuming Camden's blood since he was born. Dominic also possessed the poor boy, and you severed that connection without warning. I am inclined to believe Dominic, in this instance. But* do not trust him. *"*

"Definitely not." To Dominic I snarled, "Answer our question."

"Might you lower your damn blessed weapon?" he choked around the pressure on his windpipe. "It's searing my skin."

"The hell I will." I let out a dark chuckle. "You must be out your mind."

"I'll tell you what you'd like to know," he crooned as best he could.

"Sammy," Harper warned. "Don't trust this asshole."

I gritted my teeth. "I don't!"

"Calling a truce." Dominic raised his arms in surrender. "I'll be good. Cross my heart."

I risked a glance at Leigh. She still had Fury drawn. Her free arm was flung in front of DH, protectively baring the teen. Harper also had a white-metal knife in hand. Making a questionable judgement call, I let up on Dominic's throat enough that he no longer needed to struggle to speak.

"That a girl." Dominic's smile widened. He pointed at Helios. "Might you ease up a bit more, dear? I *do* have information you want. Think of all the Seers. All the innocents …"

"Goddamnit." Harper gnashed his teeth and stepped up close, his chest bumping my shoulder. His aura vibrated. He felt ready to blow. "Start speaking or this knife will be in your fucking kidney before your next breath."

"Easy," I murmured. He huffed, saying nothing but everything at the same time, as he pulled back a few inches.

"I can tell you more than how I got past your wards," Dominic taunted. "I have insider information, if you will."

"Gah!" I released my forearm and planted my hand to the center of his chest instead. Helios stayed at his gut. "Fine! But no shenanigans from you." I wanted answers almost as bad as I wanted to stab this freaking demon. "You've got two minutes. Talk fast."

Dominic flipped his wrist. His hat on the ground appeared in his hand and he placed it on his head. He straightened out the sleeves of his suit. "Now that we're being civil—"

"Just because I haven't embedded this in your eye socket—" I lifted Helios to his sight-line "—doesn't mean I won't. You're on my turf. On sacred ground. Surrounded by three Warriors of Light, mind you, so choose your words carefully."

"I do enjoy our sparring." Dominic smirked and faux-shivered. "Gets my black blood pumping."

"The point, motherfucker," Harper growled, "get to it."

"And you," Dominic eyeballed Harper before squinting at him. "You've Warriored up. Who's your angel, boy?"

"None of your fucking business," Harper said.

"How are you on sacred ground?" I asked for what felt like the millionth time.

Dominic smiled benignly. "The border in Shield Haven is less dense than the one in the heart of Xavier Gerena's property. *That* ward is impenetrable, but here?" He tilted his head toward the open end of the alley. "I was able to poke at it while possessing your boy—my toy—and discovered I could cross. Once we were so barbarically severed from each other, and I discovered that I had a sliver of his soul. So, I tested my limits again."

"Fuck," Harper murmured.

Holy Heaven. I wiped my mouth and glanced past Harper at Leigh. Her expression was grim and DH's eyes were still saucer-wide. Looking back at Dominic, I cleared my throat. "And here you are."

He spread his arms low and wide. "Here I am."

I released a tense breath. "Can Camden's soul be restored?"

Dominic pressed his fingertips to his chest, next to where my hand still pinned him. "What makes you think I would give it up?" His tone was glib, but his words dripped with seriousness.

"What are you planning?"

He gave a dramatic shrug and sigh, keeping his smile in place. I wanted to pinch his little head off and stomp on his stupid fedora. Part of me was willing to tolerate his manipulative ass. Most of me wanted to dig Helios into his guts and twist the blade.

"Does Aerona now you have a chunk of her son?" I

asked, diverting my mind from mutilating this conniving, murderous turd. "Not that she'd care."

"No. My chosen one draws on my Power only. No Dark Warrior shares a relationship like you do with your angel." A sly, licentious expression crossed his face. "I've finally figured out who your angel is. Seeing you fight the other day reminded me of her. My dearest Leticia has a distinct style, and she suits you."

His revelation hit me like a haymaker to the gut. Letty's presence in my soul seemed to scramble to find purchase. Her shock, more than mine, made me wheeze and I stumbled backward. *Holy* freaking *Heaven.* Harper grabbed my right shoulder. He squeezed, and I remembered how to breathe.

"Are you okay?" I asked my angel.

"I don't know. He is smarter and more cunning than most all demons. And apparently more observant."

"Enough." Harper cut in between me and Dominic. He raised his knife to Dominic's face. "No more games. Why are you here? You knew damn well that your movement would catch our attention."

"I'm so glad you asked." Glee colored Dominic's words as he adjusted his tie. "While inhabiting Camden's body, I was privy to his thoughts and interactions. His comings and goings. I gathered so many interesting morsels from those ignorant of my machinations. They told me sensitive things. And I had free rein to, ah, snoop on Andrew Shaw's property. I *learned* things."

I shook my head.

"Like what?" Leigh called, shoved DH firmly behind her, and took a step in our direction.

"The location of a safe house or two in Ireland. The approximate whereabouts of an important vault belonging to Andrew Shaw. The identity of one Timothy Patrick Quinn."

"Motherfucker." Harper slammed his free fist into Dominic's face.

Dominic doubled over, cough-laughing, and when he straightened, black blood coated his teeth and lips. He took out a handkerchief and wiped his mouth.

"Hitting me doesn't fix your problem. Though that's quite a punch. Who did you say your angel was?"

"Harper might actually kill him." Letty said softly in my mind. *"We need him alive until we can figure out this impacts Camden."*

"Right." I pulled Harper back a few feet and felt him shudder beneath my touch. With a squeeze on his forearm, I let him go and turned back around. To Dominic, I snarled. "Harper's angel is none-ya-business. Change of subject. You have a piece of human soul and some very sensitive Warrior information. What do you want?"

"To make a deal, babe." He winked.

The hair on my neck rose like hackles on a dog. "Don't call me that."

"Fuck this shit," Harper said, trying to get around me again.

Good God, he's strong-strong. His Warrior upgrade made him almost more powerful than me. I braced my back against his chest.

"Harper."

His growl vibrated against my muscles.

Leigh took several steps towards the three of us, and raised her voice. "We don't make deals with demons."

Dominic met my eyes once more. I swore he was seeing through me and directly at Letty.

"Come with me, *love.*" He held out his hand. "We'll be great together. You come with me, and I'll call off the

Mage. A decades-long battle with my Dark Warrior, gone. Just like that."

"Fuck no."

I felt Harper start to lunge. "Leigh!"

Trusting she knew what I wanted, I whirled on Harper and braced my hands against his chest. My best friend moved at the speed of light and swooped in to catch his arm. He struggled against us, his purple aura going bonkers.

Taking a risk, I laid my palm on his cheek. "Hey, hey, hey. I got you. Deep breaths." Harper froze, heaving like a winded horse, as he processed my words. Standing on my tip-toes, I reached up and kissed his forehead. "He has Cam's soul. Some of our secrets. We don't know the depth of it. So, we cannot kill him. You pulled me back from the darkness. Now let me help you."

Harpers eyes closed, all the fight leaving him. He scooped me in his arms, hugging me like I was his lifeline.

"You're right." His voice shook with restraint. "Sorry."

"Don't move," Leigh said, pointing Fury in Dominic's direction.

"Oh, my dear, I'm not going anywhere," he purred. "I'm invested."

I untangled myself from Harper and glanced down the alley to check on DH.

Only she was gone.

Nowhere to be seen.

Turning in a circle, panic climbed my spine. "Where is DH?"

28

SAM

L eigh glanced to where DH should have been. "She was just—"

"There." My heartbeat whooshed in my ears. I pointed to where I'd last seen the teen, as if that would help.

"Don't forget Dominic, Brave One," Letty reminded me.

"There you are!" I nearly crumbled in relief. *"Are you okay?"*

"Of course."

Before I could question if that were true, DH came running down the alley.

"Sam!" She held her messenger bag cradled to her chest. "Sam! I got something for you."

"Ah, there's the wee poppet now," Dominic mused. "Not to worry."

"Shut up," Harper, Leigh, and I said in unison.

I pointed Helios at him. "Don't talk. Just ... stand there. Be seen, not heard."

"As you wish, dearie."

"And don't fucking move," Harper growled.

The demon bared his teeth in a mocking grin, raised

his hands in faux-surrender, and stowed his blood-smeared handkerchief in an interior pocket of his suit jacket. "Believe me, I'm not going anywhere."

I glanced at him and tilted my head, as if to ask, "What're you playing at?"

He tapped the side of his nose then pointed at DH. She came to a skidding stop next to me.

"Where did you go?" Leigh asked DH. "You scared us, kiddo."

DH bent over, bracing her hands on her knees, trying to catch her breath. "While y'all were talking, I remembered cataloging this potion set when I attempted to get Daddo to go digital. He didn't like it, but that's not important." She took off her bag, pulled out a wooden box, and passed it to me. "It's one of his experiments. Never been tried. We kept it in his safe at the antiques shop. It's risky, but this might be an answer to our dilemma."

"Oh, this sounds interesting." Dominic pushed off the dumpster. "Color me intrigued."

Leigh, closest to him, lashed out with her sword arm. She pointed Fury right at the Crimson Creep's throat, pinning him still. He raised his hands and smiled. She rolled her eyes. "I won't kill you, but rest assured, you'll be begging for death."

The demon shivered. "I love it when Warriors threaten me."

"Risky how?" Harper barked, his expression tense.

I sheathed Helios, took the box from DH, and flipped the lid. Two crystal bottles nestled in matching compartments—one filled with silver liquid, the other with gold—and two wide-leather wrist cuffs lay inside. In Xavier's neat penmanship, on the underside of the lid, he'd written, *"Instructions for Binding Demons."*

My eyes snapped up to DH.

Hooboy.

She nodded in earnest.

"What is it?" Leigh asked.

"Some woo-woo, hocus pocus, Warrior of Light shit courtesy of Xavier." I rotated the box so Leigh could see it, too.

"Sam! Language!" Leigh scolded before reading the note out loud. "To enslave a demon, a Warrior must carefully follow the steps below."

"Holy fuck, he didn't." Harper scrubbed his face.

Leigh continued. "Step one, place the cuff with the depiction of a dragon on the demon."

"That would be me," Dominic interjected. Rising a single finger, he tapped the end of Fury. He hissed as his skin burned when he touched the Heavenly metal.

I plucked up the cuff in question. Etched into the leather was a winged dragon with a massive set of horns. Harper reached for it, but I snatched it away.

"Sammy, whatever you're thinking, don't," he warned.

"Second," Leigh read on, "the Warrior of Light must wear the cuff with the depiction of a lion."

"Wait just a goddamn minute, Kestler," Harper said. "Let me see this."

He reached for the box, and I darted away from him and closer to Dominic.

"Do it," Dominic goaded. "This should be fun."

"No!" Harper shouted. "Don't you fucking dare, Spitfire."

"Sam, we don't know the risks," Leigh said.

Over their objections, I read, "Third, the silver vial must be drunk by the demon simultaneously with the Warrior drinking the gold vial. The effect will enslave the demon to the Warrior, and it will do their bidding. The demon will not be able to lie to or hoodwink the Warrior, nor can the demon bring harm to the Warrior."

"What should I do?" I asked Letty. *"Can we trust this?"*

"If Xavier Gerena created it with Cyrus, I would venture to say that it wouldn't bring harm to you, but it is an awfully big unknown."

"Sounds like this might be the answer to our issue," I said.

"Seriously?" Leigh asked. "You would chance this?"

"This is some insane shit, even for you." Harper dipped his head, trying to get me to meet his eyes. "I won't let you do it."

"You guys, we can't let Dominic go." I stepped closer to the demon. "Sending him back to Hell while he carries a part of Camden's soul is unconceivable to me."

"True," Leigh said slowly. "Why did Adviser Gerena make this and not tell anyone about it?"

"Xavier doesn't need permission to create objects of Power." I shrugged. "It's his gift"

Harper narrowed his gaze at me and inched closer. I made sure to keep the same amount of distance from him that he low-key tried to gain and prayed to whoever in Heaven would listen, *"Let me be faster than him. Than Leigh. Let me channel the cheetah."*

"I'm conflicted," Leigh said.

"You guys, this might be our best chance." DH looped the strap of her bag back over her head and gripped it tight. "He knows too much."

Harper shook his head. "Short stuff, it's untested."

While the three of them discussed the risks, Dominic caught my eye. His slow smile and lifted brow said he *wanted* this. He must have been amping his chaotic energy, because everyone started talking over each other. Leigh even lowered Fury in her distraction. I heard questions about the how's and why's, and what if's of using Xavier's demon enslavement potions.

But this beef with Dominic?

No one would have control over him but me.

He created mayhem just because he damn well felt like it. He'd defaced holy places, and possessed someone I cared about, and killed Andrew. But worst of all, he'd invaded my mind, toyed with my emotions, and played games. If I could stop Dominic, if I could have power— actual Power—over him? Yeah, I'd made up my mind.

One look at the red demon who plagued my life, and I knew beyond a shadow of doubt I'd take the risk and shoulder the consequences With some quick slight-of-hand, I pocketed the potions, quietly set the box at my feet, and took out the Warrior's cuff with the lion.

"Zugzwang, love," Dominic purred. "Your move."

Dominic thrust out a hand. I slapped the dragon cuff on him, the lion band on me, and pulled out the vials. He was still playing chess while everyone else was playing checkers.

I knew and didn't care.

"Sam! No!" Leigh shouted. Her voice echoed in the alley. Harper moved at me with more speed than I was used to. A burst of Power shot through my legs.

"Too late." I ducked away. "I'm doing this."

"The fuck you are," he said, lunging for my wrists. "*I'll* do it. I can't risk you. Not again."

"Harper." I danced out of his reach. "You're a powder keg ready to blow. Your Power, your anointing, your conversion—it's too much for you right now. *I* won't risk *you*."

With that, I tossed Dominic the silver potion. He caught the vial, uncorked it, and chugged. Harper took one last lunge at me, but I tossed back the golden liquid as his solid body collided with mine. He wrapped me up in his arms to keep me from toppling over and held on tight.

"Jesus Christ, Sammy," he groaned in my ear. "You'll be the death of me."

Seconds ticked by as we waited.

"Maybe it expired?" DH suggested.

I met Dominic's eyes. Completely black orbs stared back at me. "The almighty Cyrus seems to have failed—"

Then it kicked in.

Dominic collapsed onto the ground. He let out an unholy wail like a screeching barn owl, putting every nerve of mine on edge. The onset of what felt like an ice cream headache ripped through my forehead and temples.

"Shit, shit, shit." I buried my face into the crook of Harper's shoulder. "That's like the worst case of brain freeze ever."

I focused on sucking in stupid calming breaths like Nigel had taught me while Harper held me close, one hand pressing into my back and the other stroking my hair. Dominic screams bounced off the brick walls, and was punctuated with short bursts of demonic language.

Everyone grew quiet except for the howling demon. Goose pimples rippled over my skin. I peeked out from where my face was buried.

Dominic writhed on the ground. His fingernails bled as he continually clawed at the asphalt. He suddenly sat up and ripped at his clothes, his hair, the invisible collar. His frantic motions started slowing down. His whole body heaved as he pulled in breath after breath.

"Bullocks!" he yelled and threw his head back. "Death must be easier."

"Can't believe you did that," Harper murmured against my ear. "So fucking impulsive."

"I know," I muttered into his shirt.

"Jesus, you're batshit nuts," he whispered.

"Maybe. The brain freeze is starting to go away."

"Super." He didn't let me go. I found that I didn't want him to.

"Miss Kestler," Dominic moaned and grabbed Leigh's ankle. "End me with that sword. Now."

"Pipe down," Leigh snapped, shaking him off her leg.

"Letty, you there?" I asked. *"How's it going? We good? You cool? Are my innards okay?"*

"Yes, but that was rather uncomfortable. I will have to study this new connection, but I detect no harm done to you. It seems to be a sort of restraint, like a leash, but you control it. However, Dominic?" The sneer in her voice was almost visible in my mind. *"He'll not have such a peaceful transition to being enslaved."*

Waves of hot and cold energy burst out from the suffering demon. I untangled myself from Harper's embrace in time to see Dominic attempt to stand, fall back to his knees, and wail again in utter agony. He flung his fedora at the brick wall across the alley, gripped his black hair, and rocked back and forth.

A spiked collar, with teeth on the inside, materialized, clicked shut around Dominic's neck. He clawed at the restraint, to no avail. Black blood leaked down his throat. I gasped as a golden thread of light, like a leash, spiraled out from me and snapped to his collar. Both immediately disappeared into thin air. Everyone looked from Dominic to me.

Dominic continued to howl, grabbing at his chest, ripping fabric, and popping buttons from his posh suit. He writhed on the dirty asphalt, then he went still, groaning and huddled in on himself. After a few more heartbeats, he settled, quiet and unresponsive.

"What the fuck happened?" Harper asked.

"Y-you didn't see that?" I asked, surprised. "The leash and collar?"

"What're you talkin' about, Sam?" DH asked.

"The stabby collar." I jabbed at my throat with my fingers. "The leash of gold?" I waggled my digits from my neck towards Dominic. "The blood?"

Leigh's brow furrowed, and she shook her head. Harper's gaze bored into me, trying to understand what the crap I was talking about.

"I don't think we can see what you see," DH said. "Must be because you made the connection. What else happened?"

"Nothing," I answered.

Dominic stirred with a pained moan.

"Adviser Gerena is going to be wondering where we are." Leigh said. "What are we going to tell him?"

"The truth," Harper said. "Just go up to the manor. Take DH with you. Sam and I will join you soon."

Leigh crossed over the alley, pulled me from Harper, and gave me a brief hug. "You sure you're okay?"

"Yeah."

DH gestured to my new pet demon. "What about him?"

Harper strode over and toed Dominic, rolling him over. A gasp escaped me. Dominic's red flesh had been replaced with bronzed, tanned skin. Under his ripped suit was solid muscle. I felt an internal tug of something like panic, but it didn't belong to me.

It was Letty's frantic alarm.

"No, no, no!" she wailed. *"This can't be possible."*

"Slow down." Had I ever needed to calm down Letty? Never. Even when Aerona commandeered my mind, she'd consoled me.

"He's been missing for so long ...lost to everyone," my angel

muttered, more to herself than to me. *"We'd wondered——"* A jittery breath echoed in my brain.

"Don't leave me hanging, Letty."

"Look, Brave One," she snapped, using a tone she'd never used. *"Really* look *at him! Think back to your vision!"*

Harper hauled Dominic to his feet and propped him up against the dumpster. The demon groaned and gripped the dirty bin. Neither seemed to want to touch each other longer than necessary. I mentally stripped away Dominic's tattered suit and replaced it with a white chiton. In my imagination, I added a massive set of black wings spreading from his back.

My head tilted as I studied the formerly crimson-skinned demon before me. His black hair was now a dark chocolate color. His face was perfection—quite possibly the most gorgeous being I'd ever seen—even with a busted lip, black eye, and *golden* ichor dripping from his neck.

With a breathy chuckle and said, "Well, that was … *something else…"*

He winced but still managed to give me a half smile. And, holy shit, did it make him fifty billion time hotter. It was only when I met his eyes that I accepted what I was seeing before me. Instead of black voids, molten brown irises peered at me. I sucked in a breath as dizziness washed over me. My knees buckled.

Harper immediately rushed to my side and slipped an arm around my waist. "What's wrong?"

When he saw me gaping, Dominic glanced down at himself. He studied his hands, flipping over his palms. He felt the bones of his face. He caught his reflection in a broken mirror across the alleyway then he howled a delighted laugh.

I wavered on my feet. Harper held on strong.

"Sam," he growled. "Answer me."

"I can't," I gasped. "Do you see—does he look different?"

Harper glanced at Dominic. "He looks like he did five minutes ago."

"Well, my dear Samantha," Dominic crooned. He gingerly pushed off the dumpster and stiffly straightened his ruined clothes. "It seems this binding spell has stripped all my glamor powers away just for you. You and I can see me as my true self."

Letty let out a scream deep inside my soul.

The demon before me was no demon.

He was an angel.

The most beautiful of all of them.

The Prince of Darkness.

The Morning star.

Lucifer.

ACKNOWLEDGMENTS

First off, I have to recognize the life events that tried to break my creativity but didn't succeed. Screw you! Warrior's Betrayal was written during one of my hardest seasons of life. Add in editorial delays, and it felt like this book would take decades. Every word, every sentence, has been battle. But here she is *published*... later than I'd intended, but published nonetheless!

Katika Schnider and Sam Parrish, I quite literally do not know where I'd be without you two. The both of you came to my rescue the *moment* I asked for it. Zero hesitancy. Full send. I am so humbled and so grateful. Also, thank you for reminding me that me I don't suck even when I've had my umpteenth author meltdown. And to not let that bitch, Imposter Syndrome, win. Your unfailing friendship and tough love are what I need to survive this writer thing. Love you both.

Anne Larsen, thank you for your edits on Betrayal, and helping her become the book she is today. I'm profoundly grateful for all the writerly things you've taught me and guidance you've provided over the years. I truly appreciate you investing your time into my craft.

To my cover artist, Frina Art, you preformed literal magic. When I saw the rough draft of Betrayal's cover, I had a full-scale come apart, in the best way possible—like you plucked the image straight from my brain. It. Is. Everything. I'm still not over it. I love it so much.

Kaitlin "Eagle Eye" Kino, your attention to detail is

unparalleled. Thank you for using your magic powers to proofread Betrayal so she is as clean as possible. Besides being good at what you do, you're one of the bestest friends a girl could ask for. Love you lots!

A special thank you to Sarah Smith. You are a gem of a human. I owe that damn clock app for bringing us together. Thank you for letting me pick your "reader" brain on the regular. I genuinely appreciate your perspective and your thoughts. But more than that, I'm proud to count you as a friend!

My parents are quite literally the best humans on this earth. They raised me to believe that my imagination was something to be cherished. That I should chase my dreams, but stay grounded so I could do something about them. My parents are *always* in my corner, no matter what, and that kind of support is precious, intangible, and rare.

Jacob, husband mine, you provide me with that real life, practical support. As a creative, sometimes my head is in the clouds and you keep me grounded. Yes, I've probably forgotten to send you the grocery list and move the clothes to the dryer as I type this. There are a million little ways you show me you love me. I see you. I love you, too.

Casey, you left me in December of 2020, and I still miss you all the time. You were the best horse I didn't know I needed. But God knew. You took a piece of me when you passed, and I find that I'm okay with that. I'll honor you in every story I write, because you're tattooed on my heart.

ABOUT THE AUTHOR

Megan is Floridian by birth, Nebraskan by marriage. She currently lives with her husband and their two dogs in a little stilt house on the Anclote River. She has been obsessed with horses since she learned to walk. So much so that she quit nursing school to pursue something more horse-centric. In 2007, she graduated from St Andrew's University in North Carolina with a degree in Equine Business Management—doing things her way, as per usual.

A life-long reader and vivid dreamer with an overactive imagination, Megan decided to use her powers of story-telling to write a book. That book took her on a fantastic journey. Now, she loves creating worlds to share with others.

Megan also enjoys tea (because coffee hurts her stomach now), horseback riding, cardio, Denver Bronco football, Nebraska volleyball (#GBR), roller coasters, and theme parks.

She'd love to connect with you. Hit her up on the socials:
Facebook & Instagram: @mmchromybooks
TikTok: @mmchromybooks0
Email: mmchromybooks@gmail.com

www.ingramcontent.com/pod-product-compliance
Lightning Source LLC
Chambersburg PA
CBHW030548260626
47157CB00006B/2234